CW00376930

The S
Price
Mysteries part 2

The

Death of

Carol

Richards

Joseph and Linda Pye

Best Wishes from the Author

[signature]

J A Rye

we would like to dedicate this

book to Carol and all the staff at the library on Canvey Island, for their help in producing our books via their computers and printing facilities, we would like to say a big,

Thank You

The names of the people that appear in this book are fictitious, apart from the group The Graduates which is real. They play in and around the clubs and pubs in the London area and their bass guitarist is Joseph Pye is one of the author's of this book. He is also a well known artist with his artwork selling worldwide which as helped to raise money to help the sick children on Canvey Island.

prologue

This story starts one Friday night in the summer of 1958. Two young girls were walking along arm in arm after an evening out.

They looked pretty and fresh in their summer attire. Seventeen year old Carol wore a white and green floral dress with a soft pink cardigan and her long mousy brown hair hung loose down her back. She was happiest without make up, whereas, her friend, sixteen year old Rose Finnegan with her long curly ginger hair, preferred heavy make up. Rose wore her usual black eye liner and deep blue mascara with a deep red lipstick coloured her lips. She wore a red pencil skirt and a white frilly blouse and tottered along on matching red high heels. They had just been to the pictures, the ABC cinema in Romford town centre to be precise.

Having been let down by their boyfriends, they visited the local fish and chip shop after the cinema closed and they had seen the film. The girls later purchased six penneth of chips each and headed for the bus stop on the opposite side of the road.

Happily puffing on a cigarette and swigging from bottles of Coke, the girls laughed about their evening as they waited patiently for their respective buses. Rose lived in Collier Row and needed the 174 bus while Carol needed the 66 bus to take her back to the Marks Gate estate, where she lived with her family which consisted of a couple of brothers and a younger sister, Susan.

Rose was lucky her bus came first and after a quick kiss on the cheek's and a quick cuddle they wished each other well and parted. Rose shouted from the platform of the bus as she clung to the bar of the open route master bus, shouting that she'd catch up with her the next evening in the Harrow Pub on the Marks Gate estate. Carol was heard to have shouting back, "Love you! Ok See you there Rose."

That was the last anybody saw of Carol, until her blood stained body was found in the alley that ran by the cemetery in Romford Market, she had been raped and stabbed several times. It was an unfortunate young stall holder who stumbled on her body around four o'clock that morning, as he was walking to the yard where he kept his stall.

Nobody was ever brought to justice for that murder......

Chapter 1

Steven's mind dwelt on the prospect of spending some precious time with Angie in his cousin's caravan, which was situated just east of the town of Weymouth, in a caravan park known as Seaview Holiday Park. The caravan had originally belonged to his aunt, Johnny's mother and he and his cousin had spent many a happy time there.

In his weary mind he felt it had been a lifetime since he last played around on the soft, sandy salt like beach that seemed to stretch on for ever. It was a lovely seaside resort and he had loved rambling over the high cliffs, then sitting on the top of one of those high cliffs happily watching the comings and goings of the cross channel ferry as it edged itself in and out of the quay.

Steve had utilized one of the empty bedrooms to use as an office, complete with a wooden desk and even a metal filing cabinet. He realised that now he was back in the force it would be of use as a place to keep his files etc; however there was also the new arrival to consider as it would then be needed as a nursery. He was also wondering where he would end up, now he was back to his old status in the force, as he had previously been working alone.

Suddenly the telephone rang out, on the side of his desk, "Yes!" he replied calmly, as he averted his eyes for a brief moment to pick up the receiver and answer the call, "Hello Johnny I was just thinking about you," he smiled returning his eyes to the paperwork he was trying to complete for the Major, with pen in hand and the relevant police paperwork in front of him.

"I thought you were coming to pick up the keys for you know what Steve."

"I am Johnny," he said as he gently laid his pen on the surface of the paperwork making sure the pen didn't affect the paper. "I have just got to fill out my report for the force regarding this little matter with the case I was working on, as you know I'm back in the force... not by choice mind you, I had to rejoin again to find out the truth, via a witness, if you know what I mean," he said as he leant his elbows on the edge of his desk. "I will drop this little matter off to the office in the morning then head over to see you, probably late morning. Ok."

"Ok I'll see you then," Johnny replied casually, "Why don't you bring Angie too, it's been a while since we last saw her."

"Sure why not...I'll treat us all to a meal in that restaurant we went to before... what d'ya reckon... it will be my treat," he smiled as he leant back in his chair and placed his elbow on the wing of the swivel chair that he sat on.

"Sure! Providing you let me get the wine."

"I'll see you tomorrow Johnny," Steve laughed to himself then added, "I'm sorry but I've got tons of paperwork to sort out for the company, if you get my drift."

With that, they gave each other the usual farewells and Steve returned the receiver to its correct place, just as Angie entered the room with an air of inquisitiveness in her voice when she asked who was on the phone. Steve replied calmly, as he picked up his pen, that it was only his cousin Johnny asking him when they were going over to get the keys to the caravan. Then he informed her that they were all going out for a meal at the restaurant, that she had fallen in love with the last time she had met Johnny and his other half.

She smiled and asked him if he would like a coffee, then added that she was now looking forward to the meal. She added that she would have to avoid the wine, as she gently patted her bump. Then bowing her head slightly she gave Steve a cheeky sly glance and a wink, with the raising of her eyes.

"Cheeky monkey!" Steve laughed as he threw a piece of rolled up note paper that had lain on the edge of the desk; he managed to hit her on the shoulder, then added, "Just go and get my coffee babe," he continued to laugh then returned with the simple, "please!" With a sad puppy dog look on his face. It was in response to this that Angie gave him another slight fleeting glance, before picking up the rolled up note paper and threw it back to Steve, who caught it then tossed it into the waste bin beside his desk.

Minutes later Angie stuck her head around the half open door to ask if he wanted his coffee in there or in the lounge.

Steve just simply smiled and told her to put it on the coffee table and explained that he'd be in there in a short while, as he had nearly finished the paperwork, he was just crossing the T's, and dotting the I's.

"Your coffee's getting cold babe," Angie shouted a few minutes later.

"I'm coming babe," he said with a brief, half hearted smile, as he carefully placed the finished paperwork into a brand new beige coloured, loose leaf folder, this in turn was finally placed into his nice new black briefcase, which he decided to leave open. Then he left the bedroom cum office to go and spend some time with Angie. She was seated on the settee with her barefoot legs tucked up beside her as she slouched against the arm of the settee, her coffee mug gripped firmly in both hands. On the television was some documentary programme.

"So Steve," Angie started casually, still holding on to her coffee as Steve sat down at the other end of the settee. "What's going to happen now?"

"What d'ya mean babe?" He asked as he retrieved his coffee.

"Well now you're back in the force, where does that leave us regarding this flat?" she enquired.

"We won't know until we get back off this little holiday sweetheart, I don't know where I'm going to be stationed. I could be stationed here in Basildon nick, I just don't know...I do know this Aussie detective wants me to help him solve a case that occurred in Australia," He informed her then added jokingly, "Who knows babe we might even get to go to Oz to investigate it."

"Yeah sure," she sighed, "You've got more chance of me becoming the Queen," she giggled, as she used the remote control to turn the sound down on the television, "So Steve, what are we doing then about this so called holiday to Weymouth then?" she pursued.

"Well, we will be going at the end of the week," he replied casually then went on to explain, "I want to go by train like we did when I was a kid," he said coolly as he took a sip of his coffee. "I've got to go into the office in the morning to hand in the report to the Major regarding this last case."

"I see!" she replied turning her head to look at the screen. "You are aware that I have to go the hospital for my check up."

"Why!" he replied with a curious look on his face, "Do you want me to go with you?"

"Nah, it'll be fine, it will be over quickly, they'll just do a couple of tests on me to check to see if the baby is doing fine. I also want to do a bit of shopping with Julie. You know her next door," she explained hastily when she saw the look on Steve's frowning face.

Steve felt an air of déjà vu about Angie's words as he remembered the last words of Sally all those years ago, he tried to make his mind believe it couldn't happen twice in his lifetime. "Lightning doesn't strike twice in the same place," he muttered.

"What you going on about?" she said with a curious look on her face.

"Oh it's nothing, just a memory, you know a touch of déjà vu regarding what you just said about shopping with a friend, that was the last thing Sally said to me years ago, only she said she was going to have lunch at a new restaurant in the town," he explained.

"Yeah well we were going to try out the new restaurant that has just opened where the buses stop," she smiled then went on to add, "Come on Steve that was six years ago. I don't think it is going to happen again, so shut up and drink yah coffee," she smiled as she turned up the volume on the television, Steve stood up and said he was going to have a bath and have an early night.

....
....

Steve walked through the entrance of Scotland Yard the next day wearing a light grey suit with a navy tie over a clean white shirt. He wore black patent shoes and held his new brief case at his side. He was met by the Major, who was wearing a pair of black trousers and a white shirt with a university tie; he'd left his jacket on the back of a chair in the office where he led Steve to.

"Here's the report you wanted," Steve said once they were in the confines of that office and both men had found their respective seats, he had removed the file from his case and casually tossed it onto the desk.

"I understand you're off on a holiday Steve," the Major said in passing.

"Is that right?" he asked as he picked up the folder and removed the paperwork from inside and briefly checked its contents.

"Yes your informants were correct boss, so what's happening now sir?" Steve quizzed, wondering where in the country he was destined to end up.

"What's happening now," The Major said quietly to himself as he carefully studied Steve's report. "This looks good Steve, well done," he returned tossing the file back onto the desk. "I understand you were working with the Aussie," He finally said after a moment's silence.

"Well, you should know, it was you who asked me to work with him, if you remember," Steve said leaning back in his seat, having placed his case on the floor beside his chair. "So! What are you saying Major."

"I think you and he could solve this case together, don't you? after all it was that was one of the reasons for him being here," he said as he began to place Steve's file into his brief case.

"So, what's it all about."

"Apparently a couple of Brits got themselves murdered in Australia," the Major expressed as he rose to his feet having dealt with Steve, then said calmly as he slipped into his jacket, "and the motive seems to have some connection to this country. If it turns out that there is a connection to this country Steve, you'll find out what it is, and sort it...you'll find the Aussie in the canteen," he said as he headed for the door, "good luck Steve and have a good holiday and don't forget..."

"Yes I know, report on your desk a.s.a.p.," Steve interrupted knowing what the Major was about to say, as he too left the office to meet up with Ian in the canteen.

The Major made for the exit whilst Steve found Ian sitting by one of the large windows, staring out into the streets of London, clasping a mug of coffee.

"I was told I'd find you up here," Steve said as he joined Ian after getting himself a coffee and finding a chair on the opposite side to him and placed his briefcase on the floor beside him.

"Ah Steve, it's good to see you again mate," Ian returned as he turned and faced Steve. A brief case stood on the floor beside him and he was wearing fawn coloured trousers with a dark brown jacket. A blue Aussie tie complete with a kangaroo in a badge at the base completed the ensemble.

"How did the family take the news about Janet?" Steve enquired.

"They didn't, they were very upset about the reasons behind it all, but they know they can't bring her back. At least she didn't die a drug dealer as it was portrayed by the media; they are going to put out an apology and explanation."

"Ok mate!" Steve expressed his sadness then went on to enquire, "so what's this case about?"

"Two Brits were killed..."

"Yes I know that," Steve interrupted him, "They were found on a beach in...Where did you say...somewhere you called Townsville, I believe that is where you said. Am I right?"

"Yes!" He replied as he picked up his briefcase and removed a folder that he had brought with him from Australia.

"So what's the m.o.?" Steve asked as he took a sip of coffee.

"The two men were both stabbed several times in the chest," he explained as he removed a piece of paper from his folder. "This was pinned to the blood stained shirt of one of the men", he said, as he handed a heavily stained piece of paper to Steve.

It simply read, 'revenge is sweet', in capital letters.

"So what makes you think this has something to do with Britain."

"They were staying in a hotel in Townsville...the owner said there were three men staying there at the time, the third has gone missing. We know he left the country later according to the airport officials who said he boarded the plane alone and didn't appear to be concerned about the fact... Heathrow later confirmed the person left the flight there. After an investigation it was discovered that the person had been using a fake passport."

"I see," Steve said softly as he glanced at the paper and the words, "What was the reason for the note and what did those men do to warrant such an violent end," he said leaning back in the chair, before staring deep in thought out of the window, "So you believe this third man is the one who killed those two men, the question is why?" he commented after a moments silence.

Several young uniformed officers, male and female moved about the canteen with their respective lunches.

"We just don't know, he might be the killer or he might know the killer and why they were killed in such a manner."

"So Ian what do we know of the two men who were killed?" Steve said finding his posture again.

He removed a couple of passports from his brief case and handed them to Steve to look at.

"I see, we have a Mr. Ian Carter of Romford and from what this says here he is or I should say he was forty five years old in July," he remarked as he studied the first of the passports. "I see the other was a male named Alfie Green from Basildon and was forty four years of age, his birthday was April," Steve returned them to Ian who placed them into the folder. "So what we have to do is find the common denominator in this case, it is evident they did something that warranted some sort of revenge, the question is what and when are we talking about, I mean these guy's weren't exactly youngsters now were they...Do we have a name for the third guy in this riddle?"

"Yes his name is," he stated, after he removed a small black book from his case, which he opened immediately at the page that told him the name of the third guy, "Robert Philips and he comes from Hainault and he is around thirty five years old, or thereabouts, but as already mentioned he was found to be using an assumed name and there has been no trace of him since."

"So the question we should be asking each other is...what is the connection between those three men, if there is one...who had the note pinned to them?"

"Ian Carter was the one with the note pinned to his chest."

"Right then, it might mean he was the true victim in this crime, and who knows the other guy Alfie might've just got himself tangled up in the crime and the killer didn't want to leave any witnesses," Steve uttered.

"So where do you think we should start then?"

"Well I think we should direct our investigation into the homes of those involved, as there may be clues at their addresses. We should see if we can find anything that could lead us to the reasons for their deaths, assuming there is something to go on, and also did anything occur between them in Australia that might've led to their deaths."

"As far as we know there wasn't any reason for them to be killed in Australia, the hotel owner said they were going to move on to a place in Ayr and visit a friend of one of them, but I guess they didn't make it, did they?" Ian said as he continued to sip at what was left of his coffee. "I want to go and get another coffee, d'ya want one Steve?"

"Sure, what's left of this one has gone cold," he said as he stared silently out of the window again deep in thought about the case and secondly the holiday he was truly looking forward to.

Later when Ian returned with a couple of coffees, that he placed on the table and sat down again, he finally stated, "If you must know Steve. I did visit the addresses that are on the passports, and there wasn't anything to indicate why they had to die, or why somebody would've wanted them dead. Ian Carter lived with his parents and they said there was no reason, as their son was a good lad and never hurt anyone in his life. Whereas Alfie had his own flat and we found nothing there to incriminate him either. In fact the only thing they had in common was they both worked for the same company, a double glazing company, it was called 'the Credit Window Company', on the Southend Road, that's about it, oh and they were good friends."

"They could've been gay," Steve said in passing, as he put a couple of spoonfuls of sugar into his coffee.

"Nah I didn't sense any of that stuff, they were just mates at work only."

"It sounds like we have very little to go on," Steve uttered then added, "Look, I'm going on a holiday for a week or so. When I get back, somehow I'll help you solve this case, how about that, I'll have the time to think about it while I'm on holiday."

"D'ya want me to be doing anything while you are away?" he enquired as he sipped on his coffee.

"Nah have a break yourself mate you've earned it too, as you have been busy with the little matter of the death of yah sister and all that stuff, spend some time with your family, I am sure they will appreciate it."

"I wish I could come along for the ride or you could find a place in your suitcase for me."

"Very funny!" Steve remarked jovially as he got up to leave his friend to finish his coffee. "I'll catch you later; I've got to get the keys for the caravan from my cousin. Then I'm looking forward to nice meal out tonight with some good company, in the meantime if you are interested, you could go to the company and talk to the other employees there and get as much info on the two men from their other friends, Ok?"

"Will do Steve, and have a good holiday."

"Cheers mate," he replied with a reassuring smile, then proceeded to leave the building.

Chapter 2

Meanwhile

A storm had all but ebbed over the buzz of Romford market that had sent many would be shopper running for any sort of shelter where ever they could. Even into the indoor market, which tended to benefit the small cafe's that begged for customers? The lightning, when it struck, sent people screaming, out of fear of being struck down in its wake.

A clear blue sky was edging forth from the west pushing the darkened sky east ward. The rain had eased somewhat now. Several buses, one of which was the 86, headed into London, passing through the well stocked market place. There people were enticed and charmed by the voices of the sellers with their comical banter, especially from the fruit and veg stalls. 'Come on ladies, treat your old man to some lovely strawberries', was just a sample of their language.

It was a far cry from where a middle aged man named George Blackmore was dying in the local hospital, in a room of his own. He was forty six and for several weeks had been teetering on the edge of death, he was away from the large wards, due to the seriousness of his terminal illness, his family sat silently around his bed as he lay in a deep coma type sleep.

For many days now his speech had been gibberish, which tended to make him very angry because those who loved him couldn't understand him.

Nurses tended to enter the room merely to take his temperature and blood pressure; occasionally the doctor would come in and check on his progress.

That is how it had been, until that day when he woke up in the early afternoon and looked around the room at those members of the family that were present by his bedside.

"Colin," he said, as plain as day, as he held out his hand to the young lad who was twenty years old. He was a slim, six foot tall lad with shoulder length fair hair, wearing a pair of denim jeans and a plain white t-shirt. He stood by a window that overlooked a garden where below them a couple were wheeling somebody in a wheelchair now the rain had ceased.

"Yes dad?" he enquired as he took his hand, "what is that you want?"

"I want you to go to the police station and fetch me a detective please," he stammered between breaths that seemed to be getting more difficult with time.

"But why dad, what's with the copper lark."

"Just do it for my sake, please, it's important to me can't you see."

Suddenly a young woman in her early forties also wearing denims and a beige sweatshirt gently took the lads hand, and said, "Do as he said son, if only for his sake."

"But why mum," he said with tears

in his eyes that he was determined to hold back, "what has he done?" he begged. This was turning into a trial for him, having no previous experience of such an event, his mind dwelled on the dad he once knew. The dad, who had once kicked a ball about in the park with him.

"Please son, do it for your dad, 'please'. I have never asked anything of you in my life until now, go please and fetch me a copper from the nick, I need to tell them something important, and don't you see."

"I don't see it dad, but if it's what you want I suppose I'd better go and get what you apparently, desperately seem to want," he uttered as he stood up, letting go of his father's hand he was touched by the hand of his mother who looked tired and puzzled by the request of her husband,

"Don't worry Lucy it isn't all bad I feel everything is going to be just fine," he said to his wife taking a long hard breath, as if it were his last.

She took his hand with her left, while with her right hand she covered her mouth to hold back the tears out of fear of upsetting him. A doctor just looked in with a gentle reassuring smile; He beckoned her out of the room to inform her that he felt it wasn't long now and felt her husband wouldn't last out the night.

Colin headed for the market place

and the police station just past it in the high street.

Finding himself standing before a middle aged station Sergeant who was in his uniform although without his uniform jacket which was draped over his chair. He stood behind his counter, his hands placed on the counter top and his clean white shirt stood out like a beacon, "Yes sir what can I do for you?" he asked politely.

"I want to talk to a detective," the lad expressed eagerly.

"Can I ask what it's all about, as the detectives are busy?" he pursued in his text book fashion.

"It's my dad, he's dying in hospital and he has requested a copper...so do I get to talk to a detective or not."

"I'm sorry to hear about your dad, but we still need to know what the problem is."

"I don't know", he begged, "It must be something he wants to get off of his chest before he dies...what do I know, come on please, if it is so important to him surely it would be fair to him to go to his maker knowing his past has been cleared...for gods sake I don't know why he is so determined to talk to a copper."

The sergeant looked into his eyes and said hang on, as he went to a phone on his desk and requested to be put through to a detective.

"You are in luck, there is only one detective on duty in his office and that is Detective Inspector Gould, he'll be down shortly, I hope this isn't a prank."

"It's genuine I wouldn't..."

"Ok, Ok keep yeah hair on, I understand," the sergeant interrupted.

D.I. Gould appeared from a side door into the reception area, he was wearing a navy blue pin striped suit, a pastel blue shirt and a beige coloured tie with dark blue thin stripes on it.

"So you are the young man who has requested the assistance of a detective, am I right?" he said as he joined him in the room, "What do they call you?"

"What?"

"Your name...what is your name."

"My name is Colin Blackmore."

"So Colin what seems to be the problem"?

"It's my dad, he has asked me to get him a detective as it is important. I guess he must be holding something in his life that he wants to get off of his chest...I don't know...I'm just has much confused about the whole thing as everybody is."

"Ok! Ok son!" replied D.I. Gould with a sympathetic voice, "So, where is your father now?"

"His in Oldchurch Hospital, in a room of his own. He's dying that is why I'm here at his request, so can you come with me and help my dad get something off of his chest. I mean it might be just an unpaid parking fine...I don't know, can we go we don't have much time left, I have this gut feeling, if you know what I mean."

"Yes son I do understand, death isn't a nice thing to experience at any age. I guess we'd better go and not keep your dad waiting," he said as he led the lad to the door and out into the yard, "I'll drive you back to the hospital, ok."

A little while later and the two men were walking along the long corridor on the second floor, passing various rooms, until they found Lucy out side the room wiping her eyes with a tissue where she had been crying.

"We're not too late, are we?" Collin asked abruptly, fearing the worst.

With tears still running down her soft pale cheeks, she just nodded to let him know his dad was still alive.

"Ok son lets find out what this little matter is and help him move on...hopefully" D.I. Gould said as he opened the door, to find George still on his back, his heart monitor bleeped steady to one side, wires and drips dotted the room. "So Colin what is your dad's name?"

"George, George Blackmore," he replied as he entered the room.

"Are you with us George?" D.I. Gould asked calmly once he reached the side of the bed, he took his hand in his, "So George what is this all about, you know you are upsetting your family."

"Who are you?" He stammered with heavy breath.

"I am Detective Inspector Gould from the local station where your son Colin came to get help for you, ok," he said finding a seat on one of the chairs at his side.

"Detective eh?"

"Sure George, you see I know your name, thanks to your son, you should be proud of him."

"I want every body to get out, I want to speak to you only this is not for their ears, do you understand copper," he ordered abruptly, for a brief second he squeezed the detectives hand tightly.

"So George what is upsetting you...is it something you've done and you need to get it off of your chest," he enquired once the room had been emptied of people. This had included Colin's aunt and uncle who had arrived while he was out on the mission.

A cool bright sun shone through the window as the two men stared at each other for a moment. George prepared his mind, in order to clear it of any misdoing that he had harboured for what appeared to be a lifetime. He was determined to see this through regardless.

"Are we alone copper," He muttered softly.

"Yes!" he replied just quickly glancing around the now empty room, "So George what is this all about?"

"I want to clear my mind of something that happened when I was a lad in the fifties, it happened here in this town."

"Go on!"

"I'm trying to remember," He said softly as if he were in the distance, a lad again in his mind, his eyes looking to the ceiling, "It had something to do with a young girl we chatted up, my mates and I that is. A nice young girl, pretty, I can even remember a flowery type dress and a pink top, I didn't get to see what actually happened as I was in the car having a smoke, but later I read in the newspaper that a young girl had been killed in Romford Market."

"I see and do those other lads have names, George?"

"Yes but we were told never to mention it to anyone, especially the police...when I asked one of the lads what had happened to the girl they said she left to catch a bus and that was it."

"Names George we need names," he enquired having taken his note pad out to take down any relevant information that was being exposed by George.

"Don't you understand copper, it wasn't me, I'm innocent, but I'm just as guilty as those others," he sobbed as he pulled himself to the detective's side.

"Ok George I understand."

"No copper you don't understand," he said calmly as he fell back onto the pillow and the heart monitor beeped endlessly. "I am as guilty as my friends for the death of that young girl...what must her parents be going through...if it were my son I would kill for him...I'm being punished by him upstairs for not saying anything in the past...don't you see?"

"I see George and now you want to do what's right for that young girl...does she have a name too?"

"I want to be left alone to die, that's what is only right for somebody like me," his voice eased down a notch or two as if he were drifting in and out of one life and another; it was as if for one minute he was that young lad again, sitting in the car, not knowing what was happening to his friends and the girl.

"They came back to the car laughing out loud saying she had a good fanny or something along those lines," He said after a moments silence, where he seemed distant, his eyes diverted to a single spot on the ceiling as if his soul had lifted itself from his body. "They waved her knickers around their heads like a flag or something, do you see what I mean, I should've done something to try and save her."

"You're so called friends, do they have names, and can you remember the girls name too?"

He went quiet yet again then turned to look at the detective with a puzzled look in his eyes, "Who are you?" He uttered, before turning again to look up at that spot on the ceiling. Once more the monitor beeped, but it appeared to him that George had gone, as he didn't answer him when he begged him too.

The Doctor entered the room and went straight to George's side to examine him, at the same time the heart monitor went into a long drawn out noise that signified George's heart had now stopped. He was still breathing for a few seconds before his breath went erratic, and then stopped.

D.I. Gould got up and headed for the door where he was met by the family who stared at him for a moment, "What did my husband want to say, Detective?" Lucy enquired followed by Colin.

"It was something he got involved in when he was just a young lad, you know what being young is all about, and he wanted to clear his mind before he died, that's all, nothing much. I would still love to talk to you all, after the funeral, if that's alright with you," he asked politely, "Can I have your address so I can talk to you in private."

"Was it something serious?" Colin asked in passing as his mother left them to talk, whilst she went to her now late husband's side.

"I don't really know at this point in time, it could be nothing but then again they say the truth comes out when the end is near...no it's something I'm going to have to look into. I can let you know more after the funeral, ok."

"Sure give us yeah pen and note pad and I'll write down our address."

"Go and pay your respects to your father son," he ordered with a half hearted grin once he retrieved his notepad and pen, before departing the room to head back to the station.

Back at the station D.I. Gould entered the reception to find the sergeant still there.

"Reg can you remember if a young girl was murdered in the fifties, in the market place?" he enquired.

It went silent for a moment as Reg racked his memory, "Yes!" He finally replied, "If my memory recalls her name was something like Carol...yeah I remember it was a young girl named Carol Richards, if it's the same one. Why do you ask...that lad's father wasn't the killer by any chance?"

"Who knows Reg...?Who knows," he replied finding the door to the sanctuary of his office. "There wouldn't be any files on that murder Reg, would there?" He enquired as he passed through the reception area.

"Should be, why?"

"Can you get them for me please have them sent to my office."

"Will do!"

"Cheers, a nice coffee wouldn't go amiss either." He laughed to himself as he headed for the canteen and a spot of lunch.

Chapter 3

Feeling a whole lot better, Steve was now able to set out and try to impress the night in his soft grey suit, white shirt opened at the top to reveal just a glimpse of his chest, his right hand delicately perched in his trouser pocket, and the bottom of his jacket draped behind it.

Whereas Angie looked stunning in a black chiffon dress with shoulder straps, a short white and grey fur jacket that balanced out her black shoulder bag that hung at her side. Her precious bulge hidden slightly by the style of her dress that flowed beautifully from just below the cleavage of her breasts. An ornate gold necklace hung elegantly at her slender neck, her hair had been styled by the local hairdresser that she and her friend had visited that same morning. This time it was a far cry from the shabby outfit that had been the only thing she had been able to wear, the last time the she frequented the same restaurant, in the company of Steve and his cousin and his wife, who were delighted to pay for the meal then.

This time Steve wanted to return the gesture in his own way. The four of them entered the large dimly lit room that was the dining area of the elegant restaurant. With its many varying circular tables to suit the different clientele that frequented the establishment. Ornate brass wall lights with pretty pink pot type shades set on two upright light fittings delicately lit the establishment, creating a warm romantic ambience, while an array of variously framed pictures dotted the walls between the lights.

The faint smell of food being cooked touched your sense buds to encourage you to want to eat at the establishment.

Soft pastel diamond wall paper graced the walls, with an ornate dado rail that separated it from a teak wooden panelled bottom.

A young couple sat to one side, they were too engrossed in their own company to give any thought to others coming or going that night. He sat with his elbows on the edge of the table whilst she sat upright but entranced by his loving glare, a light hearted smile beamed out for all to witness their love for each other.

At the far end stood a bar, set in the centre of two swinging doors with in and out over both of them. A Chinese girl stood behind the counter of the bar with a bored look on her young oriental face, her long black hair was tied up in a bun and beautified her look. She was keen to get on with her work and smiled as the public entered the establishment, meaning her job was to serve them their relevant drinks, and that included Steve and the gang.

'Lovers,' Steve thought to himself as they entered the building to be met by a well dressed Chinese young man. Over his right arm was a white cloth over and a handful of menu's were tucked under his left arm as he led them to a table for four. This was after Johnny told him that he had booked a table for four; with a polite smile of reassurance the young man said that he was aware, and happily directed them to a table near one of the front windows, with its half draped net curtain that hung on a central rod.

They found themselves sitting at a round table with a pristine white square table cloth, its corners hung neatly between each chair. The usual condiments sat in the middle of the table. The waiter who led them to the table then handed out the menus to each of them.

"Can I get you some drinks sir," enquired the waiter.

"Can I have some white wine for the girls and couple of lagers for us, Charlie," Johnny ordered politely. "It's alright Steve, me and Charlie go back a long time," he explained then went on to add, "Don't we Charlie?"

"Yes Johnny!" returned the waiter

who then departed to get the drinks leaving them to study the menu.

It was then a small party of people entered the restaurant and they too were met by Charlie, who was told that a table for six had been booked by a Mr. Johnson earlier that day. So they were led to a table at the far end of the restaurant and the same procedure occurred with them.

"So Steve what happened to those two people; you know," Johnny asked as they read the menus then whispered to Steve, "that were you know 'murdered', in the park."

"Do we have to talk shop, I mean it is a night out for god's sake," Steve snapped irritably.

"Yeah but I'm really interested to learn about their end. I guess you now know who did it and why," Johnny pressed on eager to learn the truth.

"Ok!" Steve said as he placed the menu onto the table top as he had decided what he wanted, "I can only say I feel sorry for the idiot who half inched the money they were holding. Apparently somebody conned them into giving them thirty grand, but in the end nicked one hundred and thirty grand."

"So, why would you be sorry for the person who stitched up a couple of drug dealers like them two? I mean its only drug money."

"Not quite!" Steve replied as he leant on the edge of the table, then went on to coolly explain, "for a start, the two weren't drug dealers as people believed back then," he went on, "no, they were villains, true; but certainly no drug dealers as I have been well informed, from the horse's mouth as they say."

"So Steve what were they then?" enquired Johnny's wife Diana, "If they weren't, you know, what you said."

"Yeah Steve come on spill the beans, we're all ears," Laughed Johnny.

Still leaning on the edge of the table he went on to explain, "As I've said," he started then went on to add, "I feel sorry for the person or persons who stitched them up back then. Whoever it was sealed their fate when they nicked the money, because unbeknown to them the money belonged to the I.R.A., that is why I feel the way I do about the whole situation so let's just forget that and just enjoy our food and good wine."

It was then they beckoned Charlie over and ordered their meals respectfully. Johnny sat back in his chair and glanced deep in thought at Steve's words relating to the thought of the I.R.A., being involved in the lives of those two young kids whose lives were destroyed.

"So Steve what's happening now?" Johnny finally enquired after a few minutes of silence.

"Yeah right!" he returned casually, "I've been told I have to help this Aussie geezer with a case of two Brits being killed in Australia a little while ago, there is some connection to this area Johnny, well Chadwell Heath that is."

"Australia yeh say." Johnny uttered.

"Yeah some place called Town something, I don't know," Steve replied in passing.

"That's Townsville in Queensland you fool," remarked Angie.

"Yeah that's the place babe."

"Talking of babies, when's it due Ange?" enquired Diana.

"I think it's around February, so I'm told," she replied as she glanced up at the ceiling knowing the truth but reluctant to say so, instead she was dreading the thought of the coming event but praying that the baby would be safe.

"What's wrong babe?" enquired a concerned Steve.

"It's nothing, just a woman's thing, don't worry yourself honey", she replied touching his arm that she gently squeezed before he leant forward and kissed her on the lips, to the words from Johnny, 'get a room.'

"Ha, ha," Steve laughed.

"So are you getting ready to travel

to Weymouth Steve?" Asked Diana changing the subject.

"Yeah, Steve wants to travel down on the train, his brother on the other hand wants to travel there in the car. I guess I will be going down on the train with him," she said pointing at Steve jokingly.

"But why Steve, surely you could drive there," Johnny replied inquisitively.

"He said it was a sentimental thing... you know... something that reminds him of his youth when he used to go there with his mum and dad and your mum and dad too...John."

"You're an old softy at heart Steve," Johnny returned jovially.

Steve just grinned at his cousin's wit.

....
....

A soft drizzle was passing when D.I. Gould entered the offices in Romford, with the determination to discuss the case with Chief Inspector Cross. Armed with the information from the night before and his encounter with the now late George Blackmore and his dying confession.

He made his way to the Chief Inspectors office with the request to get involved with the alleged murder of a young girl named Carol Richards. She had been murdered some twenty four years ago and he was determined to do his best for her and George, who had died knowing the truth about the old case, inside he knew he couldn't have lied because he was dying.

He was taken aback when the Chief enquired where the alleged information came from and then enquired if George was on morphine, if so he could've been hallucinating the whole affair.

"It wouldn't hurt if I looked up the case and did some checking just to prove that George was lying about his part in her death."

"What do you think you're going to prove now, it's been twenty four years and the case was never solved? It was believed she might've been on the game and a punter got heavy handed and did her in out of lust or something."

"Still, it would be interesting to learn the truth even though it was twenty four years ago...wouldn't it sir?"

"Is it going to interfere with the other cases you are working on Inspector?"

"Think about it sir," he started, "here we have a young girl on a night out only to end it just like that," he said as he clicked his fingers. "Surely we owe it to her to find those who did that to anybody, let alone a young girl on the game or not...anyway, how do we know she was on the game sir?" he demanded.

"D.I. Gould you alone should be aware we never close a case book on any crime, no matter how long it takes or until we have the evidence that is fool proof. Ok, including that case...back then the case went cold after sometime; if you are holding the file on that case and you have taken the time out to read them, you will see that there isn't much to go on."

"Yes sir I have taken the time out to read them and from what I can see this is the first time something has come to light regarding this case, surely that amounts to something...sir," he explained as he placed the file onto the Chiefs cluttered desk.

Picking up the old tatty file the Chief found his feet and walked to the window that over looked the busy high street as a red bus drove past heading east. "Look Jack!" he said as he sat on the window ledge and faced him with the file tucked under his left arm, he went on to explain, "It was a case from 1958. I was just a young detective still wet behind the ears, when that girl was murdered, she was found in the alleyway, by the church in the market place. Her body was draped over a low wall, the grave stones close to her head. It was thought she was drunk from a good night out and ended up in that predicament, it was a young lad who eventually realized the truth of the girls demise when he tried to wake her and help her to get home...in fact we did think at one time that he might've done it, but he had a good alibi for that night so he was crossed off the list."

"I understand from the file sir that the murder took place on the 28th May that year."

"Yes you're right Jack," he replied as he returned to his desk where he placed the file in front of Jack. "Now after all these years you come in with the evidence we needed back then, only to learn the person is now dead. You alone should be aware that the crown prosecution would have a field day with that information now, wouldn't they?" he said with an air of authority in his voice. He casually strolled back to his seat, once seated he leaned back with his hands held behind his head, the usual portrait of the Queen hung behind him looking down at his posture. "At that time you would've read that the only clue at the time was that witnesses noticed an American style of car which was seen at the time...well you know with wings on the back like an American car, but it was never found."

"An American car you say?"

"Yes," he said as he quickly

scratched his forehead before returning his hands to the edge of his desk, "Yeah you know it wasn't an American, but something like one but smaller."

"A bit like a Vauxhall Cresta maybe," Jack said, as he leant on the desk and then picked up the file, "So chief what do you want me to do about this case?"

"Mmmm!" He poised, "We know that she was missing a certain piece of attire."

"That's right, George mentioned that his friend came back to the car laughing and waving a pair of knickers in the air, like a flag that had just been won."

"If that is right Jack," he leant back in his chair, "He would've served his time inside by now and we might've got the names of his friends who were involved back then."

"He told me that they were scared of the one that did it to the girl, saying he would've killed them friends or no friends."

"Some friend he was then."

"Yeah! And that bastard is still out there somewhere and he could've killed again for all we know."

"So Jack where do you intend on making your start...I mean we came to nothing back then and we investigated that case fully and came up with nothing concrete that was until now of course."

"I want to go and interview

George's family once they have had the funeral. In fact I'll give them a few days to get over the event and hopefully pick up a few clues to the killer, who knows they might have pictures from the past that might help."

"You should ask Detective Sergeant Peters to assist you... he came into the force a few years after that murder, but I can remember that he was really keen to help solve it back then. He was eager to learn of any witnesses in relation to the crime, but as I've explained the case went cold and he seemed upset. However he was happy to move onto other cases at that time, but anyway to jog their memories it was the year Brazil won the world cup, ok."

Chapter 4

That day couldn't come quick enough for all who were concerned. The holiday had already started for Bob and Peta who found them heading out earlier, before the sunrise, for the caravan and Weymouth. A cool sun was beginning to rise, set perfectly in a cobalt blue sky, with just a whisper of fluffy clouds sitting on either side, it teetered on the horizon, as if it were rising up from the roof's of distant houses and casting long shadows.

Closing the front door of the flat and with Tara safely leashed and held by an overjoyed Angie, who had been like a little girl who couldn't wait to venture out on the beach, they headed for the overhead train station at Laindon. There they headed for London and Paddington Station via West Ham and the underground, Angie commented that she wasn't happy with the underground as she felt it was a dangerous place to be in. Her idea was that the holiday started the moment the front door was locked and they headed west.

Paddington was a buzz of activity, even at that time of the day, with people heading in every direction and for every reason in the book. It was a guessing game to work out how many were actually like them and heading for a well earned rest in some distant seaside resort.

Walking through that vast station armed with a large suitcase, that Steve gladly dragged along behind him as it had wheels at the back, whilst Angie, due to her present situation was only too happy just to hold onto Tara and holding a white, supermarket carrier bag with things for the journey. The little dog seemed equally glad to be going on the journey, full of zest and eagerness as she found various new smells, eagerly sniffing everything that crossed her path.

They managed to get a coffee and a couple of ham and cheese rolls at one of the many cafes within the station and they sat outside, due to Tara. Many eating places were dotted throughout the vast open space. Taking precedence were the comings and goings of many diesel trains that hissed and shunted in and out of the long straight platforms'. These were often busy for every person had to use them when they touched down or went to get onboard trains as they stood alongside the concrete walkways.

Tara started to bark at some old gentleman shabbily dressed when he asked Steve if he had a light for his cigarette. Steve just smiled and happily gave him a light sending him on his way happily dragging on his hand made cigarette probably made from the various cigarette ends that littered the area that he had picked up.

Soon they found their relevant seats on the long train that stood silently waiting, with all its doors wide open and waiting to be boarded by all those heading in the same direction as Steve and Angie.

"I wonder whereabouts the others are now Steve?" Angie asked as they found their seats and Tara found joy as she lay between their feet.

"If I know my brother he'll be nearly there by now, I guess, knowing the speed he goes," he replied casually having taken the lead from Angie and gently tied it to the handle of the suitcase.

She placed the carrier bag on the

seat beside her as she sat opposite Steve so they both could stare out of the window.

The train shunted out of the station slowly easing away from the vast cacophony of sounds; of voices giving out the relevant information to the travellers; the sound of trains coming and going, their horns screaming out to the world to let them know of their arrivals or departures. Soon the train edged out to the realms of the city, where strings of houses lined each side of the track along with tower blocks that jostled along with factories and office blocks. Squeaks and judders propelled the snake like train into the countryside as it slowly left the streets of the city behind to those who relished in the turmoil and chaos of its busy streets. Steve stared out with just a hint of a smile, his mind drifted with the increase of speed of the train. Angie removed a book from the carrier bag.

"What book's that babe?" Steve found himself asking politely.

"Oh it's a new book by Mills and Boon, I bought it yesterday in town," she replied just giving a sneak preview of its cover to Steve.

With that she returned to her book leaving Steve and Tara to their own devices. Tara just curled up under Steve's feet while Steve returned to the view from that large window.

The sound of the engine slowly seemed to change in a few moments to that of a steam train; the ghostly sound of the whistle seemed to add a strange eerie but crazy feeling in the back of his mind. It was as though Steve had been transformed to another world. The common stream of white steam that flowed past the window, like some vast cloud, and he was now flying to some distant exotic country on a mission of deep secrecy.

The voice of his granddad echoed in his ear telling him of the criminals he had caught during the war years, especially when he and some of his colleagues raided a pub in the East End and several spivs fled out of the back but were caught. He went on to tell him of a murder of a young man in the thirties, it turned out to be his wife or so the court declared.

Now he found himself believing he was his granddad on that very mission to catch the true killer of the man, his mind seemed strange when his granddad told him the wife was hung.

Suddenly the voice of somebody calling his name from afar echoed in the distance and was slowly getting nearer by the second. He turned to find he was in the presence of his mother, a woman in her late thirties with short blonde curly hair and she was dressed in early nineteen sixties clothes. He recalled how his mother was always wearing black trousers and various woollen tops, which she believed matched the way she was feeling at the time. He remembered the time his dad bought her a beautiful white dress so she could look nice when they went out, but she never ever wore it and slung it out when his dad died a couple of years ago whilst he was up in Scotland.

Suddenly he realised that he was now that young lad of eight on the steam train going to Weymouth in the summer of nineteen sixty four. The Beatles were all the rage. And the Mod's and the Rocker's was the scene of the day to be in. Steve dreamed that he would be a rocker driving his thousand cc motorbike around the world.

"You daydreaming again Steven... just look at you, don't you know I've been calling you for ages?" She said with an air of authority in her voice that tended to scare him sometimes.

"I was just pretending to be like granddad, you know a detective," He explained calmly then realised he was the young lad again.

"You are always pretending... you should get your act together, they'll be putting you away if you carry on like that my boy."

"But mum!"

"No buts my boy, just shape up or... or you'll end up in some mental home and I don't think you'd want to end up in there would you."

"No mum, but..."

It was about then that that Steve's answer was interrupted when an elderly woman, with short curly hair and a blue rinse decided to turn and pass a comment in Steve's favour when she said to his mother.

"Did you know that all the greatest authors are daydreamers, I suggest your boy might grow up to be a new Somerset Maugham or Agatha Christie who knows," she said with a soft smile and a quick wink, before she returned to her prior posture leaving his mother stunned by her interruption in the matter.

Steve gave a conceited smile as he again turned to stare out of the window and the white steam continued to drift past, when again a voice echoed in the distance and again appeared to grow nearer by the second. The voice was calling his name over and over again until in a flash the flow of the steam vanished immediately and he was facing Angie who was concerned about his wellbeing.

"What's up babe?" he uttered as he gently stirred from his dream like state.

"It looked like you were daydreaming Steve," she replied as she held her book on her lap her finger pressed in the last page she was reading before she tried to contact him.

"I was just remembering the time I was on a train with my mum and dad, it was one of those old fashioned trains, you know you only see them in the old movies, an old girl told my mum and dad that I could be an author one day as all authors were daydreamers."

"I was going to ask you if you fancied a coffee."

"Sure would you like me to go and get a couple?" he replied finding his feet.

"Sure!" She said as she folded the corner of the page so she could have a rest from her book. Her face altered when she was interrupted by a young couple with the young mother holding a baby wrapped in a white shawl, as they were passing from one carriage to the next. The sight of the baby made her look down at her bulge, believing for the first time that something like that baby was alive and kicking inside her body.

"Would you like something to eat?"

"Yeah a couple of cheese rolls please honey," she replied, gently running her hands over the unborn child, her mind dwelled heavily on the belief that the child would be healthy and not harmed by the tumour.

Steve had just found his seat again when Angie happened to mention that he should consider writing a novel or two, "if that old lady was right back then when you were a kid...who knows you could be famous," she laughed quietly to herself, "And just think it would be a nice legacy for the little one," she said as she gently tapped her bulge.

"You are joking of course...I mean, I'm still finding it hard to write out my reports let alone even consider the possibility of writing a famous novel...besides what would I write about."

"I don't know...you could write about all the cases you've worked on over the years."

"That would take all of twenty minutes."

"Just think about it eh," she uttered casually, then with a smile she returned to the confines of her book occasionally reading aloud so Steve could hear some of the written words. He sensed it was her trying to get him interested in writing that all important novel.

A few coffees later and the train edged into Poole station where to his surprise an old steam train stood rattling on the other platform. There were a mass of people standing and chatting to each other, whilst others were happily walking about in their nineteenth century outfits.

Many wore various pastel coloured crinoline dresses that stood out like the lid of some chocolate box. They were drinking hot drinks and it looked like a series of cameras stood nearby, ready to continue to make what ever they were shooting.

Another cup of coffee and several more chapters of her book and the train edged down from the speed it had been travelling at, as it neared Weymouth. It was coming in from the rear of the town and passing gently through the streets to the dock area.

The barriers on the road bridge came down to stop the traffic and the public momentarily, it spanned a stretch of inland sea that was adorned with its many varieties of yachts, either moored on the jetties or being manned as they left the sanctuary of the harbour. A red light flashed in unison to the bell that rang out.

The train rattled and squeaked as it edged nearer to its final resting place on the quay side and the large awaiting cross channel ferry that took travellers to the Island of Jersey. Steve and Angie could only watch in awe as the heavy load eased its way through the town.

The people on the path could only watch as the train slowly crossed the road by the bridge, they were eager to continue on their journey but were now stopped for the duration it took for the snake to rattle past them.

Looking out of the window they could see the many fishing boats that lined up along the quay, some with men on board sorting out the nets and rigging of their boats. Others lay idle, having been and done their part for the joys of mankind as their early catch was now being served up in the many fish and chip shops that dotted that quaint town. Stepping down from that train they were met with the scent of candy floss mingled with the faint smell of one or two of those fish and chip shops, a smell that made you feel hungry and enticed you into the establishments.

They walked into the main road that ran by the sea where they were met with some sand art set on the beach that amazed Angie who became mesmerized by the old man's work for which he was famous for.

Taking a taxi they were soon entering the holiday park and as they passed a large pub called 'The Ship', Steve expressed a desire at some point in time that he would love to go there for a meal at least once on the holiday, as Johnny had said it was a nice joint run by some old sea dog. The white horse on the hill shone out like some beacon from an age long since past.

"I've never ever seen anything like that before Steve," Angie said when she espied the white horse in front of them as they sped along the road that ran the length of the beach before it came to the cliffs that appeared to rise up out of the sea.

Portland Bill stood out on the horizon like a discarded trilby and the cross channel ferry that was now departing appeared to be brushing its shoreline.

Once at the campsite Steve paid the driver off and then they entered the reception area where they were told that his brother had arrived, and was waiting for them in the club house. They were getting something to eat after their journey, it turned out they had not long arrived too, as the roads were so busy.

A few kisses and cuddles later and the four of them entered the caravan that was situated in the middle of the site. A wire fence separated one field and an area was left for those with dogs, so Tara had a place where she could be walked. Steve took the time out to go for a walk up onto the cliff tops taking Angie with him so they could get a feel of the place. Tara was happy on her lead as she eagerly sniffed the new territory she found herself exploring.

"I can still remember walking over these cliffs with my mum and dad and my Nan it feels like it was only yesterday Ange... A thunder storm blew up from off the sea, you could see it heading this way as it engulfed Portland Bill, that's the place out there," Steve stated as he pointed towards the odd shaped island. "I remember it scared the living daylights out of my Nan when the lightning struck the wire fence just up there," he pointed. "Yeah it did 'narf make a big bang Ange."

"I can imagine, I think it would've scared the living daylights out of me Steve," She said as she tucked her arm into his arm and pulled herself into his side.

Chapter 5

The early autumn was turning into a typical Indian summer, with its warm sunny days and cold nights. It was the early afternoon of the 6th September when Steve and Angie strolled hand in hand along the soft sandy beach. Their minds were on the great time they were having, what with the past two nights entertainment in the clubhouse on the campsite, which had been very enjoyable.

They had just spent an hour in the Ship Pub having a few jars (beers) before they eventually ventured onto the road to the town centre. Once they reached the main drag they noticed that Petula Clarke and Nookie Bear were appearing at the local theatre which was situated on the point just in front of the train station. It stood like some majestic ornament on a low ridge. They were there all that week so Steve said he felt like going along at some point to see them, if Angie fancied it too. She laughed but said, 'yes,' as she pulled him to her for a quick cuddle and a tender kiss.

Steve decided to stop at one of the many beach cafes to get a couple of white coffees for the pair of them, it was near the clock tower that stood like an Egyptian Cleopatra's needle in the centre of the wide footpath.

The smell of freshly cooked fish and chips wafted around the noses enticing them to explore more closely those quaint little shops set in the narrow lanes.

....

....

<u>Meanwhile</u>

Back in the town of Romford, on the same day, D.I. Gould had turned up for work at the usual time to be greeted by the other offices with the usual greeting of, 'Morning Jack,' as he casually made his way to his little office. There he dropped his briefcase on the floor beside his old wooden desk that was cluttered with files and unfinished forms he was supposed to have filled in. He made a start to clean his desk when D.S. Peters entered the office with a big grin on his face, he was a man in his mid forties, clean shaven and wearing a black suit with a grey silvery tie.

"Hi Jack!" He expressed casually once inside the room, "So what's going down Jack?" He enquired in passing, as he gently closed the office door and placed his hands on the edge of the desk. "The

Chief said I'm to assist you on some case you want to work on".

"Well at the moment I, or I should say we, have...hum it's a young coloured woman and her baby", Returned Jack, as he tossed a brown file onto the desk having removed it from his case.

"You mean the jumper," D.S Peters smiled as he found the corner of the desk to sit on and picked up the file.

"That jumper had a name," expressed Jack seriously.

"Yeah sure, Adele or something," commented Peters as he read through the file.

"Yeah Adele Nbada, to be precise she took her life on Romford Station on Friday evening, the baby somehow survived but she ended up everywhere along the track...I looked into the flat she lived in thanks to her hand bag being thrown back onto the platform along with the baby, that you can say was nothing short of a miracle, wouldn't you Adam and Eve it, now, what are the odds of that happening."

"So what's to look into about that case."

"Not much, all we found at the flat was a letter telling her she was to be deported back to her own country."

"I guess that's out of the question now eh," he said finding his feet. "So which case am I supposed to help you with...or have I got to try and guess what it is?" He enquired, finding the window sill comfortable for a moment.

"You joined the force in..." He paused to see what response he'd get.

"It was around nineteen sixty one I believe... why are you asking?" He asked with a puzzled look on his face. "Is it important or something," he said, rubbing his chin.

"Could be!" Jack expressed as he picked up his case from the floor, then he proceeded to stand it on his desk and went on to add, "back then, I've been told by god upstairs, that you got involved in a certain case."

"And which case would that be pray, may I ask?" He said standing up straight with a curious look on his face, "I was involved in many cases back then, which one are you referring to if you don't mind me asking?"

"A young girl was murdered in the alleyway by the church yard in the market here in Romford," he said removing the file from the case and placing it in front of him. "Well Danny does it ring a few bells."

"Christ that's going back awhile Jack, where did you dig that up from". He said picking up the file, "It feels just like yesterday when I filed work on that case with the then chief the one you so call god."

"I know, he told me the other day."

"But why now?" he said tossing the file back onto the desk. "It was never solved back then so how are you going to solve it today?"

"I had to go to visit a young man in the hospital the other day he was dying and it came to light that he wanted to get something off of his chest. Namely that case, he said he was connected to that girl's death but he didn't do it. He was concerned that those involved were scared of the person who did kill her, apparently he told them he'd kill them if they squealed."

"So did this guy say who did kill the girl back then...oh by the way her name was Carol Richards, a nice looking girl if I recall, having seen the pictures that her family supplied."

"I see!" Jack uttered as he too found his feet and headed for the canteen and a breakfast of cheese on toast and a well earned cup of tea.

"So this dying guy did he have a name?" Danny asked as they casually walked the short distance to the canteen. There a young woman in a white overall took their orders, then they both went and found a seat in the middle of the room.

"Yeah it was George Blackmore," he said stirring his mug of tea having just put two spoonfuls of sugar in it.

"George Blackmore you say?" Danny replied, his mind in thought as he stared briefly into his mug of tea.

"Does it ring a few bells Danny?"

"I don't know at the moment," he pouted, "Hum, (ugh), although I believe I have heard of the name, but you've got to remember it was so long ago...I mean it was twenty four years ago for Christ sake...get real Jack, what you are trying to tell me is you are basing your line of investigation on the words of a dying man, who, I seem to remember was never questioned about that crime back then...so why now...it doesn't make sense at all."

Just then the young girl from the counter came over and placed a plate of cheese on toast in front of Jack with the courteous response from him saying "Thanks Jean you're a diamond," he then went on to add, "Now where were we, ah yes I remember...It obviously meant a lot to him Danny, I mean he was dying as you so put it and wouldn't that be a good time to clear your mind of such a crime, eh?"

"Yeah well he might've been the person who killed the girl but was still reluctant to say so," he said as he cupped his mug of tea in both hands.

"That's true, but if he was going to die, and I do know he did die because I was there; surely he would've confessed to the whole crime, knowing he could never be tried for his crime or even get to serve his time for it...no, he had a family that he obviously adored...surely you must agree that a killer of that calibre wouldn't be like that...he'd be a loner yeah."

"I wouldn't know, all I know is there are many nutcases out there who were capable of such a crime, at that time. If I were you Jack I'd just put that case back into the archives where it belongs, it was never solved back then and I'm sure you'll never solve it now; besides we have a lot of other unsolved cases to solve at the moment."

"So what else have we got eh."

"There's that bungled bank job last week, it needs to be sorted out."

"Jackson's working on that case...no I want to get me teeth into this old murder case of Carol Richards. I feel the true villain is still out there somewhere and we know he drove a Vauxhall Cresta back then. A lovely car that looks like an American car which seems to have confused a few of those witnesses back then."

"Yeah! well, my guess is most of those so called witnesses are now like George, brown bread."

"That's why I intend going to George's home and tactfully interview his family, without giving to much away at this moment in time; I mean I don't want to go and upset a grieving family at this moment in time...now do I, who knows they might still have some old photos of him back then. There could be some clues which might lead to the killer and who knows he might've even said something to his wife Lucy or his son Colin," Jack explained as he slowly sipped his mug of tea.

"Do we have an address for this family?"

"Yeah sure!" He said as he then bit into a piece of toast having just put some tomato ketchup on both slices.

"I'm sure there use to be a George Blackmore in my old school, that's where I've heard the name from, but he lived in Chadwell Heath back then. He was one of those kids that was a bit of a nutter, always pretending to be somebody he wasn't... you know what I mean. He would always make cards and pretend he was head of MI5 or a copper and that he carried a gun sometimes; we all use to take the piss out of him... if my memory serves me right he once died his hair green, it was supposed to have been black, the silly idiot went and bleached it white, that's your George Blackmore, assuming it is the same person... in any court of law he would be seen as a time waster."

"For somebody who didn't know him a minute ago you seem to know all about him now," Jack replied as he looked at Danny whilst deep in thought regarding the case. Especially the fear that the killer had instilled into people back then.

"Yeah well, it came back to me didn't it," he leant back casually in his chair.

"In that case sergeant, you can take me through everything you found out back when you were working on the case. I understand you were working with Cross on that case, is that right?" he asked politely still munching on his toast and sipping his tea.

"That's right, I came in several years later, the girl was murdered in nineteen fifty eight for Christ's sake. There wasn't much to go on, all we had was a group of lads were in an American type car, they were drunk and out for a good night when they met that young girl,"

"What about her friend Rose?" Jack casually enquired as he bit once more into his toast.

"She came later, all she knew was they went to the flicks...pictures," he explained. Jack just smiled and nodded his head as he put another piece of toast in his mouth, his mind was alert to Danny's words. "She got the bus and left her friend and that was the last she saw of her...nah we investigated that case until there was nothing left to investigate...no it went cold quickly back then."

"So this George has shed a new light on the case. it just might be the one clue you were hoping to find all those years ago, don't you understand...can't you see the significance of this last dying wish of a man whose only dream was to go and meet his maker with a clear conscience, now that makes sense to me, doesn't it you?"

"Jack, forget it, it was a long time ago, it died a death twenty four years ago, we couldn't solve it then. So now put it away and lets get on and do some real police work."

"This is real police work you idiot, just now and again something comes to light and we get led down a new path and in time somebody does or says the wrong thing and bang the villain is caught and put behind bars were they belong. This George could be the one too put right a wrong of so long ago, besides we owe it to Carol for god's sake," he pressed home then went on to add, "The only person to know her killer is the victim herself, maybe her spirit is leading us to the murderer via this George, what d'ya think eh Danny boy."

"I think you're mad but who am I to argue."

....

....

Steve and Angie found themselves in the theatre that evening being entertained by Nookie Bear, who had the audience in stitches from the very start of the act. In fact a group of elderly women never stopped laughing all evening.

Leaving that theatre they made for one of the little pubs on the far bank of the inlet, having crossed the bridge that greeted them when they arrived, but now empty of any trains. They crossed the bridge to get to the other side, the litle pub they chose was a little old sailor's pub, with all the usual sailors knots dotted around the fawn coloured walls. Old oak beams and wooden panelled ceilings completed the old fashioned look and it was enhanced by a well stocked bar that was situated at the far end of the establishment.

"That's got to be the most funniest thing I have ever seen in my life Steve, I nearly wet my knickers laughing so much," she said as she pulled herself to his side, slipping her arm under his arm for comfort as the evening had gone cold.

"I know, it was really good to see you laugh so much as we've been through so much babe," he said as he gave her a gentle kiss on her lips.

Getting a couple of drinks, Angie chose an orange and lemonade with some ice, whilst Steve got himself a pint of lager, they then found a table in a little nook. A picture of a grand old sailing ship, in full sail on a choppy sea hung in an ornate golden frame on the wall behind them.

"So Steve what are you going to do when we go home?" she inquired as she sipped at her pint glass.

"I said I'm supposed to help the Aussie guy Ian with this murder case of two Brits in Australia," he said as he sipped his lager, savouring the moment.

"So how are you going to start that case, surely you are working on a shoestring of a case."

"If they are Brits who were on holiday out there the answer just might be connected to something back here in Britain. It would be up to Ian and me to find that one missing link that would solve the case once and for all... no, my guess is the answer is right here in this country and we will need to find it, anyway lets not talk shop while we are on holiday. Anyway you never talk about how the baby is doing, is everything ok, you know you can tell me anything."

"Of course everything is ok, I would tell you otherwise so stop worrying your little head about it. I just like to savour being pregnant at the moment, you will get your chance when the little one arrives. The we will both be too busy to think," she laughed nervously and he gently moved towards her to give her a kiss.

"O.K. Mum," he laughed and talk turned to other trivial matters.

They managed to get a taxi to take them back to the camp where they found Bob and Peta busy cooking some sausages on the cooker, with some chips to go with them.

"We're on holiday Bruv, I do love a good fry up after a few beers," Bob said as he started to pour out a beer from a can into a tall glass. Throwing a can to Steve to drink he pulled the ring pull to the hiss of the drink as it frothed over the top.

Chapter 6

It was a typical Friday, the eleventh of September. The market place in Romford, that was usually a hive of activity, had now had the stalls packed away into their relevant sheds. This just left the council's dustmen to do the dirty bit of cleaning up after them, and removing any leftover waste from the day. The faint smell of fresh fish and hot dogs and burgers still lingered in the air, although the stalls had long been put away. Some local people used the various routes around and within the confines of the market to get home or to make for the relevant bus stops.

Now the normally busy place was a vast, empty, cobble stoned area which resembled the very early market that dated from the middle ages when cattle and sheep would have been on sale.

The odd double decker red bus partially full headed rumbled by in either direction. The traffic was sparse and the sun had set, an overcast sky created a sense that rain was imminent. Even the odd drop of rain kissed the bare skin. It had been a strange day for Jack, who hadn't been feeling too well earlier in the day but did his brave bit and battled on.

"You should go home Jack and go to bed, you're not looking too good," insisted the chief who stumbled on him as he sneezed into his handkerchief.

"Yes Sir!" Jack replied soulfully as he tucked his white handkerchief back into his jacket pocket, with the intention of grabbing it fast if he needed to. "It's just that I have got to go and see the Blackmore family, apparently their house has been broken into and ransacked, as if somebody was looking for something," he explained to his chief.

"Is that the same Blackmore who confessed to you last week in the hospital, something to do with the Graveside Murder of 1958"?

"The very same one," Jack said as he bent down to retrieve his briefcase from the floor beside his desk where several files were stacked, "are you thinking what I'm thinking Sir?" He quizzed, as once again he sneezed and took out his handkerchief.

"And what might that be Jack?" asked the Chief with an intrigued look in his eyes.

"Well, if my theory is right, I feel the killer has heard of the death of our Mr. Blackmore and suddenly his demise has put a cat amongst the pigeons, as they would say, sir," Jack expressed as the two men headed for the main entrance.

"So Jack what you are saying is Carol Richards killer is getting scared of being found out and he or she is thinking our Mr. Blackmore has something that would incriminate his or hers identity."

"The very same," Jack uttered before another sneezing spell occurred.

"The question is, who at the time was aware of his death, his son, his wife, anybody that was close to him could've informed the killer unknowingly...that's the irony of this case... one things for sure

Jack, it has opened this case up again, with good prospects this time around maybe eh?"

"Lets hope so sir, if not for Carol's sake and the horror her family must be going through, even today, they must be living the nightmare over and over every year on the anniversary of her death...lets hope we can get a result this time, sir,"

"Let's just pray for that result and put this little matter to bed once and for all...so Jack what are you going to do now?"

"I don't know, I'll just play this one by ear at the moment. I know one thing that's interesting me, and that is the place where she died. I know it was in the alley by the church and her body ended up being draped over a low wall along there that is assuming that low wall is still there. So I thought that would be my first port of call. Then I'll head in the direction of the Blackmore home; the trouble is my car is in the garage having its brakes fixed so it's buses for me tonight."

"Tut! Tut! No courtesy car then Jack?"

"Nah, I'm not good enough," he smiled as they stood in the now empty reception area. Jack sneezed again and quickly retrieved his handkerchief from his pocket. A young w.p.c., in her pristine uniform stood guard awaiting a call from the public. With the time approaching ten o'clock in the evening it wouldn't be long before she would be at her wits end, with the usual fights as the local pubs cleared out. A sudden phone call came through that indicated a complaint of a domestic taking place on the other side of the town. She confirmed to those concerned that a car was on its way as she spoke.

"You'll have your work cut out for you tonight Jane, I can feel it in my bones," Jack laughed to himself as he turned to depart. She just laughed half heartedly at his idea of a joke.

"You take care Jack, and get an early night," the chief said with concern in his voice, "make sure you get something for that cold and look after yourself."

"Yes sir!" He replied softly, removing his handkerchief to stop another sneeze.

A gentle rain had left the street with a soft glaze. It was a short distance to the old, worn, cobble stoned area which was now free of the banter of the day. It was a place where you could buy anything from a bag of potatoes to a diamond ring, with the occasional wheeler dealer chancing his luck, moving on when the police arrived.

Jack stopped just on the edge of the market place, putting his briefcase on the ground for second to remove a packet of king size cigarettes from his jacket pocket and lighting one. He used an American style, silver flick up lid with the wheel that lit it via a piece of flint that was inserted in the bottom, which was then held in place at the top by a spring and a screw. He inhaled the smoke once it was lit, then he proceeded to return both items to his jacket pocket and picking up his briefcase he headed for the alley way in question. His heavy footsteps echoed across the area from the metal studs he had put into the heels of his black leather brogues.

Several people were leaving the local pub at the far end of the market square, their voices seemed like they were using a megaphone. "How loud do you need to shout just to say good night to anybody," Jack muttered under his breath as he dragged on his cigarette. It was about then the number eighty six passed heading for London. The lights at the junction of the road were red as Jack began to reach the dreaded alleyway with the church looming up in the wake of that selling place.

A young couple were sitting on a bench kissing and cuddling, oblivious of the reality of life and the movement of the night. Only their love was more important to them, so they ignored the passing of Jack who just moved his head from side to side in disgust at their frolicking.

Stopping briefly to enjoy a long drawn out drag on his cigarette he proceeded with an eager step to enter the alleyway where he hoped to find the spot where Carol Richards had been found all those years ago. It was found by one of those young lads who moved the stalls at the beginning and end of the market. Jack pondered the thought that the lad probably owns his own stall these days, but Jack knew inside his mind what the lad must have been thinking at that moment in time.

He suddenly came across some old wilted flowers at the low wall which he now believed was the last resting place of that unfortunate youngster. She didn't deserve to die so brutally, especially at that age. She could have been a mother today, or even a grandmother, Jack thought to himself, as he stood silent for a moment to dwell on the area twenty four years before. Flicking his ash to one side away from the wilted flowers, he stooped down to read a tatty card that lay amidst the dead flowers which read, 'we'll love you till the end of time,' a small light brown teddy bear lay on the top of the wall.

The clock in the square chimed eleven o'clock. Jack checked the time to look at his watch, he leant over the wall to look at the grave stones that stood close to the wall. The nearest gravestone bore the name Grace Roberts died 1968.

"Have you got a light mate," suddenly a voice came from behind and Jack, who hadn't heard the person approach gingerly, got up as he suddenly felt unsteady on his legs. He turned to see where the voice had come from, only to be confronted by a young man in his early forties holding a freshly rolled cigarette which he held in his right hand waving it near to his mouth. A white peaked cap shadowed his face. The dim light reflected off the end of his nose and chin.

"Sure Mate!" Jack replied calmly, removing his lighter from his jacket pocket and with a quick flick of the lid and as he again flicked the little wheel it lit allowing the young man to light his cigarette. Jack was just about to return the lighter to his jacket pocket when he felt a sudden shooting pain in his stomach. His voice took a tone of terror as he reeled backwards, his lighter flying across the path. Looking down he saw the hilt of a knife sticking out of his body and he realised he had been stabbed. "But why?" he begged as he held his stomach knowing he was in serious danger now.

The young man moved forward to confront the now dying officer. "You were told to drop it, but you just wouldn't listen, would you, now you will pay the price for not doing as you were told, old man."

"What have I done," Jack muttered only to be stabbed a second time as the young man removed the knife with some speed and stabbed him in the chest. This was the fatal blow and the weapon was an old scouting knife that would've been kept in a leather sheath, which in turn would've been attached to the belt of the scout.

The young man removed the knife from Jack and lifted his prey and laid the body over the low wall, where Carol once lay. Happy with his work he casually walked back down the alley to the far end where a waiting car that he'd parked earlier stood, it was a dark blue Ford Fiesta.

A short time later a middle aged couple happened to pass along that alley as they were heading home. When they stumbled across the body of Jack, but they assumed he was just drunk and were about to go when they spotted some blood on the floor near him. As a street light created a dim glow, they noticed his briefcase was still at his side. Once they reached the sanctuary of their home in a nearby road, they quickly telephoned the police to tell them of the discovery in the alley. They told the officer on the phone that they believed somebody had been attacked or worse, or simply drunk, they didn't know which as they hadn't wanted to hang around, just in case.

"Ok sir we'll send an officer to find

out, can we take your name and address just in case."

Moments later and a police car pulled up in the market place and two officers in uniform set out to investigate the problem. It wasn't long before they found the body slumped over the wall. Another couple were also there as they had been asking if he was alright, but got no answer even when the gentleman gave him a little nudge to no avail. They had been on the point of leaving to phone the police when the officers had arrived they explained.

"Ok sir we'll take it from now on," returned one of the officers whilst the other went over to the body and picked up the briefcase left by his side, "however we will need your names and addresses first please," he proceeded to take down the details in his pocketbook.

"Pete," returned the officer who had picked up the case, "I think this is Jack, Jack Gould."

"Jack!" called the officer with Jack's case, but eerily there was no answer. He realised it was serious as he had noticed some blood near Jack's foot and leaning over the wall he noticed blood on the edge of the gravestone.

"This is PC 207, can you get an ambulance here right away, to the alley at the side of the church in the market square, also we are going to need extra help," ordered one of the officers into his radio pinned to his left shoulder.

"Where are you now 207?"

"We're with the body and Jane, its Jack."

Very shortly the whole area was sealed off with the usual police ribbon and the alley became a hive of activity as forensic teams scoured the area for any hidden clues. Detective Inspector Jackson was first on the scene, a six foot male in his mid thirties with an Elvis look, including a soft, ginger teddy boy hair do and wearing a fawn jacket and black trousers and Chelsea boots with a zip up the side.

When he approached the scene, flashing his badge at the young uniformed officer on guard duty, he stooped under the police cordon where he met a middle-aged man in white overalls examining the body.

"Ok Phil what's the mo?"

"He was stabbed twice, once in the stomach, and again in the chest. I would say the chest stabbing was the one that killed him," he said as he knelt by the body.

"Time Phil. What time do you reckon?" He asked as he finally knelt beside the body.

"I guess around ten or eleven

o'clock, maybe, he's been dead about a couple of hours if that's any help Bob, ok."

It wasn't long before the chief was present at their side, investigating the death of one of his senior officers who now lay undignified on the cold tarmac path, in some dingy lit alley way that he had walked down on many occasions without any incident.

The next morning the media were keen to learn of the death of a detective, so Chief Constable Cross along with Detective Inspector Jackson entertained the media. This included the television camera's that stood around outside the police station in the high street almost bringing the area to a stand still, with people milling around hoping to get a glimpse of themselves on the television, even though it was only the news.

Finally the two officers came out to give the usual type of interview. It began with the chief telling the media that a good man had been killed in the alleyway in the market square and that they would be fully investigating his death. He then went on to tell them that he was one of the most well respected officers on the force, his loss to the community would be felt everywhere he had worked and how his presence would be missed in the office's where he would be a hard act to follow.

Suddenly there was a voice from

the crowd of journalists shouting, "Is there a reason for his death?"

"No! Although I can confirm that we are looking into anything to do with his previous cases, in case there is a clue in there. Ok, we will be letting the media know as soon as we have carried out a full investigation into his untimely death. Ok that's all for now," the two officers departed to have a discussion about the evenings work and how they were going to investigate this incident.

Chapter 7

A cool breeze wafted across the cliff tops, it was scented with the sweet smell of gorse and wild fauna which in turn was enhanced by the tang of the sea. It was a glorious day, the twelfth of September, almost the end of their first week of the holiday.

Steve and Angie found themselves strolling hand in hand across those lush green high cliff tops, they were both wearing jeans and sweat shirts. Steve's was black and Angie's was red, they also wore matching trainers. Tara was straining at her lead as the glorious smells of the wildlife teased her nostrils awakening her animal instincts, including barking at the noisy seagulls that swooped overhead.

They had crossed a field of wild overgrown grasses strolling along a well trodden path and had passed another well known holiday park. Its many varieties of chalets were over shadowed with what can only be described as a block of flats and all set in a compound near the cliff top.

Way down below, the now calm

sea splashed endlessly against the rocks, its mellow sound soothed the soul, in Steve's eyes. Portland Bill stood like an ornament that dominated the horizon, as though it was trying to entice the would-be traveller to venture onto its top and discover its true potential.

A lone cross channel ferry was returning to the port having visited Jersey or Guernsey, which ever and a naval helicopter was buzzing around like some fly flying around rotting meat, as it hovered and darted back and forth around the base on the shores of Portland Bill.

On the other side was a sight to die for, with rolling hills and the bustle of the campsite a distant memory, just the open barrenness of the countryside that echoed with wild life. A lone sparrow hawk sang as it hovered, searching for that unfortunate little creature who fails to see the danger above, its head ready to swoop down at great speed. The songs of different birds came from all around them, and mingled with the gorse and the squawking of the many seagulls drifting on the wind just off the cliff top and the odd tree stood like a sentry nearby.

A wire fence prevented the walker from getting too near to the perilous edge, as it could go at anytime and it had been reported that several people had fallen to the their deaths from the cliff tops. They said hello to several couples and the odd family group with the kids running about enjoying the fresh air, it was an idyllic holiday scene and the scenery was amazing.

They found themselves walking down a shallow slope that meandered down into a cove known as Osmington Mills. There they found what was left of some large old liner that once sailed our seas, it was now just a mere skeleton of its former life.

"It's this sort of thing that hurts me Ange," Steve said soulfully as they reached the wreck. "Can you imagine what tales it could tell if it could talk?"

"I know honey... it's a shame. I wonder what her name was."

"Who knows... my guess is the salvage company would know which ship it was". Steve expressed casually, as they found themselves walking in the bowels of the ship, being careful not to trip on the rusting beams. There was the faint left over whiff of diesel from where the large old engines had been fixed. They would've once taken up the whole of the bowels of that once fine vessel but now nothing lined their place where they had lain. Everywhere rusting metal parts looked up, Steve sensed the immense size of the vessel that had once travelled the world. Steve closed his eyes for a moment, to relish in the thought, that he was on board this once beautiful liner heading into the sun and some distant exotic shore; he saw himself walking the elegant wooden decks. Then being waited on by well dressed sailors, whose job it was to make your life comfortable.

"You seem distant Steve," nudged Angie politely.

"Sorry! I was miles away on this liner, heading westward and...Well...god knows where," he returned as they made for an exit from the decaying shell of the shipwreck.

"I wonder how it got here," Angie enquired, after a moment's silence.

"My guess is she was stripped of all her glory whilst she was at sea and then what was left, namely the empty hull was then simply dragged ashore to be finished off...I reckon if you were to come here next year; I bet you a fiver, it wouldn't be here anymore, just a stain in the ground, where it once lay, and a distant memory to all those who worked on her."

"You are an old romantic Steve, I think we should head back to the camp," Angie said holding her bump and complained of being hungry.

Steve, licking his lips, toyed with the thought of some of that bacon his brother had been cooking as they left on their little venture to help their appetite's and clear their minds.

A few clouds drifted up from the sea as the tide was still coming in with the faint smell of seaweed touching their noses. As they strolled along that well trodden dirt path with the odd bench to rest your tired legs, the thought of food prevented them from resting as they were to eager to get back to the caravan and a good fry up.

<u>Meanwhile</u>

Back at the caravan Bob was happy to be cooking Peta some breakfast of eggs and bacon on toast. Peta sat looking out of the large open window at the front of the caravan that overlooked another caravan where she casually watched a couple moving about in their little temporary home.

About the same time the Major was nearing Weymouth. He was wearing a pale blue suit with a navy and gold tie over a clean white shirt, and black leather, chisel toed slip on casual shoes that he preferred when driving.

He had driven all the way from London to the campsite with the hopeful intention of meeting Steve as he was on an urgent mission. He drove his car, a black Ford Granada, into the camp car park and proceeded to the reception to enquire after the caravan Steve and his party were staying in, producing his badge of office as proof of his rank.

"What have they done?" inquired a curious female receptionist, a five foot nothing woman with long fair hair that she'd tied up in a ponytail.

"What makes you think they have done anything," He smiled, "so young lady can I have the number of the caravan my officer is staying in?"

"Caravan 13K, you'll find it by going straight along the road you came in, go down there till you reach the middle field...are you walking sir?" she eagerly asked.

"I'll walk ok; it'll do me good as I've been driving most of the night to get here," He said with a serious voice, and then added sarcastically, "Straight down the middle you say."

She smiled coyly and nodded her head and gave a casual rising of her eyebrows sexily, just to tease him, before she slowly bowed her head and laughed to herself.

Removing his briefcase from the boot of his car he found the fresh air strange to his city nose, giving it thumbs down as he strolled along the tarmac road and acting path. He removed his jacket and neatly folded it over his right arm as he walked in the direction he had been pointed out. Soon he reached the next field that matched the one he had just left, so once there he searched for row 'K', where he then proceeded to search for number 13 as stated.

The faint smell of bacon cooking was intoxicating even to the pallet of the Major. He just followed his nose hoping it would lead him to his final destination.

Climbing the two steps to the door he knocked and a few seconds later Peta opened it and politely asked him what he wanted.

"Can you tell me, is the caravan where Mr. Price's party is residing," enquired the Major.

"Depends on who's asking", she returned with the door tucked into her side.

"Who is it honey?" Bob asked from the lounge, where he was happy doing the crossword in the newspaper and drinking his cup of tea, that he had placed onto the low table. He tossed aside his newspaper onto the long bench settee.

"Some guy wants Mr. Price."

"That's Mr. Steven Price to be precise," he continued to pursue.

"He wants your brother, Bob."

"He's gone for a walk over the cliff tops with Angie and his little mutt Tara," Bob returned as he gently moved Peta to one side and took her place at the door, leaving her to return to the cooking. "You'd better come in and wait if you like," he said as he moved back to allow him to enter. "So what's this all about then?"

"I'm Steven's boss; he works for me and the Home office. I am known as the Major, Major Thompson to be more precise, but people just call me the Major."

"Right!" replied Bob who led him to the lounge where he found a seat under the large front window, with its orange coloured curtains and white nets. There he placed his briefcase on the floor beside the low wooden table, "so Major what's this little visit in aid of, I mean, you can tell me, I am his little brother."

"It's a matter of national interest and I can only tell Steven as he his my officer in the force."

"Are you a real Major," enquired Peta who was still busying herself in the kitchen area, "would you like a tea or coffee?"

"Tea would be nice, two sugars please," he replied as he gently laid his jacket onto the seat beside him, "I see you do the crosswords in the papers," he enquired, as he stooped to look at his paper with the crossword almost complete.

"He tries to," Peta giggled. "Would you like a bacon roll Major?"

"Thanks a lot. I love you too," Bob replied sarcastically, "so what sort of work do you do Major?"

"Have you just come from London to here this morning", Peta enquired as she placed his cup of tea in front of him, to the reply of a polite 'thank you', by the Major.

"Yes you could say that, and no I don't fancy a bacon roll all the same thanks," he replied tasting his tea and complimenting her on her ability to please him.

"Blimey! It must be important if it brought you all this way so soon."

"You could say that," he replied with a smile, then went on to enquire, "this walk Steve and Angie went on is it far and how long ago did they leave?"

"They left a couple of hours ago and do you see that hill just over there," Bob explained as he pointed to the left of the caravan, "there's a path that leads you up onto the cliff tops and my guess is they would've headed for Lullworth Cove, which is east of here," Bob found himself explaining. "I suppose you want to go and find him eh?"

"I'll wait awhile," he replied sipping slowly at his mug of tea, "this tea is a breath of fresh air to my tongue after that long old journey," he expressed, as he gently undid his navy and gold striped tie, just enough to reveal a fraction of his neck, with the top button shirt undone.

"Its been rather warm down here

this week," returned Peta who leant against the back of the seat that was part of the dining table, sipping at her mug of coffee, that she had cupped in both hands.

"I can feel it Peta, you don't mind me calling you by your first name?" he said as he too sipped at his tea, Bob just smiled to himself.

"Of course you can Major... mind you I feel strange calling you Major, I mean...that isn't your first name you were born with... is it?"

"No!" he replied with a slight hint of a grin, "If you must know my first name is Alex but don't tell anybody or I will have to shoot you... no, I'm only joking," he grinned.

"Is that short for Alexander?"

He smiled, and nodded to acknowledge her inquisitive mind, before finishing his tea, and after placing the empty mug on the low table, he proceeded to retrieve his briefcase from the floor as he found his feet, and returning his suit jacket over his arm, claimed that he felt he should go and look for Steve as he explained he was a very busy man.

"Ok Major!" returned Bob who also found his feet. "If you follow the path you came up from the reception you'll come to the clubhouse, well just before you get the clubhouse, you take the path to the left, and follow it to the gate, cross the road to the field opposite, there you'll see the path that passes through the overgrown field that'll take you up to the cliff top, turn left and just follow that path, I'm sure at some point you'll meet the pair of them...ok Major."

He smiled and departed, leaving them with a worried look on their faces and hoping they hadn't put Steve in any danger.

Bob held his mug of coffee in his hand as he stood at the window and watched the Major head back to the path and casually walk in the direction of the clubhouse, as directed.

"What d'ya thinks wrong Bob?"

"I don't know sugar, it could be anything, knowing that lot, especially if he is from the Home Office as he claims therefore it's got to be a mega problem," he commented as he returned to his crossword puzzle and bacon roll.

Chapter 8

Stopping for a breather the Major placed his briefcase on the floor in front of him for a few moments, then he pulled the ring pull off his can of soft drink which made the usual hiss and froth came spouting out of the hole. He quickly sipped the froth before taking a well earned swig of the cold refreshing drink that reached his vital parts with ease.

A family group of six nudged past him heading for a caravan in another field adjacent to the one he had stopped in, just as a sudden breeze blew up from the sea.

Retrieving his case he continued on his way heading for the gate and feeling out of place in the campsite in his office gear as everybody else was well attired in their holiday outfits. Many of them wore shorts of many colours, accompanied by an array of multi coloured t-shirts; there were no suits and ties in sight, so he felt wild as he undid his tie before removing it and neatly folded he placed it in his jacket pocket.

A couple of Westie's ran past him as he finally reached what could only be described as a stile, which the Major found difficult to scramble over while clutching his jacket and briefcase in one hand and his can of drink in the other. So in the end, out of desperation, he shoved his briefcase under the bottom rail and placed his can in the now empty hand and then he was able to climb over grabbing a post at the side to steady himself.

Taking another sip of his drink he proceeded to reach the cliff top and genuinely believed he didn't have to walk too far to meet up with Steve. Closing his eyes and taking a deep breath he finally reached the cliff edge and he could now see the sea in all its glory to behold. Thinking deeply to himself that it was good to be alive on such a sad day, in his eyes, as he headed in the direction he was told too in the hope of crossing paths with Steve and Angie.

Looking up into the distance, he hoped and prayed that he just might espy them, but all he could see were several small groups with their backs walking away from him. One group was a group of girls; their laughter enchanted the air around him. It seemed a magical place for all who ventured there, for fun and fantastic memories to take back to their mundane lives, back in their own worlds, oblivious of the events going on around them in more rural areas.

Suddenly, in the far distance on a second distant hill top he spotted what looked like little Tara, who suddenly appeared over the horizon of the hill top, followed shortly by two people. However because they were still far off, it was hard to be sure in the Majors eyes. He felt he had to get a bit closer to be certain, but the incline was slow and steady to climb and heavy on the stamina and the Major began to feel out of condition. He was wishing he was like those young girls, full of vim, but found himself having to stop for a moment to recover, so he looked for one of the cliff top benches, where he could simply sit, and watch the world walk by. He could wait for them to reach him and after finding a seat he placed his briefcase between his legs and draped his suit jacket over it for safety purposes.

He was tempted to walk to the edge of the cliff and peer over to see how high he truly was, as it seemed a long way down. Several gorse bushes prevented you from getting too close, but the odd gap emerged to tempt you to be nosey. Where he sat he had a clear view of the sea and he watched as a couple of large sailing boats scurried past out to sea, as if they were enjoying the odd race with each other. One had a white sail while the other had a two tone colour sail of navy blue and red.

The droning sound of a naval helicopter appeared from behind him and passing low over his head, it headed out to sea and came down in the naval base at the foot of a steep cliff face on Portland Bill. He jokingly used his fingers like a makeshift gun and pretended to shoot it down, even to the extent of making the sound of the gun with his mouth, just like a schoolboy would.

The sun was rising higher and getting even warmer as he got up for a moment to observe the continual approach of the couple and their little white dog, who had now disappeared into the well of the two hills, making him think they may have taken a different route. He used the time to stretch his legs as he walked around the bench a few times to get his circulation back as his legs were getting numb from sitting for so long.

A faint barking seemed to bounce off the airwaves to reassure the Major everything was still ok.

What seemed like a lifetime now ebbed when the barking neared and he could now see it was the two people he had been waiting patiently for. They had failed to notice him sitting there; drinking what was left of the can. He gave a big yawn and was sorely tempted to lie down on the bench and grab some shut eye in the wake of his wait.

"Do you know what's really worrying me Angie?" Steve said as they slowly edged their way home to the sanctum of the caravan and maybe a lay down for an hour or two.

"What's that honey...what is it that is worrying you?" She enquired warmly.

"I'm worried about where I'm going to be put, I'm not really happy in Basildon, I just want to know where we are going to end up."

"Where would you like to go then?"

"I don't know," he uttered, "if I had my way I'd love to emigrate to Australia. the stories that Ian has told me are enticing," he said as he pulled her to his side.

"Here! Steve! That wouldn't be who I think it is?" she said in anticipation, when her eyes were averted in the Majors direction; even though it was still a little way off she thought it was odd that somebody dressed so smart would be out there on the cliff tops sitting all alone, with a woman yes, but not alone. "You know the one who calls himself the Major."

"Where are we talking about?" he enquired, stopping for a moment to gather his senses,

"There!" She pointed referring to the bench and the lone, well dressed man sitting staring out to sea.

"Nah, not here surely, he wouldn't know we were up here, unless... nah it can't be... can it Ange... your eyesight must be better than mine."

"Well in my eyes that's the Major," she expressed as she nudged him joyfully. Tara barked at her silliness.

"Well there's only one way to find out if it is him, we'll get a move on, because if it is him it must be important to have brought him this far. I wouldn't think it was to have a taste of candy floss or a hot dog... Nah it can't be him."

Moments later and they began to reach him, just as he turned around and found his feet, he retrieved his briefcase and jacket, then slowly he walked towards them with a smile on his face as he was really glad to have met up with them at last.

"Major!" Steve said with a curious look on his face, wondering what had brought him out this far.

"Steve! Angie! it's good to see you both and you're looking good, the sea air is good for you," The Major said as he arrived at their side and the three of them took up the width of the path with Tara sniffing the long grass.

"What brings you out here Major, it isn't bad news I hope?" Steve asked as he shook the Major's hand warmly.

"Lets sit on that seat where I was sitting Steve," he replied, pointing to the seat where he had just been sitting and admiring the view.

"Yeah, what's the problem boss?"

Steve pressed as they all found the seat and Tara was happy just to lay herself in the grass, rolling over a few times, dwelling in self glory.

"Well Major?" enquired a curious Angie who sat on her hands as the hard seat felt uncomfortable in her condition, "What's this all in aid of?"

"Yeah boss what ever she said."

"Ok Steve," he said as he placed the briefcase on the floor in front of him and began to open it to remove some files in the manner Steve had become familiar with, "You know a Detective Inspector Gould."

"Gould you say?" Steve replied with a puzzled look in his eyes, "You don't mean Jack Gould...what about him?"

"I gather then you haven't been watching any television today."

"Why what has happened, is he in trouble...I mean he is a good guy, the last time we were together was in Harlow, some six years ago we were working on the Janet Dobson case until we heard a task force was calling the shots...D.I. Lawrence I believe."

"Yeah you're right Steve."

"The last thing I remember was he got a transfer to Romford nick that was the last I heard of him, so what as he gone and done now... who has he upset?"

"Nobody Steve... well he may

have, because he is dead; killed late last night, around eleven o'clock."

"You are joking Major!?" Steve said in a shocked state putting his hand over his mouth.

"I wish I was Steve... truly I wish it weren't true, but it is."

"But how... how was he killed."

"He was stabbed twice, the second time fatally."

"What was he working on at the time?" Steve pursued for answers regarding the fate of his old friend of the early days in his troubled career.

"It is still unclear at this moment in time... in fact, it's all a bit hazy at present... they are all in a state of shock," he said as he continued to remove a file.

"Surely it is a case for the local plod to deal with," he expressed disconcertedly.

"That's true, but I want you to go there and take Jack's place," he said removing his transfer form to be filled out. He placed the form on the briefcase that he had lain on his lap and handed him a pen from his inside pocket of his jacket.

"So where are we going to be living, have you thought about that issue Major," Steve pressed his concern as he signed the papers, but still thought about their future, as he didn't relish the thought of having to travel from Laindon every day to Romford.

"If you wait a minute I'm going to give you a set of keys to a police house in Rainham, the address you will find is on the keys," he explained as he casually tossed them to him, and required him to sign some papers to make it all legal, "What is the purpose of the move?" He asked as he grabbed the keys and looked at the address on the label that was tied to the key ring.

"I want you to go there and find out how and why your friend was murdered, I'm sure he would expect you to find the truth if it is out there. There is one thing that might interest you Steve; it even might have some bearing as to Jack's untimely death. Who knows but it is a coincidence in the light of the events of this last few days," he said calmly as he took another file out of his case and removed a letter that had been addressed to the home office. "This letter Steve arrived on my desk about a week ago and when I first read it I thought it was a hoax, until I did some research, I think it could be of some interest to you... who knows it still could be a hoax... still find out... but read the letter and give it back to me Steve, and tell me what you think."

"I can see it is from somebody who is serving time at her Majesties pleasure in 'The Scrubs.'

"Read on!" He expressed his desire for answers.

"Dear sirs," it formally started.

I am serving life for allegedly killing my wife ten years ago, but I know I'm innocent of the crime, because, yes I was stoned out of my head having downed several pints of beer in the local pub where I had met a guy. He said he had a stash of heroin, I can remember taking some, and I was out of it, but this guy was boasting about killing some young girl in the late fifties. He asked if he could stop over at my house for the night, as he claimed he lived up north somewhere and needed a place to crash out. So I took him back to my gaff and I vaguely remember the wife was sitting watching the television when I got home.

The next morning when I woke up he was gone and I found the wife dead in the armchair where she had been the night before. The law said I killed her and I was put down for life but I know I'm innocent as I've preached ever since, I was banged up in this rat hole please help me.

yours sincerely
Andrew Cox

Steve read the letter then handed it back to the Major with a puzzled look on his face, "So Major what do we know of the Andrew Cox guy."

"Well according to his file...he was

convicted of killing his wife after a night out and having taken a dose of heroin himself, he went home and injected a lethal dose of heroin into the neck of his wife while she was watching the TV. which was still going on when she was found. It killed her instantly which in her case was a godsend as she would have become a dope fiend like her husband was if it hadn't killed her due to the amount injected."

"It makes some sense!", Steve said thoughtfully, finding his feet he walked to the fence and turned to face them, while he tried to get the feel for the case then went on to add, "if this Andrew Cox was high on heroin and booze as he claims, it could be said, he wouldn't have been fit enough to have killed his wife, in fact he wouldn't have been able to have done any thing to anybody," he explained then went on to enquire, "Why is it significant to me?"

"Andrew Cox lived in Romford for many years both as a boy and when he married Lucy in nineteen sixty nine. He started out in life working on one of the market stalls there, apparently he was a good little worker, he loved working on the fruit and veg stalls, in fact they said at the time he could sell ice to the Eskimos and had all the banter that went with the job."

"So what do we know about this so called murder of the fifties he mentions in the letter?"

"There was only one murder that we could think of at that moment in time and that was the one that took place in Romford in the fifties, It was a young girl named Carol Richards, she was stabbed too and in the same place as our Jack was last night, a coincidence...don't you think?"

"It's hard to swallow at this moment in time...anyway what about our friend Ian Dobson; I was supposed to have been helping him with his mystery killing in Australia."

"You carry on with that case, while I set up this transfer business for you as it will take me a while to sort everything out in your favour. You will be taking Jack's place there and that is how it must look. Then study the events of last night, in fact study everything and I mean everything, are you ok about that Steve."

"I get it you want me to go undercover at that nick just in case I end up like Jack, is that it?"

"You've got it in one; I will let you know when you start there ok."

"Got it...fancy a spot of lunch Major, I'm sure you must be hungry from your journey to this place."

"You don't have to twist my arm Steve," he replied as he returned everything to his case, then standing up he placed his jacket over his case and the three of them headed back to the camp and then on to the pub 'The Ship,' and a table for three, where they were served by a tall stockily built man who was once the chef on a naval ship.

The place was laced with relics of old ships, a capstan stood in the corner next to an old wooden ship's wheel, soft beige walls were enhanced with dark oak beams everywhere and a bar was done out like the inside of a sailing ship with light oak wooden strips on the ceiling. The Major was mesmerised by the effect the proprietor had achieved when designing his pub, the place was half full of hungry holiday makers.

Chapter 9

A cool breeze kissed the cheeks of the little group as they left the sanctuary of, 'The Ship Pub', having quelled their hunger, especially Angie who had enjoyed every minute of the culinary experience. An army tank rumbled by to Steve's amazement and it was accompanied by a couple of army trucks. These had many young soldiers perched on seats on either side of the trucks as the cavalcade headed for the Town.

The Major was eager to return to London hoping to get back in one piece. The roads were beginning to get busy with the build up of traffic on the roads that were all heading in the same direction; he had politely refused to spend the night in the caravan, claiming he preferred sleeping in his own bed and found it difficult to adjust to any other.

The group headed back to the campsite and the Major's awaiting car.

"Can you make sure that Jack's office is sealed off, so I can check it for any clues to his sad ending Major," requested a more serious Steve, feeling bitter about the concept of losing a friend he had worked with.

"Will do Steve," the Major replied, then proceeded to use his car phone to call the Romford police station to order the sealing off of Jacks office. He asked to talk to the chief and once he was put through to the chief's office he gave the order using his Home Office seal of authority to get the task done, "will there be anything else you would like me to do while I'm at it?" enquired the Major, as he returned the receiver to its rightful place in the holder on the console in the middle of the front seats.

"Not really, I think we've covered everything today. I am looking forward to getting stuck into this case Major; it feels good to be working with the police again. I did miss it over the years and Romford is a better deal then I have at present in Basildon. Besides which I am eager to find out who did this terrible thing to Jack and why?"

"I know it is a bad thing that has happened to this Jack, but to be honest it is the best thing to happen to us Major," Angie piped up putting her two penneth into the conversation, Why only this morning he was complaining about his future...wasn't you Steve?"

"Would you like me to cut my holiday short and get to work on this case?" He replied, scratching his head in thought.

"No Steve, it can wait a few more days. Besides, you are supposed to be working with, you know who," The Major commented, as he headed for his parked car. "Anyway if it is of any interest he is the second copper to have been killed in Romford... don't worry the other one was shot in eighteen eighty five, a bit before your time, and I believe his killer was caught so let's hope we can do just as good, eh," the Major bid them a fond farewell, as he tossed his briefcase on the passenger seat along with his jacket, "Oh and by the way Steve you might need this," he said as he removed a small card from his back pocket.

"What is it boss?" he said as he glanced at it.

"It's Jack's home address ok."

"That's great it'll save me going to the factory to find it...great just great," he replied joyfully giving him the thumbs up, slipping the card into his back pocket too. The Major gave him a glancing smile as he closed the door of his car, winding down the window he bid the pair of them a fond farewell as he slowly drove out of the campsite and headed back to London.

Angie put her arm in Steve's and she walked back to the caravan with an excited smile and a lightness in her step, knowing she was getting a house in Rainham. Steve's head was buzzing, as one moment he was on cloud nine at the thought of getting his teeth back into what he always knew he was good at, then he felt sadness as he realised that it had come about through the death of Jack and he knew he would do all he could to track down the killer of his friend.

....
....

Back in the ranks and files of the offices in Romford, the Chief ordered the sealing of Jacks office, once the Major had finished on the phone. Although the door was already locked by a key and the chief was in charge of that key, it was a formality regarding the entrance of the office. They used police ribbon tied around the door handle and a 'Do Not Enter,' notice on the door.

Detective Sergeant Peters just happened to be passing, carrying a set of files neatly tucked up under his right arm, when suddenly he was observing the act taking place on Jack's door. He was compelled to enquire after the reason for the sealing of Jack's office and was abruptly told it was in the hands of the Home Office and who were they to argue.

"So Chief, what's it got to do with the Home Office, don't they think we can sort out our own dirty linen, or something."

"Who are we to judge the minds of those in Whitehall," the Chief replied softly, with a lingering sigh because Jack was a dear friend as well as a good colleague to him and the others.

"Who's going to take Jack's place then," asked Peters with a curious look in his eyes.

"From what I've been told, Whitehall are sending in a good officer to take his place, we must make the new guy feel at home, ok," explained the Chief, calmly shrugging his shoulders.

"I thought I was going to sort out this matter regarding Jack... Chief", enquired a saddened D.I. Jackson, who appeared from around a corner carrying a mug of coffee in one hand and a couple of custard creams in the other.

All the officers were dressed in black trousers and black ties out of respect to a fallen comrade.

"I guess the powers to be, feel we are too emotionally connected to the case and therefore they want an officer from outside to carry out the investigation into his untimely death, that's it... as I said before... who are we to judge the minds of those in power... it is above me now... I guess they feel it might have some connections to somebody in here... who knows... don't forget we are talking about a fellow officer here. How's it going with the forensic boys, anything Jackson"?

"Nothing at the moment boss, only thing we found was Jack's lighter, it was on the floor a couple of feet from him. We know it is his lighter as it is engraved with the words, 'to Jack with love from Margaret,' there was a roll up cigarette a few feet away that had been trodden on and the forensic boys have taken it away, just in case it has a bearing on the case."

"Ok!" returned the Chief, "has

anybody else been to see Margaret since I went to break the bad news to her?"

"Yeah we have sent a W.P.C. to sit with her and help her sort things out."

"In that case I guess we have to wait for the new guy, whoever he is," returned the Chief who was keen to return to his office.

"I thought I would get promoted to Jack's rank, Chief," commented Peters wistfully.

He just turned and glanced at Peters face and gave a half-hearted grin with a shaking of his head from side to side.

"Well Chief, when do I get the promotion I put in for ?" Peters requested.

"When you've learnt to be a real copper," returned Jackson with a jovial wink, then headed for his office too. Peters was left to stand staring, with bitterness in his eyes, at the blue and white ribbon hanging from the office door.

....
....

That evening Steve walked up onto the cliff tops again as Angie was busy talking to Peta about the problems of pregnancy. Bob asked if he could join him but he refused saying he wanted to be alone for a moment. He explained he was all right, it was the case of his friend that was bugging him and he needed to be alone to dwell on the prospects of the case and that of Ian's and the two Brits killed in Australia.

The name Andrew Cox and his hand written letter played heavy on his mind. He was getting a strange feeling about the whole affair.

"What was Jack involved in that warranted him being killed... could it have been somebody he had banged up in the past, and they sought revenge,' it didn't seem possible in his eyes, but who knows what went on in the minds of some of these villains. If it were so, it meant he would have to go through every single case Jack had been involved in since he joined the team at Romford. 'What is so important about Romford', he thought to himself as he stood on top of the cliff looking out to sea, 'why am I being led more and more into believing this whole case has its roots in that place. Oh Jack what can of worms have you unearthed?"

"What's wrong Bruv," Bob said quietly as he found him staring out to sea as if he were in another world.

"Oh it's you!" He expressed with a half hearted smile on his face, "You made me jump," he said as he turned to see his brother standing there with his hands tucked in his trouser pockets and his jacket open, with a curious look on his face,

"Angie told me about the death of your friend in Romford and how you and her are moving to Rainham... that's brilliant Steve," Bob expressed his joy. "So what's really bothering you about it mate?"

"If Jack was involved with something big and he was killed for getting too close to finding out the truth, well as a result I am going to have to tread very, very carefully so as not to be found out. Otherwise I could easily end up like my friend Jack, and I don't relish the idea of the scenario in my life Bruv."

"I see!" Bob replied seriously, "that's real heavy stuff Bruv. I certainly wouldn't fancy being in your shoes right now."

"Thanks!" he snapped then added, "you really know how to cheer me up," he smiled then added joyfully, "Fancy a pint?"

"The clubhouse?"

"The clubhouse it is... let's go Bruv, your round."

That evening, when the boys returned to the caravan and a round of coffees courtesy of Peta, they finally retired to their respective bedrooms. Steve found Angie sitting up, reading her book that she'd purchased for the journey down to that little haven.

Steve got into bed beside her and

gave her a loving kiss.

"Do you think we should go home tomorrow Steve, especially now with the death of your friend?" she enquired as she lay the opened book on the peach coloured floral quilt, her hand carefully keeping it open at the page she was on.

"I know what you are after seeing and it certainly isn't your friends," Steve sat back leaning against the wall of the caravan with a smug grin on his face. Some people outside were walking past heading for their own caravan's, laughing and talking aloud amongst themselves. "No, you want to be nosy don't you," he jibed joyfully then explained, "you want to go and have a butchers hook at that new house we've been offered in Rainham, don't you babe," he smiled as he gently pushed her bare shoulder playfully before waving the set of keys in front of her gaze.

"That's not fair," she returned with a pouting look in her eye, as she made a grab for the keys but Steve was too quick and snatched them out of her reach.

"Ok! Ok! we'll go back tomorrow if it pleases you babe, and yes it would be nice to get to a look at our future home, especially as I'll be working in that area, thank god."

"Well you got your wish then honey," she replied as she lifted the book up to continue to read but just glancing at the open page.

"Sure, mind you, I will have to go and pay a visit on Margaret... Jack's wife... just to find out what's happening about the funeral, as we were friends, even though it was six years ago since we last saw each other," he said as he ran both hands through his hair.

"Yes!" she returned quickly, then went on to say, "and don't forget we will have to sort out this business of the flat," she said lowering the book slightly.

"I know, don't remind me... still it served it's purpose didn't it, and I did find out how matie's friends died, plus who was responsible for killing them," Steve uttered sadly as he turned to lay his head back against the wall, deep in thought, just as the muffled voices of a couple walking by outside, were talking about the act they had been entertained by in the clubhouse. "No! I'm more concerned about the person who killed Jack at the moment and why was he killed which is more important."

"Does it frighten you Steve?"

"It disturbs me more than anything, that if that person thinks for one minute I'm on to them I could be the next copper to die in Romford... mind you... I was told a while ago by a certain person that we know as the Doc, well he told me that I have a guardian angel watching over me, well if he was right then I hope they are truly watching over me, for real," he grinned then turned to Angie to give her a cuddle accompanied with a loving kiss.

The next morning they were awoken to the birds doing their bit on the roof that sounded like they were practicing to be tap dancers. Their heavy footwork was accompanied by the soft howling sound of the wind echoing through the overhead cables and the rustle of the trees finished it off. But most of all it was the smell of fresh bacon on the go that tingled their noses, and made their mouth's water.

The book lay on the side cabinet with a piece of thin card protruding from its pages, keeping the place where Angie had stopped the night before, ready for her to continue reading on the train later.

That sad morning was busy as Steve and Angie gathered their belongings together and packed them in to their case which they eventually placed in the boot of Bob's car, ready for him to run them to the station, after some breakfast.

Bob and Peta were happy to be staying for another couple of weeks which didn't seem to worry Steve, he was just glad they were enjoying themselves after their little ordeal, Bob was forgiving, knowing that he was shot by mistake.

A Vulcan bomber accompanied by a couple of smaller jets roared low level as they appeared to be following the coast line. Many people already on the beach were taken back by the sight of this aircraft flying so low and so fast just off the shore. Young boys watched in awe at the sight, some were pointing at it and jumping for joy, as they shouted to their parents to look.

"What are you going to do when you get home Steve?" enquired Bob at the breakfast table reading the days paper, that he went and got before anybody else was up and about, he claimed the early morning walk was good for his old ticker.

"Well Angie wants to go and look at the new house in Rainham and I want to go and see Margaret, Jack's wife, she must be devastated by this, she was the one that said she wanted him to go to a place were she believed he'd be safe until his retirement."

"Well in that case I think she got it wrong," Peta commented as she sat on the long seat in front of the long front window, it looked overcast outside as greying clouds drifted across the sky coming in from the sea.

"Maybe you're right Peta! Maybe you're right, who knows?" Steve uttered.

"When it's your time to go, you go when your number is up and all that jazz," remarked Bob who said it just as he glanced over his newspaper that he had lowered briefly. "Maybe he should've stayed in Harlow then he might've still been alive today... so who knows what him upstairs plans are", with that he returned to his paper with a cheeky rapport.

"You should get shot more often Bruv you're getting too... how can you put it... ah yes too philosophical."

"Go back to London copper".

Chapter 10

Steven's cousin Johnny, an ex-boxing champion who resigned his life in the ring so that he could run a pub, was happy to be propping up the bar on the early afternoon of Saturday the twelfth of September. He was busying himself studying the latest form in the daily newspaper, for the races of the day, which were at Chepstow and Newmarket and getting ready to put a few bets on the horses.

His old friend the Doc, who had once been his coach and ring attendant, had stayed loyal to his protégé and was there too. He was enjoying a nice cool pint of bitter, sitting on one of the few stools that lined the bar.

"What d'ya reckon on this copper's murder, Johnny boy?" The Doc enquired casually holding onto his pint.

A couple sat in the window that

overlooked the busy main road. They were talking amongst themselves whilst a loner sat in the corner cuddling a pint of lager and reading his newspaper that he had laid out on the round table.

"Yeah mate," Johnny replied wistfully, then went on to add, "I saw it on the news the other night... why do you ask?" Johnny replied, uninterested in the question because his eyes didn't even leave the page, as he twiddled with his biro in his right hand ready to write the name's of the horses on one of his many betting slips.

"Well it so happens the copper was a friend of your cousin," the Doc commented sipping at his beer.

"I see!" Johnny returned, lifting his head up briefly from the newspaper and frowning for a second but pondering over the words of his friend and pouting at the same time, "and you think Steve is going to get involved in finding his killer... is that it?"

"It makes sense doesn't it?" he replied turning on his stool.

"So Mr. Wise guy, what was the copper involved in... Do you know... or have you heard anything in your journey Reg?" Johnny pursued going to get himself a pint of bitter.

"Nothing at the moment... but it must've been something very big for him to be killed like that... what do you think Johnny?"

"So now, what you are trying to tell me is, my cousin is likely to get involved in the case... and if he was too get involved in finding the person or person's responsible for the death of his friend, this so called copper friend of Steve's... you seem to think my cousin is going to be in some sort of danger... right?"

"You said it Johnny, not me," he said taking a long mouthful of his beer.

"Here Reg!" Johnny snapped as he removed a five pound note from his trouser pocket, having just written the names of four horses and the times of their races on his betting slip, "Put a pound each way on a Yankee and an accumulator please Reg, now bugger off... yah beers safe, go on."

"I know you want to make a phone call... right Johnny," returned The Doc with a glancing smile, as he took the betting slip. "I see you've got a couple of outsiders there Johnny. I mean, 'Sloppy Joe at two thirty at Chepstow, and 'The Red King', at three o'clock also at Chepstow..."

"Just bugger off," he interrupted the Doc with a smile as he folded his newspaper and tossing it to one side of the bar then proceeded to go to the phone at the other end of the bar. There he dialled a number and a few moments later the voice of a woman came back with a simple polite, "Yes!"

"It's ok it's me, Johnny, I think you should know my cousin might get involved in the murdered copper's case, if he does, I want you to be very vigilant now... do you understand?" he ordered, then continued to explain, "The copper was killed for some reason or other, so if you feel my cousin's life is in any sort of danger you deal with it ok."

"Is that it?" returned the voice of the female.

"That's it, that's all I ask of you, ok."

"So where is your cousin now?" she continued to pursue.

"In Weymouth... but my guess is; he'll be coming back very soon to sort out the killing of his friend."

"What makes you think he'll get involved with that case" she enquired, then went on to add, "I'm led to believe that he's working with this Aussie cop."

"Let's just say it's a gut feeling, ok, it stands to reason, and he was Steve's friend" Johnny said as he leant on the edge of the bar.

"Yeah! Well that was six years ago, besides you know what I want Johnny."

Shirley the barmaid left what she was doing to go and serve a couple of builder type guys, who had entered the pub and were eager to quench their thirst, with a long cool lager or two and busy chatting up the barmaid.

"Yes! I do know what you are after, and I said I would help you when the time comes, now I must go, I've some customers to serve, keep in touch ok."

"I just wish this affair would end... do you hear Johnny... and I mean end."

"The end will be determined by your own actions sweetheart, so concentrate on the job at hand that's all we ask, your job..."

"Yes I know!" She interrupted him abruptly, and then added, "And don't I know it," She expressed bitterly as she hung up.

"There yeh go Johnny boy," the Doc said with a joyful skip in his step, when he returned to the bar bearing the betting slip and the change from the five pound note, that he placed onto the counter in front of Johnny. He now stood with a puzzled look on his face having replaced the receiver to its rightful place and then returned to his paper before propping up the bar once more.

Shirley went to clean a few tables and empty the glass ashtrays from an earlier group of workers who had enjoyed their liquid lunch.

"What are you looking so happy

about?" Johnny enquired as he retrieved his change returning it to his trouser pocket.

"My horse came in at Newmarket. I won twenty five quid mate; I put a fiver on to win at four to one... not bad eh."

"Jammy git!" Johnny smirked.

....
....

It was around seven o'clock when the train from Fenchurch Street pulled into Laindon station carrying two tired people and a little Westie. Steve dragged the suitcase while Angie cuddled a medium sized black shoulder bag and held on to Tara's lead, as they walked the long road heading north of the station to their humble top floor flat, were they couldn't wait to kick off their shoes and just crash out after their long journey from Weymouth.

Steve removed their stack of mail in the row of metal mail boxes that were on the wall at the base of the concrete stairwell. With a joyful sigh the three of them climbed the stairs as Steve couldn't wait to turn the front door key and enter the sanctity of their home. He tossed the pile of letters onto the shiny coffee table, with its empty steel fruit bowl patiently waiting to be refilled with a variety of fruit.

Once Tara's lead was removed by a tired Angie she made for her water bowl that sat in the corner of the kitchen.

"Coffee dear?" asked Steve who headed for the kitchen too, and happily put on the electric kettle having filled it along with Tara's bowl.

"Yes please," Angie said softly as she removed a tobacco pouch from her shoulder bag that she had lain on the arm of the sofa and started to roll a cigarette. Sitting down she put her tired feet on the edge of the coffee table and leant back against the soft cushion behind her.

Whilst the kettle boiled Steve returned to the lounge and pressed the button on his answer phone that stood on the window sill of the square type bay window. The lights told him that he had two messages. He stared out of the window to check on his car that had stood idle all week and was still safe in the prescribed parking space allocated to that flat. Each flat had its own parking lot and there was a parking lot for visitors to park in too, he noticed the car park was full. Some youngsters were playing a game of tennis on a small green in the middle of the block.

Pressing the message button the first message rang out, 'Hi Steve its only me, Ian, you know from Aussie, can you ring me when you get back please, ok it's no worries mate".

The second message came back saying, "Hi Steve and Angie it's me Charlie... we need to talk mate so either pick up the phone or call me a.s.a.p. ok mate you know my number".

"What are you going to do about those two honey?" She asked as she lit her cigarette,

"I don't know," he said as he headed back to the kitchen still tired but eager to make the coffees when he heard the sound of the kettle as it switched itself off; he removed a couple of mugs from one of the wall cabinets along with the appropriate ingredients, namely the coffee jar and the sugar container, he set about to make the two coffees. "I will phone them both first thing in the morning babe."

"So when are we going to look at the house then?" she quizzed, feeling good as she dragged warmly on her cigarette and relished every lungful of the nicotine smoke, I wish I had a stash somewhere". She giggled at the thought when she jovially said, "Sorry I forgot you're a copper now... are you going to arrest me for smoking a joint... or something."

"I'll just pretend I didn't hear that babe, although you really need to cut down on the smoking or even stop for the sake of the baby," Steve commented as he gently stirred the coffees after adding two spoonfuls of sugar in each coffee. Angie just glared at him briefly and stuck her tongue out at him and blew a raspberry, but then became thoughtful.

After he placed the two mugs onto the coffee table he picked up the case and took it to the bedroom where he placed it by the white Parisian style fitted wardrobe with its ornamental trim. In between the two wardrobes there was a central dressing table with an ornate, free standing mirror on a small drawer where the lady of the house could put her trinkets. Although a tall wooden jewellery box that Steve bought for Angie stood to one side of the mirror and a ladies brush and comb dominated the centre of the dressing table alongside a variety of perfumes. Underneath the unit was an ornate peach coloured draylon stool. A double bed dominated the opposite wall, accompanied by two white bed side cabinets and a row of drawer units stood under the window that overlooked the street.

Steve finally slumped into the sofa along side Angie who had now tucked her feet up under her as she dragged on her cigarette and was using the remote control to select a channel on their TV. "What are we doing about the house?"

"Don't worry babe we'll go and see it tomorrow. I have got to go and pay my respects to Margaret, but tonight I'm going to have a nice hot bath and bed, preferably in that order," he grinned as he picked up his coffee. I guess it wouldn't hurt to pay a visit to Romford nick too, it'll kill three birds in one go... what'cha say?"

"Sounds ok to me honey... in fact it sounds bloody fantastic, just think we could be living in a nice house soon and not this flat, with all those bloody stairs."

"I know what you mean," he sighed.

It was then the phone rang, to Steve's dismay as he didn't feel like answering it at first, but it seemed whoever was on the other end was determined to get an answer and as Steve had turned the answer phone off he had no excuse not to answer it, "well aren't you going to answer it honey, or are you going to let it ring its little heart out".

"Yes!" Steve said with a sigh, as he leant against the wall of the arched entrance to the kitchen.

"Steve it's only me Ian, I've been trying to contact you; I didn't know when you'd be back."

"Yeah I heard your message only a short while ago as we've only just got back from Weymouth."

"Oh right, sorry, I didn't realise,

would you like me to call you back tomorrow."

"No it's ok, you can talk, as we are going to look at a house in Rainham tomorrow and pay our respect to a friend who was killed last week," he said soulfully, finally taking one of the chairs that he pulled out from under the table and he sat down to take his tired feet off the floor.

"You don't mean that copper that was killed Steve?"

"Yeah the very same, he was an old friend of mine from old... a bloody good copper in his day," Steve expressed with some hesitancy in his voice but then went on to say, "by the way I have been transferred to the Romford nick," he informed him then went on to add, "but first I've got to go and interview a guy named Andrew Cox who happens to be banged up for allegedly killing his wife ten years ago; guess what, he comes from Romford."

"I see Steve I get the feeling we're firing on all four cylinders now you've had this little break eh."

"Too right mate, it seems we are both being drawn to Romford, what with your two dead Brits in Australia and now this guy in the Scrubs, that's a prison by the way."

"Ha! Ha! Steve I was born in

England don't forget and I'm fully aware of the Scrubs... but you're right, there seems to be something about Romford that seems to be holding all the clues," he then went on to add, "you don't mind if I tag along for the ride Steve, I mean I might find it interesting."

"Well I've been told by the Home Office I have to continue helping you to solve your little mystery... but more and more I'm getting a strong feeling like you that all the answers to everything are connected to something or someone in Romford."

"I'm getting that buzz too so what do we do then?"

"Meet me here on Monday morning and we'll go and interview our Mr. Cox, how does that grab you".

"That's great, I'm getting fed up of the never ending family gatherings, there's only so much to talk about... no I'll be glad to escape for a while and do my job."

"Ok mate Monday it is then," Steve smiled, then said, "I'll have to go now mate my bath is running over... Right?"

With that, they both bid the other farewell and Steve hung up.

Chapter 11

The morning had began with a gentle drizzle, instead of the warm summer sun that had normally greeted them every morning; it was the sort of rain that soaked you right through, should you find yourself caught out in it. It trickled endlessly down the windows of the flat.

Angie had awoken earlier having had a rough night and found herself sitting in the bay window staring out into the early morning light. She had pulled the net curtain to one side so she could observe the scenery. Her bare feet were resting on the middle run of the one of the other chairs that stood with its back to the window. Having made herself some breakfast, she sat in her dressing gown, happily eating a bowl of cornflakes, made in a large white china bowl, and a mug of coffee that stood in the middle of the dining table. Her tobacco pouch lay beside it with one cigarette lying close by where she had painstakingly rolled it.

Between mouthfuls of cornflakes, her mind drifted towards many things that worried her, especially that of the forthcoming baby, let alone the thoughts of her own life that frightened her more than anything else did. She was still afraid to tell Steve the truth of her predicament, believing everything was going to be alright and that the hospital had got it all wrong about her condition.

She was just about to take another spoonful of her breakfast when the sound to the telephone disturbed her concentration briefly. Holding back she called out to Steve saying aloud, "It's probably for you sleepy head," but with a sigh she had to pick it up it as Steve shouted back for her to answer it.

"Yes it's the Price residency," she

sighed, and then shouted, and "It's for you!" she said, quickly placing the receiver onto the table.

Steve came into the lounge wearing nothing but his red boxer shorts yawning and stretching, "Who is it?" he asked quietly so as not to be heard.

"I don't know," she frowned having returned to her place, "it's some bloke, he asked to speak to you, ok sleepy head".

"Yeah!" Yeah! but did he give a name?" he asked as he reached the table and picked up the receiver and placed his hand to cover the mouth piece, but she just took another spoonful of cornflakes into her mouth and shrugged her shoulders with a slight cheeky little grin.

"Very funny!" He yawned, "Yes who is it?" he asked calmly then added, "Oh it's you Charlie, we need to talk...I gather you got my report regarding your late friends then."

"Yes it is disturbing to believe that my friends ended their lives like they did and for what... a stupid lorry load of booze," came the voice from the other end of the phone.

"Well not just the lorry load of booze more like they upset the I.R.A., and I guess you don't upset the likes of them...do we Charlie?"

"So what's the problem that you

want to discuss with me?"

"I'll catch up with you later only we have to go over to Romford on business due to my friend being knocked off."

"Are we referring to the Copper who was murdered there the other day"?

"Yeah, well he was on the case of your dead friends, until like me we were warned off as a task force was onto them...it's all in my report ok."

"Don't tell me you are going to solve his murder now?"

"Well he was my friend, we went through Hendon together."

"Ok Steve I'll catch you later mate... and good luck."

"Yeah cheers mate," he responded as he returned the receiver to its rightful place.

"I gather that was Charlie," Angie remarked, as she got up from the comfort of the chair and taking herself and the bowl of cornflakes to the settee where she stuck her feet up under her, still eating what was left of her breakfast. Steve removed her mug of coffee and placed it on the coffee table. Tara was asleep in the kitchen area and was aroused when Steve entered the room, she rushed to him jumping up and wagging her tail.

Picking up the set of keys from the TV cabinet that the Major had given to them, Steve tossed them into the air in fun.

Angie told him the kettle was hot, and that she had left his bowl on the side, next to his mug that had coffee and sugar already in it, and was awaiting the hot water and the milk.

Within a couple of hours, they had washed and dressed and were heading off in the direction of Rainham and the new home that they couldn't wait to see and explore. Tara sat on the rear shelf looking out at the traffic following with the joyful sights of children who happily pointed at her posture in the car.

Angie sat quietly deep in thought staring out of the car window, as they drove down the A11, heading into London.

Sometime later they found themselves driving down Ellis avenue which was the address they had been given. They found the house in question where they pulled up in the driveway and embarked into the journey of the future. In Steve's eyes it was a new beginning for the pair soon to be three of them.

They found the house was empty of any signs of life with bare rooms. Some were decorated with square patterned wallpaper, whilst others had been painted with either magnolia or beige, vinyl silk paint. The kitchen had been wallpapered with a tiled effect vinyl paper. Every room had a brilliant white Georgian panelled door, with brass ornamental handles and floral scratch plates beneath them. The lower rooms, hallway and stairs were carpeted in a soft green carpet, whereas the bedrooms had soft peach coloured carpets. Steve looked at Angie and smiled, then went on to remark that they had a blank canvas to work on and a lifetime to enjoy it all.

Leaving Angie sizing up the rooms and the windows he drove to Romford police station alone, where he parked up in their car park. He headed for the market place to find the spot where the incident of his friend took place. He found the alley that had been sealed off and a couple of young fresh faced constables stood on guard duty not letting anybody enter the alleyway.

"I'm sorry Sir but you can't go down there," one of the young officers expressed his concern regarding the intrusion of Steve. He closed his eyes and smiled at the officer's comment, knowing he was only doing his job.

"This is where the copper was killed yeah?" Steve quizzed.

"Yes sir that is correct, the officer in question was killed in this alley."

"Good officer two seven four, I'm glad to see you are doing your job," Steve said warmly as he removed his badge from his pocket "I'm the officer sent to investigate this crime... ok."

"And you are Sir?"

"I'm Detective Inspector Steven Price from the Met and I'm taking over from Jack Gould, so you can take me to where our colleague Jack died," he said as he lifted the blue and white ribbon that barred the public, "Have the boys in their white overalls finished in the alley do you know?"

"Yes! For now," returned the young officer, "So you are taking over from Jack then... he was a good cop... the best."

"And you are PC two seven four?" Steve asked politely.

"My name is Mark Smith sir and my colleague is PC. Ricky Hudson, we're hoping to be detectives some day."

"Well keep yeah noses clean and you just might get there... so what do you make of this incident, as you must've know the dead officer."

"He was a good cop."

"I know that, you've already said it, but what do you say happened on that fatal night?" Steve reached the place where his friends life had been taken from him with out any mercy.

"Jack's body was slumped over that wall just there," he pointed to the spot where a pool of dried blood lay on the floor. "Apparently from what we were told his lighter was found a few feet from where he ended up."

"His lighter you say, constable," Steve suddenly remembered Jack's wife giving him that lighter for his birthday some eight years ago. Steve looked around the scene trying to take in the events of that night.

"There was one thing that didn't fit... the killer didn't take his briefcase... in fact nothing was taken, not even his wallet."

"So we can rule out robbery then?" Steve commented briefly, as he looked around the area carefully. "Where does this alley take you?"

"There is a street at the other end Sir."

The young officer led him to the other end of the alley where another couple of young officers were standing and Mark told them Steve was a detective sent to investigate the incident.

"I've seen enough son, it is obvious this was the exit of the killer, so let's get out of here, the place gives me the creeps... who knows I might have you assist me in solving this crime... do you know what our Jack was involved in?"

"Not really," he replied as they walked back to the market square and his friend, "I know who might know," he went on to add, "Old sergeant Reg, he knows everything that goes on in that office, he's like a walking encyclopaedia of crime, is our Reg," he went on to ask curiously, "how did you surmise that the killer left by the road at the other end of the alley?"

"Think about it constable," he commented then went on to explain when he could see the young PC was deep in thought over the question. "if the killer came from the market end, Jack would've seen him," he paused for a moment rubbing his chin and pondering over the scene then went onto add, "no... who ever killed him, knew he would be coming to this place at that point in time... So," he again paused for a moment to scan yet again the scene of the crime, then said softly to himself, "so Jack, now why did you come to this place... and more to the point, who else knew... that is the question?" He then added finding himself rejoining the young constable, "Cheers I'll keep that in mind," he said as he ducked under the ribbon, "I suppose they've sealed his office off too eh."

"Yes Sir we have been informed that somebody from the Home Office is coming down to look into it."

"I'm the one from the Home Office and I have been assigned to investigate this crime. I guess it's time I made my presence felt... don't you think?" He smiled, then enquired casually, "Who's in charge of the factory then?"

"It's Cross Sir, that's Chief Constable Cross Sir to be precise".

"Well! Well! If it isn't Raymond Cross eh," he grinned.

"I wouldn't let him hear you call him that Inspector".

"I'll keep that in mind when we talk," he replied jovially.

"Good luck then Sir."

"Thanks! And call me Steve... Mark," he said in passing, "Oh and by the way I was serious about you assisting me in this crime... I trust no-body, and neither should you, ok."

There was a cheeky grin that came over the young constable as he returned to his friend, with a cocky sway in his step, who just raised his eyes having been amused by his colleague's frame of mind.

The market was in full swing, regardless of the situation that had arisen in the alleyway, the sound of the stall holders and their usual banter echoed around the area. With the sale of all the different items up for sale, the place was crowded with people, making it hard for anybody to embark on a journey through the heaving mass. That also included Steve who struggled helplessly to endeavour to take up the challenge, hard as it appeared, yet necessary in his case. He was tempted to take a break at the sight and smell of the hot dog stand with the heavenly thought of a cheese burger and a cup of coffee.

Steve walked back to the police station in a different frame of mind, happily munching on his half eaten cheese burger, his mind reflecting on the whole scene. He constantly berated himself with the simple question, 'why did his friend go into that alley at that time and who was aware of his actions', he knew it wasn't a chancer out to rob him, no, he realised It had to be somebody who wanted him dead, but why, plagued his detective mind.

Steve leant on the bonnet of his car whilst he finished his burger, when a young officer approached him to inform him he couldn't park there as it was police parking only. However he was stopped dead in his tracks when a diligent Steve removed his badge and simply flashed it in the constable's face, without saying a single word in his defence knowing his status was enough to suffice in the incident. In reply came a simple, 'sorry sir, I didn't realise," from a young constable. Steve stared at the lad thinking to himself, 'is it me or are these constables looking so young these days.'

"Constable!" He finally said once he finished the last mouthful of the burger and rubbed his hands together, "is the big chief in?" He enquired as he stood up and headed for the main entrance to the old, brown bricked building that lay back off the high street like some sort of out of place converted mansion.

"I believe so Sir," returned the constable as they passed through the main door into the reception area, "Are you the one who is going to take over from Jack Gould."

"And that would be Detective Inspector Jack Gould young man," he said with an air of authority in his voice, "And the answer to your question is yes. I am here to take over from him... why do you ask?"

"Sorry Sir!" Returned the constable who led him to the reception area and Jane who managed that area well, "Jane, this is...?" he explained then looked at Steve waiting for his name and rank.

"I'm Steven Price... that's Detective Inspector Steven Price and I'm here to see the chief, who I believe is Chief Constable Raymond Cross."

Jane pressed a button to a side door that led him to the offices in the rear of the building and the home of the detectives. He was led up the stairs to a large office with the Chief's name engraved into a black plastic panel and filled with a white paint, by Jane, "Have you been in the force long Sir?"

"Long enough young Jane", he

smiled as he knocked on the office door and entered to the words, 'come in', from within.

Entering the room he was met with a room that was a home from home; with some soft furnishings in one corner and a large old oak desk where the chief sat writing up some paperwork on the green baize. A couple of family photographs stood at either end of the desk. An old black tiled fireplace stood to one side, complete with some China ornaments that stood proudly on its mantelpiece. The usual large full length, framed print of the Queen bedecked in her Royal Regalia hung above that fireplace along with some other prints of ships. They in turn were accompanied by a large map of the area that hung on the wall to his right.

"You must be our new replacement... Right," remarked the Chief who sat in his neat uniform. His greying hair, which was receding slightly, was also accompanied by a thin moustache.

"That's right Sir I'm..."

"Yes! Yes! I know who you are officer," he interrupted as he offered him a chair with his right hand held out in the direction of a padded chair on the opposite side of his desk. "You must be Detective Inspector Steven Price... am I right."

"I guess you have me at a disadvantage Raymond," Steve replied just resting his hand on the back of the chair

"Yes!" he said abruptly, finding his feet to go around his desk to join him and to shake his hand, and greet him formally. "Yes... I was informed earlier by those in Whitehall that you were going to join our little band of hero's Steven."

"If I'm to take over from Jack Gould then I will need to know everything of what he was involved in," Steve said with some authority.

"Whitehall said you were a bit of a wild card... is that right," the chief returned informally as he shook his hand, "A drink Steve?"

"Depends what you are offering Sir."

"Tea or coffee."

"Coffee would be ok... and that's the first I've heard of myself being called a wild card. I have been doing some under cover work in the past if that is what they mean, when they call me a wild card... I understand you have sealed off his office, am I right?"

"Yes you are right," He replied pressing his intercom button next to his white porcelain telephone. The secretary in the next room responded promptly and he ordered two coffees.

"I visited the spot where Jack was killed... I am curious to know why he went to that place so late in the evening, it isn't a nice place to walk through in the light of day let alone at night. I know I have just experienced it."

"I know he was working on a suicide case."

"A suicide case?" Steve repeated.

"Yeah some Asian woman chose to jump in front of the Southend express train, taking her little kid with her, thank god the kid survived the ordeal."

"And you're telling me Jack was handling that case, is there anything else he was working on?" Steve pressed.

"He was about to start work on a bungled bank job in the high street along with his Sergeant... that's Sergeant Peters."

"And that's it... nothing else?" he pursued carefully as he began to feel uneasy about the situation.

"Well! There was something that upset him around that time; it was something he was told in the hospital by a dying person who claimed to be involved in a crime in the late fifties. I suggested it had to be an hoaxer, as we are always getting them here, they think it will make them go out in a blaze of glory if they confessed to something they didn't do, knowing their death would be the end of it... you know what I mean Inspector."

"I guess so Chief... but I would like to know what that person confessed to. Just in case that person opened a can of worms by their own untimely confession."

"I guess it might be tied up in his office... when are you coming to join us Inspector?"

"I've got to sort out the formalities regarding our new home, and then I have to call on somebody in prison. It's another person who wants to confess to a crime, it seems to be a new trend with the criminals, confessing on their death beds... still who are we to judge their mentality and who knows it might solve a crime or two in the process Sir."

"So we'll expect you when we see you then?" returned the Chief as his young secretary entered the room with their coffees and a plate of biscuits on a tray. "Thanks Chris put it on my desk please."

"Have the white coats finished in the alleyway Chief?" Steve asked, finding the seat for the first time as he took one of the cups of coffee along with one of the custard creams.

"Yes!"

"Then I think we can open it up to the public again don't you, I've had a good look at that place and there isn't anything that interests me regarding that incident".

Chapter 12

The earlier drizzle had long since eased when Steve found himself leaving the confines of the police station in Romford high street. It was still overcast but clearing with blue skies coming up from the west, *'The tide must be going out,'* he thought to himself as he unlocked his car door and casually glanced up at the sky before getting into the driving seat, having also noticed the movement of the traffic, that appeared to have increased as the day progressed.

He had found the offices amusing and the Chief somebody he could just about get on with. His mind dwelt on the effects he would have on the morale of the other Inspectors he was yet to meet. He glanced back at the building before he merged into the slow moving traffic.

He was heading for the estate known as 'The Marks Gate estate,' just off the Southend Road. A housing estate built in the mid-fifties, to replace the lost buildings, due to the bombings of the Second World War. It was a relatively new estate in accordance with the rest of the area. Half an hour later he arrived at the address in Rose Lane that was on the card the Major had given to him. He found Jack's house set in a row of houses that had joint porch ways with concrete roofs over them, with bedroom windows above and below the apex roof.

As Steve got out of the car he noticed the 'Harrow pub' at the end of the road, with its sign standing on the corner for all to see and a large car park to the rear. Open fields spread out on the opposite side of the road that ran across the end of Rose Lane. Those fields appeared to stretch on for ever, with low lying hills in the far distance covered with trees. Steve smiled at the scene that greeted him and thought about his friend and how he must've loved this tranquil place. A far cry from the hustle and bustle of the likes of Romford or even Harlow.

He had noticed the parade of shops in the same road; several groups of people were walking along the path heading for the local shops and the local school.

With pouted lips he closed the car door and locking it he glanced at the house. He walked across the grassed area that ran the length of the street with the odd pathway to the edge of the road. Opening the low wooden gate he gingerly walked up the path to the maroon coloured wooden door, with its frosted glass at the top and panelled lower section with its metal knocker that encircled the letterbox and which he used to make his presence known. Either side was a cupboard where once coal would've been stored

He turned to face a low brick built cupboard unit with a concrete slab on top and being curious he opened the wooden panelled door where he was confronted with the dustbin shed. He closed it quickly when he heard the front door open; turning back to the door he found he was met by a fair haired young lad of around ten years of age, in jeans and a black t-shirt.

"Matthew!" Steve said with wide eyes and a puzzled look on his face, "it is Matthew, isn't it."

The boy just nodded yes.

"Is your mum there?" Steve found himself asking politely. He didn't need to worry as Margaret suddenly appeared. She was wearing a black short sleeved top over a pair of black slacks; a gold necklace hung over the top and carried a gold crucifix. Her soft mousy brown curly hair hung loosely at her shoulders. Pulling back the door she gently touched her son's shoulder to tell him to go in, she was clutching a damp tissue in her hand.

"I saw you coming up the path Steve... do come in," she said soulfully, gently moving back to let Steve enter the house.

Once out of the way, she led him through into the lounge with its York stone fireplace that stretched from one side of the room to the other. A gold coloured three piece suite dominated the centre of the room and an oak, oval coffee table stood in front and on it was a fruit bowl with a couple of oranges, two apples plus a small bunch of grapes in it. A large ornate mirror set into a gold frame hung over the fireplace and a medium sized TV stood on one side of the grand fireplace.

A cocktail bar stood beside the front window that overlooked the scene from the road, where she had watched him arrive. She was being comforted by a neighbour.

"This is my friend Tracy, Steve... and Tracy this is my Jack's friend Steve," she introduced, "Steve's a police officer too," she explained softly to her friend as she stood by the window, then went on to say, "he lost his wife many years ago, isn't that right Steve?"

He just nodded his head as he went to comfort her, gently touching her shoulder, "I'm truly sorry Margaret I wish we could've met again in more happier times... it came as a bit of a shock to me when I was told by somebody from Whitehall. I was on holiday in Weymouth when I was informed, like I said it came as a great shock to me, if it is any consolation, the Home Office have requested me to carry out a full investigation into his death."

"I think Jack would like that Steve," she said as she took his hand then moved to sit in the armchair facing the window.

"Would you like a tea or a coffee Steve?" asked Tracy politely.

"Thanks Tracy," returned Margaret politely.

"Yeah a coffee please Tracy, with two sugars," he replied sitting on the edge of the sofa and resting his clasped hands on his knees, "How are you feeling Marge... sorry that's a silly question to be asking?"

"Empty Steve," she replied sadly. "It's like my whole life has come to an end, but I guess you must know what I'm going through especially after losing... what was her name, oh yeah Sally eh."

"Yeah it was Sally," Steve replied wistfully, bowing his head, but then continued to add casually, "but that was a lifetime ago Marge, I've come thought the worst of it, and yes she'll always be a part of me... just like Jack will always be with you... in here," he said touching his heart.

"It's not easy Steve its bloody hard... Sorry you'll have to excuse the French."

Steve just gave her a reassuring

smile, "Did Jack say anything about his work to you especially with the events that led up to his death."

"No! Nothing I can put my finger on, besides, you know Jack Steve, he was always a very personal man and didn't give much away... his briefcase is in the bedroom if that might help," she explained then she called to Matthew who was quietly sitting in his bedroom listening to some music whilst doing some of his homework.

When he stuck his head around the doorway she asked him to go into her bedroom and bring down his dad's briefcase. To which he replied 'yes mum,' then did as he was told.

"He's a great lad Marge; I can remember him when he was a baby... how big he has grown."

"Yeah!" She sighed as she wiped her nose with the tissue she was holding. "He wants to grow up to be a policeman just like his dad."

"If you must know It was my grand-dad who influenced me to be a policeman... he would always tell me stories of his time as a policeman in the Met, he was based at Bow nick and dealt with the East End gangs before and during the Second World War."

"I was told to give his briefcase to the investigating officer and as that is you

Steve it is only fitting you should have it," she said as Mathew entered the room carrying his father's briefcase, that he placed on the sofa along side Steve, "You knew my dad?" He asked cagily.

"Me and your dad go back a long time Matthew, the last time I saw you, you were only a baby in yeh mum's arms, ain't that right Margaret."

She just gave him a half-hearted grin still wiping her nose with the crumpled up tissue that seemed to give her some comfort in her hour of grief.

"Is it alright if I just look in the case... you never know what we might find?" Steve politely asked as he took hold of the case.

"Sure! You are the investigating officer Steve, it's your job for god's sake," she wept softly to herself as a few tender tears ran down her cheek.

"I should leave this to a more quieter time Marge," Steve tried to change the scene, when Tracy returned carrying a tray of drinks.

"Just look in the damn thing and get it over and done with for Christ's sake Steve... I'm ok about it, I know it has to be done. Ok," she fell back into the chair and laid her head on it's back, staring up at the ceiling, closing her tear swept eyes in her grief.

"Are you alright mum?" Matthew

asked with a worried tone in his voice, unsure of his own inner feelings.

"I'm ok Matthew just come and give me a cuddle please," she replied lowering her head to give him a passing glance and opening her arms to him.

Steve looked through the briefcase and came across an old brown coloured folder with the words 'The Market Murder of 1958' hand written on it on an old white label, in a faint state. "Can I take this folder it might be important, who knows?"

"Is that a clue Steve?" Matthew eagerly asked.

"I don't know mate... if it is... I'll soon find out, and who knows," he said with a knowing wink, "it just might lead me to your dad's killer, who knows," he said closing the case and casually asked Matthew to return it to the bedroom, at the same time he placed the old folder on the sofa beside him, while he drank his coffee.

Looking at the carriage clock on the mantelpiece he explained that he had to go and meet Angie who he told Margaret was the new love in his life, and she was the light at the end of his tunnel. Picking up the folder he bid them farewell giving Margaret a friendly peck on the cheek, giving her their new address in Rainham, saying he'd be in touch regarding the funeral.

Returning to his car he went to the boot and opened his black briefcase, where he tossed the old folder into it, with the intention of studying it's contents at a later time.

He drove back to Rainham with an air of apprehension regarding the death of his friend and the feelings he had for his friend's family.

Arriving back at their new home Steve was surprised to find Angie wasn't there; she had left a note to say where she was, in fact she had made friends with the young woman who lived next door and he found her enjoying a good chat over a mug of coffee. She introduced the woman as that of Lisa Smith declaring her husband was a policeman too.

"It wouldn't be a Mark Smith by any chance," Steve grinned.

"Why yes," she replied with a grin, she was a young woman of five foot six and dressed in a mauve floral maxi dress with shoulder straps. Her long black shiny hair hung down her slender back, she was wearing large looped gold earrings with a gold necklace with her name on it across her chest. She had several gold ornamental rings on her fingers making it clear she loved gold, this also included a couple of gold charm bracelets on her left arm and a cute ladies' watch on her right wrist.

On the way home Angie eagerly told Steve that Lisa was going to sort out some of her old curtains for them as a start to their life in the house. Steve just nodded in response to her obvious excitement at the prospect of starting a new life. The thought of their time on the street seemed to have lulled to a mere after thought, as she sat back in the seat with a grin that could've encircled her face if it had the chance. Steve felt good seeing her looking so radiant and motherly in her attitude. He casually put his arm out across her and gently stroked her tummy, reassuring her that life was on the up for them both now. Turning his attention back to the road he missed the apprehensive glance that flickered across her face as her thoughts turned to her predicament.

Chapter 13

Steve suddenly decided on the spur of the moment not to go directly home, as planned, but instead he took the time out to drive to Charlie Smith's Snooker hall, in Walthamstow, where he carefully parked up in a nearby street.

All the way, Angie was curious about her destination and constantly asked Steve where he was taking her, in reply he simply told her politely, with a smile on his face, 'you'll have to wait and see'.

He finally led Angie up the steep concrete staircase that wound its way up to the upper floor taking you from the reality of life to the sleazier side of the profession, in the dark confines of the establishment. The only light in the vast arena was from the ones illuminating the green cloth of the dozen, full size snooker tables that stood in three rows.

The smell and taste from the hazy stale smoke drifted around the room and greeted you as you opened its only door where you found yourself entering the room. The smoke drifted across from those who sat at the little round tables that stood beside the score board. They were happily dragging on their cigarettes and drinking their beer from pint glasses.

Several groups of men of varying ages, some standing holding on to their cues like a pole dancer awaiting their turn, while others leant over the table, ready to take their shots which were being played on one of the many tables. The place was filled with the sound of balls being hit by cues, and the odd ball being knocked over the side cushion onto the wooden floor. There was the laughter and banter of those who found their freedom in the depths of this humble place, with its manly attitude.

Angie questioned Steve's motives in visiting such a place as this; she busily scanned the area and tried in vain to shun the sight of grown men indulging in this past time. Even though she was a smoker herself she couldn't help trying to clear her path of the smoke. "It's nothing like the snooker we see on the TV," she expressed, as she eventually found herself sitting on one of the tall chromium swivel stools with a low red padded back and seat, that were fixed to the floor at the bar that stood in the far corner.

An elderly gentleman was busying himself drying the clean wet glasses, when Steve asked him if Charlie was in.

"It depends on who's asking?" He returned lowering his t-towel.

"Why don't you go and tell him it's Steven Price?" Steve said as he too found one of the stools more comfortable. "And I'll have a pint of lager and my lady friend here will have an orange and lemonade please," he ordered as at the same time he took a handful of peanuts from a china bowl that stood in the middle of the counter, casually pushing them in Angie's direction.

Minutes later Charlie entered the room via a side door and immediately shook Steve's hand. "So Steve... this must be the lovely Angie you've talked about?"

"Charlie it's good to see you again and yes this is the love of my life," he said as he grabbed another handful of the peanuts. "Ange this is Charlie, the one who owns the flat we are living in."

"It's nice to put a face to a name Charlie," Angie smiled, as she too shook his hand, "Shame about the smoke in here."

He replied with a courteous kiss on her right cheek, then responded saying, "the same goes for you sweetheart... the same goes for you... I see you have ordered your drinks... they are on the house Clive, ok," he winked, "and yes the smoke, I'm sorry about that."

"Thank you Charlie," returned Steve and Angie respectfully, "We need to talk Charlie," Steve expressed. "Have you read my report?"

"Yes!" He smiled then returned to the side door. "Lets go somewhere much nicer than this smoky joint... my humble office will a lot better... bring another round of drinks to my office please Clive, you know what I like."

"Yes boss!" he replied sharply.

"And some of those peanuts wouldn't go amiss... Clive", Steve joked.

Charlie grinned and used his hands say, 'go and do as he was ordered.'

They soon found themselves in the comfort of his office, where they both ended up, sitting together, on a comfortable sofa that stood in the corner of the room. It faced the desk where

Charlie sat swivelling on his chair. Many signed and framed prints of famous snooker players hung around the walls, with its green floral flock wallpaper that decorated the room.

"So Steve what brings you and your lovely lady friend to my humble establishment"?

"We need to talk openly about your flat Charlie... if it isn't too much trouble," Steve said, "Oh! Don't get me wrong mate it's a lovely flat... but you see... I'm being transferred to the Romford nick at the request of Home Office who have given us a house in Rainham, a police house that is."

"I see!" He uttered as he leant back in his chair, placing his clasped hands behind his head. "I guess you fulfilled your part of the bargain," he said, after a few minutes silence just as Clive had knocked and entered the room with the tray of drinks and a few bags of the salted peanuts, "Thanks Clive now bugger off," he demanded then went on to inform them, "at least I now know what happened to my two friends... and yes I did read your report," he expressed as he tossed the said report onto the edge of his desk for Steve to see. "I guess we can't argue with the likes of the I.R.A., can we? I suppose it was a case of my friends... how do you put it... stupidly getting involved in something they just couldn't handle," he explained as he found his feet to walk around his desk, and found a seat on the edge of it in front of Steve and Angie, who just sat there in awe of her situation. "So Steve what is the problem?"

"Well! we'll need to move out soon to take up residence in Rainham, as I said Charlie. I'm taking the place of the dead copper in that nick in Romford."

"I see Steve... who am I to stand in the way of the law then...how are you for furniture Steve?"

"We have to start all over again", Steve replied, sipping his drink, "why do you ask?"

"The furniture in that gaff is yours for the asking, it's no good to me. I was going to sell the flat anyway...would you like it... the furniture I mean?"

"Sure!" Steve snapped joyfully. Angie just repeated Steve's words with excitement in her voice.

"In that case I have a friend who owes me a favour and he just happens to own a large white van... I'll have a word in his lughole to return that favour ok, eh."

"I don't know what to say Charlie... I guess all *can* say is you're a diamond."

"Then don't say anything," Charlie said with a grin as he dipped into his out tray on the edge of his desk and craftily removed a white envelope with the address of the flat and Steve's name on it, "I was going to send this letter to you Steve, but as you are here it's only fitting that I give it to you now," he said handing the sealed envelope to Steve.

"What is it Charlie?" He enquired taking it into his hand.

"Open it when you get home," Charlie ordered casually. "There's only one true issue that has been bugging me right now Steve".

"And what might that be Charlie... I'm all ears," Steve replied, curiously sipping at his beer and with a warm smile he slipped the white envelope into his inside jacket pocket.

"It has always puzzled me that when I was banged up doing stir... I never stopped thinking about the bastard who half inched all that dosh... all one hundred and thirty big ones?"

"What is it Charlie?" Angie continued to enquire with a puzzled look on her reddened face, due to the warmth of the room.

"Lets just say Angie... it's a gift from me, to you, for your new home, ok... now drink yeh drink... oh and by the way the car is yours too, ok, eh," he said with a sly wink and a cheeky little smile he returned to his office chair.

"The furniture is the best gift you could've ever given to us Charlie," she expressed with feelings of guilt in her voice at her good fortune.

"As for the money that was nicked back then," Steve said, "we can only surmise what happened to it... who knows, maybe one day that person will slip up and bang we'll nick him or her."

"Maybe you're right Steve, but I know I would love to get my hands on them and wring their little scrawny necks."

"It wouldn't have mattered Charlie, at the time the I.R.A. would have shot them regardless... no! They sealed their own fate when they got involved in nicking Lorries."

"Their fate was getting involved with the Younger gang."

An hour later, and they were leaving that smoky establishment knowing the future was now set with the coming of the new house and the career change for Steve.

"I was just thinking Steve," she said as they headed home in a drizzling rain, without a care in the world.

"What was you thinking babe... I thought I could hear the cogs grinding," he replied jokingly.

"Very funny ha! Ha!" She replied than added, "If we are moving to Rainham, and you'll be working in Romford..."

"I know what you are going to say babe", he interrupted, "If I'm right... are you thinking we'd be near to Johnny and Diana and their pub?"

"Yeah you got it... I suppose that's your keen police nose that sussed that out eh", she giggled with her hands held in front of her mouth as if she were praying, "This dead copper, he was your friend Steve?"

"Sure babe," He replied as he slipped the car into first gear, having stopped for a moment at a set of traffic lights.

"What puzzles me is where do you start with that line of investigation?" she enquired curiously.

"I'm not sure at the moment," Steve said hesitantly, then went on to explain, "I have to interview a bloke named Andrew Cox, who's doing time in the Scrubs; for allegedly murdering his wife ten years ago... tomorrow along with Ian... you know... the Aussie copper... he wants to sit in with me... anyway babe, what will you be doing tomorrow babe... anything?"

"Yeah! I'm going out with a friend to Basildon town centre to start getting some baby stuff... you now what I mean."

"I was wondering when we were going to get on to that stuff," he smiled as he gently squeezed her kneecap, then went on to enquire, "Will you be needing any money then babe?"

"Probably!"

"In that case you can get some

money out of the hole in the wall when we get home, will a couple of hundred do you?"

"Well we'll need a pram and the usual baby stuff" she said calmly as she stared out of the window."

"When's your next hospital appointment."

"Next Monday in the afternoon," she replied casually as she took out her tobacco pouch and proceeded to roll another cigarette, "I am going to have to tell them about the change of address... we'll have to sort out the hospital in Rainham... where ever that is."

"I think you'll find it's in Romford."

The rain eased as they neared Laindon and home after they stopped off in Basildon town centre to get some money out of the hole in the wall of their bank.

Once inside the flat Angie flopped into the sofa and tucked her feet under her hips and just leant back into the cushion.

Steve went into the kitchen to put on the kettle and at the same time he removed the white envelope from his jacket and placed it on the work surface. He then hung his jacket over the back of one of the four dining chairs in the bay window.

"What's in the envelope Charlie gave to you honey"?" she enquired as she picked up the remote control for the TV.

"We'll find out shall we" he smiled as he retrieved it and started to open it and enter the lounge at the same time.

"Well!?" Angie eagerly pressed.

He stood in awe at what he found inside the envelope. It was a cheque for the ten thousand pounds he had offered to Steve for finding the truth of Charlie's friends. He now just waved it in front of Angie, who took it to say she had held ten grand in her hand. "You can put it in the bank account when you are in town with yeh friend tomorrow, the paying in book is in the drawer... I'll get it and fill it in, when it clears, and you can have half to go towards the things for the baby ok... courtesy of Charlie."

"Charlie I love you," she laughed as she waved the cheque in the air.

Steve went to his answer phone and pressed the button, the female voice returned with the words, 'you have one new message' a beep later and the voice of the Major came back saying, 'Hi Steve it's the Major... have contacted the prison and arranged a meeting with the person we talked about, subject to his recent letter, the interview will be taped for my purpose so good luck and catch up with you later.'

Chapter 14

The morning had started with a good feel to it, with a warming sun rising up over the roof tops which shone brightly into the bedroom. Angie as usual was already up and pottering about in the kitchen making herself a coffee and some porridge.

The radio was ringing out the sounds of Radio One and the usual banter from Tony Blackburn, mingling with songs of the black bird on the roof and also of pigeons nestling in the tree tops.

Steve edged cagily out of bed, yawning profusely as he moved to the open window. He stood in his navy blue boxer shorts and looked out on the world to get a good view of the forthcoming day. The empty blue sky didn't fool him one bit, he knew the weather could easily change at a moments notice. He also knew the early morning sun was a nightmare to any would be driver.

Scratching his head and rubbing

his cheeks, he made for the direction of the scent that wafted across his sensitive nose. It came from the kitchen where coffee was on the go. He heard the sound of Angie putting two slices of bread into the toaster.

He went to the dressing table first, where he removed his bank paying in book which was kept in the narrow drawer of the centre section, where the padded stool stood. Picking up a black biro from the same drawer he proceeded to fill in the details of the cheque that had to be deposited. Removing the cheque from Angie's jewellery box where he had put it for safe keeping, he finally tucked it into the book and left it on top of the jewellery box.

Minutes later he joined a happy Angie in the kitchen where he gave her a peck on the back of her bare neck, then gently blew a raspberry in the same place that sent shivers down her spine, to the cries of 'you bastard, you know how that gets me going,' she giggled in response.

Grabbing a slice of the toast she had just buttered, he headed for the shower.

A quick shower later and in his suit trousers he returned to the kitchen where Angie was wrestling with a fried egg to go with his two slices of toast. As he approached, she jokingly wielded the spatula in his face as a warning not to do what he did earlier, especially as she was using the frying pan and hot oil.

Steve chuckled to himself as he grabbed his coffee from the work surface, then casually went and sat at the table where he gingerly looked out into the glare of the rising sun, briefly brushing the net curtain to one side.

Just as he placed his mug on the place mat on the table, the telephone rang out making him jump and curse.

"Yes!" He said politely after a silent moment to compose himself.

"Hi Steve it's me Ian... I was just phoning you to see if you were still going to the prison to talk to that drongo?"

"Yeah, you mean Andrew Cox don't you?"

"That's what I said, that drongo... back in Aussie he would be doing hard labour... over here you're too soft, it's like a holiday camp."

"I'll pick you up in an hour or so," he said as he picked up his coffee to have a sip then added, "look I'm just about to eat my breakfast, is that ok, Christ what time is it?"

"Its seven thirty Steve," returned Ian.

"As late as that eh," he laughed to himself, "The powers to 'B' said we can go and interview this... how you say, drongo...

I gather that's an Aussie expression."

Ian just burst out laughing and said simply, " see you in a while... good to talk to you mate... later... Bye," then he hung up.

"What has this Andrew Cox got to do with your friend Jack's death?" Angie said as she sat at the table in her sexy pink pyjamas with peddle pusher bottoms that tied up at her slender knees.

"God knows babe," Steve replied as he cut his toast and dipped it into the egg yolk. "I just get this gut feeling that everything is directed at something connected to Romford, but what?"

"What about this murder of that girl the Major mentioned in Weymouth."

"You're joking, that was twenty four years ago babe the killer could even be dead themselves...no I just can't see what the connection is right now...I need to get into Jack's mind and work out what it was he was getting involved in",

"It could've been somebody he nicked years ago and they got their revenge", Angie responded calmly as she cuddled her mug of coffee.

"Nah! a lag knows it's part and parcel of his occupation and they know it goes with the job... no this is something else... still I will get to the bottom of it in time Babe," he said as he tucked into his eggs on toast.

As he was leaving there was a knock at the door and Angie said, "That's my friend Sharon, can you let her in honey."

Opening the door he just asked politely, "Sharon?" She replied with a nod and a smile to say yes. She was a young woman with fair hair done up in a pony tail and she was wearing a mauve woollen 'V' neck top with short sleeves and black trousers. In her ears she wore large gold hooped earrings and a heart shaped pendant hung around her neck and across her chest.

"Is she ready?" she asked.

"You'd better go in," he replied then shouted, "Bye babe," leaving the two women to go about their business.

Sometime later.

After picking up Ian, they speedily headed for London, via the north circular road, heading west. London was no picnic at the best of times, that day was no exception as the traffic was overwhelming.

Steve explained the case regarding Andrew Cox as they passed through the wrought iron gates into the large car park with several cars dotted about the place. The prison was similar to Wembley Stadium with its two tall roundish sandstone towers.

Soon they were being led through

the corridors of the ornate establishment, along corridors that had heavy barred doors that needed to be locked and unlocked each time they passed through one. The usual smells of disinfectant and floor polish mingled with the gloom of the area and made one feel uncomfortable about being there, knowing they were innocent of any crimes.

A young prison warden led them to the Governor's office and their footsteps echoed eerily in the quietness. There they found a middle-aged greying man, stockily built, with a grey moustache, sitting at his desk.

"I understand you want to talk to our Mr. Cox, am I correct in thinking D.I. Price," he said referring to Ian.

"I'm D.I. Price Sir," Steve expressed.

"And I'm D.I. Dobson on loan from Australia... Sir."

"My apologies," he smiled and leaned back in his seat.

"You are right about the little chat I want with your Mr. Cox though", returned Steve who edged over the desk to shake his hand. "The Home...".

"Yes! Yes! The Home Office did ring," the governor interrupted as he found his feet to walk around his desk to greet them more intimately, "I was told to let you talk to him in private but it must be taped...

is that correct?"

"You got it in one", returned Steve, "and who are we to argue with the likes of the Home Office," he went on to add, "No! You must've known about the letter our Mr. Cox sent to Whitehall... and that is why they have asked me to interview him, somehow they seem to have this idea that it might have some connection to the copper killed last week."

"Yes, I saw that on the news and read about it in the paper... but I can't see how that has anything to do with Cox."

"Who are we to judge that scenario... anyway we won't know until we talk to him."

With that, the Governor pressed his intercom and ordered his secretary Roberts to come into the room. He then instructed him to escort the two men to the interview room and arrange for Mr. Cox to be taken to the same room, that had been set up as requested; he then informed them that refreshments had been arranged for them, to be sent to the room.

As they were led through the corridors of that place, the haunting sounds echoed around the grey walls that seemed to engulf those who dared to walk them. Its fearsome environment with iron bars everywhere and the clang of the warden's keys as they passed through each locked railed doorway made them feel strange. At last they reached the room, in which they found the usual old fashioned wooden desk with its four regimental legs. The tape deck stood at one end of the table which had three chairs around it, two under the table and a third by the wall.

A barred window overlooked the court yard where the inmates would do their usual daily exercises.

A few moments later and a fresh young prison warder entered the room carrying a tray that he placed on to the table. It was coffee for three, along with three white mugs were the usual large full coffee pot, accompanied by the full milk jug and sugar bowl.

The young warder smiled and left the room closing the door behind him.

"I wonder how long we have to wait to get to talk to this Mr. Cox guy Steve?", asked a curious Ian, who poured himself a coffee and spooned in two sugars, followed by a shot of milk. "What about you Steve... do you want a coffee?"

"Go on you've twisted my arm," he said as he bowed his head in thought rubbing his chin with his right hand.

"In that case you can put in your own milk and sugar," he smiled.

A couple of sips of the hot coffee and the door suddenly opened and there stood a gaunt looking man, allegedly in his mid-forties, but looking a lot older due to his misuse of drugs and alcohol. A grey ponytail hung down his back tied by an old elastic band. He was wearing the usual prison attire, dark blue denim trousers and jacket with a white shirt. He was led into the room by the first warder, who led him straight to the chair opposite the two men, who didn't move. Instead Steve slowly lifted his head to look at the sorry sight that greeted them. He looked older than his forties. The warder retired to the door where he stood upright on guard should the prisoner kick off.

"So you are Andrew Cox?" enquired Steve, after a moment to study the situation he rested his hands on the table top and stared into the prisoners eyes. Switching on the tape deck Steve introduced himself.

"For the purpose of the tape, it is now eleven thirty two am... I am Detective Inspector Steven Price and also present is..." he directed his attention to Ian.

"And I'm Detective Inspector Ian Dobson."

Steve continued with an air of authority in his voice, that was directed at the tape, saying, "Also in the room is Mr. Andrew Cox, who is serving life for the murder of his late wife."

Andrew lowered his head in shame at the statement, but placed his hands on the table too as he had learnt over the years when being interviewed or when facing a visitor.

"I think you know why we are having this meeting Mr. Cox," Steve stated.

"Would you like a coffee Andrew?" asked Ian informally, and got up to make him one when, after looking at the warder who just nodded to say it was ok, he poured him one and let him put in his own sugar and milk. "Carry on Steve," he continued once he found his seat again.

"Thank you!" Steve returned politely, then went on, "can you remember sending a letter that was addressed to the Home Office?"

"Yes!" He replied cagily. "So you are here because of that letter... I didn't even think it would've drawn any attention to it and I certainly didn't expect this sort of treatment... not by a long shot."

"Are you trying to tell me it was a hoax, Mr. Cox?"

"Hoax!" He snapped, "no way, it was real, honestly it was real."

"I see," returned Steve.

"Why do we have to be so formal Steve, the poor guy isn't on trial here, surely it would be better to refer to him as Andrew, and drop all this formality stuff, it does my head in and I'm sure Andrew would feel more comfortable about it... right?"

The room went quiet for a second

while Steve looked at both men, rubbing his head at the statement.

"So Andrew... what made you suddenly declare your innocence after so many years," Steve enquired.

"I guess it was last year when we were watching police five on the TV... they were looking into a crime back in the late fifties when a young girl was, you know, murdered in Romford."

"Are you saying you killed her or something?" Steve pursued carefully.

"I didn't kill her no way... look... I was there that's what started it all off back then. Ten years ago I was in this pub in Chadwell Heath, I have forgotten the name of the pub but I was there when some guy... a bit tipsy, just happened to mention the murder of the girl in the Fifties... I said in reply that I was in Romford at that time and I think I might've seen something... but I didn't know if I had or not, it was late and quite a few years before... I was working on my friend's fruit and veg stall. I was good even if I have to say it."

"The murder...what about the murder?" Steve pressed rubbing his chin. Ian sat silently contemplating the direction the conversation was heading.

"The murder?" he uttered, sipping at his coffee, "Have you got any fags... I'm gasping for a tailor made," he asked, his eyes were averted to a cigarette machine that stood in the corner hidden by a tall cabinet. Ian took some change out of his pocket and brought a packet of twenty and tossed them onto the table in front of Andrew who snapped them up and eagerly opened them. He then proceeded to light one up with a match that the warden had stepped forward with. A sigh of relief escaped him as he drew in the smoke, as if it was his last wish before execution.

"The murder?" Steve eagerly pressed on, looking at his watch. Ian just pushed the glass ashtray across the table for Andrew's use.

"Ok!" he returned, flicking his ash in the receptacle. "It was nineteen fifty eight, I was dating my late wife Lucy, we were sitting in the back of my car in the back street behind the church... we were, you know, otherwise engaged, when we heard some laughter coming from the alley way. Looking up I noticed to my surprise, that a Vauxhall Cresta was parked on the other side of the road, about twenty yards from me. It was a lovely pale blue bottom with a cream coloured top half... you know, two tone, I remember saying to Lucy I just loved that sort of car and that maybe one day we would have one just like it. This group of three guys came out of the alley full of joy and one of them was laughing aloud and happily waving what I thought was a pink flag of some kind... you know it was the year of the world cup and I thought they were getting ready for the big day... I later learned that flag was in fact a pair of girls knickers he was waving about, as they all jumped into that car. I didn't realise at the time that there was somebody else in the driver's seat... it sped off once all three lads got into it."

"So Andrew did you get a look at the lads... or should I say could you have identified them at the time."

"I don't know...maybe."

"So this letter you sent refers to something that happened only ten years ago and then some fourteen years later what was the idea behind that... you say you didn't kill your wife... to set the record straight, it is said that you came home late on that evening drunk and high on heroin and the court was told you injected a lethal dose of heroin directly into her neck killing her instantly... isn't that right Andrew?" Steve continued to press.

"I know it is stacked up against me," he sighed as he dragged on his cigarette then sipped his coffee, "but I'm off that crap now, don't you see. I have spent the last ten years trying to piece together the events of that night... as I said; I was in this pub in Chadwell Heath when this guy passed a comment regarding that murder. To which I stupidly mentioned that I was there on that night with my wife in a car close by and I saw some lads coming from that alley way and getting into the car...this guy got a bit concerned but brought me a couple of beers and said he had a bit of a stash in his car if I was interested. It was on the house so he reckoned, I thought I'd died and gone to heaven".

"Did this guy have a name?" Steve quizzed leaning back in his seat with a curious look on his face.

Ian sat silently with his right hand holding his chin and getting engulfed in the direction of the conversation.

"I can't remember, I know he was well dressed, you know... like a city toff. He said he had travelled down from the north on some sort of business trip and he had had too much to drink... well like a fool, I said he could doss down at my gaff for the night... he offered me some heroin as a gift... and wow it was powerful stuff, I was on cloud nine... I remember getting home in one piece and seeing Lucy watching the television, she was in her dressing gown and she was dozing off and muttered something like, 'you're home then'. I remember giving her a kiss on the head and told her that I had brought a friend home. She was surprised to meet this guy and immediately offered to get him a drink but I guess it was about then I crashed out, the heroin had kicked in... The next thing I can remember was being woken up when my neighbour came in... As that guy had gone and left the front door wide open... and that was it, I ended up being arrested and charged with my Lucy's death. They said a syringe was protruding from her neck, and as you would say the rest is history... and here I am, stuck in this joint". He went on the state, "It was when I was watching police five last year, and I suddenly remembered where I had seen that guy before. He had looked a lot older but he still looked like the lad who was waving the pair of knickers in the air that night in Romford... well... what do you think."

"I see!" Remarked Steve curiously. "So what you are saying is, this alleged guy who killed Lucy was the same guy who killed the girl in the late fifties...is that what you are saying?"

"It seems to make some sort of logical sense Steve," commented Ian casually, then went on to add. "If this guy... who he says, killed his wife, was the same guy who committed the earlier killing... and he stupidly confessed to having seen that person at the time of that earlier killing; then it would be right to assume that he would want to put our friend here in a position where he wouldn't cause him any harm in the future, after all who would believe a convicted wife killer?"

"So you think he is telling the truth Ian?"

"I think he is telling us something about the past that needs to be looked into... so Steve, what do we know about this killing in Romford in the late fifties then."

"A girl named Carol Richards was murdered in Romford in nineteen fifty eight, as he mentioned her killer was never found. She was stabbed several times after being raped and her body was discovered the next day by a young stall holder going to work. I have her report in the boot of my car."

"That's right the young stall holder was Terry Saint, he use to work on several of the stalls, it depended on who was busy at the time", Andrew suddenly remembered. "He also worked behind the bar of 'The Lamb Pub', if I remember rightly," he explained joyfully then uttered, "Yeah the Lamb pub, that was it."

"I see... can you run it past me again?" Steve asked with a puzzled look on his face, putting his hands in front of his mouth as if he were praying.

"Do you realise what we have here Steve?" Ian finally uttered.

"And what might we have eh?" Steve enquired calmly.

"What you might call a miscarriage of justice on the part of our Mr.

Cox... it sounds as if this person set him up to shut him up, the question is who was he and where is he now"?"

"I can remember something from back then, if it is truly important... I remember seeing that lad in the market a few times with his little gang. On one occasion I remember seeing the girl with her friend, who I think had ginger hair, the friend that is. I can remember my mate saying, 'you know what they say about these ginger birds, they're sex mad', and still that was in a different life time... a long time ago, eh," Steve and Ian looked at each other and then Steve indicated to Ian to switch off the machine and remove the tape from the deck. He did this and handed it to Steve who put it into his jacket pocket.

"If this is really a miscarriage of justice, and it sounds like it is, then we will have to trace this posh guy, and prove it's true. Then and only then can the law declare it really is a miscarriage of justice... but until then, unfortunately, he will have to remain banged up."

"The hardest thing is going to get this drongo, this posh git to confess to the crime or crimes and find the proof to send him down," Ian said with a grimace.

"Does this mean you believe me and that you are gonna help me get out of this place?" said an eager Andrew.

Steve responded by saying "If we

find this guy you mentioned regarding both murders, do you think you could identify him? Even after all the time that has passed."

Andrew nodded and eagerly said "Yes of course."

"In that case we need to keep Andrew under wraps so the killer will never know until it's too late." Ian said as an aside to Steve. "We need to see the Governor before we go."

Chapter 15

The sun shone brightly through the caravan window, where Peta and Bob were busying themselves enjoying their well earned holiday relaxation. Well in the eyes of Peta it was more a holiday for Bob.

Peta, having got their breakfasts out of the way as usual, hurriedly completed her chores in the makeshift room you called a mini kitchenette. She eventually found some time to relax at the table, lying back with her feet dangling off the end of the long bench type seat, her back leant against the side of the caravan. On the Formica topped table, which was now clean and clear, stood a fresh mug of coffee.

A family group walked past heading for the beach, their children getting excited at the thought of building sand castles and romping in the cool sea waters, their buckets and spades were at the ready in their tiny hands.

"What would you do if we had kids Bob?" She asked curiously holding her coffee in both hands.

"What's another word for heroic, eight letters, Pet?"

"Fearless!" she snapped, "You didn't hear what I said... did you."

"Yeah, something about kids...you're not getting broody again are you, you know what happened the last time", he said tossing his pen onto the low coffee table in front of him, "what has brought this on again sweetheart... it's not the thought of Angie having one... is that it?"

"No... Well yes... maybe, I don't know it's just something that's bugging me a bit that's all", she uttered.

"So what's bugging you... you've got my undying attention, I'm all ears and yes I'm truly intrigued to hear your explanation regarding this matter"?

"Well! You are right... it has something to do with Angie and the baby."

"I might've guessed, so you are

getting broody,"

"No!" she said with a sigh as she sipped her coffee to add to the suspense, "No... It's just something Angie said to me when you and your brother pissed off for the night, before they left to go home."

"Yeah! Yeah! I remember, what about it," he said finding his feet he went to the kitchen to join her making himself a coffee along the way too.

"Well Angie and me had a really good talk and Angie wanted to know if we could make sure the baby is well looked after, when it is born that is."

"Curious!" he said finding the seat opposite a comfortable place to sit, "what else did you girls talk about... was my name mentioned eh?"

"Why would your name be mentioned twat," she sighed.

"So! Come on, spit it out, I know you are determined to tell somebody... don't tell me, it's going to be born with two heads or something."

"Be serious for once in your life Bob," she uttered moving her head from side to side,

"Well spit it out then... I'm all ears for Christ's sake... so you and Angie had a heart to heart whilst we were in the bar having a few beers, so go on don't keep me in suspense any longer."

"What ever I tell you Bob has to

stay in this caravan and nobody else must ever learn of this conversation... promise me Bob."

"Now you're beginning to scare me Pet" he said as he found his feet again and made for the large front window where he stared out into the world. "Ok!" he said softly after a moment's silence, turning to face the situation head on, he slowly walked back to the table.

"Bob! I'm worried about Angie, she seemed troubled at first but finally gave in and she told me she is very ill".

"But! He uttered with a curious look in his eyes, "she looked so well when they left here."

"I know, Angie is putting on a brave face hoping and praying Steve don't learn the truth about her situation".

"Situation?"

"Yeah! Situation!"

"So what situation is that?"

"Promise me you won't say anything to Steve regarding this matter... promise me please, for the sake of Angie."

"God this is doing my head in, just spit it out and we'll take it from there," Bob demanded severely.

"It's the big 'C'," she said, letting go of her mug to make the shape of the letter with her left hand, still holding the mug firmly with her other hand.

"I don't believe it... what will

happen to Steve when he finds out the truth, it'll kill him, especially after Sally, we all know what he did back then", Bob said abruptly, out of feelings for his brother.

"How do you think Angie feels, she learnt the truth about her condition when she first found out she was pregnant... she was faced with a difficult situation. They wanted to abort the baby so they could do tests and operate and give her chemo. They told her that if she kept the baby she might not live long enough to see it being born. She just doesn't know what the future has in store for her now. That is why she asked me to make sure the baby has a good life and to tell the child about her and what happened to her in the light of her predicament... if Steve is tied up in his work, I would love to take the baby in and give it a good life for Angie's sake and Steve's... I'm sure he'll help in the child's welfare"

"You have really thought this through haven't you Pet? I can see why you've been so quiet since they left and there's me thinking I was in your bad books."

"No!" she sighed, "Why does life have to be so cruel?"

"I know Pet, but Angie had a choice and she must desperately want to give Steve a child, whatever it costs; she is banking on her memory living on in the life of the child. Who knows, she might make it, who are we to know what lies ahead... and yes if Steve is willing we'll take the child and bring it up as ours, if that is your wish and Steve says yes... but you are right he must never know the truth until it is all over... if that is her wish then who are we to deny her it, but I would hate to be in Steve's shoes when the truth eventually comes out. However if he decides he wants to keep the baby then we will do all we can to support him in his decision, ok?"

"Thanks for understanding," she said softly reaching out her hand.

"Do I get the feeling you want to go home too?"

"Is it obvious?"

"Then we'd better get packed and head for home then."

Meanwhile

On leaving that establishment, the two men made their way back to the Governor's office with the help of the warder. Steve wanted to inform him that they were going to suggest to the Home Office, that for the safety of Mr. Cox, he should be moved to an open prison of their choice for his own protection.

A cool breeze whispered around their ears as the two men eventually walked across the vast car park. "I am glad we are out of that place," Ian expressed his feelings.

"I know it was like walking through hell and back," Steve remarked with a shiver in his voice but expressing his feelings. "I felt more like a criminal in there than that poor sod we just interviewed."

"I know what yeh mean, I wanted to get up and run from that hell hole... I feel sorry for the young warders, they have to live with it... at least we can turn our backs on it, which is more than those poor sods back there can, eh."

"Lets just get out of this place and find a nice pub and have drink... what d'ya think, sound good to you does it?"

"Any way Steve what did you make of his story back there?"

"Very interesting, we'll just have to start digging into the past and find the truth in his story; if it is a case of a miscarriage of justice then we'd better get our finger out and hopefully get him off," he said calmly, opening the boot of his car and undoing the clips on his brief case, he was about to toss the cassette into the case when Ian spied the old file Steve had taken from Jack's house.

"So Steve, this is the famous file on the Sheila who was murdered in Romford eh," he said retrieving the file before Steve placed the cassette into his brief case then closing it right away. This left Ian holding onto the file; declaring he wanted to study it himself so he could get a better idea of what he had let himself in for having just witnessed what had just taken place.

The emergency services were busy as sirens bellowed out on the main road, "Don't tell me there's been an accident on the North Circular... lets hope it's going in the other direction," Steve sighed as he opened the car doors pressing the button on his key and watching the blue flashing lights speed across before him.

About then a large white prison wagon, with its blacked out windows which hid the criminals from the public, came through the ornate black wrought iron gates and headed for the gap between the two towers. Two tall heavy doors opened to allow the wagon to pass through and into the courtyard, to off load some more unfortunate men; who by their own misfortune happened to have got caught committing a crime. Now they too were about to trudge the same corridors they had just embarked on, but with a difference, they wouldn't be coming out for some time.

Getting comfortable in the car, Ian removed some of the paperwork from the file and began to read it, leaving Steve to edge his way cagily out into the city traffic.

The atmosphere in the car was silent, as Ian continued to study the old dusty paperwork. Steve turned on the car radio and played some soft music of the fifties and sixties on Radio two.

"Have you read this paperwork Stevie boy, it's very interesting. I think I would of loved to have met her, it seems she was a tasty bit of stuff... my sort of girl," Ian smiled.

"I did glance at it... why what's wrong with it."

"Apparently there isn't much to go on in this case, it seems everything dried up; some seemed to think she was on the game, but others said she was innocent... but it says here that she had a boyfriend named Joseph Turner... no relation to the artist, according to this."

"Do we have an address of this so called boyfriend?" Steve enquired as he carefully edged his way in the heavy traffic that greeted them. It was a case of stop start for several miles. The accident was in the opposite direction but they were caught up in the normal everyday set of circumstances.

"Yeah he lived on the Marks Gate estate and so did our Sheila."

"What about her address?"

"Yeah it's all here but there's nothing concrete to go on. I can see why they run out of steam back then," Ian said as he placed the paperwork onto his lap, "It doesn't even mention the car in it or anything of the statement our friend made in that place back there... so how do we know he's telling the truth?"

"A gut feeling Ian," Steve said bluntly then explained, "I had it the moment the Major mentioned it and I read that guy's letter he sent to the Home Office... that's why... mate!"

"I see!" Ian said sharply. "So Steve how are you going to solve this murder if there isn't anything to go on?" Ian eagerly enquired. "And according to this paperwork none of the officers involved in solving the crime at that time never solved it".

"But there is!" Steve said cockily, "You're not looking at it properly that is why I haven't taken that file seriously."

"Now you've got me really thinking about this crime", he said curiously, "What is your line of thinking Steve?"

"The killer thinks he's free of conviction...my guess is somehow my mate Jack hit on something that frightened the killer into reacting in the killer instinct again.. believing if Jack was getting close to nabbing him or her then they had to kill him to conceal their identity again... I think our killer did it twenty four years ago... the question is... how many more innocent victims has the killer killed since that incident... that is the question... who did he get to...whose lives has he destroyed in his attempt to stay free... my guess is the killer feels he has beaten the law and the system."

"So have you got a plan then Steve?" Ian pressed as he replaced the paperwork back into the old dusty file.

The traffic lights turned green again and Steve was able to move a few hundred yards again before he was stopped at the next set of lights that were on red.

"I'm going to return that file back to where it came from and start a new one by me. We have my friends untimely death to be going on with... we will need to know what exactly he was up to prior to his death... I can only assume it had something to do with the murder of Carol Richards and especially that file, but what had he learnt that wasn't in that file... that is the puzzle... perhaps if we learned the answer to that question we might learn who the killer is."

"So smarty pants, where do we start in this case?"

"It's staring you right in the face."

"Ho, it's a game is it?"

"No! Think about what has been said today, that isn't in that file... think!"

"I get it, the car."

"Bingo! you got it Ian... the car is the beginning, we need to know how many of those cars were registered in that area at that time and with those two colours... and we would need to know their names too, so we can follow it up and hopefully get this killer, whoever he happens to be."

"In that case Steve, leave it to me I'll go to the DVLA offices in Swansea tomorrow and see what we come up with... ok... eh."

"Yeah sure that'll be great Ian you'd be doing me great favour."

"Well, it will allow you to get the move on the way and get settled into your new home yeah," he said as he tossed the file onto the back seat.

"That's my main aim at present... besides... I need to make the other officers known to me at that nick."

"Who knows Steve the killer might even be a copper... (Ugh) the thought sends shivers down my spine Steve."

"And mine... that has to be considered though... but I'm laying my bets on an outsider. Mind you after what happened with Jack maybe it's best if we keep things to ourselves for the moment. They may even have some connection to the market place and they saw Jack getting involved in that alley...did you know Jack was the second copper to have been killed in Romford, a detective was shot there in eighteen seventy four, now there's some nostalgia for yeah Ian."

"What!" Ian said abruptly then added, "Have you swallowed an encyclopaedia or something?" he joked.

"Not really, the Major made a point of telling me in Weymouth, but he got it wrong, he said it was eighteen seventy five not four, I know I looked it up in the library and it was a Detective Inspector Simmons."

"Is there a meaning behind this madness?" Ian asked curiously.

"Well! It makes sense doesn't it... think about it... my friend Jack will go down in history as the second officer to be killed in Romford, and the poor sod had to die in order to be so."

"We're getting melodramatic all of a sudden Steve, that place must've got to you."

Taking a note book out of his jacket pocket Ian retrieved the file and began to write down in his book the addresses of those in the files.

"As you have those files, is there a forensic report regarding the weapon used?"

"Lets see!" He uttered as he removed more of the paperwork. "Ah yes here we are, there is a report, it says the knife used was about an inch wide with a six inch blade, with a hilt, as the knife left the mark in the skin... it says it could have been a boy scout knife."

"Well I guess that narrows it down to a few thousand lads of that time," Steve jovially remarked at the prospect.

"Who knows Steve, the guy waving the pink knickers might've been a boy scout in his youth".

"That's true, it might be worth looking into that possibility", Steve remarked curiously, then added, "There can't be that many scout groups in and around the Romford area."

"There's only one flaw in that idea, those knives could be bought in most hardware shops...why I knew somebody who bought one in Woolies when I was a kid living in this god forsaken country."

"So what made you want to move to Australia and what is it like out there?"

"It's bloody hot for a start and I was fed up with the way this country was fast going down the pan. Oh by the way everything wants to eat you out there too, all in good fun of course," Ian laughed out loud. "It's nice to visit here once in a while but Oz is where I want to be even now. We could do with more coppers like you out there Stevie boy."

"Who knows what the future may hold mate," Steve said with a smile.

Chapter 16

A shroud of gloom fell over the town of Romford, as the media moved into the once bustling market place; with television reporters from all the different channels, all talking in unison in different positions in and around the area of the police station. Each reporter eagerly hoped to get a scoop, as they chatted into their respective microphones and faced the camera's and were continually being given directions through their ear pieces. The main topic at that time was based on the big issue of the day, *'Who killed the copper'*. Some even mentioned the other copper who had been killed in the eighteen hundreds.

Many of the stall holders remained quiet, out of respect for the dead. The once noisy shoppers now quietly went about their shopping, stopping occasionally to now and then dwell on the scene; some even found themselves staring at the deathly alley where many flowers were already accumulating from well wishers.

Some of the stall holders did nothing but talk endlessly about the crime so near to home, occurring on their own doorstep. They were aware of the fact that the crime could bring sudden notoriety to the market place as death had come knocking at its door.

In the police station it was a sad time to be there. Long faces dwelled on the fact that one of their team was dead, a victim of somebody's hatred. Even some of the hardened officers were finding it hard to come to terms with the event.

The chief came out and made his usual statement to the media, once again declaring that he would not stop until he had found the culprit who had performed this atrocity in this humble town.

Detective Sergeant Peters was concerned about who would fill the vacant position, asking awkward questions of the chief. He in turn simply informed his member of staff that Whitehall had already assigned a new Detective to take the place of Jack. He went on to add that the detective was to take Jack's office and lead the inquiry into Jack's murder. He told him it was orders from above, but Peters was upset as he had visualised it being him who would be promoted to that post, then he could lead the inquiry into the untimely death of his mentor.

"So this new detective, does he have a name Chief?" enquired Peters, determined to know who his future boss would be, as the two men walked to the canteen for a fresh mug of tea for the chief and coffee for Peters.

"Yes!" the Chief said with a half hearted smile, "his name is Price, that's Detective Chief Inspector Steven Price being transferred from Basildon. He specializes in murder cases...he is moving into a police house right now and will be joining us in about a week's time... ok Peters eh."

"Next week you say Chief?"

"Yes Peters, next week," the Chief confirmed as he got himself a tea adding a couple of sugars before returning to his office which then left Peters to get a coffee and go and sit with D.I. Jackson.

"Have you heard about this new officer Sir?" he said finding a seat opposite Jackson.

"Yeah we all have," Jackson said as he carefully read his daily newspaper and didn't even take the time out to look up in Peters' direction.

"What do we know about him, anything?" Peters eagerly pressed, "And when are we going to sort out Jack's killer?"

"I gather you are referring to Detective Chief Inspector Steven Price. From what I've heard he's good, he knows his job."

"If you are talking about the new guy," came the voice of a young female officer in her pristine uniform and carrying a tray of coffee and a plate of tuna and mayo sandwiches, who had just heard Jackson mention Steve's name.

"You know of him Jane?" Peters enquired as she found a seat at the end of the table.

Jackson just raised his head for a second to acknowledge her presence, but he was all ears too.

"From what I have found out he lost his wife six years ago, she was murdered and her killer was never found. Steve had a reputation of being a very fair guy and very good at his job... apparently he felt if he could've got involved in finding her killer he might've wrapped it up years ago."

"The law wouldn't have let him.... he would be personally involved and as you are aware of... in the eyes of the powers to be they say it could jeopardize the outcome of the case", Jackson returned placing his hands onto his paper to talk openly, "and as you are aware of Peters, there are many cases where the killer has got away with the crime, the trouble is one day they make a silly mistake or on their death beds they confess to the crime... but no case is ever closed until the culprit is caught and banged up."

Peters sat drinking his coffee, while Jane bit into her sandwich.

"I met the new guy the other day, he dropped in and had a chat with the Chief," Jane remarked between bites.

"What was he like?" Peters enquired excitedly, whereas Jackson was more laid back when he asked the same question.

"He was a bit of aright actually...very polite... I could quite easily fancy him... oh yeah and for your information he has already been and studied the scene of the crime."

"Why haven't we been informed of his actions, oh and by the way Jane we all know you fancy anything in a pair of trousers," remarked Peters.

"Well at least I don't have to rely on old slappers like somebody I know," she said cockily averting her eyes in Peters direction.

"Now that wasn't called for," Jackson remarked with a serious voice. "Come on children we've got work to do", he said as he neatly folded his newspaper and rising to his feet he took his mug back to the counter.

....
....

The morning for Steve and Angie started out with tired eyes and a growing nightmare, as they busily finished packing everything up in the boxes that Steve had managed to get from a local mini supermarket on the estate. Charlie had arranged for his friend to be there on the Tuesday, to assist them with the move.

Little did they know that when they woke up that bright sunny morning all hell would break loose? The phone seemed to want to walk to hell and back, as it continued to ring time and time. One such call was from the Major who wanted to meet up with Steve, as he had a file on the murder of his friend and he felt he would need it in the light of his investigation work on the case. Other calls came from the friend's of the last person to live at that address and Angie had to tell them that the person didn't live there anymore. Every time the phone rang or the buzzer went little Tara went into a frenzy of barking and jumping about. She was sniffing at the boxes and sometimes retreated to her bed where she looked sad eyed at all the coming and goings, as if wondering what her fate would be.

The door intercom buzzer rang out and when Steve answered it he was somewhat surprised to hear the voice of his Brother and Peta. They had decided to come and see for themselves the situation and offered their help in the quest to pack and sort out their belongings.

"I thought you were staying down in Weymouth for another week or two, Bob," Steve said joyfully, having given Peta a kiss on her cheek and his brother a hug.

"We were", he said calmly then went on to explain, "but it was lonely without you two down there... so we decided to come back home and give you a helping hand with your moving... you don't mind do you Steve?" Bob said as he entered the lounge to be faced with all the big cardboard boxes being stacked up in the corner, "what are you going to do about your bungalow bruv."

"No bruv I don't mind you helping and as for my bungalow, you keep it". Steve said as he went into the kitchen where he found Angie sorting out the cupboards in there.

Peta had joined her and offered to take over the task at hand but Angie was reluctant to budge, saying she was alright.

"Coffee anyone?" Steve asked politely.

"I'll make it Steve," returned Peta

helpfully.

"His lordship has got to go and pay a visit to the Major...they're to meet up in one of the local cafes in the town centre of Basildon," Returned Angie.

Sometime later Steve headed for the rendezvous with the Major in the cafe in the bus terminal with its American style set up. Finding a quiet table for four in the far corner, out of the way of prying ears, the Major sat gently stirring his coffee with his right hand while his left elbow rested on the edge of the table. He busied himself watching the world walking by as he gazed out of the large window that overlooked the buses which were coming and going.

His usual brief case stood rigid at his side; he was smartly dressed in his navy blue pin-striped suit and navy tie and not a hair out of place as it was held in place with hair cream.

"How are you coping Steve?" the Major enquired as Steve joined him, making the sign to the young waitress as he created the letter 'C' with his left hand and gave her a wink, she acknowledged his request with a gentle nod of her head and an accompanying smile whilst she was busy making some-one else's tea and coffee.

"Yeah it's going swimmingly Major... the little brother and his wife are helping us to move... so Major what's the meaning of this little secret meeting."

"I gather you have ordered you drink?" he stated as he picked up his coffee and took a sip.

"Yeah they know me in here, I normally come in here every morning for my breakfast," he said as he toyed with the glass sugar shaker. "I'm going to miss my little visits to this establishment."

"Enough of the sentimentality Steve, let's get down to the business at hand," he continued once the young waitress had left Steve his coffee and asked politely if there was anything else, holding her little note book and pen ready. Steve just smiled and said, "Not yet babe."

She gave him a glancing smile and left them to go and serve a middle-aged couple who had entered the cafe and sat at the other end and were placing several shopping bags beneath the table.

"So Major, what's wrong?" he enquired putting two sugars in his coffee.

"I have the file on your friend Steve... there isn't much to go on as yet but its useful reading," he said as he lifted his briefcase up and laid it on the table to remove the said file. "while we are at it Steve we at Whitehall feel that you would be better off being promoted, you will be, as of now, a Detective Chief Inspector, ok. Eh."

"You are joking," Steve snapped he then went on to say, "me a Detective Chief Inspector, that's going to upset a few people Gov."

"Yes and as of immediately, he handed him a form to sign, you keep me informed regarding this case of Jack Gould."

"I have the tape of the interview with our friend Mr. Cox if you are interested," he said as he removed the tape cassette from his jacket pocket and placed it on the table, and then he gently slid it to him.

"I'll listen to it later back in the office... I was made aware of your visit to the prison by the Governor, he phoned me while you were interviewing him... what was your opinion on the matter."

"I get the feeling he was telling the truth, we are looking into the matter right now to see if it is of any importance."

"We you say?" he enquired, "I gather you are referring to our Aussie friend?"

"Yes he was with me in that interview, there are certain issues raised at that interview that need to be looked into very, very carefully. Because of Jack's untimely death which looms in our face it is going to be hard to keep this under wraps... oh, by the way we feel that Mr. Cox should be moved to an open prison for his own safety's sake... I don't know, it is just a gut feeling about his interview". Steve got up to leave having finished his coffee, he turned briefly.

"Oh! by the way Major, the Detective shot in Romford was in the year of eighteen seventy four not five."

"Why do you think we made you what you are today D.C.I. Price."

Steve left that cafe with a big broad grin on his face. It was like he had just been told he had won the Football Pools. With a kick in his stride at the thought of his promotion, he couldn't wait to get home and tell Angie the good news.

....
....

Ian drove to Swansea with his brother John who fancied some time away from the bustle of life at home. Ian had said this was a formal trip, with business on his mind regarding the statement of Andrew Cox, with reference to the car he painstakingly mentioned.

The M4 was quiet as they headed west. It was a few hours later and a couple of pit stops on the way had helped to quell their thirst and hunger in one of the motorway cafe's. It took a while to actually find the place which turned out to be a tall office block. They drove into the place and parked up before heading for the main entrance reception area where they were met by a pretty young girl who enquired after their arrival in her presence.

"I'm Detective Inspector Ian Dobson and I am working on a crime that took place in nineteen fifty eight."

"And what do you require from us Inspector," she asked courteously.

"A few names of people who owned a certain car in that area at that time is it possible?"

"Why didn't you just telephone the office, it would've been simpler than driving all this way Inspector."

"Yeah well I fancied the drive. No, this information has to be secret ok," he said calmly then went on to explain, "you see we didn't want anybody getting wind of what we were doing."

She pressed a button on her desk and moments later she said to somebody on the other end that there was a police officer who needed help in solving a crime. She then told Ian that a Mr. Dawson was coming to speak to him, regarding his plight. "Would you like to take a seat sir", she returned politely, pointing to a row of chairs by the wall where some old pictures of vehicles lined the wall, with one of them a gold coloured Roller.

Moments later and the receptionist called to him to tell him he could go to the third floor where they would be met. She pointed them in the general direction of the lift.

As the lift doors opened on the third floor, they immediately found themselves standing before a man in his thirties, with a distinctive receding hair line. He was well dressed in a grey double breasted suit with a fawn coloured tie which was done up in a full Windsor knot, This had the effect of making the knot seem bigger and looked good under his large, buttoned down collar.

"So Inspector what can we do for you?" he said with a Welsh accent, as he led them into his office which was just off to one side of the lift. The corridor was quiet and a woman walked past holding a large file and a couple of books, she was wearing a pink knee length skirt and a white blouse. She did not bat an eyelid at their presence.

"The receptionist says you are acting secretly on a case, how interesting...do take a seat."

"Yeah we, I mean I, am trying to trace the owner of a Vauxhall Cresta in or around the nineteen fifty eight era."

"I see", he said as he leant back in his swivel chair, "do you have a registration number or anything to be going on with?"

"No!" he uttered, "all we have to

go on is the make and the colour, which was a light blue bottom and a cream coloured top half."

"Bloody hell Ian you don't want much, do you? that's an impossible task you are asking of this gentleman," John cracked.

"Not really sir," Mr. Dawson responded. "We are looking at post war time when most of the cars back then were drab and you could say boring. What you are after was a new wave car; the question is how many were registered... where abouts are we looking at?"

"In or around the Romford area", Ian piped up.

"Nineteen fifty eight, a Vauxhall Cresta two tone colour and you say in or around the Romford area?" He enquired. "Now I can tell you that could take me a few days to search for the answer to the question", he said with some air of excitement in his voice, "Have you got anywhere to stay for a few days and somewhere I can call you when I'm ready?"

"No we thought you might get it right away."

"In that case, Mrs Evans has lodgings in the town centre. I'll give you her address; she always has rooms to let," he said joyfully. "So this case you are working on, what is it?"

"Oh it was a young girl who was

murdered back then and that car was seen leaving the scene of the crime."

"Why wasn't it looked into back then?"

"Because the person chose not to say anything until now, that's why. It's all pie in the sky at the moment but we still have to do our job, because no case is ever closed."

"In that case Inspector I'll see you in a couple of days...ok," he said, as he handed the piece of paper with the address on it.

Chapter 17

Having been told to get out of his new home by Angie, Bob and Peta after Angie had declared her ultimatum, by telling Steve to get his finger out and leave the home to them. She added with a wry smile that it was time he got on with the job he was good at and bring in the killer of Jack Gould.

Finally, under duress, Steve came to his senses and agreed with their ideology, declaring that they were right all along. So under that sort of pressure, he finally made his mind up to make his presence felt in his new position, at Romford police station. There in the high road, with the market in full view, with all of its usual sounds and smells that greeted you as you stepped off of any of the buses that ventured into the area Steve finally arrived and parked up. The market was in full swing as traders were profiting well under the circumstances surrounding the place. He felt strange to be venturing into this new position, which had arisen because of the sad situation of his friend's death. He knew his future was based upon him finding the killer of his friend and only then would he be able to settle into his new life there. He knew he had to be alert and aware of what was happening around him but his mind was still occupied most of the time with the grief surrounding Margaret, Jack's bereaved wife, and their family.

After driving into the place via the side gate where he had parked up, he was met by some of the other younger officers in their uniforms moving about doing their relevant jobs.

A Black Maria arrived at this point in time, bringing in an unfortunate burglar who had been caught committing a robbery on a house in a nearby street, having been spotted by a vigilant neighbour.

Stepping out of his car and retrieving his attaché case from the boot of his car, he endured the odd glance from those officers who suspected he was their new replacement. He stood resplendent in his pale grey suit with a neat striped tie for a moment before heading for the entrance. A police car drove slowly by and headed out of the gates he had just come through. He noticed out of the corner of his eye a young W.P.C. who was in the passenger seat, she gave him a glancing smile, then appeared to turn to her driver and made a comment about that being the new officer taking over from Jack.

Passing through the side door he found himself in the booking in foyer, where a middle-aged sergeant in uniform enquired after his reason for being there. He was taking down the details of the young offender in handcuffs who had just been brought in by a couple of uniformed boys. Steve simply showed him his badge and passed easily into the heart of the establishment. Stopping for a second or two before he passed through the doorway he placed his case on the counter and removed the old dusty file, placing it onto the counter he asked the acting sergeant what he should do with it. He said it was one of Jack's old ones.

"Leave it with me Sir," he replied

as he was writing down the details of the lad, "I will see that it gets put back to where it belongs, was it of any importance Inspector?" he asked as he carefully took the file and placed it under the counter, putting his attention back to the young lad he continued to question the poor chap who stood silently by still handcuffed, who seemed upset by his own actions. He then turned again to Steve and retorted, "I will put it back in a while, there is some big time villain being brought in very soon."

"I see...Jack's office ..."

"Steven Price come along with me," he was abruptly interrupted by the sudden presence of the Chief in his clean, smart uniform, befitting a man of his stature, "I spotted you coming through the gates Mr. Price."

"As I said Inspector I'll see the file gets put back in its rightful place," the sergeant returned informatively.

"File Steve?" enquired the Chief as they headed for his office to formally introduce him to the station, "which file would that be?"

"Oh! It was just some old case file that Jack Gould had in his brief case... It is ok, I did pay my respects to his wife Margaret. The Home Office asked me to go and give the family their condolences, as I knew them so well," Steve explained cagily then added, "I hope you didn't mind

Chief?"

"Mind? Why should I mind... I mean you are taking his place in this police station, I feel it was only right you pay the family your respects," the Chief said casually.

"Good morning Sir," came from a young fair haired W.P.C., who was passing through and gave the two men a glancing smile as she headed in the opposite direction. She seemed to manage well with juggling a few files tucked up under her arm and a cup of coffee in a polystyrene cup in her hand.

"The file was an old case from nineteen fifty eight the murder of a young girl..."

"The Carol Richards murder", the Chief interrupted and stopped in the corridor for a moment, "I remember it like it was only yesterday, it got renamed the churchyard murder".

"I know you were the acting Inspector working on the case...that's right yeh... I did read its content's sir?"

"That's right", he expressed as he led him into his office, "you'll have to tell me what your opinions are regarding that case," he said as he found his seat.

"What is there to say," Steve said as he found a seat too. "You had very little to go on back then", he remarked, crossing his legs and placing his attaché case on the floor beside him, resting his hands on his knees, "I could see she was raped and murdered with a six inch knife, similar to a scout knife... yes I did read the forensic report too, as I said...not much to go on... Yeah... I could see why it all went cold back then... I saw that an officer named Peters got involved later and after some time interviewing people he too came up with zilch."

"Yeah Peters was wet behind the ears back then... he's improved a bit since those days... I can tell you now Steve, that case has always bugged me...I can say without fail...I really thought we would nab that bastard back then, but as you say, it mounted to zilch; nothing; not even a sniff of a likely suspect in the case. It was as if the killer had vanished into thin air."

"He might even be out there now living a normal life believing he has beaten the system."

"Or even dead for all we know."

"Even dead as you say Chief... I have a gut feeling though that he is still alive and out there, just waiting to be caught... still who knows, one day his guilt might catch up with him," Steve expressed calmly, then went on to enquire, "The question I keep asking myself is, why did Jack have that file in his possession?"

"I'll guess we'll never know the answer to that question now, eh Steve."

"I have got to look into Jack's untimely death...I have already studied the area, it looks to me like it's beginning to be a bit like our Carol Richards scenario Chief...a murder with nothing to be going on with," he then went on to state, "I know you told me he was working on a bungled bank job as well as a girl who topped her self on Romford Station, isn't that correct?"

"That's correct... but neither of those would warrant him being killed."

"Not unless he was onto those who were involved in the bungled bank job. Still I will have to look more closely into his last actions; somehow the killer knew he was going to be at that place and at that time, the question is, who knew and why did he need to go to that spot? We know he had the file of the Carol Richards murder case in his possession, or should I say the Churchyard murder, nineteen fifty eight; so could he have been interested in looking further into that case, hoping to pick up on something that might've been overlooked back then, who knows? I gather she was killed quite close to where Jack was killed, am I right in thinking that?"

"Yes you are quite right there Steve, he was quite close to where the girl was murdered, but that was twenty four years ago," the Chief replied calmly.

"Well something led him to that spot at that precise moment in time... you agree?" Steve expressed.

"I can assume then that you are going to try and solve this case?"

"I'll do my best Chief... I am on to it and I'm looking for any leads to come to light... who knows there might even be something in his office."

"Ah yes his office, I suppose you'll want to look into it as it will be your office from now on... you'll want the key", The Chief replied as he removed the door key from the top drawer on his right and tossed it onto his desk in front of Steve who picked it up along with his case.

"I'll see what we can find," he said as he found his feet and made for the door. "Keep me informed of your progress Steve."

"Will do Chief... will do!" He replied in passing as he left the Chief's office and made his way to the office of the late Jack Gould. Unlocking the door he stepped into the world of his late friend, it was untidy, with papers everywhere on his desk.

Leaving the door wide open he studied the loose paperwork that was strewn on the desk. A picture of Margaret and Jack standing out side the church they were married in stood directly in front of him on the desk. A large map of Essex hung on the wall to his left and the window overlooked some gardens at the rear of the building. On examining the papers there didn't seem to be much to go on, in Steve's eyes, although a couple of pieces of note paper caught his interest. One of them referred to him being asked to go to the local hospital to talk to a dying man, the other was of a break-in of a house in Park Lane, Chadwell Heath.

He was putting the paperwork in a neat pile when Peters happened to be passing and noticed the door open so he popped in to find Steve doing his chores. "You must be Detective Chief Inspector Price, am I right?"

"And you are?" Steve enquired raising his head for a second.

"I'm Detective Sergeant Peters Sir," He politely replied, "So you are going to solve Jack's murder are you?" he asked, as he stood by the desk.

"I guess I will have to, eh," he smiled.

"So!" He said eagerly, "Where are you going to start in this case?"

"Who knows?" He replied as he continued to clear the papers on his desk. He picked up the photo of the couple, "I gather this was Jack eh?" Steve asked, feigning interest.

"Yes," he replied taking it from him to look at before returning it to the desk, where Steve just picked it up again and gently placed it into the waste paper bin at the side of the desk, along with everything else that didn't interest him.

He then came across another couple of pieces of paper that did interest him but he couldn't understand the writing on them, as they were written in a form of shorthand only known to Jack. He remembered it from the time they worked together, all those years ago. He had tried to explain his formula to Steve for reading it, but it went right over his head. Well at that time he hadn't expected his life to end so soon; especially when you considered he moved to Romford for a quieter life hoping to retire in one piece. He wondered if Jack had taught the code of writing to anyone in that office.

"Shouldn't you be working sergeant?" Steve enquired wishing to get on with sorting things out.

"I am Sir, I was Jack's right hand man," he replied calmly trying to look busy picking up a few files and placing them into the bin along with the stuff Steve was putting there,

"So where were you on the night he died?" Steve enquired as he busied himself trying to clear his office.

"I was busy with D.I. Jackson, staking out a possible bank job, it was a waste of time, nothing happened".

"Sods law then eh."

"You could say that sir... can I get you anything?"

"Yeah a coffee wouldn't go amiss... two sugars sergeant", he smiled at his young detective's eagerness to please.

A couple of young uniformed officers stuck their heads around the door to greet Steve as Peters squeezed past them to go and get the coffee for Steve.

"Good morning sir," rang in his ear, looking up he found he had been joined by a young W.P.C., standing in the doorway, "so your the new Inspector everybody is talking about sir," the soft voice sent a shiver down his back, only for a second though, as he gave a little shimmy to gather his senses, the sight of this young blonde haired beauty took him back for a single moment in time.

"Ah yes! W.P.C. Fuller," he said noticing her badge pinned to her breast, "you wouldn't happen to be familiar with shorthand?"

"Yes it is part of our training sir," she said as she edged into the room.

"There look at that then and you tell me what it says", he said eagerly pushing two sheets of paper across his desk in her direction.

"Sir! This is Jack's writing," she remarked as she picked up the sheet of paper and studied it carefully.

"Yeah but can you understand what it says, it might be important, the date on the top says it was written on the day he was killed," he said finding his seat where he sat twirling around like some kid on a new ride. "Well Miss Fuller... what do you make of it?"

"Well sir, it appears to be some sort of home made speed writing, our Jack was famous for it," she replied, returning the sheet of paper to Steve who just placed it in the bin with everything else to be dumped, then on second thoughts he removed the slip of paper and the photo from the bin and slipped them into his attaché case.

"What can you tell me about the night Jack was killed...anything."

"I wasn't on duty that night, Jane was, would you like me to call her... I'm pretty sure she would want to meet you."

"I think we've already met," Steve uttered then added, "but yes I would love to talk to her regarding the specific night in question... I've got to try and piece together the events that led to that dreadful night, or anything that might've happened leading up to that night."

"I know he was working on the case regarding the Asian woman who committed suicide on Romford Station, oh and there was a bungled bank job."

"I am aware of those incidents and

neither of them warrants him being killed, no, it has to be something else".

"You mean like somebody wanting revenge for him getting them banged up?" she enquired.

"That did cross my mind at first, until I found out that he had the case file of a murder that took place in nineteen fifty eight."

"A bit before my time sir, that was when I was a twinkle in my mum's eye, so she says that is," she giggled. "You'll find Jack's old fashioned electric typewriter in the bottom of his cupboard. He used to have his own kettle in here somewhere too as he hated using the canteen...which by the way it is at the back of the building, the food isn't that bad, they do nice sandwiches though... Mary and Joyce are good, they run it like clockwork."

"I'll take your word for it; (ugh) Miss Fuller is there a first name for me to remember?"

"Its Wendy sir", she said warmly, as she headed for the door, where she stopped briefly placing her hand delicately on the wooden upright of the door frame and half turning she added, "Wendy Fuller," she replied with a cocky wink. "Oh and by the way your coffee is coming."

"Cheeky monkey," he said under his breath as Peters entered with his coffee.

The sound of the telephone made Steve jump as it cut through the moment's silence. "Price!" he said, once he retrieved the receiver.

"Hi Steve, I was told you were there... we need to talk soon. I gather you're in Romford now," he said

"So who told you I was here as I've only just started?" He said curiously, then turned to see Peters entering the room with his coffee, "thanks Peters... it's alright Peters it's my partner in crime, we work together... no not really he's on loan from Aussie."

"Yeah brother told me when I tried to ring you at your flat... who was that you just talking to Steve? I heard what you said."

"It's ok Ian, that was Peters, another Detective sergeant... so mate... I think that might've been my old landlord you were talking to Ian; my bother is at our new address sorting things out with Angie... so what is new then mate?"

"Where can we meet up? I'm still in Swansea but I'm heading home in a few minutes, I'm just waiting for my brother to sort himself out then we'll be off... I have found a few things out while I was here, it hasn't been easy, the boys in the D.V.L.A have worked bloody hard and took a few days to get the relevant information I was after, but thankfully I got it now; it cost me a few quid to get it but it was worth it in the long run."

"That sounds good mate... So when will you be back this way then?"

"I can be with you by tomorrow lunch time if that's any good... so are there any good little pubs in that area where we can meet up."

"Sure! Meet me in the pub they call the Lamb, it's in the market place... lets say around twelvish tomorrow, will that be ok with you... you won't be too tired from your journey."

"No way! It sounds good to me Steve...I hope you didn't mind me phoning you there? Come to think of it... I was only hoping you'd be there."

"I'm trying to sort out my new office."

"Ok then I'll let you get on mate and I'll speak to you tomorrow in The Lamb Pub."

"So this Aussie guy he wouldn't be a cop or something?" Enquired Peters who sat silent on the edge of the desk sipping his coffee."

"He's a Detective Inspector Ian Dobson on loan from..."

"Yeah yeah said... is he helping you on a case or something."

"Yeah you could say that! No! He's working on a case from Australia and I was helping him to sort it out. I sent him to

Swansea to get some info on a motor that was involved up north in an incident."

"Why didn't he just telephone them instead of driving to there?"

"I don't know... perhaps he wanted the pleasure of driving to that place... who knows what's on the minds of these Aussie's, anyway Peters haven't you got anything to do, if not get rid of this rubbish and we'll have some lunch."

"Sir!" He replied picking up the bin.

Steve just gave him a smile as he left to do as he was told. Rubbing the upper lip with his finger and his thumb under his chin, Steve had a puzzled look on his face feeling something didn't feel right with Peters' conversation, but he couldn't put his finger on what was puzzling him so in the end he put it down to nerves on the part of Peters.

Chapter 18

Steve spent most of the time studying the contents and layout of his new office. He finally opened the double metal doors of the cupboard, all the time aware that his friend had opened that same cupboard no end of times in his stay in that office. He found Jack's trusted old electric typewriter, sitting on the bottom shelf as Wendy had foretold and where Jack had placed it.

Taking it out of the cupboard and placing it on his nice clean desk he removed the lid, instantly he was confronted with a document that had already been started as it was set into the roller and already had lines of words typed onto it.

Lifting the duplicate set of papers that had lain across the keys in the typewriter he pulled out the two sheets of paper along with the carbon paper so that he could read its contents. Straight away he knew he was looking at the beginning of what was to be a typed statement that Jack had started to draw up. From the date typed into it, he realised his friend had started to type the statement on the day that he was killed.

Steve stared at the document with a puzzled look in his eyes, realising this was to be the beginning of a statement by the late George Blackmore. In his eye's, it was a case of who was this George Blackmore anyway? And he knew this was the last thing his friend did in the office on that day.

There were several unanswered questions swirling around in his head, the first question on Steve's mind was... what had stopped Jack from finishing this statement... secondly, what was this statement in connection to; he searched his mind, thinking to himself did it have anything to do with Jack's death. He removed the papers, one that had the speed writing on was especially interesting, that he had found earlier, from the drawer and studied them carefully, thinking to himself that these papers may contain the clues to the statement that Jack was going to draw up, if only they could talk, he thought to himself.

It was about then that a young W.P.C. popped her head around the office door.

"I was told by Wendy that you wanted to talk to me sir," she enquired as she found herself carefully embarking into the room.

"Jane, it is Jane I presume?" He said, lifting his head for a brief moment to see who had trespassed into his realm and remembering her from an earlier encounter.

"Yes sir, I'm W.P.C. Jane Fuller," she said abruptly, remembering her status.

"Cut out the formalities, I don't bite. I just want some advice that's all, nothing too difficult," he said with a smile.

"I see sir," she uttered.

"Take a seat Jane," he offered as he found his feet and went to the window to sit on the sill, with the paperwork in his hand, which he occasionally glanced at.

"Thank you sir," she said politely, her eyes glued to this new man in the building, finding the chair opposite him she sat down and tended to fidget about feeling slightly uneasy about her situation.

"Look Jane I understand you were on duty the night Jack was killed, am I right in saying that?"

"I was on duty that entire week sir, on the eight till six shift," she replied formally.

"So young lady", he said casually returning to his desk where he laid the paper back on the keyboard of the typewriter, then enquired, "can you run it past me, the events that led up to that dreadful night... the night Jack was murdered that is? Oh, and by the way, my name happens to be Steve, ok... I hate all this formality crap at the best of times."

"I'm sorry to hear that sir," she uttered, "but as for our friend Jack I can say it started the night when a young lad came into the office demanding to talk to a detective and at the time Jack was the only detective available," she said leaning back in the chair and she crossed her legs lady like, her clasped hands rested on her slender knee cap. "The young lad was determined to get a detective to go with him, to the hospital, declaring that his dad was dying and needed to tell a detective something that was very important... but when Jack asked him what it was he wanted to tell a detective, the lad went silent, then said he didn't know but was adamant that he needed to tell him something important... he started to get a bit angry declaring he didn't have much time has his dad was at death's door."

"This person wouldn't happen to have been George Blackmore by any chance?" Steve said as he picked up the papers he had lain on the typewriter.

"Yes I believe that was the name the lad gave Jack in the end... the lad said his name was Colin Blackmore", she said as she glanced at the paperwork.

"Is there anything else?" Steve pressed.

"I know when he came back to the office he met up with the chief where he explained the situation of the hospital visit, but the Chief tended to poo poo the idea, saying that many idiots confess to a crime to make them feel good. Declaring that the crime was never solved back then and he told Jack to put it to bed where it belonged, the Chief just told me it was a hoaxer trying to make a name for him self before he shuffled off this mortal world."

"I guess Jack took the matter seriously then... that is why he pulled the file on the Churchyard Murder."

"It was a bit before my time Steve."

"I guess it was...now was there anything else you want to tell me, or is that all there is on this subject."

"I know the next day the house of the dead man was broken into while they were out sorting out the funeral".

"What a bastard thing to do under the circumstances. I can see they didn't have any feelings for that poor family, so what was taken, anything?"

"That's the irony of the case, nothing was taken," she expressed then added, "The person responsible just trashed the place and took nothing."

"Or were they looking for something, the question is... did they find what they were looking for or not."

"The lads want to know. Are you only here to find out who murdered Jack?"

"No I'm here to replace Jack, but yes, I've been asked to solve this murder if it is possible. Who knows, I might get to the bottom of it somehow but don't ask how, it won't be easy that's all I can say."

"We've heard that you are one of the best murder detectives in the force", she said, acting on behalf of her colleagues, "and that is why you've been sent to us from Whitehall."

Steve chuckled to himself at her choice of words.

"I am Detective Chief Inspector Steven Price. I joined the force ten years ago and yes I specialize in murder cases". He explained formally, "and no I'm not married, but I live in sin with my girlfriend... we are having a baby, well my girlfriend is the pregnant one (he gave a little laugh)... I was on my holidays when Jack was killed that is why I wasn't here any sooner, but I did start to solve this mystery while I was away."

"I'm sorry this case has cut your holiday short, but you should be careful. If the person who killed Jack was connected to a crime he was working on, then that person might take offence to you taking Jack's place and you could be putting your own life in the same danger Jack did."

"He's a cop killer, don't forget that

Jane...a bloody cop killer... and I want him... Oh and I want him badly... and I intend on getting the bastard. Right! Besides; I've been told I have a guardian angel looking out for me".

"I think you are going to need it in this case Steve... if this person can kill Jack with out any feelings, he isn't going to find it too hard to kill you, with no feelings what so ever, when he does so," she said as she found her feet , "you just watch yeah back Steve".

"I intend too," he said calmly, scratching the back of his head, and then he repeated it quietly to himself, as he watched her leave the room.

"How's it going Steve?" said the Chief who had suddenly walked into the room. "I see you have met Jane, she works on the front desk... a good worker, cousin of Wendy, who I believe you have already met... anyway Steve would you like to meet the crew, and they're waiting in the board room wanting to meet the new member."

"Ok! And yes I can see Jane was good," he said as he returned the lid to the typewriter but leaving it on the edge of his desk where he could get to it at a moments notice.

He was clapped as he entered the room where he was met by all those who worked in the team at the station.

It was a fair sized room, with

several wooden tables and chairs. Cream coloured walls all around with a couple of windows that over looked the high road. At one end of the room stood a large white board, near a door, with a picture of Jack on it and various photographs taken at the scene where he died. Many framed prints daubed the walls, mainly pictures of Romford throughout the ages; there was even a photograph of the Detective killed in the eighteen hundreds. For a second, Steve felt he had been involved in a time warp and he was now walking in the footsteps of that late Detective, as he carefully looked at the portrait just as he was being introduced by the Chief.

"This is Detective Chief Inspector Steven Price, he has been appointed to take the place of Jack, who will be very much missed... D.C.I. Price will be carrying out the necessary work involved in Jack's death, he may call on you to assist him in that quest."

"Hi there everybody," he said, "I'm looking forward to working with you all in these sad times. I am aware of the pain of losing a colleague like you have in the death of Jack Gould. I hope I can live up to his name. I understand he was a good cop and I can say that I have started to sort this mess out and hopefully can bring this sad case to a satisfactory conclusion."

"Isn't it right your wife was

murdered six years ago?" enquired Peters.

"Why, you didn't kill her did you, besides that has no relevance to this case; but seriously, our priority lies with a lost friend, as I'm sure Jack was to many of you if not all of you... we should be concentrating our time and patience on the funeral...I have paid my condolences to his wife Margaret and his family... has there been a whip round or something? If so I would like to put in twenty quid," he said soulfully.

"Yeh we had a whip round, we have raised just over a hundred and eighty quid so your donation will give us two hundred," replied a young male officer who sat on the window ledge with a fellow friend.

"Ok! Right! Here we are twenty quid it is," he said as he removed the money from his wallet and handed it to the young P.C. who came forward to take it.

"Right let's get back to the business at hand. I have studied the area carefully where he was killed; there isn't much to go on so I'm relying on asking questions everywhere. Knock on some of the doors in the immediate area and in neighbouring streets and go into the local pubs, you never know somebody may have seen or heard something. I thought you might like to know that I started my investigations when I was on holiday, courteously of the home office... I have now learned something about his last known movements, prior to his death and I will be looking into those actions in due course... are there any other questions?"

"As a D.C.I., have you any ideas as to his killer yet," Peters once again quizzed.

Steve walked around the room cagily looking at the faces of those present. You could've heard a pin drop. "From what I can make out", he said when he stopped at Peters' side, "I believe Jack was looking at a cold case from nineteen fifty eight known as..."

"The Churchyard Murder", replied Peters calmly.

"That is right sergeant 'the Churchyard Murder.' For those unaware of the case it was the murder of a young sixteen year old girl murdered in that alley on the twentieth of May of that year... and yes sergeant I am aware that you were involved in that case some three years later...and yes I am aware that it mounted to nothing...not a sausage; zilch; as your Chief so put it. He was a detective chief inspector of the day back then... so the question that bugs me is, what was Jack up to with the file on that case. Had he found something out and was acting on it... I don't know...maybe he did...maybe he didn't... the answer to that question died with him."

"Are you suggesting the person who killed Jack had something to do with the death of that young girl?" enquired a curious W.P.C. who had sat glued to Steve's talk.

"And you are?" Steve enquired warmly.

"Trudy Lane sir."

"Well Trudy, under the circumstances I would say that the likelihood of that being true, is highly improbable, there is no evidence to support it... I have spent some time studying that old case. They couldn't solve it back then, so how can we solve it today, besides he would've had to think very highly of her parents before he tried to solve that murder. He wouldn't have wanted to build up their hopes again, not after this length of time. I can only come to one single conclusion at this moment in time and just say it was somebody who just had a hatred for cops... from what I can make of the evidence, Jack was either lighting a cigarette or somebody asked him for a light and when he lit his lighter he was stabbed, sending his lighter across the floor, it's seems unlikely for Jack to have been caught out like that."

"I'm Christine Meyers Sir, I know he was suffering from the flu on that day Sir," returned another W.P.C, who was drinking a cup of coffee, "He came to me looking for something to help him relieve his plight... I had to go and get him some Paracetamols from the local chemist that afternoon."

"Ok so that would account for his lack of hindsight... no, this killer was a psycho, and at that moment in time they acted out of impulse, that's all we have to go on", he said as he rested his hand on Peters' shoulder with a gentle squeeze, knowing he was Jack's working partner and probably feeling it more than the others. Steve too was feeling the pain of those in that room, knowing Jack was his friend too, although from the past.

"So Sir who are you going to get to help you in this matter?" enquired a curious Peters.

"That is something I'm going to have to look into sergeant... I do know you were close to Jack, so in theory it would only be right that you would be my partner... but I will need to think about it, as I'm working with a colleague from another area who is trying desperately to solve another case elsewhere. I'm tied up with bags of work at the moment but don't worry, I am intent on solving Jack's untimely death...so in answer to your question sergeant I just don't know yet... but as soon as I know you'll be the first person I will tell. Mind you I am looking at some of the young female constables who might make a good Detective, who knows", he said looking around the room at those present. "Right, are there anymore questions, if not then lets get on with some work... I want some doors knocked on in that area where Jack was killed, do I make myself clear and report to me with anything of interest, however small and insignificant it seems to you, now let's get out there and do some work. We won't find Jack's killer in here will we."

"No Sir" came the resounding cry from all gathered there as they began to make movements towards the door that led out of the room.

Chapter 19

The morning had started in the usual manner with the house still unfinished, with stuff still packed away in boxes and walls half painted as Bob had been busy decorating. Angie was eager for the arrival of Bob and Peta who were keen to get the house in some sort of order, as it was still in a mess. You could see the place was beginning to take some form of shape although there was still the odd cardboard box littering the scene.

Steve sat down to embark on his usual breakfast. Wearing his dark grey suit trousers and a clean white shirt, his top button undone; prior to him putting his tie on. He began tucking into his couple of eggs on toast and his coffee, staring out into the back garden as the morning had just awoken. There was a cool overcast feel about the air, in his mind, he felt strange to think that he'd been down this road before and now here he was right back where it had all begun. He was once again on the trail of villains, like he had done so in what he could only describe as a different lifetime. Yet here he was as if nothing had ever changed, only the area had altered. Maybe this was his destiny; his true vocation and Jack had led the way, ready for him to take the place of a good friend, in Steve's eyes.

He endeavoured to try and tell Angie about his meeting later that morning with Ian, with respect of his friend's untimely death, something that should never have happened in his eyes.

Holding her mug of coffee in both

hands and leaning back in the chair to relieve the pressure of the baby, that was now giving her some discomfort, she explained to Steve that she had to go to the local hospital to make arrangements due to the change of circumstances, regarding the move and for the future of the little one that was growing inside her.

Steve did offer to take her to the hospital but she declined, saying that he had more important things to be getting on with. She went on to explain that she'd tell him about it later that evening. He just nodded from side to side with a little grin on his face as he put on his jacket and donned his light grey tie before heading for the front door, remembering to give Angie a loving kiss on her lips.

A dizzily rain greeted Steve as he left the confines of his new home being created by his brother and Peta along with Angie who kept being told to take it easy. That morning he was finding it a far cry from travelling to work in Basildon, having mastered the heavy laden roads with the many workers all in the same boat as they too were heading for their place of work; he was so glad when he finally reached his destination, turning into the car park at the rear of the station. By the time he got to his destination the rain had stopped but it remained overcast.

That morning he was feeling alert

and impetuous knowing he had a meeting later that morning in the Lamb Pub in the market place with his Aussie friend Ian, whom had said he had some good news but for his ears only.

As he entered the rear of the building he was met by Wendy who was carrying some files close to her chest and heading for the stairs. "Morning Sir," she said politely.

"Thank you Wendy," he smiled, "it is Wendy, isn't it?" He said as he stared at her badge that was hidden by the files.

"Yes Sir, I am Wendy, can I help you at all?"

"Yes come to my office in a while so we can talk... ok," he said as he left to make his way to his own office.

"I have just got to deliver these files to the Chief's office Sir then I'll be free... Ok."

"Right... Ok," he replied calmly.

On the way he met the Chief with a cup of coffee in his hand heading back to his office but stopped for a moment to talk to Steve who was removing his jacket as the station was rather warm.

"So Steve 'ugh', what's happening 'hmm' you know, regarding this Jack incident, bit of a real messy business from what I've heard, so how's it going. Is there any progress yet?"

"I'm still working on it Sir. If you

are interested, I have a meeting with a fellow colleague who's been working on a hunch of mine and we are to meet up lunchtime in the Lamb pub. This guy claims he's got something of interest in relation to the crime... who knows what facts he has found out for me," he replied.

At the same time a couple of uniformed P.C.'s squeezed past them heading to the incident room, where Steve politely apologised and moved over to allow them to pass.

"This so called colleague of yours, does he come with a name, I presume?" The Chief curiously enquired.

"Actually!" Steve explained abruptly, then added, "he is over here from Australia on a case... you see, two Brits happened to get themselves killed while they were out there and a third is said to have returned to Britain and subsequently went missing, so you see he came over to sort the mess out and that's when he met me... I was helping him with it Sir... he is known as Detective inspector Ian Dobson and by the way the two dead Brits were from around here."

"I'd better let you go D.C.I. I shall look forward to your briefing later," returned the Chief who headed for his office and his already cooling coffee.

"Yes sir, but I want to see what happens later today... I feel it might be of some use, who knows... it might be nothing at all, we can only pray."

The Chief stopped briefly and turned to face Steve again, "In that case Inspector I'll leave it up to you, but keep me well informed of your progress in this case...you know I have the press breathing down my back, eager to learn the truth at what ever cost", he said expressively when Wendy appeared.

"By the way Sir I would like W.P.C. Fuller to assist me in this case and maybe P.C. Mark Smith if that is alright with you Chief."

"What about Sergeant Peters, I would've thought he'd have been a better choice of partners in this case as he was close to Jack, Inspector?"

"I've put those files on your desk Chief," uttered Wendy politely.

"Thank you W.P.C," returned the Chief with a half-hearted smile as he left them to return to his own duties adding as he moved away from them, "as I said Inspector keep me informed of your actions".

"I shall consider that request with regards to Peters Chief!" Steve replied in acknowledgement of the Chiefs actions as he turned to confront the now curious young W.P.C. who stood with a puzzled look on her young face, "You can start by going and getting me a coffee, with two sugars, then we can get started on this case...Ok Wendy?"

"Yes Sir!" She sighed, raising her eyebrows in contempt of her duties, thinking to herself, how she would love to be a detective some day, as she left to get the coffee for Steve.

Moments later Wendy entered Steve's office where she found him moodily staring out of the window with a puzzled look on his face and deep in thoughts of where this case was going to take him, at one point he said to himself, 'Jack if you are out there can you tell me who did it and why', but he knew he was only dreaming when he turned to thank Wendy.

"Your coffee Sir!" she said softly as she placed it on his desk, "What's next Sir... you said you needed my help in solving Jack's murder".

"Yeah! That's right Wendy," he said as he took his coffee and tried it, complimenting her with a smile, "sit down," he ordered pointing at a chair on the opposite side of the desk.

"What would like me to do Sir?" She uttered softly, unsure of her position in authority.

"I want you to do some research for me...Ok."

"Research Sir. What sort of research are you referring too."

"I want you to get the file on The Carol Richards case and study it carefully... I want you to look for every other case Jack worked on while he was here."

"This Carol Richards business Sir, what is it you want to know?"

"I want to know where the people in that file are today, you know her friend Rose Finnegan and any members of Carol's family, if they are still alive."

"I am not familiar with that case Sir, but do you think it has some bearing on Jack's death," she pursued.

"Then look at the file", he ordered as he sipped at his coffee leaning back in his chair, with a slight grin on his face then went on to say, "and I think an article in the local paper might not go amiss; you never know, it just might stir somebody's mind and shed some light on the subject...who knows it just might create something that was overlooked twenty four years ago... by the way... to jog anybody's memories, it was the year Brazil won the World Cup... Ok?... and as for it having something to do with our Jack's murder, well we can only dream, my bet is on something more recent that he was working on and as we have no clues to go on we can only guess, but we have to start somewhere don't we? And as Jack was holding that file in his case we can only speculate on it's meaning in this instance."

"Is it true Sir that your wife was murdered?" she asked curiously and out of context with what was going on and with her pad in hand where she'd been writing down her tasks for him.

"Kidnapped, raped and murdered, and yes the rumours are true, but why do you ask?"

"Just curious, I gather her killer was never caught," she said openly.

"That's right W.P.C. the bastard is still at large out there somewhere, aware of his actions and with no conscience. I know he goes by the nickname of 'The Maverick."

"It sounds like a name one would use on the C.B's Sir... you know breaker one nine, that sort of thing. My brother is into it in a big way, he spends half the night chatting to all sorts of people, you never know this so called bastard might be stupid enough to use it as his call sign assuming he is on the C.B. circuit, would you like my brother to see if he can find out if there is somebody with a call sign of the Maverick?"

"That really is a long shot," Steve said calmly leaning forward onto the desk placing his elbows on its edge, then added, "but go ahead it can't hurt now, can it? whatever, give it a go Wendy; yes, you get your brother to try and see if this Maverick is stupid enough to use it, I can only repeat myself when I say it's a long shot but what the heck. Who knows, it might solve a six year old murder to boot and put my mind at ease and who knows it might put a feather in your cap", he said as he removed an old tatty photograph from his inside jacket pocket to show her the picture of his late wife, not before he spent a minute or two to ponder on his thoughts, looking at it himself with sadness in his eyes.

"So Sir, you want me to study the file on this Carol Richards, find out the cases Jack worked on while he was here and get my brother to scour the airwaves for a character with a call sign of the Maverick?" she said with her little note pad bulging to the brim with words.

"So Wendy, what's holding you back?" he grinned, drinking his coffee and leaning back in his chair as he studied his watch to see what the time was, "oh by the way, if anybody wants me I'll be getting myself a bite to eat in the market place. I understand there are some good burger bars there and who knows maybe. Just maybe some interesting gossip."

"It's alright for some," she uttered under her breath as she left the comfort of the office to carry out his requests.

A soft sun shone through his window shedding some light on his presence as he got up and headed for the door and the so called fresh air and the busy market place.

He found himself mingling with the masses all out to get a bargain or two. The place was full of life with the yells of, 'Come on darling treat your old man to some lovely fruit; here yeh go girls some lovely bananas, only twenty pence a pound,' mingled with the sound of, 'Fresh strawberries girls, twenty pence a pummet.'

Drawn by the smell of food being cooked he was soon enticed by one of the few burger bars that dominated the market place, he found himself ordering a quarter-pounder cheese burger with mushrooms and a coffee. A middle-aged man in his white overalls and receding grey hair took his order, but his female partner with her hair tied up in a bun took over and set about to cook his order.

"You've got to be the bill?" Questioned the stall holder who leant on the counter, after giving a young lad his burger.

"What makes you say that," Steve quizzed.

"I can smell them a mile away. But you're new around here, you taken over the post of the dead copper."

"You knew the dead copper then?" Steve asked politely.

"Yeah! Sure! He would always stop for a burger just like you, only in his case he loved his hot dogs with lots of mustard and tomato ketchup and a cup of tea to boot," he grinned. "That'll be one pound twenty please mate."

"So this copper, did he talk to you?" Steve questioned him as he handed him a five pound note to change.

"You even sound like the bill; mind you, come to think of it, the day he died, he did come to me for his usual hot dog and tea and asked me if I knew anything about the murder of some bird in the fifties."

"You're talking about Carol Richards?" Steve pursued.

"Yeah! That's the bird," he replied as he handed Steve his change. "I remember now I told him it was a bit before my time," he explained casually as he wiped down the counter, then added, "I told him that I was a milkman back then up in the Midlands, but I remember reading about it in the newspapers back then, it was when Brazil..."

"Yeah I know, they won the world cup that year," Steve interrupted him, as he left to serve a young couple who wanted two coffees. The stall had a couple of metal tables and chairs with sauce bottles and sugar shakers which had a regulated nozzle to give a spoonful with each pour.

"Here is your burger sir," said the cook, who was a middle-aged woman. "Don't let my hubby worry you sir he's a good man really. I heard you mention the business of the girl in nineteen fifty eight. I knew her from school, she was a really nice girl. You know, polite, she was going out with a young lad from the school, I can't remember his name... I do know she had a lot of admirers but she loved this guy, I'll think of his name in a mo... Yeah I think it was Joe somebody... at the time I was going out with a guy named John but he died and a few years later I met and married Gordon."

"And she is still married to Gordon", was the cheeky remark that came back, "and what do they call you mate?"

"Me?" he grinned, then casually explained, "my name is Steven Price, that's Detective Chief Inspector Steven Price to be precise, and yes I'm here to take over from the copper who was murdered and my first job is hopefully to find his killer."

"Good luck with that task Detective Chief Inspector Steven Price, I can tell you now you've got a real job and a half on your hands with that case."

"I know what you mean there is very little to be going on with... my first opinion was that it's some-one he had banged up and they sought revenge."

"You don't know much about lags do you? a true lag takes prison as a downside to his life of crime... revenge is the last thing on his mind, well not unless you happen to be the Krays that is", he went on to comment, "what do you think about this government building this new motorway, what's it called the 'Hugh' I'll think of it in a minute."

"The 'M' twenty five," his wife said as she busied herself scraping down the griddle.

"Yeah that's it, the bloody 'M' twenty five."

"Yeah well that's a different kettle of fish," Steve said jovially, "as for this new motorway business you mention I wouldn't know... my guess is, this government will only scrap it because it will cost too much... but who am I to judge their reasoning."

"A!" he said sharply then added cockily, "I bet you have a field day with all those female cops I mean some of those babes are right little sexy dolls," he said joyfully pouting his lips and leaning over the counter to say softly to Steve, but out of earshot of his wife who was busy cooking some fresh burgers.

"Don't listen to him sweetheart, he's a dreamer," said his wife aloud for the whole world to hear. "He fancies himself a bit of a Casanova, but..."

"Yeah whatever," he replied interrupting her in midstream, "women eh," was his ultimate response to his wife's jibes.

"How long have you been around here then?" Steve asked as he took a bite of his burger.

"Too bloody long," she yelled with her back to the crowd.

"Take no notice of her, we've been here for about ten years, give or take a few, where we were in Bishop Stortford for a couple of years. I sold the business to a couple foreigners for a song... moved down here and bought up this lot," he smiled as he leant on the counter, and added, "Wife not included," he said softly before laughing.

"It's alright sweetheart he says that to everybody."

It was about then a group of people turned up all wanting burgers and cans of drinks which created work for the busy couple.

"I'll catch you later," Steve said as he took his coffee and sat at one of the empty tables close by.

"Yeah sure, good to talk to you mate," returned the male trader.

Steve sat enjoying his burger as he watched the world go by; the sounds and smells of the market wafting around his ears and nose like a bee around a flower, making him feel good to be alive.

A young couple walked by pushing a pushchair with a baby crying loudly and its parents at logger heads over the fact of the place being so busy. It was making them get frustrated, it was clear the fella was eager to get out of that place as he preferred the quietness of a pub. Their argument brought Steve back to the reality of his plight. It was eleven thirty five when he found himself automatically glancing at his watch.

Chapter 20

Steve finished his burger and downed the remains of his coffee and wiping his mouth with a tissue he noticed it was closing fast on twelve o'clock. The sun chose that time to show its face, coming out from behind a grey cloud that seemed to want to dominate the day. The rendezvous with his friend Ian in the Lamb Pub loomed heavily on his mind.

Opening the door to the Lamb Public house, he found himself stepping into another world, far calmer than that on the street market. The sights and sounds of that place now drifted into the past once the door had slowly closed behind him. Casually he had one hand tucked into his trouser pocket and he felt at ease once he found himself beyond that door and into a world of beer and lager. A couple of elderly gentlemen busied themselves with a game of dominoes on one of the many round tables that decorated the scene, whilst a young couple of lovers sat in the window chatting and eating some sandwiches.

A group of four lads in their early twenties were heavily engrossed in playing a game on the pool table, with a series of pint glasses lined up nearby, some full while others were half drunk.

He was met by the soft classical sounds of the Beatles music drifting around the room which was decorated in the usual pub decor of green diamond flock wallpaper with a cream coloured background. This was set against the heavy draylon green curtains that met the oak panelled bottom and oak wooden furnishings. A green floral bench ran around two of the walls. To one side of the pool table stood a large dormant fireplace with its mantelpiece decorated by several ornamental china vases. A print of the green lady hung above it in a light oak frame and many other framed prints of old Romford and racehorses adorned the walls. Reaching the counter he was met by a young woman with short ginger hair, she was wearing a pair of black trousers and a soft peach coloured sleeveless top, a gold crucifix hung around her neck.

"Can I help you Sir?" She enquired as she placed a damp cloth underneath the bar which she had been using to clean down the bar area.

"A pint of yeh best sweetheart," he ordered as he took a handful of peanuts from a china bowl that sat on the bar and then sat on one of the bar stalls that lined the bar area.

A pint of beer stood unaccompanied at one end of the bar.

"That'll be one pound ten please sir," asked the barmaid when she placed his pint of beer in front of him, handing her two one pound coins, he thanked her.

"Who owns the pint at the end of the bar sweetheart?" He asked politely taking a sip of his beer.

"It's mine Steve," returned a voice from behind him who approached him quietly.

"Oh it's you Ian... you made me jump then 'Hugh' I didn't hear you coming," Steve returned once he had turned to meet the voice that had made him jump.

"Lets go and sit over in the corner Steve, we need to talk mate," Ian commented as he went to retrieve his beer and walked to the far corner in the opposite window where they could look out into the busy world of the market place.

"So mate what's with all this cloak and dagger stuff?" Steve found himself asking once he had sat on the long bench that dominated two sides of the wooden square table.

"As you know Steve I went down to Swansea, with my brother for company, you know what I mean?" Ian said once they both had found the comfort of the bench.

"So! Carry on... I'm all ears", Steve replied sipping at his beer.

"It took nearly a week to get the answer but we are in luck mate."

"How come?"

"Well mate," he started, "It turns out, as I said a lucky break on your part... you see mate... it just so happens that the car happened to be a prototype car and one of six cars made for the company. Each car was a different colour scheme...now comes the best bit... your one was a gift to a car company; and guess where from... Steve you ain't going to believe it."

"Try me!"

"The car was registered to a company calling itself Blackmore Motors and based in Chadwell Heath high road."

"Now that does interest me somewhat", Steve said as he leant against the cushioned back.

"I guessed it might well do, and you know what... you guessed it... that company still exists today, but today it is now called Blackmore and Sons, that car was scrapped in June of nineteen sixty nine when it was involved in an accident and written off by the insurance company."

"This Blackmore Company interests me greatly, you see it just so happens that my counterpart, namely Jack Gould was about to write up a statement by a George Blackmore...it now makes me wonder, what if there is some uncanny connection to this whole affair tied up in the past of that company".

"Yeah, and what are the odds of that happening eh Steve?" He said in passing as he drank some of his beer.

It was then when one of the lads who had pocketed the black ball chose to celebrate with a hearty cheer, which made Steve smile slightly as he too drank some of his beer.

"You are right mate the odds of that are astronomical to say the least... you couldn't have written it in any of the text books. If they had known about the car back then, who knows what might be... they may have solved the case back then... who knows... the one waving the girls knickers could just be our killer, or knows the killer."

"You could say it is one of those situations that could've changed the course of history for everybody involved... you know one simple act could alter the future. You know if Carol Richards had met up with her boyfriend or changed her mind about going to the pictures and stayed at home, she could still be alive today and might even have had kids. Who knows, him upstairs maybe... and who knows if that was true your friend wouldn't have needed to look into the crime and it wouldn't have upset somebody... therefore your friend would've still been alive today...assuming that is if his death was connected to the killing of the girl in nineteen fifty eight."

"That is a very philosophical statement you are making Ian old mate, a statement that is very superficial...the business about the car is something that would have to be proven in any court of law, especially after so many years... and what you are saying is it could've also changed my future with Sally... No! We are now being silly, and going down the wrong road...in my opinion. I think we should finish these drinks and go and find this Blackmore and Sons Company and find out the truth, what ever it is...and who knows it just might hold out some clues to the truth."

"Whose car shall we go in...? Mine or yours?" Ian calmly said as he finished his beer quickly, downing the bulk of it in one mouthful, ending with a big sigh and the words of how better British beer was in comparison to the Aussie substitute, which he claimed was more chemical than hops.

"Are you parked nearby as I don't fancy heading back to the yard to get mine?" Steve found himself asking as he too finished what was left in his glass, but at a much slower pace.

Moments later and the two men were heading out of Romford in Ian's car in the general direction of Chadwell Heath. They passed over a set of traffic lights into its long high road with its rows of shops, interlaced with houses and a church. The road itself is a road that runs right into London. Passing the Bingo hall that was once the local cinema, they found themselves heading out of the area briefly until they found the car lot with its many rows of cars of various shapes and sizes. The sign over the entrance read ['Blackmore and Sons Motors', declaring that they were the cheapest and the best in town; HP available with a small deposit.] A portacabin served as a makeshift office that stood near a ten foot wire fence which backed onto a railway line which ran parallel to the road. A train rattled past on cue when the two men reached the entrance to the car lot, leaving the car parked nearby.

They pretended to act like a couple of would be buyers looking for a bargain as Steve looked eagerly at a few of the cars and imagined driving one of them.

He toyed with the idea of returning to that car lot at a later date to pick a new car in exchange for his old one, despite it being a gift from Charlie.

"Can I help you Sirs?" was a polite response from a young, well dressed man with short cropped brown hair. He was wearing a pale blue suit with a white shirt and navy tie and black shiny slip on shoes on his feet. He was a young man in his early twenties and he had left the office to introduce himself to them, rubbing his hands at the prospect of a sale.

"Mr. Blackmore?" Enquired Steve who averted his attention to the approaching young man, leaving Ian to continue to browse the many cars on offer.

"I will say this mate, If I weren't going back to Australia I would be interested in buying one of your motors young man," Ian joked.

"Very funny sir," remarked the lad, then added, "no! I'm not a Blackmore. I am a partner of theirs if you must know...they are all away at this moment in time and I'm just standing in for them while they are sorting out a funeral...you sound like the filth...are you?"

"You're the second person to have made that wise crack", Steve replied cautiously, "this funeral it would be for a George Blackmore I take it?"

"You got it in one...now can I,

'Hugh', interest you in a motor, I have the very thing for you Sir."

"This funeral business, where can we find those in charge?" Steve pressed then added, "You were right I am a copper", he said removing his badge, and then went on to inform the lad. "I'm Detective Chief Inspector Price, ok, so where can we find the Blackmore clan right now, it is important?"

"Well it can't be anything George has done...well I mean if he did do anything wrong it's a bit too late now, his dead, you can't stick him in jail he'll stink a bit... oh well I guess you'd better follow me into the office there's no pleasing the filth these days is there... oh by the way don't mind Gladys, she is harmless enough."

"You are a very funny man", Commented Ian.

"Goes with the territory man from down under. I fancy going to that country one day," replied the lad as he led them into the sanctuary of the portacabin.

"That'll be the time when it will be full," Ian laughed with a slight wink, as he entered the cabin which was like stepping into another world, it resembled a perfect little office with a woman in her forties manning the telephones.

"Can you get me Big Dave on the phone please Glad?" He said as he found his seat behind a wooden desk. A couple of grey metal filing cabinets lined the end wall; the usual office equipment donned the desk including a family photograph of the Blackmore family. Some official documents were framed and hung on the wall. Behind Gladys was a large map of the area and a radio system sat in front of the woman.

Steve walked around the clean, well decorated space looking out of the window at the yard and the traffic going past, including an empty bus which was heading towards London. The sound of a siren echoed the area as a police car sped past with its blue lights flashing.

"I have Dave on the phone for you Chris," Gladys expressed as she handed the lad the phone.

"Hi Dave!" He said coolly, "we have a slight problem that needs your immediate attention."

"What's happened now Chris?" returned a voice curiously.

"I haven't done anything Dave... it's the old bill, they are here and they want to talk to you... I think it has something to do with your brother George."

"Ok I'll be there in a while...alright."

"Would you like to talk to them over the phone?"

"No! I said I'll come down there and speak to them personally".

"Roger Dave," he said, casually replacing the phone back onto its receiver, "the boss is on his way Inspector, so what has our George been up to now then?"

"What makes you think George did anything," Steve replied calmly as he removed a chair from the side wall; replacing it in front of the desk so he could sit and wait for the arrival of the brother named Dave, "How many so called brothers are there in this family?"

"I'm not sure how many brothers there are, so chief whets the beef on George then, was he a naughty boy in his day?"

"Not that I'm aware of son... besides you're a bit too young to be of any interest to me in this case."

"I see!" he said calmly then noticed a young couple entering the yard, "I'd better go and do my job, we have customers mate" he said as he rose to his feet and headed for a board full of car keys. where he took a couple, then politely enquired if they would like a coffee while they waited, but they declined, leaving the lad to do his job, "It's alright chief these people were in the other day looking at a motor, they said they'd be back... you don't mind do you?"

"No you carry on, don't let me get in the way of your work," Steve returned as he too stood up to look out the window, eager to watch the lad at work. The lad busied himself chatting away to the young couple who seemed keen on a particular car.

"Have you been with the company long Gladys?" Steve said turning his attention to the room as he leant against the wall by the window just as another train whistled loudly as it sped past.

"Don't the trains get on yeh nerves?" enquired Ian who seemed eager to study the local map on the wall beside her.

"Too bloody long, I think," she uttered softly, then went on to say, "no I've been with the company for about fifteen years, give or take a birth or two", she giggled, then added, "and as for the trains...you get used to them", she explained, "that is my son Chris, his twenty now and loves his job here thanks to Big Dave. You see I joined the firm when he was five years old and he went to school so you see he grew up in the business you could say", she said as she started to remove some files from one of the metal filing cabinets. It was obvious she was aware of the ability of her son.

"So...this Big Dave's a good guy then?" Steve pursued casually.

"The best", she replied openly, "he hasn't done anything wrong Inspector."

"Not that I know of," Steve reassured her, and then moved to the desk, where he added, "I think that coffee wouldn't go amiss," he smiled as he casually sat on the corner of the desk.

Eager to please she left her post and made for the kitchen area.

It was then that Chris entered the office with the young couple who were dressed like hippies, the lad was wearing jeans and a t-shirt with anarchy daubed across it and she was wearing Goth type clothes black all over.

"They are after the little light green Vauxhall Viva Gladys," he said once they were in the office area.

"The paperwork is on the desk son," Gladys's voice echoed from the kitchen, popping her head around the door she went on to ask if the customers would like a coffee too, they both said yes.

"Let them have ours," Steve returned when he saw a car pull up on the car lot and a big guy got out.

"That's the one you want to talk to," explained Chris who seemed to be busy, but had enough time to spot his boss coming into the lot.

Steve and Ian left the comfort of the office to talk to Dave out of earshot of his customers.

They were met by a tall stockily built man in his mid forties with a skinhead look, he was wearing jeans and a nice clean white t-shirt that gave him the hard man look, which it seemed obvious to Steve was a look that tended to go with the territory.

"You've got to be the filth my associate mentioned," he commented as they approached each other.

"I'm Detective Chief Inspector Price and this is Detective Inspector Dobson," he said as he held his badge before him, then went on to enquire, "You are David Blackmore?"

"The very same, so Inspector what's the beef then, I haven't done anything wrong, well I hadn't the last time I looked and I know I haven't any unpaid parking fines, so what's up."

"This isn't a formal interview Mr. Blackmore," Steve replied calmly replacing his badge of office into his jacket pocket.

"Call me Dave, I hate formalities, it reminds me of the bloody tax man and we all know what they can do, the bastards...so Inspector, what can I do for you, not sell you a motor on the cheap by any chance... because if so you could've dealt with Chris, he's a good lad," he laughed as he closed his car door.

"No!" Steve replied with a grin. "I want to talk about a certain car."

"Wow that sounds ominous," he returned, leaning on his car, "a certain car you say... and what certain car are we talking about."

"A Vauxhall Cresta, two tone blue bottom and a cream coloured top," Steve pressed.

"You've got me there inspector."

"Is that right... well apparently it was a gift to your company in nineteen fifty eight," Steve explained calmly, as he stood with his hands tucked into his pockets.

"Nineteen fifty eight you say Inspector... that was a bit before my time Inspector, I would've been about fourteen then... you want to talk to my big brother Kevin... now you come to mention it, if my memory serves me right," he said as he gently rubbed his chin and turned to walk away from his car and head for the office, "now you come to mention it there was a car back then that caused some kafuffle in the family. I think it had something to do with Kevin and George, I can remember it causing a bloody big fight between them and from that moment on they never spoke to each other ever again. I can remember the car was like a miniature Yankee car... yeah come to think about it, it could've been the car you mentioned... go on, now you are going to tell me it was nicked".

"No you're alright; it was a gift to your brother for sales of Vauxhall cars."

"Yeah that was when I was a kid. I used to wash the cars for some pocket money from my big brothers," he said as he stopped for a moment.

"This brother Kevin, can we talk to him?" Steve enquired as the stood by the office door.

"Yeah sure but only if you've got bongo drums," he laughed as he opened the door to go in.

"What are you talking about?" Steve pursued as they too entered the office where Chris was finishing his sale to the hippy couple.

"I've just sold the little Vauxhall Viva boss," smiled Chris as he handed the couple the completed paperwork for their purchase and was about to go and get it out so they could drive away with their car.

"Well done Chris, you bought a lovely little runner there friends", he said as he shook the young mans hand with a courteous smile. "Right Inspector let's sort this little mess out shall we."

"There is no mess to be sorted out Sir; we just need to talk to your brother Kevin, so where can we find him today?" Steve pressed eagerly wanting to get on with the day.

"Australia!" He snapped.

The word woke up Ian who became all ears. "You said Australia mate?"

"That's right... he moved out there about ten, twelve years ago and started his car business out there, that's when I took over the company."

"Do you know an Alfie Green or an Ian Carter by any chance"?

"Hmm! not that I can remember... is it important or something?" Dave pondered for a moment, "Mind you my brother may know of them, you'll have to ask him."

"He isn't coming over for the funeral then?" Steve enquired.

"You are joking, they hated each others guts, the last words they had was when Kevin wished him dead... I suppose he got his wish in a way eh," he laughed.

"Is there an address in Australia?" Inquired Ian curiously.

Gladys removed some note paper and started to write, "There you go," she uttered as she handed Ian the slip of paper with the address in Australia. It read. *'Twenty two, Charles Avenue, Ayr, Queensland four eight zero eight'.*

Chapter 21

Ian instantly pocketed the address as the two men left the confines of the car lot and headed back to Romford.

"I think I need to go back to Australia and get all the info on this Kevin guy and the file on the two Brits case Steve, but there's a real problem regarding the journey," Ian remarked as they got into the car.

"Leave that to me Ian... I'll have a word in the ear of the Home Office. I'm sure the Major will pull a few strings in this matter mate, it's the least we can do; besides it has turned into a joint case and it appears to be connected to an old murder case... the question is to what extent does it relate to the death of Jack and is there a link to that crime...no mate you've got to go back to Aussie. You need to bring back everything, including a statement from Kevin, what ever he has to say. Who knows you may have to bring him back with you to answer those questions personally, regardless of his opinions about his brother... and at whatever it costs."

"What will you be up to while I'm away then Steve, you know it could take me some time to get there and interview this Kevin Blackmore and then get back here in the fastest time possible?"

"I'm fully aware of that problem buddy", Steve said with a smile, as they drove on back to the turmoil of the market place. "Don't worry I'll have my hands tied interviewing those in connection to this Carol Richards business... god knows where that is going to take me... and I've got to look into everything my mate Jack was involved in. You know, just in case this crime has no bearing on the reason for his death."

"So you'll be busy then?" Ian said as he stopped at the traffic lights.

"Yeah, that address, you don't mind if I take a copy of it for the files. You never know it might be important and then again it might not. So who are we to judge the future, besides our Mr. Kevin Blackmore might not even be alive today".

"I'm sure if he were dead his brother would've known. Nah, his still alive, I can feel it in my bones," he smiled then added, "I'll be glad to be driving in Aussie again, these roads are crap, driving around England has done my head in."

"So the roads are different out there then?"

"Too bloody true mate, we don't know about these bloody traffic lights or your roundabouts. The Aussies would be going mad by now if they had to tackle your roads. Nah, give me Aussie anytime. I will have to drive down to Ayr from Townsville, it's a good couple of hours drive to there, then I will have to trace this address. I'll check in at their local post office in the town centre, I have been there once, some guy was selling a boat so I went there to have a butchers at it, It needed too much work on it so I left it alone".

"How do they drive out there then. I mean what side of the road do you drive on?"

"Same as here mate, in fact I'll tell you now, out there if you were to drive down our roads you'd think you were in England except for the sugar cane fields that is, they stretch for ever."

"Who knows mate I might take you up on that offer."

"You would only need your air fare mate, I would take good care of you and you could drive one of my cars while you were out there. I'm sure your lady friend wouldn't mind the holiday, especially if she is expecting a baby."

"That is something to look forward to mate, but let's get this case sorted out and who knows where it could lead us. I wonder which car that lad was thinking about when he said he had a car just right for me."

"My guess it was the two seated sports car that was sitting in the far corner", he laughed, then added, "or the Capri; mind you, I did take a shine to that little baby, I wonder how much it would cost to have it shipped out to Australia?"

"Very funny! ha, ha!"

Some time later the two men entered the police station having manoeuvred their way through the market place. Entering via the back of the station the two men made for Steven's office where Steve automatically picked up his phone and requested to be put through to the Home Office. A couple of minutes later and the phone rang; it was the reception of the Home Office.

"Can you put me through to extension two six, six please," Steve politely requested, "I'll talk to the Major on behalf of this little matter", Steve explained as he put his hand over the receiver. "Ah Major it's D.C.I. Price here," he said when the phone was answered.

"Yes Steve what is your problem?"

"I need a favour and a chat about the death of Jack."

"So Steve. What is the favour?"

"I need to get Detective Inspector Dobson back to Australia to get some info regarding the two Brits murdered out there and also to interview an ex-pat living out there, it is in connection to the murder of Carol Richards, you know the girl..."

"Yes I am fully aware of that case in question," he interrupted Steve then went on to inquire, adding, "so what is the problem?"

"How soon can you get him on a flight to Cairns in Australia, he needs to get to Townsville in a hurry, that's a return fare?" Steve pressed.

"It could take me a while or so but if it is so important... I'll do my best and get back to you ok."

"Thanks Major."

Returning the phone to its rightful place he was greeted by the entrance of the Chief who enquired after the presence of Ian.

Steve explained calmly that he was Detective Inspector Ian Dobson on loan from Australia. Then went on to tell him that thanks to him they had uncovered some useful information that could be linked to Jack's death; but at that moment in time it needed to be more refined and telling the Chief that was why he had to speak to the Home Office in respect of the unearthed information.

He explained to the Chief that he was going to be following up on that new information; by interviewing certain people in this country, while Ian went back to Australia in order to get the other half of the information that was somehow connected to somebody from Britain, who now lived and worked in Australia.

"It all sounds so confusing Inspector," returned the Chief with a confused look on his face then added, "I hope you know what you are doing D.C.I.... so what you are trying to say is that Jack was killed in connection to somebody who now lives in Australia."

"It's a start in the right direction Chief. I'm sure of it. We need to talk to the Blackmore family of whom, one of them lives in Aussie. Now does it make sense?"

He just nodded his head in disbelief as he left the office to the company of Ian and Steve, who eagerly awaited the call from the Major.

Steve decided to lead Ian to the canteen and some lunch of a bacon sandwich and a cup of coffee. They soon found a table where they sat and Ian prepared himself for the journey home.

"I'm looking forward to getting back to Townsville and the lads. I will have to travel down to Ayr to interview Kevin...you should come out there Steve, Australia could do with more coppers like you mate. It's a good country to live in and you'll get a good house to live in, it'll make these houses look like sheds, every house is huge."

"It would be nice to visit that country," Steve uttered.

Ian went on to inform him that everybody should visit that country at some point in their life time.

Just then Wendy turned up and joined the two men at the table standing beside Steve she stated, "I have done as you asked Sir... I've studied that file and found out where some of those in question are now living... shall I tell you now, or later?"

"Come to my office in about half an hour's time ok W.P.C. Fuller and talk to me there," Steve said with some authority in his voice, between mouthfuls of his bacon sandwich.

"I will need to go back to my brother's house and put a few things in a bag ready to fly back to Australia," Ian explained soulfully.

"I get the impression you're not looking forward to going home."

"Going home is the best thing; it's

the bloody travelling I hate."

Returning to the office they found Wendy waiting patiently for them to finish in the canteen.

"Ok W.P.C. what do you have for me?" Steve enquired politely once he found his seat. Ian went to the window and carefully watched the traffic outside. "Don't let Ian worry you, he is Detective Inspector Ian Dobson..."

"On loan from Australia sweetheart... you're a bonny Sheila," Ian interrupted.

"I can only assume that's a bit of Australian lingo," She replied with a slight grin.

"You're a bright little Sheila... could do with some female coppers like you out there."

"Alright! Alright! What do you have for me W.P.C.?"

"I told you I have studied the file on Carol Richards as you requested and I've located some of those in the file, apparently her mother is still living in the house on the Marks Gate estate. This Rose Finnegan married a Edward Bright and they moved to a bungalow on Canvey Island; by the way that's on the east coast not far from Southend Sir. Her boyfriend Joseph went on to marry a girl named Susan and they moved to Mildenhall in Suffolk about sixteen years ago". She explained in detail then went on to add, "As for any crimes Jack was involved in, I have made a list and I'll leave it on your desk for you to examine personally and Sir, the only person Jack had banged up for murder is still in prison serving life for killing his best friend."

"Thanks W.P.C.," Steve replied politely.

The telephone rang out making them jump.

"D.C.I. Price. Ah Major what's happening."

"You are to take your friend to Heathrow airport and go to terminal two for seven o'clock tomorrow evening, there you will be met by a courier from the Home Office, he will give your friend his tickets... he will be booked onto the nine o'clock flight to Cairns where he'll get a joining flight down to Townsville... the return flight will be governed by his time needed to get the necessary information and return to this country... is that alright for you Sir."

"You're brilliant Major; I will put you on my Christmas list. It will be a pleasure, the person in question is here with me, I shall inform him right away, so he can go home and pack a few things in a shoulder bag."

"Right Steve... you keep me informed of the progress in this matter alright. I understand you are onto something that appears to be very important in this case regarding D.I. Gould."

"Will do Major, and yes I have a gut feeling about this whole affair Major, the question is where is it going to take us."

"By the way I read your report from Andrew Cox, it looks promising. I agree he should be moved to an open prison so I'm sending him down to the open prison on the island of Portland Bill ok, I understand you are working on this Church yard murder business regarding the death of Carol Richards, if so... you be careful, we wouldn't want another Jack incident. I mean we wouldn't want three coppers killed in the same area."

"Three! Oh yeah, I forgot the one in the eighteen hundreds... ok Major I will take care... and I'll keep you informed of the progress," Steve politely replied, then went on to say once he replaced the receiver, "it looks like you'll be heading home tomorrow night at nine o'clock Ian...in the mean time, you should go home and pack some things for the journey, me old china."

"In that case I'll be off", he said with a hint of joy in his step as he made for the door with one hand in his trouser pocket.

"Come back here tomorrow

around fourish and I'll get you to the airport...even if it means a police escort... now go on bugger off," he ordered with a little laugh. He found himself following Ian out in to the yard.

Returning to the building after having said farewell to Ian he met up with Wendy, who was carrying a pile of files and heading for Steve's office, "Ah W.P.C. Fuller do us a favour and get Southend nick on the phone and ask them to locate this Rose character on Canvey Island. Explain to them we need her to be interviewed by me at some point in the very near future."

"I have done that already Sir," She replied calmly, then went on to explain, adding, "There is a slight problem... well there is and there isn't."

"Now you are confusing me...what is this problem that's bothering you?" Steve quizzed as they both headed for the office.

"Southend wants us to go to Kimbley Road and take into custody a Keith Paterson, they said he is wanted for jumping bail, a month ago for GBH and drug dealing. They say he has gone home to his mother's house at that address but something has come to light, they said his mother phoned them the other day... apparently he is wanted for beating up a copper in the Kensal whilst he was being arrested for drug dealing," she explained then went on to add, "I've taken the liberty of getting the Ilford boys to go and get him sir and we are awaiting their call telling us he's been arrested... they said to be careful as he is a big guy... the Ilford boys said they are looking forward to meeting him in person."

"Well done police constable Fuller," Steve complimented her as they entered the incident room where several young uniformed officers sat either typing or on the phone. The board was decorated with the pictures of Jack and the scene of his death hung heavy over the board. Steve started to write in there the fact that Jack had spoken to the stall holder that same day and enquired after the death of Carol Richards, but with little response.

"The question of this old murder plays heavy in my investigation into Jack's death... I don't know there is something strange about this whole affair regarding this murder... we are talking about twenty four years ago for god sake... and yet here it is staring at me as if somebody wants me to solve it... from what I have so far uncovered there is a connection to a family known as the Blackmore family with connections to Australia...what the hell did Jack unearth and did it cost him his life, if so then we had all better watch our backs, this killer isn't too bothered who he kills in order to remain elusive... I mean he has got away with it for the past twenty four years. Right listen up everybody, I told you before I want to know of any incidents relating to women being raped or injured in this area over the past twenty four years and I want it yesterday ok. I'm sure this person wouldn't have stopped at Carol Richards, especially with him believing he's got away with it for so long...I think he has made one stupid mistake and our Jack may have stumbled on it, to his cost," Steve said as he rubbed his chin.

"Jack's funeral is tomorrow Gov," was the voice of a young male uniformed officer sitting at his desk.

"Where is he being buried constable, do you know?" Steve returned eagerly.

"In the Chase Cemetery Sir in Dagenham."

"In that case we should all be present in our best for our fallen colleague... I know it will be a sad time so let's do him proud and make it the best of honours for the day... I'm sure Jack would've loved it," Steve ordered.

"We have got him a lovely wreath sir," remarked Wendy.

"Come to my office Inspector," Ordered the Chief as he left the incident room.

"Ok Chief!" He said expressively,

then turned back to Wendy and ordered her to take a police car and go to Chadwell Heath nick and fetch him back the report of the break in at the Blackmore house in Park Road.

In the Chief's office Steve stood looking out of the window at the car park at the rear of the building deep in thought.

"So Inspector I understand you are re-opening the Carol Richards case?" inquired the Chief who sat at his desk with his elbows on the edge of it, "that case was never solved back then so what has come to light now Inspector?"

"The home office received a letter which caused some concern, they thought it was a hoax at first but I was sent up to interview an Andrew Cox. He is serving a life sentence for allegedly killing his wife with a lethal dose of Heroin, injecting it into his wife's neck."

"So Inspector... what has that got to do with this case?"

"Well at the time of Carol's death he was sitting in his car in that area when he spotted a group of lads coming from that alley. One of them was waving a pair of pink knickers in the air and they got into a Vauxhall Cresta car which happened to be a prototype owned by a Kevin Blackmore who now lives in Australia."

"I see," the Chief mumbled as he found his feet and headed for the window, "and you think our Jack may have stumbled on that clue and was about to open the case himself and it upset the killer, because it would've meant he would get caught... so who did he upset, it could've been anybody... I know he became interested after he came back from the hospital having been asked to go to a dying man."

"Yes I know it was a George Blackmore, apparently his funeral is in a couple of days time... I have spent the afternoon talking to his big brother David... I want to interview the family, especially his wife... and I also want to interview everybody connected to the case, including her friend Rose who lives on Canvey Island, the Southend boys are going to trace her for me."

"Our Sergeant Peters has asked for a transfer to another station, somehow he seems scared that he might end up like Jack... so I've put his request forward, at this moment in time he has asked for a break as he isn't feeling too good... so I've suggested he should go away for a couple of weeks... I have arranged for another Sergeant to take his place."

"I'm happy to be working with W.P.C. Fuller; she is proving very useful to me."

"Ok then Steve but watch your back," replied the concerned Chief, "So you think George Blackmore was the killer of Carol Richards then."

"No I think he knew who the killer was... and the killer may have believed that George had told Jack who did kill her, hence Jack had to die to stop it getting out," he said as he sat on the window ledge.

"Do you think this Kevin in Australia has anything to do with Carol's killer and that is why he emigrated to Australia thinking he got away with it"?

"I was told he had a blazing row with George a short time after Carol's death... which sounds suspicious... I do know that your report doesn't mention the car and that could be the one clue the killer overlooked. The fact that it was a prototype meant it was easily identified by Swansea. It was a gift to Kevin who ran the car lot in Chadwell Heath."

"A nice gift", The Chief expressed as he returned to his desk, "If that piece of information had come to light back then... who knows... we might've caught her killer back then."

"Yeah and Jack might be still alive and Father Christmas might be real... I'll keep you informed of the progress, besides Chief it might put a feather in your cap knowing you solved the murder despite it being twenty four years old."

"You've got to catch this killer first

Steve, don't forget that and make it stick because of the time lapse your evidence has to be foolproof, anything less and the lawyers will walk all over your evidence... you've got to convince the Crown Prosecution service you have a water tight case, or you know what will happen...they'll simply kick it out... but I guess you are aware of that problem Inspector?"

"Too bloody true, that is why I want it kept under wraps for now, but this car business could be the killers Achilles heel, the one thing he overlooked."

"I hope you are right Inspector."

"So do I," Steve sighed then went on to add, "But there are so many underlying coincidences and they are all leading me right back to Carol Richards, it's as if she is guiding us to her killer."

Chapter 22

W.P.C Fuller was driven to the police station in Chadwell Heath by a young police officer named Mark Smith, who happily drove the police car. Having driven along the high road, they turned into the one way system which ran along the side of the Victorian brown bricked building that was the local police station. Chadwell Heath train station dominated the scene in front of them which was situated on top of the bridge that spanned the railway line.

Parking up the car in the police car park the young male driver said he wanted to go to the local newsagents on the opposite side of the road, as he wanted to get some cigarettes and a bar of chocolate.

"Hurry up then P.C. I'll meet you inside," Wendy ordered, then left the car and headed around the building to get to the main entrance where she was met by the receptionist.

"Yes W.P.C. What can we do for you?" enquired a middle-aged man with a good head of grey hair, his uniform brandishing his rank of sergeant on his arm.

"I've been sent from Romford nick to get some paperwork from here regarding a break in of a house in Park Road, a day or two after Jack Gould was murdered," She explained calmly but with some sense of authority.

"Ah yes you'd better go through, you'll want D.I. Pullman, he handled that incident, you'll find him in his office, room five, ok W.P.C."

"By the way, my driver will be in shortly he was gasping for a fag so he had to go and get himself some cigarettes from one of your local shops," she expressed as she passed through the electronic door that the sergeant opened by a button under the counter.

"So who's dealing with Jack's murder then. I would've thought Jackson would've dealt with it?" Remarked the sergeant nosily.

"They've sent us a Detective Chief Inspector Steven Price and he's the one who sent me to get this paperwork, because he seems to think it might have some bearing on Jack's death", she replied half-heartedly

"Whose they?" He pressed.

"The home office of course," she replied.

"Then surely they must've chosen the best man for the job".

"I suppose so Sergeant."

"Who are we to judge the minds of the detectives, eh girl"? He replied with a half hearted grin, and then repeated it to himself.

She entered the world of the police in that station, seeking room five, with the usual guilt edged number on it. As she roamed the corridor with a puzzled look on her face she was met by a young, plain clothed man in the usual dark grey pin stripe suit with a navy and cream striped tie over a clean white shirt. He had soft, light brown hair parted on the side and with a slight quiff and was carrying a couple of files tucked under his left arm.

His right hand was casually tucked into his trouser pocket and his jacket was unbuttoned.

"Who are you looking for W.P.C.?" he asked casually, stopping to talk to her.

"I'm looking for Detective Inspector Pullman, I was told..."

"You've found him," he interrupted politely, with a soft well spoken voice, and "so what's the problem?"

"D.C.I Price from Romford wants the paperwork you did for the robbery of the house in Park Road," she explained.

"There wasn't anything taken from that robbery, the place was trashed a bit but the family declared that nothing had been taken. So you see, there isn't much to go on."

"Who am I to judge but D.C.I. Price wants everything you wrote down, because he believes it might have something to do with Jack Gould's murder."

"I can't see how a robbery in Chadwell Heath can have any bearing on the murder of Jack, not unless he knows something we don't," he said as he led her to his office on the upper floor, "I can't say I've heard of this D.C.I. Price, constable."

"I can tell you now, he's got the office buzzing with his actions in this case and he appears to be on the ball regarding Jack's murder. He has the idea that the house and that family has some connection to the killer of Jack...according to what's being said, he lost his wife six years ago, they say she was raped and murdered by somebody who called himself the Maverick."

"Would he like us to bring the Blackmore clan in for questioning regarding this matter then eh?" He enquired when he reached his office and his sturdy desk where he finally sat on its corner. Leaning back he removed the said file in its fawn coloured card folder from his desk and handed it to her.

"Perhaps you should ask him yourself," she said jovially then added, "but my guess is he has his own plans regarding that matter, which is why he sent me to get this paperwork", she commented, as she waved it in front of him jokingly, then added as she made for the door, "I'll have the paperwork photocopied and send them back to you Inspector."

"Any chance of a date tonight W.P.C.," he said aloud.

"In your dreams lover boy; in your dreams. I have a boyfriend," she smiled as she closed his office door and headed back to the car where she found her driver puffing on a cigarette and leaning against the driver's door.

"Are you hungry Wendy? I've seen really a nice cafe just along the road there. I fancy a nice jacket potato with cheese and mushrooms," he said as he righted himself from leaning against the side of the police car.

"Go on then," she said as she tossed the file onto the floor of the front seat, then proceeded to lock the door before heading off for some lunch.

"What do you make of this new Detective?" The P.C. asked dragging on his cigarette as they cagily crossed the high road heading west.

"Are you referring to D.C.I. Steven Price by any chance constable?" She enquired casually.

"The very same."

"I like him. He seems to know his job and I think he is working hard to catch Jack's killer, even though it sounds weird what he's getting up to in order to do so... but who are we to judge him yet... let's just see how he concludes this case, then we can judge him... I'm eager to learn from his way of working... this cafe you mentioned, does it have a name?"

"Yeah the Kontiki bar, just up here," the constable replied, and "So who do you think killed Jack then?"

"That is the million dollar question, there are no clues to be going on with, but I guess the Inspector believes the answer lies with this bungled house break in. But who are we to make assumptions regarding his technique in solving crimes, as I said it will be interesting to say the least to see how he solves Jack's murder. That is as much as I can say at this point in time, but I'm sure we'll all be the wiser before long, assuming he has all the answers, and from what I've seen so far he seems in control and certainly confident that he will solve it."

"I gather you like him then?" He giggled, as they entered the Greek styled restaurant with soft green walls and cushioned high bench type seats and a light oak Formica style table. On the walls were pictures of giant vegetables and one of a Latte.

Later back in Romford nick, she found Steve's office empty so she placed the file on his desk so he would find it when he came back to his office. If she came across him in her duties she would inform him of the whereabouts of the file.

The reception was now getting busy, with an elderly woman being led in by a young female W.P.C. and a male constable. She was brought in for shoplifting in one of the local superstores; there was also a young man in handcuffs having been caught drug dealing in one of the market place who was being taken to an interview room.

That evening Steve arrived home around seven o'clock in the evening to the smell of fresh paint and the gang relaxing in the lounge. Bob slouched on the sofa with a cushion tucked under his arm, he held a can of beer in his other hand as he watched some football on the television, which stood by the ornate marble fireplace. He had been busy most of the day painting the lounge a clean looking magnolia colour and had laid a grey carpet. Everything was beginning to look homely again, but some boxes still dominated the space. Some were partially empty, while others lay untouched.

Angie was in the kitchen with Peta talking amongst them selves. Angie was telling Peta about the trip to the hospital that morning saying that everything was fine, as she noticed Steve enter the room with the usual, 'hello babe', which made Peta smile as she stood by the sink unit.

"So your hospital appointment went well then babe," Steve said as he undid his tie then his top button of his shirt having tossed his jacket on to the arm of the sofa. "In that case gang how about lunch on me, at that Chinese restaurant you liked so much babe."

"What that restaurant we went to with your cousin?" Angie replied eagerly, "You don't have to ask me twice," she laughed out loud for the whole world to hear her joy. Then she noticed Steve's face light up with his cheeky grin and his eyes widened with joy, kissing the first finger of his left hand he pointed it at her with a broad smile.

"So Bruv. How many criminals have you banged up today?" Bob enquired jovially as he tossed the cushion into the corner of the sofa and found his feet, "did I hear the sound of a meal on offer from you Bruv?"

"For your information brother, I haven't nicked any criminals today. Some I might've wanted to strangle, but none put away... anyway what makes you think my days are out there nicking the villains, most of our time is investigative work, you know interviewing suspects and piecing together a crime scene."

"In other words you do sweet FA," Bob taunted jokingly.

"Yeah you could say that Brother."

"I thought you were working on the case of your friend who was killed," Bob said changing the subject to a more sombre one.

"I am and we are trying to piece together the event that led up to his death, that's proving difficult to say the least."

They were soon heading in the car to Romford market that had become dead now, just an empty wasted space with music coming from one of the local pubs where a band was performing. A sign outside read - here tonight, 'The Graduates live, with the sounds of the sixties.'

"They sound like my cup of tea Steve," Peta said as she tucked her arm into Bob's for comfort, while Angie did the same to Steve. She was looking more and more pregnant by the day.

"Dinner first, then we'll play it by ear... in other words... if the music sounds good, then we go and end the night there... how does that grab you, gang?"

"Sounds good to me Bruv."

Later, as they were leaving the company of the restaurant, they could hear the sound of music coming from the Kings head pub at the far end of the market place, where the group the Graduates were playing, they could hear the sound of 'Johnny Be Goode,' being sung.

Entering the pub they were met by a good crowd who seemed enthralled by the band's musical skills. A young girl with long black hair and wearing a black top and leggings, was working hard on the drums, while a tall, stockily built guy with black curly hair sang and played the lead guitar which showed he was a master. He in turn was accompanied by a couple of shorter, slightly older guys, playing rhythm and bass guitar. The men were smartly dressed in black waist coats and trousers, with white, short sleeved shirts and a red tie to set off the ensemble and gave the group a semi professional look.

The crowd were wowed as they listened excitedly to the sound of the sexy female drummer hammer out the drums to the classic 'Wipe out.'

Before the evening ended the lead singer introduced the band, starting with the incredible female drummer .

"On the drums we have Julie".

The crowd yelled out, especially the women in the audience as they happily cheered her ability, while the men wolf whistled their approval, as she stood up and waved her drumsticks in acknowledgement to the yells and whistles of her fans.

"On the bass guitar is Joe," the audience again showed their eagerness to show approval with cheers and whistles.

"On rhythm guitar we have Paul," this was accompanied by loud claps and shouts of approval from all those surrounding the band.

"On lead and vocals we have Gary, yeah". Expressed Paul in acknowledgement of Gary's status.

The crowd yelled even more and then went on to beg for more, clapping and cheering and asking the owner to let the band continue.

The rest of evening went well until

finally they disembarked from the pub to the sound of, 'Save the last dance for me', being sung by Paul the rhythm guitarist.

"That was a great night Steve, good band too," Bob happily expressed his deep feelings that echoed in the night sky; for it had turned out to be a great night out, with good company, great food and fantastic entertainment. As they entered the open space and headed for Steve's parked car their every footstep echoed over the cobbled surface. The night was calm and peaceful and they all felt they were in a good place at that moment in time.

In Steve's eyes, it was hard to believe that this area would become the busy market place again, as it did every morning around four o'clock. That would be in just a few more hours from then, as it was one o'clock in the morning, as indicated by the clock on the church tower which chimed the hour for all to hear in the openness of the town square. A night bus drifted by heading for London, the otherwise empty road still echoed the changing colours on the traffic lights that refused to cease their actions in the night.

A bright moon shone out in a clear sky and the stars looked great too as the four happy people cuddled and giggled gently. The great music was slowly drifting into the past and you could faintly hear the cheers of more from a contented crowd who had been well entertained by such a brilliant band as the Graduates, who had said they would be back the following month.

"Lets get home for a nightcap, I've got a busy day ahead of me tomorrow morning," Steve said with a warm smile on his face as he held Angie close to his side. She just looked up to him as they stopped briefly and Steve just gave her a long lingering kiss on her lips and whispered 'I love you babe.'

"Get a room", Bob said aloud, as he cuddled Peta.

"You never do that to me Bob," Peta laughed.

"We're a married couple you fool, we can do that anytime in the right place," Bob responded and laughed gently as Peta poked her tongue out at him in a loving way.

"You sound like a couple of old fogies; young or old, married or not you shouldn't stop showing affection in public, within reason, if you really love someone," commented Steve giving Angie another gentle kiss and hug as they continued on their way back to the car.

"I see you managed to get the group's autographs Ange," Peta remarked.

"You know me, I loved getting autographs of the few bands I went to see, besides that band was magic."

"You can say that again," commented Bob. As they all got into the car and headed home for a well earned nightcap.

Chapter 23

Steve entered the police station, dressed in his dark grey suit with a pale blue tie. His hair was well groomed but he was still feeling the effects of the previous night in the pub. The vibrant music was still ringing around inside his head, his weary mind still rocking and rolling.

The marketplace outside was momentarily a quiet haven now, unlike its true potential which would come later as the public embarked on their business. As he had driven through the heart of the market place he had passed the now dormant pub, its bill board removed and back inside where it belonged, with no sign of the events of the night before. Now it was replaced by the usual sights and sounds of the bustling market, which were quickly replacing the pleasures that had unfolded the night before which in turn had bought a great deal of pleasure to a great evening.

Tapping in the code on the

electrical door security pad which was on the main door, he passed through into the workings of the place. The reception was already a buzz of activity as a few people waited to be seen by somebody on the desk. Most of them there were connected to the usual crimes which were often related to some simple motoring offence, where the driver had to produce their documents having been stopped sometime before.

One young man was giving some sob story about his girlfriend booting him out into the street, complaining about how she had stolen his belongings, mainly his TV and stereo system along with his records. He appeared to be in a drunken stupor, even at that hour of the day and was demanding some sort of action, but the duty officer on the desk was an elderly officer who wasn't having any nonsense.

"I'll get a few of my mates in and trash the place and get back my things," the lad slurred in a menacing voice.

"Now sir, we won't have any of that talk... and if you did do that you would be arrested and charged with assault... now, how long have you lived with this young lady sir?" asked the duty officer politely.

Steve hung back out of sight just in case this idiot kicked off in any way.

"About a month ago, I gave up my

flat for that bitch and now she has kicked me out... ME! Do you understand she kicked me out, the bitch?"

"So! Sir! You tell me why she kicked you out then ah."

"All because I accidentally hit her for having a go at me that's all and all because I got drunk the other night. So what I told her I was sorry, but the bitch didn't want to know, she just got her brother to come and get me out... And the bitch just chucked all my gear out on the grass, that's assault that is," he drunkenly proclaimed.

"Did her brother hit you? And will you kindly stop calling her a bitch, she must have a name so use it or I will have to ask you to leave ok."

"So the bitch is going to get away with it then?"

"What did I just tell you sir," the police officer glared at the drunk, then politely added, "now if you will listen carefully, I will take down the lady's address and I will send a police car around there to have a word with the lady... so if that is what you want then just give me the details and we'll soon sort this mess out."

Still with a smile on his face he looked forward to doing a day's work, especially on the Jack Gould case, he left the duty officer to do what was right for that idiot of a guy who obviously liked the sound of his own voice.

"Hi Gov. I put that file on your desk sir," W.P.C. Fuller explained when they met in the corridor as she was going to get a cup of tea for the Chief.

"Thanks constable," he said with a slight yawn.

"Good night last night, eh Inspector?" She went on to say as they walked together heading for the office.

"What'cha talking about Miss Fuller?" Steve enquired stopping briefly and stared at her presence with some element of surprise.

"Last night Gov in the pub, remember... Hmm, you know it was a bloody good band, weren't they sir... I saw you with your friends... I gather the pregnant lady was your good lady friend," she smiled then added; "would you like a coffee sir?"

"Are you saying you were at the pub last night watching that band? I would've thought it was out of date for the likes of you and your friends."

"You're joking Gov, we love the old rock and roll stuff, in fact I got a friend of mine to go and ask the band if they would play the song, 'Little Children,' by Billy J. Kramer, Sir, for me that is. I do love that song, they said they used to play it but they had forgotten it, but they promised me that they would learn it for the next time they appeared there."

"I see. So where were you then... I remember the guy who asked the band but I didn't see anything of you there."

"I was at the far end of bar Gov, you know with my boyfriend. It was the third time I'd seen 'The Graduates,' live, the other times were in the football club in Rush Green,"

"Ok Constable, now on a different matter, do you have any conservative outfits to wear?" Steve enquired changing the subject for a moment as he found his office and standing momentarily in the doorway, holding on to the handle ready to go in.

"Yes sir I do. I have a nice navy blue pin striped ladies suit, a skirt and jacket. Why do you ask Gov?"

"If you are going to work with me constable, you should look the part. 'Acting Detective Constable,' So young lady we'll get this funeral out of the way and then we'll nail Jack Gould's killer... what do you think?"

"I can't believe it Gov; you are promoting me to a Detective. I've always wanted to be a Detective Sir... it's been my one ambition, you know my one dream... you wait till I tell my mum, she'll hit the roof with joy, that is...she knows I dreamt of being a detective ever since I was five years old. I used to watch all the detective show's."

"Then trust me Constable I'll see what I can do about making it a more permanent position, maybe even to Detective Sergeant Fuller, if you do a good job that is," Steve said as he entered his office, with a calm smile on his face rubbing his nose with pleasure at his choice of judgement regarding Miss Fuller.

"Wow!" She exclaimed out of joy of her new found fortune, "My stars today read that my work status will take a boost for the good... by the way Gov, Detective Inspector Pullman wanted to know if you wanted them to bring in the Blackmore family for questioning regarding Jack's murder."

"I see," he remarked as he sat down at his desk leaving Miss Fuller standing at the corner of the desk. "So, what makes him think the Blackmore family had anything to do with Jack's murder... does he think he was lured to the hospital to be killed by one of that family... it's hardly likely," he explained as he picked up the file she had brought back and placed on his desk, "I gather Constable this is the file you bought back from the factory in Chadwell Heath?"

"Yes Gov...I'll go and get that coffee you wanted and the Chief's one", she said as she left the office.

Steve quickly glanced over the

statement taken at the crime scene, pouting his lips as he studied its contents.

'Oh well not much in here so the question is why didn't the villain take anything, he obviously believed there was something there that was important to him, that could incriminate him... but what... that is the real problem... what am I looking for...more to the point what were they looking for,' he repeated quietly to himself, rubbing his chin with his left hand he stared at the file hoping to get a feeling for its meaning.

Getting up from his chair he went to the window and stared at the high street as a row of buses drifted past, going in different directions, "For god's sake, help me out a bit here Jack," he said to himself again, "I'm confused. I am getting the feeling that the answer is staring me in the face and if so...god I'm going mad," he smiled ruefully to himself.

He returned slowly and casually to his desk only to find that the file was open and the name Blackmore calling out to him from the front page of that file. He was surprised to notice the page he had removed from the Jack's old typewriter, was now poking out from under the file. It was declaring the statement Jack had been about to type up prior to his death and after his visit to George in the hospital.

He knew from the interview the

day before that the car had been owned by Kevin Blackmore and that it had been involved in an accident several years later. Picking up the unfinished statement that was being typed by Jack; he noticed it indicated that George was somehow connected to something to do with the death of a young girl in nineteen fifty eight. However and more to the point was how was he connected to it, somebody knows the answer, but the question heavy on Steve's mind was who.

Still, there was a funeral to attend later that day, which included him also having to run his friend Ian to the airport later that day.

"Here's yeh coffee Sir... I still can't believe what you are doing for me, is it real, am I going to be a Detective?" She said joyfully.

"Acting Detective Miss Fuller, ok Wendy," he smiled as he took his coffee in his hand and took a sip, then handed her the file and told her that they were going to interview George Blackmore's family. It would be regarding the reason for Jack visiting him in the hospital, because he believed that was the place to really get started in solving Jack's murder, but told her to keep it under her hat.

"I think my friends are going to get suspicious if I turn up in a suit and not in my uniform, especially the Chief."

"Don't worry about the Chief; I've cleared it with him. I told him it was either Mark Smith or yourself and as you may have guessed you won. I look forward to us working as a good team, so young lady what did you make of the Carol Richards case?"

"Not much to be going on Gov, so what is the plan... I mean D. I. Pullman of Chadwell Heath feels you are barking up the wrong tree going after the file on the break in of the Blackmore house," she explained as she sipped at her own cup of coffee. She sat at the edge of the desk, having retrieved a chair from the far wall.

"So what else did he say?" Steve asked, as he stood up to go to the window again.

"He said you must know something that they don't Gov", she said calmly as she crossed her legs tucking her feet under the chair and holding her cup of coffee in her left hand whilst her right hand rested on her knee.

"I do Detective..."

"Wow that sounds great," she interrupted.

"What does?"

"Detective... it sounds strange to me Gov."

"For the time being you are only an Acting Detective constable... anyway what I was about to tell you is that this case I feel has a strong connection to the murder of Carol Richards. Jack was about to reopen the case when somebody decided to kill him in order to stop him from finding out the truth."

"But we are talking about a crime that took place, what, twenty four years ago Gov. I mean surely her killer would be long gone by now and we have still got to find the killer. It could be just about anybody connected to that Girl... so Gov what have we got to go on?"

"There was one forgotten clue that was overlooked all those years ago and that was a prototype car that was owned by a Kevin Blackmore, who now lives and works in Australia... Jack on the other hand interviewed a George Blackmore in the local hospital the night before he was killed, so anybody who was at that hospital could be our killer."

"So that is why you wanted to know everything about those involved in the file of that old murder case; for example her friend Rose who now lives with her husband on Canvey Island. Oh by the way Gov, the boys from Chadwell Heath arrested the guy Southend wanted and they are transporting him to them as we speak. He was arrested in the local pub in Seven Kings High Road last night, he didn't put up much of a fight, why couldn't Southend mob come and get him themselves?"

"Because we are the Met and they are not, it is as simple as that... we do not tread on their turf; just as they wouldn't tread on our turf. Well not without permission that is".

"So Gov do we have to notify them if we want to talk to Rose."

"Only if it meant we were interviewing her in their nick."

"But not in her home?"

"That will be between me and the gate post, besides she hasn't done anything wrong has she?" Steve said as he casually leant against the wall of his office, still drinking his coffee.

"Do you think this Kevin Blackmore in Australia that you mentioned... do you think he had something to do with Carol Richards murder?"

"We won't know until my friend, Detective Inspector Ian Dobson goes back home and interviews him to see if he can shed some light on the matter... besides he is still out there in Australia so there is no way he could've known Jack was involved, or that the case was to be reopened... so my guess is somebody thought George had grassed them up to Jack, hence the reason why Jack had that file in his possession. I believe the killer may have believed he had left evidence at George's house and broke in hoping to find something that would link them to Carol Richards killer, who ever he happened to be, the question now is...who 'hum,' who stood to lose the most if the truth was to come out."

"The killer of course."

"Well there you go, it will be our job now to interview everybody connected to the Blackmore family. Also all those in the file and yes that would include Rose too and that would also include the dead girl's mother... I want you to locate in Mildenhall the whereabouts of Carol's old flame Joseph. I will need to talk to him despite him saying in his statement that he was fixing his car with his mates, and then getting ready with them to watch the World Cup on a new TV that he and his mates had brought between them."

"So Gov, where do we start then, if you don't mind me asking?" she said as she placed her empty cup onto the edge of the desk.

"I think we should start with this Lucy Blackmore," he said as he returned to his desk and calmly opened the file that Wendy had brought back from Chadwell Heath. Placing the first finger of his right hand specifically on her name which had been written on top of her statement. He began to read about how she had arrived home in the afternoon only to find her home had been trashed, but then went on to declare that nothing had been taken. "What time is Jack's funeral today?"

"Two o'clock at the Chase cemetery Gov."

Looking at his watch he saw it was now nine thirty seven as he closed the file and tossed it into his out tray that dominated the edge of his cluttered desk.

"I think constable we should go and have a little chat with Lucy Blackmore, in respect of her late husband and the connection regarding Jack... ok... lets go then," he ordered as he pushed away from the wall and they headed towards the door.

Chapter 24

The drive from Romford was a quiet affair as Wendy stared out of the window day dreaming about her good fortune. She was looking forward to getting out of the police uniform and into civvies ready to take her place in the ranks of the Detectives. She was acutely aware though of the fact that it was only in an acting capacity.

Arriving at the nineteen thirties, three bedroomed terraced house which was situated in a short road which ran up to the park, they both got out of the car and approached the house. Steve knocked on the green wooden door with its half moon glassed top window and silver accessories.

After a few minutes the door was opened cagily by a tired looking, slim woman with brown hair which she had tied up in a ponytail, complete with a red ribbon just tied in a knot leaving the two lengths dangling amidst her long flowing hair that hung down her back. She was wearing denim jeans with a white t-shirt and a gold crucifix hung around her slender neck, she wore flip flops on her bare feet.

"Yes!" She uttered carefully and with a curious look on her face at the sight of the two people standing in her doorway, "I hope you're not Jehovah's Witnesses?" she asked.

Steve looked at Wendy with a slight smile before turning to the woman.

"No we are not Jehovah Witnesses... you wouldn't happen to be

Lucy Blackmore by any chance?" Wendy enquired.

"It depends on who's asking," she uttered cagily.

"If you must know," Steve said, as he searched his pocket for his warrant card and badge of office, waving it in front of her then added, "I am Detective Chief Inspector Price and this is acting Detective Constable Fuller... can we talk?" he explained with a smile as Wendy flashed her official badge of office too.

"So what brings you here today Inspector," she asked holding firm against the front door, then enquired with some authority in her voice, "if it has anything to do with the break in I've already made a statement in respect of that incident."

"Yes we know! I have read your statement regarding that incident as you say... no my visit is in respect of your late husband and an interview he had with one of my colleagues."

She paused for a moment to redress her stature before adding, "You're talking about the copper that was killed yeh?" She said as she desperately held on to the door.

"Yes that's right madam; can we come in and talk about that event?" Steve pressed.

"It isn't a good time right now, you know family problems linked to the funeral... but if you really want to talk I will walk through the park with you, where we can talk if it is alright with you... my place is a mess at the moment, I have been so busy sorting out the funeral of George as he wanted to be cremated. I'm glad the family is close by to help me in this time of sadness... I'll just get my jacket ok."

"Is everything all right mum?" enquired a young man from just inside the door.

"It's ok son it's the police, they want to talk to me about yeh dad so don't worry," she reassured her son, gently closing the door behind her, having put on her little grey jacket.

The entrance to the park was at the end of the street. It had ten foot high metal gates and the name of the park arched over both gates which were now open to the public. The three of them passed through them into another world, a tree lined wide path led across the open space. To the right they could hear several people playing a game of bowls on the elegant green which was behind a modern pavilion built in the sixties.

"So Inspector what is this all about?" Lucy enquired calmly, as they strolled along the straight path. On the way they passed on the right a children's play area. Many young children played on the swings and on a roundabout. They were enjoying themselves running about and jumping on and off it with laughter. A tall slide was being well used by a couple of lads running up and down the slope.

"I understand your husband requested the presence of a police officer whilst he was in the hospital in Romford, the trouble is that the police officer was killed before he could draw up the statement based on what your late husband had told him... so you see I was wondering if you could shed some light on the subject as you were his wife."

A young couple were running through the park, sweating under the pressure of the combination of the warm overcast weather. The three of them finally sat on a long wooden bench on the edge of the path, a row of tall trees stood on the opposite side, the grass spread out before them like a giant green blanket. In the distance you could hear the sounds of more children playing, their laughter dancing on the breeze. There was the sweet smell from the floral arrangement behind them. It was a place of tranquillity.

"I was the one in the end who got him to tell the police the truth, while he was in hospital and still alive, otherwise it would be too late if he died before he repented his sins... I wanted him to tell your lot so he could die in peace and release the truth about his past, as I know it really did weigh heavy on his mind for decades, in fact it was affecting his life before we met in the June of nineteen sixty two. We had a three year courtship, but he always hated going to Romford. I didn't know why until many years later, it was much later that I learned the real truth as to why he so hated Romford."

"So what do you know about his past, if he told you about it then?" Steve asked politely, not wishing to rattle her.

"Yes I know the truth," she uttered soulfully lowering her head in sadness and twiddled with her fingers in her lap, shaking slightly out of worry.

"It's ok Lucy," comforted Wendy as she put her hand gently onto her shoulder and gave her a gentle squeeze, "You are not in any trouble sweetheart."

"You were saying Lucy... that this started before you met George, would you like to take it from there", Steve carefully pushed, seeing her sense of stress in relation to the situation. The young couple that had jogged past earlier now returned, heading in the other direction. A group of people strolled past talking about going to the cinema that evening, the sun started to show its face casting a shadow over the scene.

"It started... well from what he told me... it started in the nineteen fifties when he was a lad in his late teens, he took his older brother's car without his consent...I can tell you now it caused a lot of trouble with his brother when he found out."

"Are you referring to his brother Kevin? From what I've heard they never spoke to each other ever again after that stupid act... sorry carry on," Steve asked in passing.

"Yes he was a car salesman and the car was a gift so George said and he believed it was a gift for the family. He reckoned it could be driven by any member of the family, but his brother still beat him up... and beat him up rotten from what his mother told me a few years after we married."

"So the night George borrowed the car, which I gather was in fact a Vauxhall Cresta ... a prototype registration number RYE 333."

"You already know that Inspector?" remarked Lucy who lifted her head and a sense of some relief could be seen in her eyes as she stared at Steve.

A middle-aged woman walked by with a black and white collie on a lead, she let it loose when she headed across the vast open green, a flock of birds in a 'V' shape headed south on their migration and they squawked loudly in the sky.

"So Lucy... did he tell you what happened the night he as you say, he borrowed his big brother's car... I gather it was that story you wanted him to tell the police isn't it or wasn't it I should say."

"You're right Inspector", she said reaching out with her left hand to gently touch his hand in an act of reassurance.

"That night he drove around Romford with some of his friends, he was out looking for some fun and maybe pick up a girl and enjoy a good night out... but something happened to change all that didn't it... was it something to do with the death of a young girl named Carol Richards by any chance," Steve spoke softly to her egging her on to add to the story.

She went silent for a moment, still toying with her fingers, again out of fear, close to her lap. Wendy sat the other side of her with her hand softly placed on hers.

"You must understand Inspector my George didn't have anything to do with what happened to that girl, in fact he didn't even know anything about it, until he happened to read it in the local news papers later, that is another reason why his brother beat the crap out of him."

"What you are saying is his big brother had some idea that his brother was involved in that murder... the murder of a sixteen year old girl and he also kept quiet about it too."

"He had no choice in the matter, don't you understand Inspector the killer threatened them all with the same knife he used to kill that young girl."

"I see, so did he tell you the name of her killer?"

"No! That was something he took to the grave with him Inspector, I'm telling you the truth that name was taboo in our house."

"So what did he tell you in respect of that evening?"

"He said that night they were looking for some girls to flirt with, using the car was a bird puller... he said it started with a couple of girls waiting outside the local cinema. There was a girl in a floral dress with long brown hair... he said he fancied her something rotten, but the other girl was like a tart with her ginger hair and heavy makeup and her tight skirt and boobs to die for... not his cup of tea he reckoned... I told him... I wouldn't know about that, I mean he chose me didn't he and I like putting on the makeup."

"You are referring to Carol Richards and Rose Finnegan", returned Wendy who remembered reading the file.

"Was that their names?" she said curiously then went on to add, "he never knew their names...he did say that he believed they went to the same school he went to...in fact he reckoned they were in his year, but they had grown outward since he last saw the girl who was murdered".

"So what else did he tell you, anything else that will help us?"

"He said he stopped in the road that ran behind the church in the market place and his three mates ran off in the direction of the town centre. He sat listening to the radio because he wasn't interested in chasing girls not after seeing that girl outside the cinema... she had told him she was waiting for her boyfriend... but it was obvious he never turned up, to his disappointment, had he known he said he would've gone back and tried to chat her up... who knows if he had have done so she might've still been alive today."

"It's that old, 'if only scenario' ," remarked Wendy.

"You could say that Constable," Lucy reassured, then went on to tell the story; "George was sitting in the car listening to the music on the radio when his friend Ian came running out waving a pair of pink knickers in the air. He was saying he'd just shagged a girl in the graveyard and it was magic, he was followed by his other friend Alfie, who Ian said had picked the girl up and got her to go to the graveyard with him."

"So did either of those two kill Carol?"

"George said they didn't kill her and I believed him, he was a good man. He said his friends had sexual fun with her which was bad enough, but they didn't kill her, they told him that and they were adamant about it, she was alive and kicking when they left her... no!... my bet is on the killer who is still out there and his identity died with my George. It was his so called friend, who no-one would grass up out of fear of his life or theirs... that bastard had a strong hold over everybody he met from that night, telling them that if they grassed him up he would make sure they too would face a murder charge and be banged up for life."

"Ok Lucy, would you be prepared to put this down on paper and make a statement to those facts?" Steve enquired politely. She nodded in return with a look of relief on her face.

"This break in Lucy... you don't think it might've had something to do with that murder, possibly the person might've been looking for anything that could've linked them to Carol's murder?" asked a curious Wendy, Steve looked on with a quiet smile on his face.

"I don't know constable; if they were they would've been out of luck."

"Why is that Lucy... what aren't you telling us?" Steve asked with a puzzled look on his face.

"Because George had everything relating to him put in to boxes and stored in Colin's house," she replied soulfully.

"Colin! Who's Colin then?" Wendy asked inquisitively.

"Our son, that's who", she replied sharply. It was a case of, she hadn't wanted her son to get involved in any of the past; out of fear that the killer might get wind that Colin was now involved in his game of charades.

"Is there an address for your son, so we can eliminate him from the scene; I have a feeling it is what George was wanting... knowing the police would find it and take that stuff and piece it together and lead us to the killer."

"Are you all right mum," enquired a young man who suddenly appeared from nearby.

"This is my son Colin," she said finding her feet to join him, she then added, "These are the police son, this is Detective Chief Inspector Price and the lady is Detective Constable Fuller, they want the stuff your father left with you in those boxes."

"I see mum", he replied warmly, "I will get them for you".

"You could fetch them to Romford nick if you want, if anybody asks, its my belongings ok...that way it will take the heat from your son, will that suit you Lucy?"

"Yes I can't wait to get rid of the stuff," Colin uttered.

"Ok then fetch it to me after the funeral if you want and talking of funerals, we have to go now, we also have a funeral to go to, our fallen comrade," he said looking at his watch as the four of them returned to the gate.

A few minutes later and they were heading back to the Chase, only Wendy had to guide him as he didn't know where the cemetery known as the Chase was. It was around one o'clock when they arrived at the place as Steve drove down the country lane passing a large flower stall at the junction on the bend. She showed Steve the reason why it was called the Chase when she pointed out to him the lake, named the Chase, to his left, they soon came upon the car park just outside the grounds and Steve quickly found a parking spot.

The pair of them entered the grounds and found several members of the station already waiting by the red bricked building. It stood like a castle in the middle of an open field; empty fields awaited future graves to be dug. Passing through a privet fence that was next to some portacabin toilets they found the hole that had been dug the day before, by the men and their mechanical digger, and which was now awaiting Jack's remains to be interred into it.

Steve commented on the

tranquillity of the final resting place, declaring it was the sort of place he would want to be buried in, as and when he died of course. Several tall elegant trees dotted that place of peace.

The solemn group stood talking quietly while they waited for the funeral cortege to arrive. All too soon the hearse slowly entered the grounds followed by a line of black limousines full of his family and friends. Looking at his watch he saw it was almost two o'clock. He stepped forward with five other police officers and they solemnly carried Jack's coffin into the chapel for the service.

The Chief and several other officials and senior members of the force were there in abundance, proof of the respect that Jack had commanded in his job.

Before the coffin was taken into the chapel Margaret and other family members were led into their respective places and finally the coffin led by the priest was bought into the quiet cool area. The service itself was very moving and many people stood up to give their thoughts on the loss of a great man and friend.

Finally Steve and the other pall bearers stepped forward and they carried the coffin back to the hearse which would take them to the graveside. Soon the hole was alive with the congregation mourning the death of a friend. The priest was doing his bit as the coffin lay over the hole on wooden boards; green ropes lay to its side awaiting their role in lowering the coffin in to its last resting place. His police hat lay on a Union Jack flag that covered the coffin, to be removed once the vicar had performed his duty.

Steve looked up to get a sudden shock that rattled his whole body. He spotted a tall woman standing by a tree with long blonde hair and wearing a soft pink outfit. When she spotted Steve she walked away, disappearing behind the tall green privet hedge and was heading for the exit.

"What is wrong Gov?" Wendy asked curiously.

"I'm not sure, I think I've just seen a ghost or something over by the tree, but it can't be".

"A ghost you say, of who?" Wendy asked as she tried to see what he was talking about.

"The ghost of my late wife Sally... but it can't be she is dead."

"Well she wouldn't be a ghost if she were still alive now would she."

"Well in that case she has got a double and it isn't the first time I've seen her, there was one time. No... It can't be... it's nothing Constable forget it, I have, so lets just listen to Jack's funeral.

Steve comforted Margaret once the formalities were over and they had lowered the coffin into the grave. Many of his friends cast roses on to the coffin, as well as a handful of soil, including Steve who simply said, 'see you around old friend.'

"Will you be going to the wake Steve?" Margaret asked sadly

"I have got to take a friend to Heathrow Airport soon because he is flying to Australia. I will meet up with you sometime in the future Margaret, you just take care of your self and the family, if not for me but for Jack, you know he loved you more than anything, he used to tell me that nearly every day and I believed him."

"He thought the world of you Steve, he said he would've liked you to have joined him at that office," she said as she lovingly tugged at his arm, before heading for the awaiting limo.

Wendy joined her friends from the office, she couldn't wait to tell them her news.

'See you in the morning Wendy,' he said to himself as he headed for his car and some lunch in a local cafe.

Chapter 25

The trees rustled gentle in the breeze that whistled around the cemetery. Steve was touched by the whole affair and casually watch Wendy, who he could see had become overwhelmed by his orders. She just couldn't wait to tell all her friends the good news regarding her new status within the force, albeit temporary for the moment. Inside her feminine mind she dwelled on the prospect of not having to wear the uniform of her rank again, well not while she was working with Steve that was, she looked forward to being recognised as a plain clothed officer.

All through the ceremony, Jackson and Peters had stood at the back of the crowd, close to the tall evergreen privet, where their presence could be seen by everybody. A small group of people were walking along the path, they were carrying large bunches of flowers that they had purchased from the stall at the junction. They were heading to another part of that quaint silent place, heading to a grave of one of their family which was in another field.

"Say Jackson... what do you think of this new guy, D.C.I. Price then," enquired Peters quietly.

"What is there to say, he has to be good to be a D.C.I., besides, he has only just arrived and I understand he is working hard on finding Jack's killer, although I have heard through the grape vine that he is also working on the Church yard murder... you know... the one you worked on all those years ago sunshine."

"I see! But that case was never solved. I should know, I worked on that bloody case for sometime and there was nothing. Not even one bloody solitary clue that led you to her killer...no, I think he's barking up the wrong tree."

"In that case Peters, I dare you to go and tell him that... go on," Jackson smiled cockily, just as another hearse drove past with a floral draped coffin inside it. At the sides of the coffin the word Granddad was spelt out with wreaths covered in white flowers. A large bouquet on the roof of the coffin was apparent as it slowly edged its way to the chapel in the centre of the graveyard, followed by two limos.

"He is only going to come up against the same brick wall we did all those years ago... if there were any clues back then surely we would've found them, eh."

"Yeah well that might've been true in those time Peters. I mean you will agree that we've come a long way since those days, so don't forget that, but apparently something new has come to light... something that was overlooked twenty four years ago."

"That's impossible... if it has, then why now for god's sake and not over the years since that girl was killed". Peters uttered angrily, "ok then, if there is new evidence relating to that murder, what that might be?" Peters enquired curiously.

"I wouldn't know Peters... but my guess is... well, I think what ever it is... it's what cost Jack his life."

Unknown to them the blonde haired beauty that Steve had seen earlier standing by a distant tree, was now standing on the opposite side of the privet, glued to their every word.

"I know from fact that any clues to that girl's murder was checked and double checked, if there were any clues about then those concerned were keeping very quiet about it," Peters insisted.

"You mean like somebody had got to those concerned and put the fear of god into them in order to shut them up," Jackson responded more serious.

"That sounds about right mate... somebody put the fear into those concerned and we couldn't get through that barrier," Peters said wistfully.

"And you would know that then Peters...no mate... what if somebody saw something back then and didn't realize that what they actually saw had anything to do with the girl's murder," Jackson replied calmly.

"Why now then... why... no it can't be... we checked everything out back then... this is crazy why couldn't they just leave it alone and let sleeping dogs lie. For god's sake Jackson this crime died a death twenty four years ago."

"Watch out Peters you're letting your colours show...besides, if you continue like this they'll think you might've killed the girl yourself...for Christ's sake...give it a rest, this is Jack's day, don't forget your place". Jackson commented quietly.

"Yeah well I'd like to know who it was then... who knows it might've been somebody I... or I should say we, might've interviewed back then."

"From what I've heard it has something to do with the Blackmore family of Chadwell Heath... if anybody asks it wasn't me who told you ok... now give it a rest."

Peters went quiet from then on and appeared to be in deep thought over the conversation he had just had with Jackson.

....
....

The blonde girl pouted her lips in thought at what she had just overheard; as she slowly noted down what she had been listening to onto a little pad. This she had removed from her petite little silver shoulder bag which hung delicately over her left shoulder and was held tightly at her side. After she had put away the note pad she headed for her parked car close to where Steve had parked his earlier.

Some time later she stopped at a phone box and then made a phone call to the Home Office, where she calmly asked to be put through to extension two, six, six.

"Hello Major," she said after a moment's silence, "it's Tinkerbelle."

"So Tinkerbelle, what is it you're after now?” enquired the Major inquisitively.

"I need you to pull out any files on two people for me?" she asked curiously.

"Who and why would that be

Tinkerbelle, has somebody upset you eh?"

"The who Major is Detective Inspector Jackson and Detective Sergeant Peters... and the reason is, that I'm concerned for the safety of D.C.I. Price sir, as you are fully aware of my concerns for his safety."

"Are you saying that Price's life is in any danger from those two officers?"

"I'm not sure. Ugh. Well... hmm... well not until I've looked at their files that is Major...it's a case of well you know. Ugh... woman's intuition, that sort of thing... it's just a hunch... something I happened to over hear".

"In that case Tinkerbelle I'll do my best...come to my office in a couple of days from now... and Tinkerbelle don't go and do anything stupid, well, not without my consent that is, are you ok with that then, if so I'll see you when I said and I should have the information you require."

"Good!" She uttered and hung up.

....
....

Steve left the graveyard to the dignitaries to carry on their loyal duty to a fallen colleague. Finding his car he headed back to the office, where he was to meet up with Ian and help him on his epic journey home. He toyed with the dream that one day he just might make that journey himself.

The office was quiet for once, only Reg was on duty to man the phones and answer any queries.

"Ok Reg how's it been?" Steve politely asked as he passed through an electronic door into the workings of the building.

"It's had its moment Inspector...not stopping at the funeral then?" Reg enquired out of curiosity.

"No Reg! Too many dignitaries for my liking... they tend to give me the creeps mate," Steve responded casually.

Just then a young man entered the reception area brandishing a piece of official paper, with what was obviously an address the person wanted to know the whereabouts of. He politely asked for directions to the Harrow public house in Rose Lane on the Marks Gate estate.

"I'll leave that for you Reg," Steve gently smiled, as he headed for his own office and to await the arrival of his friend Ian. "Is the canteen still open Reg?" was the last thing he asked for before disappearing into the belly of the peaceful establishment.

A polite smile and a nod was how Reg politely replied to his request and to inform him that, yes it was open, as he was giving directions to the lad.

Steve retired to the canteen, where he managed to get himself some lunch and a coffee. He found a seat by the window where he could eat and watch the world drift by. A hazy sun shadowed the day; a few scattered clouds seemed to be gathering in the skies above. Out of the window that overlooked the local park area he saw some people sitting on the grass reading their book or newspapers.

Business men walked through there carrying their elegant briefcases and handling their brollies like army officials marching home. Their brollies were a weapon to shove aside the weary traveller should one happen to get in his way. What made him smile most of all was seeing a young couple and the man was pushing the pushchair with a baby in it. To his eyes he felt he was looking at a perfect utopia, something he was soon to get involved in with Angie and the new member of the family, once it arrived.

For a second he closed his eyes and believed he was seeing a mirror image of himself in the park arm in arm with Angie; proudly pushing the baby in it's pram, their little baby in that very same park, or somewhere like it, with the whole world at peace with itself, and the baby being the centre of their universe.

Looking at his watch brought him back to reality as it was a quarter to four and he was still downing his lunch and his mug of coffee was waiting patiently for his attention. The number eighty six bus drifted past heading for London like clockwork.

He finally found his feet at around a couple of minutes to four and he found himself headed for the reception area in hope of finding his friend waiting patiently. However, only Reg was sitting there, drinking a mug of tea and dunking a custard cream into it at the same time. When Steve joined him and asked what he was up to with his tea he responded by saying he was dunking it to soften it. Steve held onto his mug of coffee which was still in his hand and smiled as he sipped at its cool contents.

"So what's happening now Inspector?" Reg inquired contentedly.

"Not much Reg," Steve uttered soulfully, "I'm just waiting for a friend. I've got to run him to Heathrow Airport and get him there for seven o'clock, we have to meet somebody from the Home Office for his tickets to Australia... don't worry Reg it is on police business; well I mean, the person returning to Australia is actually one of us, you know a copper, he might have some vital clues to Jack's killer."

"Are you saying that Jack's killer is from Australia?" Returned Reg sharply.

"No mate!" Steve returned frankly,

"A crime that happened in Australia could be linked to the reason why Jack was killed here... get it?"

"Not quite Inspector, but I assume that you know what you are doing". Reg replied curiously as he sipped at his tea.

"Look! It's simple. Two Brits were found murdered on a beach in Australia, and they came from around this area. A third person disappeared and they sent over a Detective from there to try and find this third person... but something else has come to light in the process of finding Jack's killer... it is felt it has something to do with the girl that was murdered in nineteen fifty eight."

"Are you saying that the person who murdered Jack is the same person who murdered Carol Richards?"

"Could be... who knows, but it is a strong possibility that somewhere down the line something came to light...and I believe Jack had got wind of it too... which led to his demise."

"Wow! It sounds a bit like a movie set."

"Maybe Reg...but keep it under your hat for now... I can tell you that something new has come to light... we just don't know where this is going to take us at this moment in time," Steve stated casually. It was then that Ian entered the building after his brother had dropped him off, it saved him from leaving his rented car there. He entered the building with his rucksack slung over his right shoulder.

"Ok Steve my little brother brought me here because I had to hand back the rental car as we don't know how long I'll be gone... right then Steve, so what now?"

"Reg meet the Aussie Detective," introduced Steve with positive hand gestures which showed respect towards his friend.

"Yeah, I'm bloody Detective Inspector Ian Dobson," he returned in a distinctive Aussie accent, dropping his rucksack on the floor nearby, "All you bloody Pommies coming over and.," he laughed out loud, then added, "I'm only joking mate," he returned in a more subtle accent, as he looked with amazement at Reg, who simply stared at him with wide eyes before giving a slight laugh. Then Ian in his jovial manner asked openly, "any chance of a coffee mate?"

"Not now Ian, we have to get you to Heathrow Airport for seven o'clock don't forget we have to meet this person from the Home Office with your tickets."

"Yeah I know sunbeam, it was nice to have met you Reg maybe another day and we could have a beer or two, who knows", he said as he shook his hand before the pair of them left the confines of that humble workplace.

Steve left his empty mug on the shelf beside Reg who said he'd ensure that it got returned to the canteen; at the same time the telephone rang out making them all jump due to it being quiet and peaceful until that point in time.

Steve edged out of the car park to join the main road and the emerging traffic, which had now become very busy. Many people who had finished their daily toils were now heading home to their other lives what ever that happened to be. It was a stop start affair as Steve managed to overcome his anger at the traffic in his way, thinking to himself that he should've left a lot earlier. However he was soon on the dual carriageway heading into London where he hoped to join the north circular road that took him around the outside of the city.

"So Steve how's it all going mate?" Ian enquired as they drove out of Romford.

"I spoke to Lucy Blackmore this morning and she mentioned something of interest and it might be useful to you mate...she mentioned two names connected to her late husband...she said that two of her late husband's friends just happened to be your dead bodies in Aussie mate...well I believe so. Ugh... you know she just said their first name's, Ian and Alfie."

"That's interesting Steve," he pondered, "then we must be on the right lines... what are the odds of that happening in any murder case."

"What are the odds of that happening in any part of life... we have three murders and it appears they are linked to one murder twenty four years ago... I feel we might just have to bring this Kevin back here to answer some questions... because I feel he might know something about what has been going on in your country as well as this country... I would like to know why he emigrated to Australia after the accident way back then."

"You don't think this Kevin could be the killer of the girl in the fifties."

"No! If I my theory is right, he wouldn't have known anything about his brother's death because he didn't want anymore to do with him and as he never come back here he wouldn't have known about Jack being involved. No the killer is still here and if my hunch is right this Kevin might know who the killer is... that's the killer of Carol Richards that I'm talking about."

"If you are right Steve I would've solved two problems while I have been here, something I would never have done if it weren't for you and your connections with the Home Office... if this is true then we can release the bodies of the two dead Brits so they can be buried here in their respective homeland."

As they arrived at the entrance to the airport as usual many people were coming and going. Convoys of taxi's edged back and forth either dropping travellers off or picking them up and in some cases, even both. Overhead could be heard the roars of the jumbo jets as they took off or landed on the runaways a short distance away from where they were.

Steve pulled up near one of the main entrances where he spotted a young man leaning against the wall with one leg bent and his foot pinned to the wall. A briefcase stood beside him as he was casually smoking a king-size cigarette, he started to move forward, picking up the briefcase when he spotted Steve pulling up with his precious cargo.

Removing the rucksack from the back seat where he had tossed it when he got into the car, Ian slowly opened the car door and stepped out.

"D.C.I. Price?" asked the young man dressed in a light grey suit and a pale blue shirt with a silvery grey tie. He had short fair hair and had come from the Home Office, having discarded his half smoked cigarette and clutching his briefcase he headed for Steve and his parked car from which he was now disembarking.

"Yeah you found me... you must be the man from the pru... sorry Home office, just being facetious young man...so have you got the tickets for my good friend here, yes?" Steve said in a joking manner, it was his way of overcoming the feeling of sadness at saying farewell to a friend he'd come to admire.

"Yes!" returned a more serious young man, "May I put my case on your bonnet, Inspector?"

"You know you can't park there sir," came the voice of an airport official smartly attired in his uniform.

Steve removed his warrant card and badge of office and the young man flashed his Home office badge then told the security guard to disappear.

"You may use the bonnet of my car young man from the Home Office," he smiled then went on to add, "Just watch the paintwork."

"Inspector!" He uttered as he proceeded to place his case on the bonnet of Steve's car and opened it to reveal a large brown envelope that he removed and handed to Steve, before he closed his case and placed it onto the floor. Turning to Ian he stated with authority in his voice, "Right, in the envelope you will find your tickets, you will have to get your boarding passes for the flight in side. You are booked on to Cathay Pacific... your return flight can be arranged as and when you are ready to come back... the Major has notified your office back there in Townsville, so Inspector Dobson have a safe journey and we look forward to seeing you when you get back," he said with a posh accent as he closed his case and shook Ian's hand with a gentle grip.

Steve put his hands to his face and sighed at the thought of leaving his friend, but he hated farewells so he too shook Ian's hand. Ian just smiled and said he wasn't looking forward to the journey and he couldn't wait to get back to England again. Then each went in different directions, Ian towards the terminal doors, the Home Office gent to his car and Steve got into his car and with a final wave to Ian left the area.

Chapter 26

Entering the office the next morning Steve was greeted by the sight of young Wendy out of her usual uniform in favour of a mid grey, pin striped suit with a knee length skirt and short jacket, which was worn over a white blouse. A smart black shoulder bag hung at her left side. To complete the smart business, no nonsense look, she wore her hair tied back in a bun. It was something she'd longed to wear before, having purchased it about a year previously, when she had often dreamed of becoming a Detective like her father before her. Despite the right moment never arising she had however kept it in her wardrobe for just such an occasion, but as the time slipped by, she begun to believe that such a time would never come.

Steve, dressed in his usual attire, stared briefly at her with just a slight hint of a cheeky smile, reassuring his choice of assistant and pupil. He was in awe of her new appearance as she stood in the main entrance of the block awaiting the arrival of Steve. "You look good Constable," Steve commented.

That morning to her surprise and delight she had even got a few wolf whistles from some of the young male officers who happened to pass her by, on their way to do their duties in the field.

"Thank you Inspector," she uttered with her head slightly bowed out of respect and to show she was still unsure of her new position.

She had even been admired by some of her female colleagues who had stopped in passing, to eye her up and down and wishing her well in her new found fame. "What are we doing today Sir?" She pursued as they both headed for Steve's office.

"She scrubbed up well Steve," commented Reg softly so as not to be heard by Wendy. He was still on duty at the front desk.

Steve gave him a glancing look accompanied with a slight wink of approval at Reg's comical banter. "We are going on a little field trip to Canvey Island. I want to interview this Rose," Steve explained as they neared his office.

A young male officer was passing and gave her a wolf whistle, for the third time that morning she had been whistled at by various male colleagues. "Ok constable that's enough of that nonsense, remember your place".

"Sorry Inspector," he returned shyly.

"Ok then! Back to business; I want to go and interview this Rose and learn everything from her regarding the time that led up to Carol Richards' murder," he expressed calmly, he then added, "lets get a coffee first... business later, shall we Constable, or should I say Acting Detective Constable Fuller, eh Wendy?"

"Sounds good to me Sir," she uttered, clutching her bag, "would you like me to find out where she lives from the Southend nick Gov?"

"No we'll find it out when we get there later. I understand there is a nick on Canvey itself, we'll try there first. Besides Canvey isn't that big an island so it shouldn't be that hard to find her."

"I didn't think I'd be doing this sort of thing right away Sir," she said joyfully.

"Stick with me and you'll go far Constable, sorry Acting Detective Constable, as I said; lets have a coffee, then we'll hit the road... I do fancy a drive to the coast, don't you?"

"Sir!" she replied joyfully, and then went on to say, "Would you like me to find out where the nick is on the island, assuming there is one?"

"I'm sure it wouldn't hurt Constable. I'll leave it in your capable hands but you could just look in the yellow pages for Canvey Island."

"Will we have to notify the Southend boys of our intentions?" she enquired as they both got their coffees and headed for an empty table by the window.

"Nah! Only if we wanted to interview her in the nick... no we will interview her on the island, assuming we can find her at home to start with."

"This will be my first time on the Island, my brothers said they go fishing for Cod off the sea wall...they told me it is a dump, not much goes on there... well that's what they say Gov."

"Well! I guess we'll soon find out if they are right... won't we, eh Constable."

"I always wanted to go there with my boyfriend, but my brothers put him off the idea," she said as she put a couple of spoonfuls of sugar in her coffee.

The break was interrupted when Reg entered the canteen and headed for Steve's table. "Yes Reg, what is it now," Steve enquired as he took a sip of his coffee.

"There's a young lad in the reception, he said he has a couple of cardboard boxes for you, he claims they are your possessions... what do you want me to do with him?"

"Get somebody to help you to take them to my office... here are the keys," he said frankly then went on to add; "can you return them when you've done, ok. I know who it is and what's in the boxes," he turned to look at Wendy who also was aware of their contents. "By the way Reg, the lad's name is Colin Blackmore all right... just see to it, but don't say anything to anybody about them ok... and don't forget to lock it after you. I don't want anybody being nosy, ok Reg."

"Yes Steve!" He smiled as he tossed the keys joyfully in the air.

"I guess that's George Blackmore's belongings Gov?"

"You guessed right Constable," Steve said clasping his mug of coffee and leaning on the edge of the table, "we'll look into them when we get back," looking at his watch it told him it was now nearly ten o'clock.

....
....

Later they were heading for Canvey Island in Steve's car using the old 'A' thirteen. This was a country road that twisted and turned until it reached the junction that split one way to Benfleet, the other was marked up to Canvey Island. It was a road that led him onto the island and was known as Canvey Way. It was a long road with an oil refinery looming up on the horizon, making those going there believe that was all Canvey Island was famous for. However they were very wrong, as the oil refinery was off the island in a place called Coryton.

"Where do we go Constable?" Steve remarked casually giving her a fleeting glance as she stared out of the window at the scenery that greeted them as they drove over the bridge, with the tide neither in nor out, but there. Soon the sight of many masts of boats that were moored in the quay loomed out at the base of a steep hill that occupied the town of Benfleet.

Coming down to a large roundabout the sign showed that in one direction and straight over led you to the town centre, whereas the other way to the right would take you to the seafront. Leaving Steve with no option but to head for the town centre and the possibility of finding the place which they were hoping to find.

On reaching the town centre they discovered the one way system that encircled the main town centre, where Steve eventually found a parking space in the large car park area at the rear of the town centre, where he had to pay to park up.

Getting out of the car to the slight taint of seaweed in the air and sea gulls squawking high above helped to create the seaside effect that was so related to the sea. Wendy even remarked on the feel of the place. Groups of school children in their uniforms laughed and talked politely as they too headed for the town centre and a place where they could gather and chat openly about what ever they felt keen to tell.

"Where do we start then Inspector?" Wendy asked as they headed for the entrance to the precinct.

"We just have to play it by ear and hope we can get the information from a shop keeper," Steve said calmly as they waited for other vehicles to pass on their respective ways.

The sun dipped under the shroud of a passing cloud that changed the scene into a sudden dullness. Some people were pushing supermarket trolleys to their respective cars.

Passing through a set of electronic doors that opened automatically, they soon found themselves inside the workings of the shopping precinct. The first place they encountered was a stall where the stall holder was selling videos and cassettes, along with some framed oil paintings of old Canvey by an artist J. A. Pye. There were also some watercolours of old sailing ships that lined the floor in front of his stall. The owner of the stall was a short, stockily built guy in his mid fifties wearing a Russian style, black furry type hat with tassels either side and a grey bomber jacket and jeans, "Can I help you sir/madam?" he uttered, with a broad grin on his face once he noticed Steve admiring some of the paintings on show, while Wendy curiously searched the vast selection of video films that the stall holder had on offer.

In front of that stall was a flower stall, which was being run by a couple of women who seemed engrossed in making wreaths for a future funeral, as there were several circular wreaths and one long one that spelled Granddad. A short gap away and in front of them was a fruit and veg stall being run by a short middle-aged woman with short blonde hair.

The whole area was alive with people of all ages as they wandered around that place in a world of their own. Some were laden down with supermarket carrier bags, while others stood talking to friends etc by some of the windows of the shops. Others were just happy to be out in the company of life as they sat on the benches, either munching on some chocolate bar or reading a book whilst watching the masses pass them by, hoping that one or two of their friends would pass by and stop for a chat.

"Yeah mate," Steve returned, rising to his feet, "these paintings are really good, do you know the artists?" he asked as he picked up an oil painting.

"Yeah they both live on the Island... and the one you have in your hand is of the Lobster Smack as it was in eighteen ninety."

"Right," Steve uttered curiously as he found himself studying it carefully with the eye's of the stall holder looking on protectively, "the police station."

"What about it?" returned a wary eyed stall holder, who suddenly felt uneasy as if he now believed he had done something wrong?

"Whereabouts is it?" Steve asked quietly, returning the painting to its rightful place, leaning up against the leg of the stall.

"Christ I thought I. ugh you know... done something wrong... the police station you say, do you have a car?" asked the stall holder curiously, now feeling more relaxed.

"Yes," he replied calmly.

"Well you should drive out into the one way system and turn left at the top and then...ugh...turn right at the junction where the Haystack pub stands on the corner...

you travel down that road for about half a mile or so and you'll find the place you are looking for on the left hand side... you can't miss it mate, it kind of like, you know... stands out a bit like a sore thumb...a big old Victorian building... your not coppers are you?" he asked with a glint in his eye.

"All we wanted to know was where the police station was, that's all mate," Steve replied with a casual wink, "Your paintings are really good...in fact they are brilliant".

"Eighty quid to you Gov."

"Maybe another day, who knows."

Shortly after they had left the stall holder and his wares they arrived at the police station in Long Road. As had been told to them, they saw it was indeed a large Victorian building, set in the rear of a car park where Steve finally came to rest near the station wall. A couple of police cars sat side by side. The delicious smells from a local fish and chip shop drifted on the air and people hurried about, in and out of the local shops that added to the place. A post stood nearby with Canvey police station on it with the usual badge. At the far end of the building were a set of wrought iron gates that were shut to the public. Entering the building via a glass panelled door they entered a lobby with its counter and a button to press for attention.

"A bit primitive Gov," Wendy

commented.

"You're telling me," Steve returned pressing the button for attention, only to be greeted by a thirty year old blonde haired woman in a clean well pressed police uniform, who suddenly appeared from a closed door, with the usual formalities of, "Yes, Can I help you sir?"

"I am Detective Chief Inspector Price and this is Acting Detective Constable Fuller," he introduced, as both parties showed their badges of office.

"And what can we do for you D. C. I. Price?" enquired the duty officer with a blank look on her face.

"We are looking for a couple named Rose and Edward Bright; we believe they moved here several years ago from Collier Row."

"What is the purpose of this interview with this person Inspector?"

"We just need to talk to her, that's all," Steve explained casually, then went on to add, "So can you help us locate their whereabouts, or not Constable?"

"I'll just check," she returned as she headed for the door but just briefly she turned to say, "Rose and Edward Bright you say?"

"Yes, today would help," Steve toyed with her straight faced look.

"She's a bit of a stuck up bitch, Gov."

Steve just smiled and gave her a wink. "Lets just hope she can help us find this Rose," he remarked in passing as he scoured the cream coloured walls of the reception area. He noticed a row of metal chairs under the front window, that overlooked the main road where a couple of buses passed in either direction. On the walls were the usual police notices, especially ones about drug dealers and how they were the rats of our society, "there's not much change here then," he smiled to himself, with one hand in his trouser pocket.

A few minutes later and a young female officer came out of an electronic type side door, "Inspector come with me", she ordered, taking the pair of them into the workings of the place where they were led into a room that had a window which overlooked the car park. "I understand from our duty officer you are interested in interviewing a Rose and Edward Bright, can I ask on what grounds?" She asked as she sat on the edge of a wooden table.

"It has something to do with a case that goes back to nineteen fifty eight if you must know," returned Wendy who seemed on edge regarding the officer's approach to this simple request.

"Yes Officer," Steve returned walking to the window where he briefly looked out before turning to face the young female officer, adding, "My officer is right about the facts regarding that case in question. As my colleague so said the case was in fact a young sixteen year old girl, who was murdered back then and Rose, the one we want to talk to, was the girl's best friend and the last person to have seen her alive on that day in May of that year... does that answer your question Ma'am... and before you ask, she isn't suspected of being her killer?"

"I see," she pondered for a moment, pouting her lips with a curious look on her face; "you wouldn't be from the Met by any chance?"

"What if we are?" Steve quizzed.

"Then surely you of all people should be aware of protocol within the system... Sir," returned a stern faced female officer who twiddled with her pen having placed her note book on the desk beside her.

Wendy found standing by the door more comfortable having been familiar with that role, prior to becoming an acting Detective.

"Do not question my knowledge of protocol ma'am," Steve replied sharply then added, "I wasn't born yesterday and as for protocol, as you so pointed out; it only refers to people we ask to be arrested, due to a crime that has been committed by the said person or persons in the Met area

and we need him or her to be arrested...
then yes protocol would require me to
contact you and request you arrest that
person and hold them for me to interview
them; or give you the details of their crime
so your lot can interview them on our
behalf, then feedback to us with the
answers... in this case the person we
require to talk to hasn't committed any
crime...so therefore, the protocol you
mention with so much authority doesn't
apply in this matter, ok eh."

It was at this point a knock came
at the door. Steve turned to look out of the
window again with a sigh, briefly turning to
see the entrance of the female duty officer
who entered the room with a folded piece
of paper in her hand. This she handed to
the young female officer who remained
seated on the edge of the table.

"This is what you requested
Ma'am," explained the duty officer.

"Thank you," returned the female
officer who was unmoved and on opening
it she just gave it a glancing look, pouted
her lips and fumbled with the piece of
paper in her hands while the duty officer
departed from the room. Rising to her feet
she headed for the window where she
handed Steve the piece of paper and
muttered quietly, "This is what you were
after Inspector," she then returned to the
desk where she sat back down in the same

place again.

"I see they live at 10, Tilburg Road," he said as he opened up the piece of paper and studied the contents before heading back to the table, "so Ma'am, where can we find this address then, if it isn't any trouble that is?"

She again rose to her feet and headed for the window that overlooked the main road where she pointed to a road that was opposite the office, "That is Tilburg Road, you can just cross the road and there it is, the house you require is this end of the road ok... let's hope you get what you are after Inspector."

"So do I Ma'am," he smiled as he headed for the door and freedom to the relief of Wendy. Stopping briefly he turned and stated with authority, "When protocol requires me to have a person arrested for a crime I will honour that protocol and ensure your lot will do your job properly, just as we would should you require the same of us... oh and by the way Ma'am, we are all in the same boat... I'm not the criminal, ok."

Stepping out into the fresh air which they noticed was still fragranced with the smell of fish and chips from the local chip shop. The shop dominated the end of the block of shops and the dead end of the road which was known as Tilburg Road. A small grassed area greeted them as they were tempted to enjoy some seaside fish and chips but duty called and besides the shop was packed.

So they walked down the middle of the road looking for the house in question. They didn't take long in finding the address as there were only five houses on the right hand side of the road and it turned out to be a bungalow which seemed to dominate that side of the road. A dark blue Ford Fiesta was parked off the road just outside the bungalow as they entered through a single gate which led to two separate homes, with a garden either side, the garden of number ten was well established with various flowering plants. Entering the covered porch area, Steve knocked abruptly on the green wooden front door, but there was no answer except from a dog that barked from behind it.

A few minutes later, as they headed for the gate, a tall thin elderly woman came out of the more modern bungalow opposite and headed for them. "Are looking for the Bright's?" she enquired.

"Yes!" Steve said casually, "do you know when they'll be home?"

"Later... your not one of those, you know who, Jehovah's Witness people are you?" she enquired curiously.

"Do we look like them then?" Wendy asked politely.

"A bit," she smiled back.

"No we are from the police ok and we need to talk to Rose," Steve explained.

"Nothing has happened to Edward, you know her hubby?" she pursued eagerly.

"No!"

"In that case, if it is important you might like to know that Rose works in a cafe on the sea front, known as Foodfayre, opposite the Monaco pub, you can't miss it," explained the elderly woman as they all stood in the middle of the quiet road, two cars were parked in the large house next door.

"So how do we get to the sea front then madam?" Steve pressed.

"If you are in a car then you drive back to the town centre turn right at the end of the road and follow it down to the end where you'll find a large open field, go left at the roundabout and you can't help but find what you are looking for, the cafe in question is on the right hand side, next to the amusement arcade... you can't miss it."

"So you have said madam," Steve uttered.

"I hope I have been of some help," she said with a smile as she turned and headed for her home leaving Steve and Wendy to go about their business.

They headed for the parked car in

the police car park.

Chapter 27

Walking back to the car, Wendy commented briefly on the woman, claiming she was a nosy old cow, but Steve pulled her up and said she was a good woman who looked out for her neighbours. Steve gave the woman a fleeting glance, looking back over his shoulder in the direction of the elderly woman who was heading for her next door neighbour's home, to wave an informal thank you in response to her kind gesture.

The sun made its reappearance from behind the cloud to brighten the day once again, clear blue skies beckoned.

"I do like this place, it is so laid back and friendly, in fact, you could say...if it were any more laid back you'd fall over", he laughed as they crossed the road, after a number twenty two single Decker bus had rolled past to stop at a nearby bus stop, before heading off in the direction of the town. "Who knows Wendy, I might like to end my days on this island...I could happily see Angie and me pottering around in our little garden and the grandchildren coming to visit us at the week-end", he said as he stood by the car with a slight sigh and a glancing smile, as he looked around at the calm peaceful air of tranquillity that embraced everything that was Canvey Island.

"Did you find what you were looking for Inspector?" asked the officer who had interviewed them earlier as she joined them in the car park, having exited the building via a private door close to the parked car.

"Oh it's you officer...and no, the person was out, but we were told the one we want works in the cafe on the sea front ok.

"You must mean Foodfayre, it is run by an Italian woman named Dol, good luck" She smiled, as she headed for the local shops, leaving them to continue on their quest for knowledge.

They were soon entering the world of the seaside as they neared their destination. The sea wall loomed up on the horizon, across an open field a tall chimney stood like a statue and appeared to stand just on the other side of the grey concrete wall that ran around the island. It had been built to hold back the sea after the great flood of nineteen fifty three. A group of lads were kicking a football about on the green. Going left, they began to see the scene that had been described to them earlier.

The Monaco pub stood out like a relic of the nineteen thirties which was when it was built. A white monster set against the blue skies.

"There's Foodfayre Gov", Wendy pointed out as they headed for a nearby car park. The cafe was set beside an amusement arcade. A cafe with long windows either side of a door with six metal tables and chairs either side of the door. A couple sat at one of the tables nursing a little brown coloured puppy dog on a long lead as they were drinking from white mugs.

Steve found a parking place in a partly full car park in front of the sea wall. Several people were heading for a bank of public toilets to the left.

"I guess the sea is on the other side of that wall?" Steve casually remarked as they stepped out of the car and taking a long breath he embraced the fresh sea air that was wafting off of the sea.

Wendy grabbed her shoulder bag with the necessary items of her position, she flicked it over her left shoulder and headed for the steep grassy slope, with laughter in her footsteps.

They both agreed to climb the grassed slope that led up to the seawall and the sights of that seaside resort. Reaching the wall they were greeted by a gust of wind that felt good as the tide was halfway out and the beach was there in full view with children playing near the waters edge. A stairway the traveller down to the lower path and slope which in turn led down to the beach. The view in the distance was the Kent coast line with the tall rubbish disposal chimney of the Isle of Sheppey in full splendour on the horizon. They eventually walked towards the cafe to the right along the path.

They finally came back down from the wall via a narrow path. The couple who was at one of the tables with the little puppy was now heading up the same slope heading for the beach area and excitement for the puppy who just wagged his tail.

Opening the cafe door they entered the establishment where several groups of people were busy eating their meals on marble effect laminated tables and metal chairs with maroon coloured PVC covers.

Three women were busy working

hard behind the counter. One was a middle-aged woman with short black hair and she was cooking on a griddle in the front corner and she occasionally waved at somebody walking past her window. Another was a youngster who seemed destined to clean the tables and generally keep the place clean; she flittered in and out of a back room. All of them were wearing dark blue tunics.

"Yes! Can I help you sweetheart?" asked a bubbly stout woman with short ginger hair, her pen delicately poised in her right hand and a numbered notepad at the ready, she was wearing large hooped gold earrings.

Steve turned and looked wide eyed at Wendy who just smiled and nodded side to side joyfully then asked politely. "We are looking for a Rose Bright?"

"I am Rose", she replied, her eyes danced curiously to and fro from one to the other, "What is this all about...why...what have I done...mores' the point, who are you?"

"You have done nothing...nothing at all". Wendy explained.

"You may have won the Pool's Rose", laughed the woman cooking on the griddle.

"Leave it out Dol...It's not my kind of luck...besides it's been years since my

Eddy did them...no...So what's this all about then sweetheart".

"Sorry madam we forgot our manners", Steve returned with a smile, each of them flashed their respective badge's in her direction before informing her, "I am Detective Chief Inspector Price and this is my colleague Detective Constable Fuller and we would like to talk to you in private...if we may that is?"

She looked at Dol who just shrugged her shoulders and just nodded to tell her to go and sort it out. "We can go for a walk along the sea front...if you like, that's if you want to...it should be a bit more private this time of the year", she said as she removed her tunic to reveal a 'V' necked and sleeveless pink top and black trousers, she also wore black flat slip on shoes, "I can have a fag at the same time", she said in passing, as she took a packet of king-size cigarettes and a lighter from her tunic pocket.

Once outside in the fresh air she removed a cigarette and lit it, clutching the two items in her left hand she dragged on the cigarette using her right hand to handle it. "So Inspector what's this all about...it ain't my Eddy is it, what has he gone and done now?"

"What makes you think your Eddy has done something?" Steve stated calmly, he's not a criminal by any chance?"

"No!" she snapped taking a quick drag on her cigarette.

"So why do you assume he has done something wrong then?" Steve pressed curiously.

"Because!" She said stopping for a second to look at Steve and Wendy with some curiosity in her eyes. "I don't know...Ugh...you must realize...hum...you have got to understand I just haven't...Ugh...been in this sort of situation before in my whole life", she uttered cagily before continuing on the journey to the sea front.

Many seagulls squawked and flew in varying circles, some chasing others for the mere morsel of food that one of them had managed to grab on the quick. A coast guard helicopter flew low over the sea front heading for Southend.

Once on the path below the wall they walked westward to a more private area where only the hardened fisherman would go to catch cod and bass if they were lucky, but this day it was empty.

"So what is this all about then, if it isn't anything my Eddy has done and I know I haven't done anything wrong...never".

"Ok Rose", Steve said openly as they walked along the path passing a white round structure known as the Labworth cafe. However it was shut up with grey steel panelled shutters protecting the long glazed window area and door. "I want to take you back twenty four years ago to one night in Romford".

She stopped for a moment to stare at him and his words, "You wouldn't happen to be talking about 'May the twentieth in nineteen fifty eight', by any chance", she uttered with a hint of sadness in her voice, "that was a lifetime ago", she said.

"Yes I'm talking about the night your friend Carol lost her life". Steve said calmly.

"Why now?" she snapped, as she dragged more slowly on her cigarette. Her eyes dulled at the thought of something that happened in another lifetime. "A lot of water has passed under the bridge since that time Inspector", she said as she bowed her head momentarily.

"Yeah well that may be true Rose, but another incident has brought it to limelight again", Steve said softly.

A Dutch cargo ship edged its way up the river estuary, its large engines droned out over the sea, as it majestically passed them, heavily laden with stacks of metal containers four high, headed gracefully for the port at Tilbury. A couple of men were enjoying themselves wind surfing, while a couple in a speedboat skimmed across the gentle waves that lapped the sandy beach.

"So what do you want to know?" She said stopping for a moment and lent against the sea wall out of the wind propping her right foot against the wall.

"Look why don't we go and sit on one of those benches over there", Steve said pointing to a couple of metal and wooden benches situated on a concrete bed but on a lower level, on the corner of the wall that lead around the corner to a popular beach area.

The two women sat on the first bench, while Steve stood and lent on the top rail of a metal railings made of three round bars that ran in front of the benches. "Why don't you tell me what happened back then Rose...I know you were the last person to have seen your friend alive other than the killer himself"?"

"You know you are asking about something that happened a long time ago...but I told the police back then, it should be in my statement that I made back then".

"Just try and remember, you might be holding a clue which could be something small and seems insignificant that could lead us to her killer", Steve said as he turned to face them propping one leg on the middle rail and his elbows rested on the top rail. Just then the sound of a motorbike roared down the stretch of road behind the wall.

"How far back do you want me to go?"

"When ever!"

She removed a fresh cigarette from her packet and lit it carefully, poised to talk and finding her feet she joined Steve at the railing, leaning on it as she stared out to sea. The past played heavily on her mind as she found herself having to remember so far back.

"I suppose I can never forget that time in my life...truly Carol was my best friend, we worked together in the chocolate factory in Hainault all week before and we had planned to go to the flicks you know pictures...cinema".

"Yeah I get what you are saying, pray continue", Steve smiled running his hand through his hair.

"Ok! You see we wanted to see the film, 'One Hot Summers Day', staring my all time dream boat...mmmm...yeah...Paul Newman. I remember having his picture on my bedroom wall above my bed...I use to dream about me and him out on a date...well we all can only dream of things like that...yeah...as if that could ever happen...but it never does, so what the hell...we were going to do some shopping that morning. Carol wanted to get herself a new dress for a party we were going to a couple of weeks later but there was nothing that interested us especially. Carol, she was always fussy about her clothes...I guess I was the wild one of us...I felt guilty at the time".

"Why did you feel guilty Rose?" Enquired a quiet Wendy.

"I have just told you, I was the wild one...if anyone should have copped it, it should've been me...Carol was the sensible one of us, she was very clever...she had a dream that one day she'd be famous", she said as she dragged on her cigarette, leaning over the top bar.

"Well her fame lives on and she is now known as the Churchyard murder", Steve remarked.

"The churchyard murder...what a legacy", she sighed.

"Tell me about that fatal day...try and remember as much as you can, that's everything that might be of some use". Steve eagerly pressed.

"As I said we had planned that day all week before...we were supposed to have met up with the boys that afternoon but they never turned up because Carol's other half had trouble with his car...we so wanted to see the film so we went and queued up outside the cinema as I said, to see the Paul Newman film.

We had decided to take the time off work to do some shopping as I said, we were planning to go on holiday that summer and she wanted some going away clothes as well as her party dress...we were going to go to camping in Devon with the boys...it was a really good day.

We ended up standing in the queue for the film, when a group of lads decided to come up to annoy us, they said they wanted to talk to us, claiming they had seen us in the market place that day...one of them was a bit arrogant to say the least...he pestered me to go off with him, saying he wanted to give me a good time...I remember thinking; I know the sort of fun he was after, although there was one of them that Carol said she did fancy, he was very quiet and hung back, but he was giving Carol a long leering look and I'm sure she had the hots for him. He stood toying with a set of keys; spinning them around on the first finger of his right hand...it was as if he was trying to show her he had a car.

The arrogant one tried to convince us he had just passed an exam and that he was off to do a course in a college that was in Hendon...we just thought he was a bit off a prat to tell you the truth".

"Hendon you say...did he say what college he was going to?"

"No! and I wasn't about to get into a conversation with him over it, in fact I told him to piss off and leave us alone, he began to get irritable, as if he was letting me know he was god's gift to mankind because he believed he was so clever...I got the impression he believed no woman should turn him down and if they did he would get cross...his friends dragged him away but he kept on shouting out, calling me a slag...I just stuck my two fingers up at him".

"What happened next?" Wendy asked quietly, taking in everything she was saying and drawing her own conclusions about the story that was unfolding.

"Did you know any of the boys Rose?" Steve enquired as he continued to lean on the top bar of the railings.

She flicked the end of her cigarette onto the beach having stubbed it out on the metal rail, she turned to face the wall and to look at Wendy, "I didn't know any of them but Carol reckoned she knew them from her school days...she went to the Warren County Secondary School in Whalebone lane, she told me it was a rough school...but I don't know...all I know is a few minutes later they drove past in what looked like a small Yankee car. That prat leant out of the window and shouted abuse at us, others in the queue looked at us and smiled at the way we handled the situation...I can tell you it was scary at times. I got the feeling this guy could hurt me or any woman who turned him down".

"This prat you talk about, can you describe him?" Steve pursued relentlessly.

A elderly couple walked down the set of concrete stairs that led down to the beach where they let loose their little Jack Russell who barked at them as he ran down to the sea, at the same time the lad on his speedboat roared past heading for Southend.

"Vaguely", she uttered as she took out another cigarette and lit it up, "He was a tall, slim boy, with cropped hair...I can remember him wearing a white shirt and denim jeans, by the way he stank of Old Spice aftershave, that's all I can remember...sorry".

"You mentioned the car and you said it was like an American car...yeah...tell me...it wouldn't have been two tone by any chance, you know with a pale blue bottom and a cream coloured top?" Steve pursued carefully.

"Again you are asking a lot of me Inspector", she replied, dragging yet again on her cigarette, "mind you...now you come to mention it, I think it was as you said, two tone...but how come you know that, I never said anything about that incident in my statement back then...I mean I didn't think it had any bearing on the death of my friend".

"I told you that something has come to light in the last month...so lets talk about the driver of that car, you say your friend fancied him because he was how did you put it, dishy?" Steve remarked.

"You could say that...she said if she wasn't going out with Joe she'd have let him chat her up".

"I see! Your friend Carol wouldn't have decided to go off with him if he had seen her standing alone at that bus stop now would she?" asked Steve with an hint of curiosity in his voice.

"Are you saying that guy could've killed her?" She snapped, "But he looked so innocent...I would've said he was more like the gent in the midst of idiots...no way do I think he would've killed her. But as for getting in his car, if he'd seen her waiting for the bus, well your guess is as good as mine...to tell you the truth I wouldn't know...she might've done...she did say she liked him while we were in the cinema and she hoped he might still be around but on his own...but she was only dreaming at the time. I would've believed the idiot who called me a slag was the one to kill...but who am I to judge, it was for Christ's sake twenty four years ago...I can tell you both that every twentieth of May I raise a glass or two of wine and call out her name and yes I missed her so much back then...I wanted to join her but you can't can you", she said softly with sadness written all over her face. She wiped a tear from her eye and sniffed loudly. Steve offered her a hankie but she refused and sniffed again.

"Ok Rose, you've been very helpful to me, you should get back to work", Steve said as he made his way up the short slope behind the benches, he helped the girls up the slope too.

Wendy slipped her note pad into her bag and took Steve's helping hand as he pulled her up that tiled slope.

"Have I helped you Inspector?" Rose enquired as they walked back along the path. A young woman approached walking her little Westie and some lads were standing at the top of some stairs pointing at another large ship laden with metal containers heading into port.

Some people found sanctuary sitting on towels and leaning their backs against the sea wall as they sat in their swimwear, him in shorts and her in a brown bikini, both enjoying the warm sun that shone.

Some girls were running on the beach chasing another little dog who barked profusely at their play.

"You've been a great help in more ways than one Rose, all I can say is thank you", Steve remarked warmly.

"But I feel like I was just wasting your time", she replied sadly, "But how did you know about the car and the lad driving it?" She asked stopping for a moment for an answer.

"If you must know Rose, the driver of that car died a short while ago and he admitted he was connected to the death of Carol, or he was there but didn't get involved. He died without saying who killed her but you may be right, it could very well have been the one you called a prat...the one we have yet to discover the name of as those concerned are reluctant to say his name as if he has a hold over every one of them".

"I know there were four lads outside the cinema trying to chat up the girls, in fact one of them nearly got beaten up when he tried to chat up a bloke's girlfriend".

"There you go, you held the truth all along but failed to see the significance of the crime back then...certain things you have said today is what was needed twenty four years ago, you failed to see it, along with the police of the day...who knows where this could have led back then...I will let you know of the progress in this case. I feel it's time we put this case to bed and her killer behind bars where he belongs...right?"

"Did the driver have a name?" Rose enquired curiously.

"Yes, he was called George Blackmore, why do you ask; does the name ring a bell?" Steve responded.

"I was just curious that's all and no I don't recognise the name but Carol may have known it but she can't tell you can she?" she said as they walked back to the cafe.

"If I draft up a statement regarding what you have told us will you be willing to sign it for us and for Carol's sake?" enquired Wendy.

She invited them into the cafe for a drink and something to eat before they headed back to London.

Chapter 28

Steve and Wendy decided instead to return to Romford, having spent quite some time on the island with a warm sun that had made their visit and day out worthwhile. The interview had been carried out in style by the sea, a gentle sea that had lapped softly onto the soft sandy beach. However the job and the comfort of the station canteen beckoned them rather than the offer from Rose of a meal etc in the cafe.

"How did you think it went Gov?" Wendy enquired as they headed for the car park.

"It was very interesting what she had to say about the incident back then Constable", Steve replied casually as he removed the car keys from his jacket pocket, "I don't know...to tell you the truth but...do you...ugh...know something. I think she unknowingly said a few things that really interested me in more ways than one; still...ugh...we will have to wait and see later, let me know when you have drawn up her statement. I want to just read it through and hope it contains the things that interested me most about the things she said...there was something she said that puzzled me...still we will have to look into her whole statement as it doesn't resemble the statement she wrote twenty four years ago, I know because I have already read it". Steve said as he unlocked the door of the passenger side to allow Wendy to get in first.

"I know what you mean Gov. I too have read her previous statement and in this one she has been rather more articulate".

Feeling rather confused, Rose quietly returned to the friendly ambience of the cafe and to her place within that humble workplace. She donned her tunic and returned to answer the needs of the hungry day trippers who were queuing up, waiting to give them their respective orders.

A group of holiday makers sat against the far wall which was complete with various pictures of old Canvey just waiting to be admired. They were busying themselves studying the menu before going up to the counter to make their respective orders. A middle-aged couple were sat quietly eating their meals by the window, a number twenty one bus had stopped at the nearby bus stop and was being boarded by a girl with a baby in a push chair.

Turning her head from the griddle, Dol briefly asked her if everything was alright, whereas the youngster asked jovially if she had really won the Pools.

Rose found herself quietly laughing and then said softly, "If only that were true sweetheart, if only that were true". She replied, and then went on to tell Dol that she'd tell her later when the place was quieter.

Later when they were shutting up Rose explained to them that it was about something that had happened in another lifetime, a long time ago but somehow it had been dug up again. The law somehow believed she may hold a clue to the murder of her friend, all those years ago she said, as she cleaned the tables, while the youngster was doing the washing up in the back kitchen.

....
....

In the meantime.

Peta and Angie were busy in the house still trying to put things straight. Most of the house was in order with just the odd part needing to be put in its place. Bob had decided to go to the D.I.Y., shop to get some more paint to finish the hallway and some more wallpaper paste.

Angie was feeling a bit tired and decided to go and make a coffee for the pair of them.

"How are feeling Ange?" Enquired a concerned Peta who sat on a stool by a breakfast bar in the large kitchen come diner.

"I am getting tired", she uttered softly, "It's the baby, he or she is getting to me".

"What have they said at the hospital then?" Peta found herself asking with some interest in her future. "Have you told Steve about the situation regarding your problem?"

"No!" She snapped sadly, "and I don't want him to know...well not yet that is".

"Surely he should be the one person who should know the truth, who knows, maybe he'll understand if you had to abort the baby in order to save your life".

"That might be true Peta, but the doctors said it would be a slim chance I might survive the operation, if I aborted the baby...don't you understand; under those circumstances I feel it is my duty as a mother to preserve the life of our unborn baby. Anyway it is far too late to go down that road now anyway. I have to give the baby a chance to live even if it means I don't".

"So at what point in time do you intend on telling Steve the truth about your situation...it will be too late when you're dead, even you have got to admit that", Peta expressed her concern for the future of her brother-in-law and the situation that Angie faced.

"Don't you understand, I am protecting him from his feelings...I know about Sally and what effect her death had on him and I am afraid the news of my problem might destroy his future. More to the point it might prevent him from doing his job properly, especially right now when he is trying to solve the murder of his mate".

"His mate?"

"Yes, Detective Inspector Gould was Steve's best friend and for that reason alone I feel compelled to keep quiet about my own problems...The less Steve knows about my problems the better detective he'll be ok...OK!"

"Ok! Have it your way Angie...but you know how I feel about this whole affair...and as for Steve we'll be here to help him just as we were when he lost Sally...anyway if you were aware of your situation why didn't you leave Steve in the beginning, that would've solved all the problems".

"Do you love Bob?"

"Of course I do, what a stupid question to be asking me...but unlike you Ange I would've told him the truth of my problem, irrespective of the outcome, we would work at it and face the end together, what ever the end would be...now do you understand the seriousness of your attitude regarding Steve and the babies futures".

"I do understand what you are saying, but I have to think about the lives that would be affected if he suddenly knew now".

"Yeah but you knew before he got

involved in this case...in fact you must've known when the pair of you lived on the streets...remember Ange...look I'm not trying to get at you, it's the last thing on my mind...but I am thinking of the consequences when this comes to light and we can only hope the baby lives and is perfect".

"Then look for me in the life of the baby, I believe it will be a girl, if so give her my name so I will live on in her".

"I see", Peta uttered, and then asked politely, "Would you like her to have your surname or Steve's?"

"Steve's would be right, don't forget he will be the baby's father...besides Angela Philips wouldn't be right...no...I would prefer her to be called Angela Price, in fact it would be nice to know she'd have my middle name too...yeah I like it, Angela Karen Price".

"Well Angie I just hope you know what you are doing, because you know my feelings on this matter", She remarked as she sipped at her coffee.

....
....

"Did you manage to get everything she said written down on your little pad Constable?" Steve enquired as he edged out of the car park and headed for the exit off the island.

"Yes Gov", she remarked as she tossed her shoulder bag into the well of the front seat and got into the car in a lady like manner, "I managed to get it all down on my pad. I can write it up when I get back to the office". She expressed casually. "What did you make of her statement Gov...?Was it of any use to us?"

"There was something that interested me and it might just be nothing, but it could be something the killer may have foolishly overlooked. In fact he may have never given it a thought and thinking it would never come to light and be long forgotten with time". He replied as he headed off of the island. "So Constable, what did you think of the island then?"

"I don't know Gov, it wasn't anything like my brother said it was; in fact, I was taken aback by what I saw Gov", she replied casually as she stared out of the window at the various types of houses that decorated the island. "I can't believe how many different types of homes there are here on the island".

"I know what you mean", Steve replied as he just gave her a fleeting glance before returning to the road ahead. Steve turned on the radio to Radio One and the music and chat dominated the main part of the journey back to the office, with Wendy engrossed with the songs and the views out of the window along the way.

Steve concentrated on the busy road whilst Wendy's mind was now working on the business of drafting up yet another statement. She had already spent the time before the visit typing up the statement that had been made by Lucy Blackmore previously.

"I'll get the coffees in Gov", remarked an eager Wendy as she grabbed her bag and headed for the canteen whilst Steve parked up.

Steve could only smile as he too made his way to the canteen where he found Wendy nursing her coffee by the window and Steve's coffee sitting there awaiting his presence.

"Well Gov what did you make of Rose then eh?" She asked as she leant back in the chair and sipped at her coffee.

"Like I said, there was something that really interested me with what she was saying, or I should say, what she said in that statement. Unknowingly she may have given us the one clue we never expected".

"You've got me there Gov", she said curiously. "What was it that interested you...I mean I found her statement bewildering to say the least"?

"Something she said in passing that shed some light on this whole sordid affair", he said with a slight glint in his eyes, "Everything is becoming clear",

Steve said as he gently stirred his coffee. Wendy eagerly clutched her coffee with both hands as she rested her elbows on the edge of the table with all ears to hear Steve's surmise, "we know that Jack was told by George Blackmore the story about the murder of Carol Richards, we know this because Lucy confirmed that in her statement and in her own words".

"Are you saying Gov, that Jack was killed by the same person who killed this Carol Richards girl in nineteen fifty eight?"

"It makes sense, don't you see. We must assume the killer heard that George Blackmore had needed the assistance of a police officer...so we can assume the killer became scared in case George had grassed him up...but he couldn't kill George because he was already dead...so the only person he believed knew his identity was Jack and therefore the killer had no choice in the matter, than to kill Jack in order to protect his little secret".

"What about George's house being broken into then?" She pursued.

"The killer had to find out if there was anything at George's house that could lead the police to him, but of course he hadn't realised George had removed his things and stored them up at his son's house...so...that must mean there must be something that he was after...something that would lead to his capture...then we talked to Rose and she said something which sent the alarm bells ringing in my ears".

"And pray what was it she said that interested you?" Wendy enquired curiously.

"She said the person who was trying to chat her up mentioned he was celebrating the fact that he had passed the entrance exam to go to the college in Hendon...think about it Constable, what does that tell you".

"You've got to be joking Gov", she replied with wide eyes at the statement Steve seemed to be implying. "Are you saying our killer could be...you know...one of us?"

"I too find it hard to believe constable and I know it doesn't bear thinking about", Steve said in a serious manner then added, "but we must look at that possibility that...Ugh...yes I am aware about the prospect of the killer being a police officer, but we are still none the wiser to his identity...remember that Constable...and for the sake of our sanity and safety I suggest you keep it under your hat for the time being...ok?"

"Yes Gov", She said softly bowing her head with sadness in her voice at the prospect that somebody in the force was a killer, "it's like somebody burglaring your home, it makes you feel sick inside to even think about it Gov".

It was about that time a couple of male young constables entered the canteen and ordered a couple of coffees. One ordered a couple of eggs on toast while the other ordered a tuna sandwich. One of them gave Wendy a wink before heading off to another table on the other side of the room. Once seated, one of them had grabbed a newspaper and started to read it while the other lit a cigarette and sipped at his coffee briefly looking over his shoulder at Wendy.

"It looks like you've got an admirer constable", Steve muttered with a smile on his face when he saw the look on her face as she gave the lad a fleeting glance as he too sipped at his coffee. "Remember constable the killer wouldn't be one of the young officers. No, my guess is we are looking for the answers from one of the older officers, that's assuming we are right. The killer could be a copper who must by now be in his late thirties or even in their early forties...so now let's assume the killer was around the age of seventeen or eighteen back then in nineteen fifty eight...he would be around forty one or two and don't forget, he might not even be in this area anymore, he could be anywhere. Beside when you come to think about it, he might've even given up the force years ago...no...Ugh...my guess is we are going to have to prove it without any question of doubt to succeed in getting the killer to justice. If he is or was a copper that is going to be very hard to prove and besides you must understand the consequences of the outcome, should we accuse a fellow officer of murder, remember he could be in this office".

"Right Gov that is going to be very difficult to keep quiet, especially in this place", she said calmly as she slowly sipped at her coffee and staring out of the window she went on, "if what you are saying is true and the killer is one of us, you know, in the force, then he would know you are out to capture the killer of Jack. Therefore, he would be more than keen to keep a sharp eye on your progress in this case and you must realise that if for one moment he got wind of your progress and he believed you were getting too close to the truth you could quite easily end up just like Jack...I mean it is evident from what happened to Jack that he doesn't care about killing anybody who gets too close...so Gov...what you're saying is the killer knew Jack had talked to George Blackmore and the killer believed George told him who the killer was...but if that were true and the killer was a copper and Jack knew that then surely he would've arrested him there and then?"

"That could be one of the killer's downfalls...having listened to what's been said by those involved it would be very easy to see the mistakes that had been made in the past".

"Are you telling me that the killer who as you say is a copper, could've covered up his tracks over time, hence there is nothing to go on to convict him, unless somebody with guts stood up and confessed in our favour", Wendy explained in some detail.

Just then there was some disturbance in the station which reached the ears of the officers in the canteen and they headed with haste in the direction of the yard. In the yard several police vehicles had gathered and officers in riot gear were preparing to go into service.

"I wonder what's going down Constable." Steve said as he too became transfixed by the occurrence in the yard.

"It's a raid Gov", Wendy remarked casually as she too stared at the action outside.

"A raid you say?"

"Yes Gov they are going to raid The Black Hat night club in Upminster....you know it's a drugs bust. Apparently they have had an undercover operative working in the club for the past year, because every time we got a sniff of drugs somehow they got wind of the actions of the police and when we raided the place there wasn't anything to be found".

"Who's running the show?" Steve enquired as he returned to his coffee.

"It's a task force from the city, code named operation seagull". Wendy returned wisely.

"It wouldn't by any chance being run by a Detective Chief Inspector Philip Lawrence", Steve uttered.

"I believe you may be right Gov...I get the feeling you and he have crossed path's in the past, by the way Gov me and couple of my mates have found a new cafe in the high street and we were thinking of trying it out...", She expressed as her voice slowly drifted into the background.

Steve's mind drifted away as he stared out of the window. The past slowly began to drift back into his life as he began to remember the day it all started for him so many years ago. In his mind he found himself at that table again, in his home with Sally preparing his usual breakfast, as if nothing had happened. In his eyes it was as real as it was back then and Sally was there, as if time had no meaning and she was alive and everything was how it had been before.

It felt like time had gone backwards and here he was again sitting at his old table, eating his toast and Sally's voice echoed in his mind, just as it had when she was excitedly telling him that she was meeting her friends Leslie and Grace and how they had planned to go to a new cafe in the high street of Hoddesdon in Hertfordshire. He could even smell her perfume floating about in the air.

Within a flash he was talking to Philip Lawrence regarding the Sally situation when he suddenly heard a voice in the distance calling out to him. The word Gov was being repeated in the background, over and over again and slowly getting louder; until like a bolt from the blue, he was again staring out the window and the noises of the time rang out in his ears as he suddenly faced a concerned Wendy who was trying to gain his attention.

"What is wrong Constable?"

"You were miles away Gov, I thought there was something wrong with you".

"It was you mentioning the new cafe in the high street that made me suddenly think of the last day I saw my late wife alive...you see...she too was going to try a new cafe in the high street in Hoddesdon with a couple of her friends...anyway I'm back now so who runs the Black Hat night club then?" Steve enquired.

"They do say it is run by a mob from the coast but at the moment we know it is being run by a guy named Peter Locke. He has got a bit of form from the past, but as far as we know he has done nothing for a few years, that was until a year ago when a young female drug addict was found dead in his car park".

"This female did she have a name?"

"Yeah! Her name was Sarah Roberts, a known prostitute working in the Romford area. Some say she wouldn't be missed but she was once somebody Gov".

"Well you are right Constable she was once a real person and like Carol Richards she had a life irrespective of the reasons for their meagre existences. They deserved to live their lives and not have some low life take that gift from them...who was on the case?"

"Jackson was on the case and said there was nothing to go on, apparently she OD'd on heroin", she explained, then added, "The pathologist's report said there was evidence that she had had sex some time prior to her death, maybe her last punter's money paid for the fix".

"Do we know by whom?" Steve asked inquisitively.

"No Gov".

"I think we can safely say we will

be looking into her death, if anybody asks, so you can get me everything you can lay your hands on about her, right".

"What about the murder of Jack then?" Wendy pressed. "You said the killer has made so many mistakes but doesn't realise he has".

"Yes Constable that's right, he hasn't seen them but they are there...you see it is like a jigsaw puzzle that has been thrown into the air and come down in bits all over the floor. It is our job to put that jigsaw puzzle back together again, piece by piece until we have the full picture...the trouble is at this moment in time...is that it is easy to see that all we have are bits and pieces of the puzzle...it will be our job to find out in which order they all go in and don't forget we have twenty four years to cover in order to come to a final satisfactory conclusion to this case".

"You are saying the killer is searching for anything that could link him to both killings, assuming he was the one to have killed Jack". Wendy said then added, "Another coffee Gov?"

"Go on Constable, you don't have to ask twice but you know we have work to do...but go on". Steve commented.

Chapter 29

Entering his office with a smile on his face and a cup of coffee in his hand, he suddenly remembered the packages belonging to George Blackmore that had been carefully placed in his office by Reg, as requested earlier that day. Reg had placed them on the floor behind his desk nearly causing him to trip over.

Wendy followed him into the room, placing her shoulder bag over the corner of one of the chair backs and immediately picked up of the first of the two medium sized boxes. She gently placed it on to the desk top to be examined, to see if it's contents contained anything of real interest. Something that could be of any interest and which could be related to George's past and could be useful in their quest. Something that could be a link to the killer; maybe something he was so desperate to find; that had caused him to break into the Blackmore house, believing there might've been anything, even something small that could reveal his true identity.

Most of it was his personal things, like various papers from his bank and job that he felt he needed to keep just in case; for legal purposes only. There was an old driving licence along with an old passport, but in Steve's eyes they meant nothing to him.

It was when Steve picked up the next box and opened it that he came across some old photographs in a large brown envelope that had been opened. Most of them were old photos of him and his wife and son when they were all young. But as he slowly shuffled through them and was just about to give up looking when a sudden smile came on his eager face. He stumbled on an old black and white photo that bore the picture of the car that was at the centre of the evidence given to him by Andrew Cox and Lucy. The photo contained three young men leaning against the bonnet of a two tone Vauxhall, it was what Steve had hoped for and suddenly it became real for the first time, not just a vision in some bodies mind.

Studying the photo, Steve suddenly realised it could be the very thing the killer was after, believing any evidence of the car could lead them directly to him, even though it had long since gone.

"What is it Gov?" Wendy asked curiously, as she began to replace the useless things back into her box.

"I believe this is what the killer was after", he replied, handing her the photo to look at.

"I gather Gov...This is the car Rose talked about in her statement too...what is so important about that car...I mean...it must be long gone by now".

"You don't understand constable that car was a prototype with only six of them in the world, back then, so...er...you see it wouldn't have taken the plod back then that long to have found its owner. Somehow and maybe, just maybe they would've linked it to our killer, but had it been any old car we might never have found it...I would imagine at that time the killer must've been young and might not have realised the importance of that fact".

"And how do you know all this Gov?" Wendy asked curiously.

"Lets just say a little birdie told me before I came here, so you see constable I was working on this case prior to getting to this office", he said as he took the photo back and put it into his inside jacket pocket for safety purposes. Giving her a quick wink with one of his usual cheeky smiles, "the rest of this stuff is just junk", he remarked as he found his feet, and then added, "You can see that it gets taken back to his son to be disposed of as he wishes".

"Yes Gov...I'll get P.C. Smith to help me take it back". She said joyfully, by the way Gov I've been meaning to ask you...why have you chosen me to do this and not Mark, or better still we all believed in the typing pool that you would have chosen Peters".

"That's a silly question to be asking, for a start Peters is working with Jackson so I didn't want to tread on Jackson's toes and yes I had to choose between Mark and yourself...anyway don't you like it then...the job that is then?"

"Yes!" She snapped, "It's just that...Oh darn it...of cause I wanted the role and I'm enjoying it for Christ sake".

"Well then lets hear no more about this and lets just take these boxes down to the front desk...I'm sure Reg will take care of them until you get the chance to return them to their rightful owners. I have what I was hoping to find, you see that car was a mere vision, until now that is".

"What if the killer was to see them...the boxes that is Gov?"

"You forget if he does he doesn't know I have what he'd be looking for safely tucked away in my pocket and in my possession...but should anybody find themselves asking after them there wasn't anything of interest in them...ok", Steve said still with that cheeky little smile on his face as he hung his jacket over the back of his chair. He then man handled the boxes back to the front desk, accompanied by Wendy who managed one of the boxes, which they then placed by the back wall in the reception, having carried them to the front desk.

"What's going down Reg regarding this night club business?" enquired Steve as he lifted himself up having placed the boxes in the corner.

"The raid on the night club was a success Inspector, apparently they have arrested four people on drug dealing charges and they found two cars that contained guns in their boots...what a blag eh", he grinned. Just then a middle-aged man entered the reception with some paperwork declaring he had been asked to produce his driving documents at this station. He had been stopped the day before but he didn't have them on him then, hence the need to be there now. "So how's the investigation going regarding our Jack?" Reg asked politely.

"I'll tell you later Reg when you're

not too busy", Steve remarked seeing the man coming through the main door into the lobby, "it looks like you are going to be very busy tonight Reg. I hope the cells have been cleaned, we don't want a diplomatic incident now, do we", Steve laughed as he headed back to the office. "Oh by the way Reg those...er...cardboard boxes are to go back to the Blackmore clan ok. By the way if anyone is interested, there wasn't anything of real interest in them, they were just a waste of our time; still we could only hope that something useful might turn up, eh".

"What's on the agenda now Gov?" Wendy enquired casually as they headed back to the office.

"Well there's the little matter regarding the two statements that need to be drawn up and get them read by those concerned then signed and filed", he replied as they entered the realms of his office, "I want you to find out all you can on this Sarah Roberts' business and I want to know if there are any clues that were overlooked back then...then I want to go and visit Carol Richards family, maybe tomorrow that is", he said as he sat behind his desk and leant on the edge of it, toying with his chin with a puzzled look on his face, "I think we should also go to the Warren school and see if they have any records of those boys in the photo...I just have this gut feeling about this whole sordid affair...I get the feeling the killer is so close. I sense I could feel him breathing down the back of my neck...like a ghost floating around and laughing at us; thinking he's got away with the perfect murder", he expressed as he gently rubbed the back of his neck.

It was just then the telephone rang out making the pair of them jump.

"Yeah D.C.I. Price". He said politely, once he picked up the receiver.

"Yeah this is Southend nick, I'm W.P.C. Banner here and I am led to believe that you were wanting the address of a certain Rose Bright who lives on Canvey Island...is that right Inspector", returned the voice of the female officer on the other end of the phone.

"It is ok W.P.C., we found the address, alright...they informed us at the nick on the island...but thanks all the same for your help. I shall inform my colleague of your call...we hope you got your man that we arrested on your behalf".

"Yes Inspector thanks for your help too...this Rose Bright is she wanted for anything...I mean...there wouldn't be anything that we should be made aware of?" returned the voice.

"No she was just a witness to an incident in relation to her friend some twenty four years ago, that's all. We were just looking into that old case, nothing more nothing less you might say, so don't worry, we have the situation under control this end, ok...Again we thank for you co-operation in this delicate matter ok, bye". He said politely as he hung up the phone. "By the way that was your friend from Southend Constable, with reference to the address of Rose you enquired after", he smiled.

"A bit late Gov I think don't you".

"My opinion too", he replied cheekily.

"In that case I'll leave you and I'll go and get on with typing up these statements for you Gov", she said eagerly as she retrieved her bag and slinging it over her left shoulder she eagerly headed for the area of her own desk in the typing pool. There she met up with some of her female colleagues busying themselves with their own typing. She removed her note pad and placed her bag under her seat and set up her typewriter ready to do her job.

There was a lot of talk amongst the girls in the typing pool; mainly it was about the raid on the night club and the horde uncovered. This was thanks to an undercover team who had spent the whole year working on the case.

Wendy sat at her desk, where she retrieved the right forms for the statements from one of her drawers and as normal she placed the paperwork, plus carbon paper so that she could get triplicate copies, into her electric typewriter and prepared herself for the task ahead, this was something she was used too. The last time she sat in front of that typewriter she was in uniform, she wasted no time in preparing to draft up those two statements. She placed her suit jacket on the back of the chair so she could feel free and proud of her present situation.

Looking up from her duty she realised she had been approached by her cousin Jane who was surprised to see her back in the usual place behind the desk. The friend had believed she would be out there doing detective work.

"We didn't think we'd find you back in here Wendy", remarked the uniformed W.P.C., who stood in front of her holding a mug of coffee in one hand and a half smoked filter tipped cigarette in the other.

"Why is that Jane?" She said casually, briefly lifting her head to see who had entered her field of concentration.

"Well you being a detective now", she said jovially, then added sarcastically, "you know you're the envy of the station".

"You forget Jane, we all work together in this office and my job is to type up statements just as I have always done in the past...which is exactly what I am trying to do right now...and for you information I feel great about my job".

"I see Wendy...so...eh...what's this new guy like then...hum...he seems dishy, how comes he chose you, surely Peters should have got the post", she enquired with a sexy glint in her eyes as she slowly dragged on her cigarette.

"Peters is working with Jackson and if you must know he had to choose between Mark and me and he chose me is that alright with you".

"You look so different out of uniform Wendy", commented a fellow male officer as he passed her desk carrying a stack of files.

"Thanks John, I needed that", Wendy responded politely before returning to the inquisitive Jane, who was perched on the edge of her desk, but not before she had retrieved an ashtray from another desk placing it on Wendy's desk, "And you know my feelings towards Peters, he's a creep and I'm sure the Gov would've seen that".

"Well there you go Wendy old girl why don't you spill the beans on the new guy", Jane said with a grin on her pretty face, then added, "He seems to be a bit of all right".

"Anything in a pair of trousers is all right in your eyes Jane", Wendy responded wisely, "If you must know he is good, he knows his place and he is out to solve the crime of who killed Jack. He told me he had been working on that very case long before he came here", she said softly then went on to inform her cousin, "Look Jane I know you want to talk to me but I have a lot of work to catch up with, so I'm sorry to say this, but bugger off and let me get on with my job", she said politely, waving her away with her right hand, "and take your ashtray with you".

"Oh blimey we can tell you ain't one of us anymore missy, you don't want to know us anymore, we'll remember you at Christmas time".

"Whatever!" Wendy replied cockily, returning to the job at hand.

There was an air of silence that entered the area with the only noise that echoed was coming from Wendy's' typewriter as she speedily typed up the contents of the statements. Each statement stretched to a couple of pages in triplicate and on police forms ready to be signed in the appropriate place on every page by the witnesses concerned.

Steve found his feet and stood by the window staring endlessly out into the busy world below, a bus slowly drifted past heading for London and there were the usual sounds echoing from the market place. In Steve's mind he was in turmoil by the present events with reference to the task at hand, especially with his involvement in the capture of Jack's killer. He had been drawn by the words of Rose that somehow seemed to make him believe that there was a possibility the killer could easily be a fellow officer. This fact, if found to be true, would make the situation a powder keg waiting to explode that could take either of them up with it.

"Everything alright Steve?" came a voice from behind.

"Oh, it's you Chief", he replied as he quickly turned to face the voice that had entered the world and was now standing by the desk with his right hand resting on its edge, "You made me jump Chief...I didn't hear you come in", he said as he slowly returned to his chair.

"So Steve how are you getting on with the case of our Jack, have you made any progress in this little matter", He asked finding a chair by the wall that he slid over to the desk.

"I'm making good progress Chief but you must agree I have to watch myself...I know the last thing Jack was on was related to this George Blackmore situation; you know the one who confessed to him regarding the Church yard murder; so I'm looking into that case and I'm hoping it will unearth the truth;

because I strongly believe the killer thought George grassed him up before he died".

"You know we worked hard on that case back then and unearthed nothing, so what could you possibly unearth now that would change things". The Chief pressed, "Certainly not from the words of a dying man who has since died and even more since Jack's death meant that link went too".

"I know you worked hard on that case Chief, but there were certain facts back then that weren't known but have since come to light recently and it's on those grounds I'm working...I want you to go back to that era after Carol Richards was murdered, can you tell me who joined this police station from Hendon, can you remember, I need to know", Steve said as he placed both elbows on the edge of his desk and twiddled with a pen that he picked up.

"Why, is it important by any chance Steve?"

"I'm not quite sure chief, but I need to know who joined the force around that time, it was something that was said to me today that's all, ok eh".

"I see...well...eh let me see now...I can tell you there were four young recruits who joined us back then, the first was a John, John Denison, and a Philip Watts I believe...yeah...they came together. John Denison became an alcoholic because his wife left him for one of his friends and he was the one who always said he had the perfect marriage...well I guess he got it wrong. Now Watts on the other hand stayed for a few years then got a transfer to the West Country, you know Cornwall or Devon; I know it was something like that. From what I've heard he's now a Detective Inspector...now the other two were Roger Benson and of cause there was Danny Peters who helped on that very case...I think he's upset because you didn't ask him to be your side kick".

"What happened to Roger then?"

"He is at the Chadwell Heath office now I believe, he too is a Detective Inspector...what's all this about Steve, are you telling me you think the killer is...no...I...eh...no, I can't believe you would think a fellow officer would or even contemplate committing such an atrocity".

"I know but it was something that was said to me today, by Carol's friend Rose, who left her at the bus stop, remember?"

"How could I ever forget that Steve. I worked on that case as you know. I always believed I would solve her murder in my lifetime...Are you now saying that the same officer killed Jack...but why?"

"As I have said the killer believed

George Blackmore had grassed him up. He also broke into his home hoping to find anything that could incriminate him, but what he didn't know was George gave all his stuff to his son to look after. Now that stuff is in our lobby waiting to go back to his son, oh and for your information there wasn't anything of interest in his belongings, so now I'm back to square one, up the river without a paddle, you could say".

"So Inspector where do you go from here then, I'm all ears?" The Chief pressed as he leant back in the chair.

"I'm going to pay a visit to Carol's mum tomorrow".

"Do you think that would be wise at this moment in time? I mean we don't want to be waking the dead now and give them false hope".

"I would normally agree with you on that issue Chief", Steve said as he leant back in his seat, then went on to add, "but because we are faced with a murderer that could be a link to both killings", he explained as he returned to leaning on the edge of his desk to be more diplomatic adding, "I need to know if Carol had known this George Blackmore guy by any chance. I believe he was in her class at school, you never know they may have a school photograph with her killer on it, we just don't know...and besides if Jack's killer is the same person who did Carol in, surely her family should be made aware of that...don't you think Chief? Besides you said yourself you hoped to get her killer before you retired" he said then added, "There are a few little loose ends I need to tie up and I hope to nail the killer soon. But I am aware that because of the time factor the case would have to be water tight, so until then I just need to learn what happened in both incidents. I need to know what happened on both days. I have some clues and a series of events regarding those two days...it is like a jigsaw that has been thrown into the air..."

"Yeah I'm aware of that scenario Inspector, that was my theory back then twenty four years ago", the Chief interrupted, then added, "you are missing the most vital piece of that jigsaw puzzle Inspector and that is the name of the killer and the events that led up to him committing the murder".

"Well I can tell you I am that close to getting the name, as for the events that led up to that murder it is in the palm of my hand and when I know the name of her killer and Jack's I will crush him with one hand", he replied using his right hand held out in front of him where he articulately showed the Chief his feelings by slowly closing his hand to resemble a fist.

"So Inspector are you going to

enlighten me to your findings?" The Chief enquired eagerly, "I'm all ears Inspector".

"I have said Chief that there are a few loose ends that need to be tied up and then I think we'll have their killer bang to rights...I can tell you the killer the first time round was a youngster, in his mid teens and because he was young he forgot what he said and didn't believing there were witnesses, only his friends who he could manipulate...but I have proof there were or are witnesses who never came forward until now and it wasn't George Blackmore, now...I'm going to leave it at that Chief".

"So Inspector, what can I tell the media regarding the murder of Jack?"

"I dun know Chief, just tell them we are still working on the case and are making good progress in finding his killer, ok".

"I can tell you Inspector on the day Jack copped it, as you put it; he wasn't very well so I told him to go home and take a few days off, we'd understand; but you know our Jack he had to press on regardless".

"I know what Jack was like", Steve remarked then added, "We worked together for several years in the Harlow area. I remember the day he told me he'd asked to be transferred to this office and all because his wife was afraid he might get killed by the gangs that were getting into that town...I can tell you it was getting a bit messy at times back then...still, it just goes to prove, it doesn't matter where you live, if your number comes up, it's good night from me and in his case it was good night Jack, however painful it seems Chief ".

"In that case Inspector as you seem to have things under control I will leave it all in your capable hands", the Chief said as he prepared to leave the office.

"For obvious reasons Chief, if it turns out to be a copper or fellow officer, don't you think we need to keep what we have already discussed under wraps, for now that is, of course. I will let you know more when the time is right".

The Chief just nodded his approval and left the office.

Chapter 30

A warm hazy autumn sun was gently setting in the west, as the clock on the church tower chimed six o'clock which echoed out across the emptiness that had only just recently been a bustling, busy market place. Now the only noises were of discarded newspapers rustling in the breeze as they wisped along over old well worn cobbles and the sound of a stall holder or two wheeling their now empty barrows to the holding shed. Steve had decided it was time to go home as he was feeling a little tired.

With his jacket undone and his tie flapping in the breeze he decided to go for a little walk first and to pay his cousin a visit in his pub, maybe grab a pint before heading home. The traffic was now light and some people were still milling about in the market place. On the air lingered the smells from the various burger bars, other fast food stalls and fruit and veg stalls which had littered the market place but which had now been put away for the night ready to begin again the next day.

Leaving the office behind him, he pouted his lips and tucked his hands deep into his trouser pockets for comfort. His footsteps now echoed over those same old cobbles, where his mind suddenly began to reflect on his friend Jack. He knew Jack had walked these same cobbles the night he lost his life to who ever had killed him; as he walked his mind toyed with the prospect that the killer could be still out there watching him; especially if they knew he was actually working on the same case as his friend. He began to wonder had been going through his friend's mind as he too had walked the path, had he been trapped in the web of the Churchyard murder, having sat and listened to George's confession on his death bed the way he had, had Jack even become aware of the identity of the killer without fully realising it, only for it all to be lost upon his death.

Stopping for a brief moment in his walk in the early evening he removed the tatty old photo from the inside pocket of his jacket and stared at it longingly, trying to imagine the day it was taken. Trying to see if there was something in that picture that would suddenly smack him in the face and the name of the killer would suddenly appear, turning the photo over he noticed the name of the company that had developed it. It was a firm in Chadwell Heath and the date it was developed was the fifteenth of May nineteen fifty eight.

It was obvious the photo was taken prior to Carol's death, when the time was good. Everyone that had been involved in the crime that was to unfold and probably change their lives for ever and was unaware of the facts. George had found the only way to have escaped that nightmare was to die. One single person's act had caused so much damage to so many lives; especially to an innocent young girl's life; one who had the right to live religiously. However she had been denied that one gift of life at the hands on an idiot. Steve knew that some where in the photo was a clue, he toyed with the idea that the killer was the person taking the photo on that day, when they all had a life to live.

Slipping the photo back into his pocket again he put on a smile and headed off to the pub and a chance to have a couple of jars with his cousin and try to forget his job for a short while, the eighty six bus passed him heading east.

Opening the pub door Steve entered the world of the drinker with the sounds of people enjoying themselves on one side of the bar. There were several people who were busy drinking at the bar, totally oblivious to Steve's sudden intrusion into their little way of escaping the rigours of the day and before heading home to face those problems too.

"A light and bitter please", Steve ordered, once he reached the bar, "Is Johnny in?"

"Yeah he's in the cellar checking the dates on the barrels", she replied as she pulled him his pint. Half filling the pint glass with the bitter before she opened a bottle of light ale which she left for him to add to the glass. "Would you like me to give him call him for you?"

"No it's alright, I'll wait for him to come back", he politely replied pouring the light ale into his glass and handing her a five pound note at the same time. A couple of men just gave him a fleeting glance with the usual, 'evening mate', Steve just nodded with the hint of a smile in response to their politeness.

He stood patiently foot a moment waiting for his change before moving to the far end of the bar where he knew his cousin would always sit. He finally sat on the far stool with his back to the wall so he could lean back more comfortably. He gently sipped at his drink and just studied the happy crowd enjoying themselves in his cousin's home.

"Well if it isn't the prodigal child come home", Johnny said jovially when he returned to the bar and immediately poured himself a pint of bitter, "So Steve what's the reason for this little visit then?"

"I see!" Steve responded, "Not, Hello Steve how's the new house going or how's Angie and the baby".

"Alright what's got up your nose then sunshine? Johnny said coolly as he sat on his stall clasping his fresh pint and taking a long mouthful to refresh his dry throat.

"Ah...it's nothing" he replied soulfully then went on to add "it's just this case I'm on, it's beginning to get to me you know what I mean".

"And what case is that or is it taboo?"

"It's the murder of the copper", he continued sadly then went on regardless adding, "and I'm faced with another murder that took place in the nineteen fifties, when a young girl was murdered right here in Romford market", Steve said as he too sipped on his drink.

"So what's the problem Steve?" Johnny quizzed, having picked up his newspaper from under the counter before placing it opened on the surface.

"The problem I'm up against Johnny is that it appears that both murders could be linked to the same killer and that's my problem, don't you see", Steve explained sadly, "I had to go to Canvey Island today and interview a friend of the dead girl who was the last person to have seen the girl alive".

"A bit before my time that is Steve", he casually smiled "The one you need to talk to is a guy called Frankie, he usually sits in the far corner over there", he said pointing to the left.

"So who is this Frank then?" Steve enquired.

"You could say he's a walking encyclopaedia. I can honestly say without a doubt...there isn't anything that guy doesn't know, especially about...well...ugh...you know that's everything to do with Romford...in fact he's usually in this time of the night...they say he lives alone having lost his wife a few years ago to the big 'C'...so they say that is, but I don't know", he replied looking at the clock on the wall.

"In that case I look forward to meeting this walking encyclopaedia chap if he is so well versed in the day to day running of this area".

"Yeah, legend has it that he came to Romford to work for British Gas, but retired a few years ago after an accident on site, he was injured in a gas explosion in Hornchurch late one evening seven years ago. He then became like he is today, because of it the locals keep telling him to write a book but he just laughs the idea off".

"Is that right you want Frank?" Asked one of the guys from the bar who overheard them talking about him.

"Yeah that's right Pete", Johnny returned politely, then went on, "why, do you know where he is?"

"Yeah he's outside talking to a couple of guys" he replied, then enquired, "would you like me to go and get him for you?"

"Please!" Returned Steve who nodded politely.

Moments later Pete returned,

bringing with him the one Johnny called the walking encyclopaedia.

He was an elderly man in his early sixties with long unkempt mousy brown hair going grey in areas. He was wearing shabby clothes that consisted of a torn grey tweed jacket unbuttoned, underneath which was a dirty pale blue un-ironed shirt, in turn covered by a V-necked patterned jumper which he wore over dark grey trousers that also looked as if they hadn't seen an iron in years too. He was led over to Steve and Johnny and Pete introduced him to an eager Steve, who offered to get him a pint, which he didn't refuse as Johnny was already pouring it out for him, as he was aware of his likes.

"I understand you want some information regarding Romford...lad?" He said as he leant against the bar, putting his right foot on the brass bar that ran the length of the foot of the bar, as his drink was placed before him the faint whiff of tobacco drifted from his being.

"You could say that", Steve replied coolly.

"So Sonny what information do you seek and thanks for the drink?" he said politely as he took his first long sip of the drink.

"You're welcome", Steve replied, then added, "What do you know of the murder of the fifties?"

"You are talking about the murder of Carol Richards in May of nineteen fifty eight if my memory serves me right I presume".

"Well...what do you know about it?" Steve pressed.

"Me, I know nothing", he uttered then went on to add, "But I do know somebody who does know things about that murder", he replied as he took out a tobacco pouch from his tatty jacket pocket and proceeded to roll a cigarette.

"So Frank...you don't mind me calling you Frank?"

"Well that is my name isn't it?" he smiled as he put his fresh cigarette into his mouth and using a slim line lighter he proceeded to light it.

"Ok so this person, does he come with a name?" Steve continued to press for answers.

"Of course he has a name stupid", He snapped jokingly then went on to add, "He's called Sid or I should say he is better known as Alchie Sid. He is a tramp who normally sleeps in the grounds of the church in the market place, that's if he doesn't get to sleep in one of the sheds where they store their market stalls first".

"So how do I get to talk to this Sid then?"

"You don't, he is scared of the police, as I gather you are the new boy in the factory am I right? You are looking for the killer of the copper who was murdered a few weeks back, am I right inspector?"

"Yes you are right, so are you going to tell me how I can talk to this person named Sid?"

"You leave it with me inspector. I know all his little haunts, so I can get him to come to you in the factory where you work", he said as he held his pint in his left hand while his cigarette hung precariously in the other. "How does that sound inspector?"

"I guess I have no choice in the matter then, do I?" Steve sighed. "So who is this Sid then?"

"He was a victim of the second world war mate", Frank said informatively, "you see, when the poor sod got, 'ugh', back home he found; like many of them returning home; his family had perished in the blitz; something he had not known about. It hit him even harder when he found his old house was left as just a pile of rubble. Because he had spent many years living off the land, along with thousands of his mates, of which many of them were killed...meant he couldn't cope with Blighty, unlike many of his mates who just about managed it. No...Not our Sid it...ugh...hit him for six, so, in his grief, he turned to drink, hoping it would drown out the sound of those bombs going off around him. Making him remember a time where he, along with everybody else, believed the next one could be good night sunshine...and that as they would say was his life...so you see he was a victim of his own destiny".

"I can see why they say you are the encyclopaedia of this area", Steve said as he sipped quietly at his beer. Knocking back the last mouthful of his beer he got up from the stool and said calmly, "I suppose I'd better get off home, Angie will be wondering where I am...I'll catch up with you later Johnny alright...and Frank don't forget to tell this Sid it is important and who knows what he might know, if you say he has been around since the end of World War two",

Tucking his right hand into his trouser pocket having placed the empty glass on the counter he made for the door, after a brisk walk back to the station he retrieved his car and headed home to Angie and he smiled as he knew Tara would be wagging her tail when he finally got home.

Angie had made herself busy preparing him a meal of spaghetti bolognaise accompanied by a nice bottle of red wine which was being chilled in the fridge.

Later sitting at the table, in the now newly decorated dining room and whilst eating his meal, he happily told Angie of his little trip to Canvey Island that day. He went on to inform her he would love to take her there the following week-end for a day out. Angie was overjoyed at the prospect of escaping the work on the house and the usual routine of a normal day for her. The sight of the growing life inside her was now showing signs of its existence, its kicking sending shudders through her body.

There were still several cardboard boxes waiting to be unpacked and which were left in a corner of the room with lounge written on them.

"I see you've been busy in here today sweetheart", Steve remarked between mouthfuls of spaghetti.

"Yeah thanks to Peta and your brother", she said softly as she held her fork in her hand, ready to scoop up some of her spaghetti too, then went on to explain saying "I did do some work, even though your brother and his missus pestered me to rest up because of the baby, but I want to help I told them".

"Well you should rest up, you forget you're pregnant", Steve replied as he gently poured two glasses of the red wine into a couple of fine crystal fluted glasses.

"Before you ask", she said as she picked up the glass of wine, "your brother is taking Peta to the pictures tonight, that's why they aren't here".

"It feels good to be alone tonight. I feel like putting my feet up and watching one of our DVD's how does that grab ye?" he said, taking a mouthful of the wine.

She just smiled and nodded her head in approval, "This Rose what was she like? I gather that's who you went to see, yeah?"

"She was ok, a bit of a wild one you might say, she could easily be the life and soul of any party, and you know the sort of woman. If you are good and we go to the island next week-end you might get to meet her as she works in one of the seafront cafes".

"That's nice love I'll look forward to that experience". She said with a big grin on her young face.

....

Around the same time Tinkerbelle and the Major were meeting on the steps of St Paul's Cathedral. The sun was setting and several groups of people, mainly tourists were busy snapping away with their cameras taking the memories of that grand place home with them. A Japanese tourist asked the Major to take a photo of his little group standing in front of it so he could also be in the picture; the Major smiled and did his duty. There was the faint aroma coming from the many coffee houses that abounded around that great place.

The Major approached Tinkerbelle, who was sitting on the middle step wearing a knee length green floral skirt with a pastel green blouse. She also wore a plain green jacket that was open and her long blonde hair hung loosely down her slender back. A dark green shoulder bag was slung over her left shoulder and to one side as she waited patiently for his arrival. She only rose to her feet when she spotted him carrying his usual briefcase. He was wearing his usual dark navy suit complete with his double breasted jacket which was done up, the whole effect was finished with a navy tie set against his clean white shirt which looked totally out of place where the normal attire should have been a more casual affair.

Pigeons scurried about coming and going as if they owned the place.

"So Jenny what is the interest in those two officers then?" He said stopping at the base of the stairs leading up to the main entrance to the cathedral. Placing his right foot on the first step and holding his briefcase on his knee. "Why don't we go and get a coffee and you can fill me in on your assumptions, I can assume this is all to do with Steve", he said as he turned to head for the place where the enticing aroma of coffee was coming from, joined by Jenny, code named Tinkerbelle.

"Of course this has everything to do with Steve...Major", she said sharply, "I am right in assuming that Steve is working on the murder of Jack Gould, am I right in thinking that".

"As always Jenny you are on the ball", he replied, and stopping briefly to answer her, "so what is the beef then?"

"If he gets into that case the killer could strike again, especially if they think Steve is getting too close...that's my beef...don't you see?"

"Yes Jenny I do understand and why do you think I chose you to be his shadow...his ghost. The killer wouldn't know anything about you, would he? You are what Jack Gould needed but he didn't have and...Well you know I'm just as fond of Steve as you are Jenny".

"Yeah well you know what I really want Major?" She said as they again headed for the coffee shop nearby.

"Yes Jenny we do know what you want and I'm sure Steve is working on it too...but you are aware it takes time and that's something we have plenty of...I'm sure in time the truth will emerge".

They managed to find a table in the far corner of one of the coffee houses, where he undid his jacket before sitting down and Jenny placed her bag on the next seat, before the Major ordered a cappuccino while Jenny asked for a latte.

Removing a couple of files from his briefcase he placed them on the table top.

"So, now are you going to tell me why you asked me to pull the files on those two officers?" He said as he placed his clasped hands on the top of the files.

"You could say it's a case of women's intuition...no there was just something about those two that worried me Major...I just can't get my thoughts around it".

"Ok then", returned the Major as he lifted the files. "Looking at Jackson's file there is nothing bad about him, he is squeaky clean, in fact he is heading for higher status in the force as he has a perfect record, but...when it comes to Peters there's a different story...it appears he's got a bit of a reputation with the female officers, in that they are afraid of him. Some say he gets angry if they refuse to go out with him but comes back later and says he's sorry...I can tell you Steve is also working on the Churchyard murder".

"Is there a file on that murder then?"

"Of course...I'm not the Major for nothing you know", he said as he lifted a third file from the briefcase and he held it out to her, "You should read this Jenny, it might be of some use to you...and you may be right about Peters, Jenny. He joined the force three years after that murder and actually worked on the case as a young rookie...the case is of a young girl who was murdered in the churchyard in Romford, so now you know why Steve is there. He believes the two murders were carried out by the same person and somehow Jack was onto it and it cost him his life".

"So...where does that leave me?" she enquired taking the file.

"You are special branch Jenny, act accordingly...you know what to do if you feel Steve is in any danger...then you think about what you say you want when you do it, right".

"What if the killer turns out to be a fellow officer?" She said curiously.

"You destroy him and save face does that answer your question".

"Loud and clear Major...loud and clear".

Chapter 31

The busy canteen was a hive of activity with little groups of officers dotted about the room chatting over their respective beverages, oblivious of the two of them. Steve explained casually to Wendy over a coffee or two how they were going to go and talk to Carol Richard's family, giving reference to the old case regarding the death of their daughter.

Wendy casually reported that the mother was still living on the Marks Gate Estate and requested it should be a low key affair, considering the reasons for their grief. Even though she was aware that it had been twenty four years since the incident had occurred, she strongly felt the pain would still be very evident, especially for the mother.

Angie and Steve sat at the table that night, he was feeling great inside, telling Angie about the visit to the pub and seeing his cousin again. He even told her about the tramp named Sid and how he lived his life, which was something the pair of them could relate to.

The pair of them found comfort that evening curled up on the sofa and a bottle of the red wine. Their glasses sitting on the coffee table lay testament to the scene, which was to while away the evening watching a romantic movie on their DVD recorder, whilst curled up in each other's arms. Steve would occasionally give her a warm tender kiss, usually accompanied with a soft lingering look as their eyes joined and with the soft words, 'I love you' being uttered. With a gentle pat on her bulge as they cuddled under the dimmed lights, the simple action would bring a warm smile to Angie's face as she returned the same words with intense feelings that welled deep from inside her. But there was still that nagging problem lingering around in her head, but as usual it was times like this that she tended to shun the problem, leaving it to fate. The world of crime seemed a distant memory and the very thought on Steve's mind was the future of their unborn child and all that it would mean to them as a family.

The evening ended with Steve taking Tara for her last walk of the day, as he walked along he felt like a millionaire and all seemed right with his world.

The next morning was a rush, with Steve in a hurry having slept in slightly. Now he hurried to put on his jacket and grabbed a slice of toast as he headed for the door still putting on his jacket, but Angie enquired casually if she was going to get her usual good morning kiss before he departed. He turned quickly and grabbing her gently in his arms he apologised and gave her a peck on the lips declaring he would make it up to her that evening. She smiled and nodded contentedly at his words.

Still trying to adjust his jacket and taking a bite of the toast at the same time, he stumbled over the keys to his car, declaring to himself, 'less haste more speed'. Taking a deep breath he opened the car door, got in and continued to eat his toast as he started the car up, finishing it before he set off for work. He felt the traffic was against him as he tried in vain to get to his work. Arriving there ten minutes late, he was surprised to see the office was working as normal and was totally unaware of his predicament; the place was too busy to be worried by his lateness. He hurried to the canteen to get himself a coffee having missed it at home.

Wendy was in the canteen too and called to him to join her. She was in a soft grey suit and white blouse and wearing a pair of grey, flat slip on shoes and white tights. Her hair was tied up in a ponytail. She was happy to have to tell him he had some crumbs on his chin from the toast earlier, he just smiled and brushed them away as he sat opposite her near the window as she knew that was his favourite spot.

"I gather sir, we're going to interview this...ugh...Mrs. Richards this morning, eh Gov?" She said as she sipped her coffee.

"You gathered right young lady", he replied as he gently stirred his coffee having put a couple of spoonfuls of sugar into it, "I hope you are feeling all right about it constable, as you seemed anxious about it yesterday".

"I have taken the time out to locate exactly where her address is Gov, I hope you don't mind".

"Why do you think I chose you to be my side kick and nobody else"? He explained, with a slight grin on his face as he gently returned to his coffee, his egg on toast, which he had ordered, was coming along soon as he hadn't had his breakfast due to his lateness that morning and he didn't feel right if he missed that start to his day.

A folded daily newspaper caught Steve's eye as it lay on another empty table nearby beckoning him to read it, picking it up, Wendy passed a comment of there's a good picture on page three, but Steve retorted that it wasn't his scene, after he found himself checking out the page that revealed a half naked woman posing on a park bench.

"I've managed to type up those statements Gov", she said pouting her lips as she watched a member of the canteen staff place his eggs on toast and a fresh coffee in front of him," if it's alright with you I thought we could go and get Lucy's statement signed after we've visited the mother of Carol, what do you thing Gov?"

"If you want to leave them here and let me browse through them that's ok" He said, having thanked the person who placed the meal before him. He refolded the newspaper and placed it at his side and applied some salt to his eggs.

"I've got to go and fetch them Gov and leave you to your meal", she uttered as she found her feet and headed for her desk to retrieve her work.

"While you're at it constable", he said, removing his car keys from his jacket pocket and placing them on the table in front of her, he went on to add, "check to see if those boxes are still there; if so get one of the lads to help you put them into the boot of my car; then we can kill two birds with one stone, ok constable".

Picking up the keys all she could muster was a quick, 'Sir!' With a slight bow out of respect, as she then departed leaving Steve to return to his eggs on toast. He just gave her a fleeting smile as he returned to his meal and began reading the front cover of the newspaper at the same time.

Later Steve found Wendy by his car waiting for him, along with her trusty shoulder bag and a pink folder under her left arm. She was twisting Steve's car keys around on her slender first finger of her right hand with a smug grin about her pretty face, her ponytail danced in the breeze.

"I got Peters to help me with the boxes Gov", she said as she tossed him his keys, "he wasn't going to Gov, well not until I told him who they were for and he became really interested in what was in them, in fact, at one point he wanted to rummage through them in the car park".

"So constable, what did you tell him?" Steve enquired as he stood by the car door on the driver's side.

"I told him there wasn't anything of any interest, just as you told me to, Gov". She replied.

"Good!" Steve snapped in reply as he opened the driver's door, telling her the door was open so she could get in as it was central locking. "I see you have the statements that need to be signed, it looks like I'll have to have words with our Mr. Peters, constable".

"I think it might've been because he was on the case all those years ago", she expressed as she got into the passenger seat of the car then added, "don't forget Gov", then went on to add, "when I look at it I guess I would be the same if it had been one of my cases too".

"Yeah I guess you're right", Steve remarked as he sat at the wheel, before adding, "it's my mind...it's this case it's getting to me", he sighed as he started up the engine, then headed off in the general direction of the estate known as the Marks Gate Estate.

The estate was so named after one of four lords who lived in and around that area, those being Lord Urswick, Lord Harvey, Lord Mildmay and of course Lord Marks. The estate had been built around the early nineteen fifties for the families who lost their homes after the Second World War, meaning that Carol's family could've been one of the earliest families to have occupied them, once they had been built.

It didn't take them long to make the journey to the still newish looking estate. The road they wanted ran straight through the middle with a row of shops nearby, reaching the end of the road they reached the address required. The house was a semi-detached with a joint porch way that had a brick built dustbin shed in the centre of the two front gardens. These were well tended too, with an array of roses outside the home where Carol Richards had lived.

Steve found himself knocking on the red, wooden front door that had a frosted glass top section and a silver letterbox and knocker. A white net curtain gathered in the middle decorated the entrance. After a moment the door was opened gingerly by a bare footed lady in her early fifties. She had short mousy brown hair and was wearing a pair of black trousers and a beige coloured T-shirt, a cigarette hung loosely in her right hand.

"Yes, Can I help you?" the woman enquired softly and with a curious look on her face.

"Before you ask", Steve returned softly, "we're not Jehovah's witnesses...ok. I am Detective Chief Inspector Price and this is my colleague, Acting Detective Constable Fuller and we would like to talk to you if that was alright with you, assuming you are Mrs. Richards that is", he explained as the pair of them carefully flashed their respective badges of office. "Would it be alright if we came in"?

"The police you say...and yes I am Mrs. Richards", she uttered as she stepped back. "What's happened now?" She continued to ask fearfully as she led them in to her lounge. This was to the left of them as they entered the building and floral wallpaper lined the hallway and up the staircase.

A three bar gas fire dominated the old tiled fireplace and her television stood on a wooden corner unit, with a video recorder beneath it and set in the left alcove. It was tuned into a morning programme which she had turned down with her remote control.

Green, leather, three piece suit took pride of place before a glass top coffee table that sat on a white rug. A large oil painting hung over the fireplace consisting of a mountain scene with a rushing stream flowing down the valley, passing through a forest with the sun rays penetrating the trees.

The mantelpiece was the home of several ornaments, including a brass horse, several white vases with flower scenes on them and a miniature statue of a boy and girl, behind which stood a white envelope.

Several pictures of her family dominated the walls on the two beige coloured alcoves either side of the fire place. Silvery, striped vinyl wallpaper covered the other three walls. A tall wooden cabinet with glass doors stood behind them and it housed more ornaments. On its top was an array of photo albums. The view from the window would've meant she must've seen them entering via the gate that had softly squeaked.

"Would you like a cup of tea?" She enquired as she indicated to them to sit down.

"No it's ok", Steve replied with a warm smile, Wendy just nodded to express her refusal as he sat in the armchair to the right.

Wendy found a seat on the settee, clutching her bag on her lap and leaning back against one of the three floral cushions that were carefully placed uniformly on each piece of the suit.

Mrs. Richards also sat on the settee, albeit at the opposite end, with her hands clasped between her knees and sitting on the edge of the seat with a fearful look on her face, as if she feared the worse.

"It's ok Mrs. Richards you haven't done anything wrong, not by a long shot", Wendy explained in a warm fashion, also now sitting on the edge of the seat.

"So what is all this about Inspector?" She finally quizzed after a moments silence, as they all composed themselves, she finally turned her attention to Steve who sat with the warm smile still on his face.

"We just need to ask you some rather delicate questions Mrs. Richards" Steve returned with an air or authority about his voice, but not wishing to cause any upset at this point in time. He was fully aware of the delicacy needed regarding his words at this point in time.

"It's Caroline actually...less formal; besides Richards was my married name. I'm divorced now if yer must know", she sadly explained, as she turned to briefly face Wendy before turning to look at the window.

"Ok Caroline, as I said, we just need to ask you some questions", he said still feeling unsure of his self then added, "we are here to talk about your late daughter and her last day..."

"You mean my Carol", she interrupted him, slowly finding her feet she went to the window, her left hand caressing her mouth as she bit gently on her finger. A strong sense of the past was catching up with her as she carefully toyed with the net curtain; her eyes were searching for the right words to say at this moment in time. "It was the death of our Carol that caused the divorce you see; he found it hard to come terms with her death; you understand Inspector", she uttered, turning to face them again but not before she removed a framed photograph from the window sill. She clutched it tightly in her hands and held it close to her chest as a hint of tears filled her eyes.

"Are you ok Caroline?" Wendy asked, as she reached out and touched her hand.

"Why have you brought this back up again after all these years Inspector", she enquired as she glanced down at the photograph. "it was a lifetime ago you see...I've searched for the truth ever since that terrible day when I was told by one of your officers that her body was found in Romford...it was a job to get my head around the words being said at the time. I thought it was a dream and I was going to wake up and she'd be in bed getting up for her breakfast as normal...but it wasn't normal was it...no...I couldn't believe it... you see not then...well not until I saw her body in that horrible place", she expressed soulfully, her voice quietened as she added; "she looked so peaceful. I half expected her to open her eyes with that usual smile she always had...she was always the good one, the best...it should never have happened to the likes of my Carol...I guess their right what they say...the good always die young", she said as she stared at the photograph.

"May I?" Steve politely asked.

She looked at him briefly a tear running down her cheek.

"What has happened Inspector to bring this about", she asked sadly, as she slowly handed the photograph over, feeling unsure of the situation.

Steve took it gently from her to look at it, only to find it was a picture of a young attractive girl sitting on a low wall with a field behind. There was a long wooden gate and a low hedge. The girl was wearing a floral dress with a pink cardigan and she was also wearing white ankle socks and a pair of black patent shoes with a buckled strap. Her long hair hung over her slender shoulder.

"Where and when was this taken Caroline, if you don't mind me asking?" Steve enquired as he returned to the comfort of the chair.

"On the wall outside 'The Harrow Pub' which is only over the road", she replied as she leant against the cabinet under the window, "She could always be found in that pub with Joe, her boyfriend that is".

"Yes we are aware of her late boyfriend", Steve replied.

"They were engaged to be married, they were planning to get married a couple of years later, after they had saved up enough money to put a five thousand pound deposit on a house, it got used to pay for her funeral instead".

"I see!" Steve remarked then went on to add, "Why don't you tell me about that day in nineteen fifty eight"?

"Why?!" She snapped curiously then went on to ask, "What has happened...are you going to tell me the killer has come to light after all these years?"

"We don't know yet, all I can say at this point in time is something has come to light regarding that situation, we have to follow it up for Carol's sake", Steve explained carefully trying not to give her false hope. "A few weeks ago a middle aged man was dying in hospital and he requested to speak to a police officer...he ended up telling him a story about the situation regarding your Carol...so I have been sent in to solve this case and that is why I want you to try and remember that day, so I can get a clear picture of the day...we have already got a statement from her friend Rose and...Well as Carol isn't around to tell me her side of the story we really need your help".

Wendy had already removed her notepad and pen from her bag which she then placed on the floor at the side of her.

"I will get a cup of tea first Inspector if you don't mind", she uttered as she made for the door.

"In that case we'll happily join you, ok". Steve returned with a smile as he carefully studied the photograph.

"You should be careful Gov", Wendy said very quietly.

"I am aware of the situation constable...but thanks for reminding me", Steve said biting his bottom lip and placing the photograph on the top of the coffee table with the picture facing the settee.

Wendy reached over to glance at the picture with a slight smile, "She was a good looking girl Gov". She said as she gently turned it in her direction.

"She was constable that's very true", Returned Caroline having re-entered the room briefly. Returning the picture to its rightful place on the window sill she went on to add., "She was also a very clever young lady, she had two GCE 'A' level and three 'O' levels and she wanted to go to university to study art and design".

"It was a shame she didn't go", returned Steve.

"Yes!" She said sadly, "that day you ask?" she said as she stood behind the settee, her hands trembling on its back.

"Take yeh time", Steve said softly, "why don't you go and make the tea and we can talk about whilst we drink".

A few minutes later she returned carrying a tray with a white and floral tea set on it, complete with a large teapot with steam that slowly drifted out of the spout, like a miniature chimney. There was a matching sugar bowl full of sugar lumps and a full milk jug which accompanied three cups and saucers with silver teaspoons. She carefully placed it on the coffee table then returned to the kitchen briefly to fetch a plate of biscuits which she also placed on the table before returning to her place on the settee.

There came the usual formalities regarding the teas with Steve sitting back in the chair holding the saucer in his left hand whilst drinking his tea with his right hand. He sensed this was her way of quelling the intense emotional feelings that were going around inside her head.

"So Inspector, you say there are new developments regarding the death of my Carol?" She asked as she sipped at her tea.

"You could say that", Steve returned, placing the cup on the saucer that he carefully held on his lap, "I was hoping you might enlighten me to the events of that day, assuming you can remember them that is".

"Remember them", she replied sadly gently placing her tea on the coffee table so she could stand up. "I live that day every day Inspector...hoping something might trigger the truth of the day...it is a case of 'if'...if only we had done something different, what if Joe's car hadn't broke down, what if they had changed their minds about the pictures or if the buses were more reliable...who knows", she remarked as she went to the cabinet under the window and opened one of the three drawers where she removed an old newspaper that she stared at for a moment, before returning to the settee.

Steve placed his half empty drink onto the coffee table before asking to look at the newspaper that was an old Daily Mail dated the twenty third of May, nineteen fifty eight and on the front page the heading read 'Young girl murdered in the churchyard', and read 'The death of a young girl named Carol Richards', and so Steve read to himself the story before Caroline started her side of the events of that day.

She sat on the edge of the settee, her hands clasped tightly in her lap and began..."That day started as it did every day with Carol getting up around ten o'clock in the morning, she had taken the day off to go out; she had her breakfast of cornflakes and a glass of milk; she hated tea and coffee; she claimed they made her feel sick.

It was around about eleven when her friend Rose phoned her to tell her to meet her in Romford market around one o'clock that afternoon. She had a shower and got dressed, it was a lovely day and she was worried about what to put on. She ended up choosing the green floral dress with a pastel green cardigan. I still have those clothes laid out on her bed; in fact her bedroom is as she left it, I can't bear to go in there these days.

She left before twelve to catch the bus and she gave me a kiss on the cheek and said she'd see me later.

I asked if she would like her dad to come and pick her up but she said Joe was meeting her that afternoon and felt sure he would make sure she got home safely. She gave me a warm smile as she waved goodbye that was the last time I saw her alive.

She did phone me around four o'clock to tell me about Joe and the situation regarding the car, but said she was going to the cinema with Rose instead and not to worry about her...but how can you not worry these days...She did say that there had been some trouble with a group of lads in a flashy car but that was it, she said Rose sent them packing...she was the wild one you know",

"Yes I read the statement she made", Steve replied calmly, he was glued to her every word. "Do carry on Caroline".

"Yes", she remarked with pouted lips and a lingering sigh, "There wasn't anything else, well not until the next morning when we were informed by one of your officers, who sat us down and told us of her death in Romford market...the other half broke down and said he wished he'd gone over to the cinema and picked them both up...you see Inspector he blamed himself for not being there for her...she was the apple of his eye".

"Can we talk to your husband about this?" Steve pursued cagily.

"Not unless you're a medium", she replied with a slight grin. "He was killed in a road accident several years after her death...you see, he couldn't come to terms with her death".

      "You said she mentioned a flashy car and a group of boys pestering them", Steve remarked, then went on to add, "I can tell you the driver of that car is dead himself, due to a fatal illness, but he confessed to a fellow officer how he, along with his friends, tormented your daughter and her friend Rose and as you rightly said Rose saw them off...but later they came back and when they saw her at the bus stop they offered her a lift home, while she was waiting for the bus as you said. The girls had some chips and Rose got on her bus first, but the driver of the car liked your Carol and said he didn't have anything to do with her death. He stressed that he had sat in the car and waited all the time and he remembered his friends returning to the car and laughing, so he assumed all was well. He didn't know what had happened, not until he read the newspapers a few days later", He said as he picked up the paper again. "I believe your Carol knew them, from her school days maybe, and that's why she went with them thinking they were going to take her home. I can confirm that, as I have a witness who saw them returning to the car and speeding off in what they thought was an American car".

      "What was the name of this

driver", asked a voice from behind them. They spun around in surprise as they had not heard anyone enter the room.

"It's ok Inspector this is my son Michael".

"What was the name of this driver you talked about Inspector?" he repeated, eager to learn the truth. He was around five foot six inches tall, slim with short cropped hair and was wearing jeans and a black t-shirt with 'Anarchy' written across it.

"His name was George...George Blackmore...why do you know of him?" Steve questioned.

"Hmm!" he smirked as he leant on the back of the settee. "I know of him, he used to go around in a gang of about six or seven of them at school. They were in a class two years in front of me and the school was scared of them, especially one of them, I believe his name was Danny something...he fancied himself a bit. He would always beat you up for looking at him and you didn't grass him up for fear of getting hurt...but George was alright, he used to bring flowers every year on that day saying he knew her and she was in his thoughts".

"Do you know any others in that gang who might be able to help us get to the bottom of this once and for all", Steve tried to reassure them.

"You want King...Johnny King; he

was one of them who scared even Danny...who by the way fancied himself with the girls. I heard back then that if he didn't get a girl for the night he'd get mental thinking he was now ugly and that was why the girls hated him...he believed he was god's gift to women".

"Sounds like another Danny I know", commented Wendy who was noting down everything on her pad.

"And where might we get to talk to this Mr. King?" Steve quizzed.

"He owns a car lot in Ilford, at the back of the station". The lad replied.

"In that case we'll leave it at that then, but we just wanted you to know that we haven't forgotten about your Carol, not by a long chalk. I believe we have a lead to this case and I feel sure we'll get to the bottom of it Caroline", he said as he found his feet and after retrieving a custard cream biscuit that he dipped in the remains of his tea he and Wendy made their way to the front door. "I will personally keep you informed of the situation and you'll be the first to know who killed her, ok eh", he reassured them of his concern regarding their loss.

Chapter 32

They headed for the home of the Blackmore's, due to it being on route to Ilford, where Steve had decided to pay this Mr. King a visit. His mind dwelt on the comments that had been made regarding this person, whose name happened to be Danny, a name that even made Wendy remark about how she knew a Danny.

He found himself doing a balancing act with what he believed were crazy notions about the missing person being a Danny.

"What did yeh make of that little episode Gov?" Wendy enquired, once they were on the road, as she clutched her hand bag in her lap.

"You mentioned something about a Danny that you know constable", Steve enquired curiously, keeping his eyes firmly fixed on the road ahead as they headed out of the estate, "to whom were you thinking of may I ask?"

"Sergeant Peter's of course Gov", she replied openly, with a smile on her face.

"Why do you mention him then?"

"Because he's a creep that's why", she snapped, turning briefly to look out of the window, "besides Gov, all the girls in the office can't stand him. He tends to think he's god's gift to women and he thinks he can order us girls to go out with him at a flick of his fingers".

"And what do the girls do about it?" Steve asked with a slight snigger under his breath.

"We just tell him to get stuffed...I know a couple of the girls went out with him and they said he was so arrogant and there were times when they felt intimidated by his actions. I know one of the girls felt that she could get physically hurt if she turned him down".

"I see Constable, it looks like I'm going to have to look very carefully into this Danny or I should say Sergeant Peter's. He seems to interest me a little...it seems to me to be an impossible thing for me to consider regarding his police background, eh constable", Steve remarked cagily, glancing at Wendy as he slowed in traffic, then went on to add, "I know he was on this case of the dead girl in the sixties when he joined the force at Romford...he could've...no it is impossible to even go there", he hesitated at the very thought of a fellow officer being the killer, "tell me constable, have any of you girls ever heard of or encountered a tramp named Sid by any chance, on your rounds?"

"Stinky Sid!" She replied with a quaint little smirk.

"I gather that is a yes then?" he replied with a serious tone in his voice.

"Yes Gov, we all have encountered him, he is a cheeky sod", she replied jovially, "he's forever trying to chat us up".

"A bit like Danny then eh?"

"You're joking, Danny scares us silly but with Sid it's an act on his part...you know a bit of harmless banter, we can imagine he was quite a lady's man in his youth, it's a shame he ended up like he has".

"That is because he lost his family in the war and his house too, that is why he has ended up like he has constable".

"Then you know him Gov?"

"Nah! His name was mentioned to me by a friend who claimed he knew everything that has happened in the market since the end of the war that is. Now I want to meet up with him and talk about the past; who knows, he just might know the truth about the past and I know it sounds strange, but I have this gut feeling, he might even unknowingly know the killer of Carol Richards, however he may have been overlooked back then because he was a drunken idiot".

"The last time I saw him he was drinking a cup of tea at the burger bar in the market square, that was a few weeks ago though...he was looking a bit red faced and busy talking to a couple of old gentlemen who seemed keen to hear his stories...that's right Gov, he is forever telling stories of the past...I think those old guys were interested in writing a book on Romford after the war, so I was told when I enquired after them whilst I was on duty that is".

It wasn't long before they reached the home of the Blackmore's and soon removed the boxes and returned them to the family, declaring there wasn't anything of interest in them but thanked them for making the effort of getting them to the station as requested, and so promptly. Lucy having read her statement that was now typed up said she was happy to sign it, hoping this would be the end of it for the sake of George. He had lived with this story throughout his entire adult life, afraid to tell anybody out of fear of meeting his end in the same manner as that young girl who had been murdered by a ruthless killer.

Steve got the feeling that the whole family just wanted to put this whole incident behind them with the hope of finding a new future for everyone.

Lucy expressed her deepest feelings of despair, by declaring that somehow she had to come to terms with the past. Now she knew the truth of why George had so desperately wanted to emigrate to Australia years ago. At that time she believed it was just to join up with his brother out there. Little did she know at the time it was because he believed that it would end the nightmare of the past? However because Lucy was totally unaware of that past at the time, she was unable to understand his reasoning behind his determination to do it. But now as she stared deeply at his framed photograph she said to herself, *'why didn't you tell back then...I would've understood...you fool',* the photo was originally on her mantelpiece, but now she held in her hands and pressed it against her heaving chest, as she faced the wall over the fireplace with tears in her eyes that slowly trickled down her face because she was feeling guilty for not believing in him.

Steve went to her side to give her some comfort and asked her if there was anything she required, as he touched her gently on her bare shoulder. She declined as she softly touched his caring hand, giving it a gentle squeeze to thank him for his concern.

"If you have any trouble don't hesitate to call me...you hear Lucy", he reassured her by placing his card on the mantelpiece. She just returned his gesture with a weepy smile and a nod of the head to thank him.

With the first of the freshly signed statements neatly tucked away in the file and now laying on the back seat of the car where Wendy had tossed it, they were back in the car and on their way again.

They were soon heading for Ilford and the encounter with this Johnny King character in his car lot. Steve casually asked Wendy if she fancied a coffee, as he had seen a cafe on the outskirts of the high street of Chadwell Heath, in the direction of Goodmayes. It was amidst a parade of shops that he had noticed with Ian, sometime earlier in his travels, which had lead up to this moment in time.

Wendy's reply was a simple relaxed exchange of words with reference to the situation at present, in relation to the interview with Mr. King. She felt it would be better to get the interview out of the way, before they had a coffee. In her mind she was determined to find a result to this case, especially regarding the so called dead girl, now referred to as simply 'the churchyard murder'.

She still had some doubts about the direction that Steve was taking her towards, because at the start of this she was led to believe they were on the case regarding the recent murder of Jack. She was edging in the direction of confronting Steve over his actions, as there was a gut feeling that she wanted to question his motives and hopes of solving Jack's murder.

It wasn't long before they came face to face with the car showroom that had a series of boats also on sale in the forecourt. The cars were more upmarket here with an office to the left of the overhead line. A nearby lay-by on the main road made good use of by Steve who stopped there. Leaving the car locked the pair of them headed for the car lot, unaware of the situation which was about to present itself. Wendy had removed the file and placed it under her seat out of sight and out of mind as they would say.

They were met by a young enthusiastic lad in a crisp new, navy suit and a navy tie over a clean white shirt, with the usual banter that accompanied his position, "Can I help you sir?"

"Yeah is the boss at home lad?" Steve said with a slight cough and a smile.

Wendy stood silently by, tucking her bag tightly under her arm and looked on with an air of authority in her face.

The lad led them through a set of glass panelled doors into an elegant showroom with an array of prestigious cars ranging from BMW's to a couple of Mercedes. They were led to a desk where a young, well dressed young girl was typing.

"Clare can you take care of these people, please, they want to talk to the boss", returned the lad who pointed to the girl in question, with a shrug of his shoulders before returning to the forecourt and another would be customer who would be engrossed in his banter. Prestigious cars needed sale staff to match was the forte on the establishment.

"Follow me!" She ordered as she found her feet and headed for a frosted glass panelled door that led them into a corridor with four offices on either side. Reaching the end she knocked gently on the door and waited for the usual return of 'enter!"

"There's a couple here to see you Mr. King", Clare said politely, allowing them to enter the office

The office space was rather minimalistic in its appearance, with cream coloured walls and a large picture of a yacht sailing in the sea hung on the wall behind him. A window overlooked a narrow river where a couple of small boats were moored. Behind them and against the facing wall was a small coffee machine.

He was holding a phone in his left hand with his elbow on the desk; his head partly bowed averting his attention from the present intrusion; as he supported the phone that he held to his ear. Their entrance interfered with the phone call that made him explain to the person on the other end that he would call them later.

He was a big man, heavily built with cropped hair and a roundish clean shaven face. He was wearing a dark grey, pin striped suit with a pale blue striped shirt and a blue and white striped tie. His suit jacket was neatly draped over the back of his cushioned chair, "What can I do for you", he enquired having returned the receiver back to its rightful place and turning his eyes in their direction, resting his chin on his hands as his elbows were placed on the edge of his modern wooden desk.

"You are Johnny King I presume?" enquired Steve, as he stood by the desk. Wendy stayed back slightly, leaving Steve to do the business.

"Do I get the feeling you two are the filth?" He said, with a pouting of his lips as he found his feet and headed for the coffee machine where he proceeded to make himself a drink, "Am I right or am I right", he grinned

"You are right Mr. King", Steve replied casually, "I am Detective Chief Inspector Price and this is my colleague Detective Constable Fuller", and he said flashing his badge.

"It doesn't mean a thing to me Inspector", he said with a cheeky little grin, "Right then what's this all about then?" he asked as he made his drink, "Coffee anyone?"

Just then there came a knock on the door and it was opened by the lad who said, "There's a guy who wants to talk to you about that Merck boss".

"Tell him I'll speak to him later, can't you see I'm rather tied up at the moment, this is the police by the way", he explained as he made for his desk again, this time sitting on the corner of his desk.

Steve removed the photograph from his inside jacket pocket and gently placed it on the desk before him.

"What do we have here then?" he replied, after a moments silence broken only by his reply, having lifted the old photograph off his desk to study it more carefully. "Where did you get this from Inspector?"

"It was in the effects of a George Blackmore who died a few weeks ago".

"Well I never", he uttered, then went on to add, "poor old George, he was a good lad, I knew him years ago...it's been a long time since I last saw this picture if you didn't know. I was a bit of a lad in those days...well we all were back then...wild that is. I guess that's how I got into this game, I mean George's older brother was in this game as well and you could say he taught us all to sell cars...but my god I can remember this car, it was fantastic for its day...but today it would be seen as a crap motor, but I guess that's the way of the world for you these days...so Inspector what has this got to do with me?" He enquired curiously as he rose to his feet and headed for the open window, having returned the photo back onto the surface of his desk.

The sound of an express train heading to Southend rattled through the nearby station, causing him to close the window.

"I understand that back in the fifties you were part of a gang that haunted the streets, is that right?" Steve continued to question him. Picking up the photo to replace it back into his pocket for safe keeping.

"I told you I was a bit of a lad in those days, in fact we all were", he said as he returned to the corner of his desk before picking up his coffee and taking a sip.

"In the photograph there are some lads, can you name them for me?"

"Show me it again", he sighed.

Steve had to remove it again to let him see it, this time he seemed different regarding the photo as he took it from him to study it more carefully. "Well!" remarked Steve after a moment's silence.

"Let me see inspector", he said as he again found his feet and this time he made for his seat where he removed a pair of glasses from his jacket pocket and proceeded to put them on, pouting his lips as he studied the photo. "You've got to remember Inspector, this was taken in another lifetime, but yes I do recognise them. They are, or were Alphie Green, Ian Carter George Blackmore and I believe the other one is Kevin Blackmore", he said before handing it back to Steve and removing his glasses then replacing them back into his jacket pocket.

"I understand there was also a lad named Danny, who was afraid of you, is that right?"

"Bloody hell Inspector we are digging deep now...again that's a name from the past, you are talking about Danny Peters. He thought he was the king pin until he came up against me that is...we were in school one day and we all took ropes in the gym and he demanded I give him mine, when I said no...He got angry and punched me right in the face, but he got a big surprise though when I replied to him saying 'is that all you've got?' That really did get right up his nose you could say, he turned his attention on taking it out on another young lad, that was until I stepped in and threatened him".

"Then what happened?"

"He tried to punch out my lights again; but I was too much for him. I just rammed his head into the wooden horse, knocked the poor bastard out cold...the funny thing about it all we...Ugh...became good friends after that little incident. I think he wanted to be on my side in the gang".

"So Mr. King tell me about this Danny Peters then?" Steve hedged his bets on what the outcome would be, as he walked to the window to see the view.

"It's Johnny ok, only business men call me Mr. King especially when they want my money, so why all the interest in that picture and the events in that time?" he enquired as he drank some of his coffee.

"It's in reference to an incident in the late fifties that interests me Johnny, there happens to be something somehow in this photo that is linked to that little incident and we are just following up the lead in regards to this photo you see", Steve remarked as he turned and sat on the window ledge leaning back against the window with his arms folded in front of him.

"The late fifties you say?" he said rubbing his chin and pouting his lips.

"Yeah that's right", he replied casually.

"That was when that photo was taken and if my memory serves me right it was Danny who took it", he said hesitantly, "I was supposed to be in it but I was rather busy with some bird, we were doing the business...if you get my drift".

"So who was the young lady you were having fun with?" Wendy asked curiously.

"Don't say anything, but it was George's missus, you know, Lucy, it's a shame, I did like her, still George was the winner in the end". He said with a smile on his face, he then went on to enquire, "This, by any chance wouldn't happen to be connected to the time George's brother beat him up for borrowing his car".

"And where were you when he...as you say, borrowed his brother's car".

"Me!" he snapped, "I was up West with this tasty bird. I took her to the flicks in the city; she wanted to watch that new Paul Newman film".

"One hot summer's day", returned Wendy.

"She's good Inspector".

"And that was the year Brazil won the World Cup".

"She really is good", he said with a surprised grin, so Inspector", he uttered with a slight cough and a little grunt. "What is it you really want to know"?

"Danny Peters, tell me what you know about him, for example do you think he could...Ugh...let's say...hmm...kill some one".

"I see!" He remarked finding his feet again he made for the coffee machine in order to gain his sense of normality, utilising the time to recall the past. Not before making that offer to them if they wanted a coffee too, but they both declined as he returned to the desk with his fresh coffee in his hand. "In school some of the pupils said he would threaten them with a knife if they didn't give him their pocket money...but as for actually killing somebody, that is a very difficult question to answer",

"Why is that then?" Steve pressed.

"Well...there's a fine line between threatening and actually killing somebody, unless it was an accident that is. But anyway I have heard through the grapevine that he's one of your lot these days...so why don't you question him personally".

"Oh I intend to", Steve remarked sharply, as he found his feet and headed for the door but was briefly stopped by Johnny.

"By the way Inspector I know I met up with Danny a couple of years later and we had a few jars in the local, whilst we were playing a game of pool he boasted about shagging some bird in the cemetery in Romford market".

"And what did you do?"

"I laughed at him and took it with a pinch of salt...the idiot was always making false claims, he was a bit of a laugh eh".

"Yeah you're right Johnny, that's

the impression I get too", Steve laughed, "I'm sorry for taking up your time Johnny. I don't think we need to continue this conversation any further", he remarked as he left the office and made his way to the exit and fresh air. The question that weighed heavily on his mind was where did he take this case now, as he started to put the case together, "Coffee Constable?" he said as he crossed the road to retrieve his car, "What did you make of that little episode then eh", he continued as they walked to the car.

"I get the feeling Gov that you know more than you are letting on".

"Maybe you're right Constable", he said calmly before repeating it with a softer tone, then went on to say, "but there's still that little niggily bit that is annoying me", he said stopping briefly and went on to add, "and I just can't put my little finger on it and that is, 'Why' constable?" He remarked before continuing on his way, "why did they have to kill her, why not just leave her or better still take her part of the way home...it just doesn't make any sense and if Peters was involved, as it appears to be so, he of all people should've been more careful about his actions, in fact he should never have been involved in such a crime...but I don't know, somehow it does make some sense I guess...still we'll chat over a coffee ok", he remarked once they reached the car.

Chapter 33

"What has this car business got to do with the two murders we are investigating Gov?" enquired a concerned Wendy, as she gently stirred her coffee in the cafe, appropriately named Sloppy Joe's.

It was an English run establishment with walls decorated in a pastel green above and a darker green panelled bottom which in turn were separated by a white glossy dado rail. Above this there were pictures of various sights of London. They sat at a table in the window which was half covered by a net curtain which was mounted on a thin metal pole placed on appropriate hooks screwed into the woodwork. The table was decorated with a gingham table cloth and the usual condiments supported the menu.

"The car is the Achilles heel of the killer in this case constable", Steve said informatively.

"What gets me Gov is how you come to know all this. I mean if they didn't get it back then in their investigation, especially in the beginning mainly, well I just can't get my head around it. What has this got to do with the murder of Jack, surely that car has long since gone?"

"You're right about that Constable", Steve replied as he put a couple of spoonfuls of sugar into his coffee, then added, "The killer knows the importance of that car because it was a prototype, only six of them were ever made at that time. One of them was given to Kevin Blackmore, the oldest of the brothers of George. We now know he borrowed the car on that terrible night when Carol lost her life. Something Kevin never knew about, as it was never mentioned".

"So! How did you learn about it then?" She pursued carefully, all ears eager for the answer.

"What the killer didn't know, at the time of their little exploits...was that not far from them they were spotted by a young man sitting in his car with his girlfriend. When he saw the car he was in awe of it, never having seen anything like it before, well I said it was a prototype...but then he saw the lads fleeing from the alley by the church. One of them was waving some girls knickers in the air and laughing out loud, before they sped off".

"And how come you know all this

stuff?" she enquired, with her elbows on the table and clutching her coffee in both hands, enthralled by the line of conversation which was taking shape.

Steve leant back in the chair toying with the silver spoon on the table, then went on to explain, "Actually I didn't want this job regarding the murder of Jack, in fact I told them to leave it to the local plod", he said half heartedly bowing his head.

"So what changed your mind then", Wendy enquired, feeling puzzled by his sudden change in attitude.

"Well it was something that happened at the Home Office; you see, they received a letter from a person serving time in prison for allegedly murdering his wife...it was said he injected a lethal dose of Heroin into her neck that killed her out right in seconds. She had been watching television when he came home...he claimed. He brought home a friend, who needed a bed for the night, but when he woke up the next morning he found her dead in the armchair and no sign of the so called friend. The law claimed he was making the story up in order to clear his name, but in the eyes of the law it didn't work as he is now serving life for his action...but having spoken to him, I believe his story about that unknown friend who went missing to be true".

"Does this person have a name?"

"Of course he does; his name happens to be Andrew Cox and before you ask, he was the lad who was in the car that saw them lads back then. So you could say he is a key witness in this case, he saw the killer more than once...I believe he met him in a pub and unknowingly he told him the story of that night and how he fell in love with the motor they left in...He was totally unaware about the killing.

But the killer realised for the first time the significance of that car, so he had to eliminate him from the scene. However at the time he couldn't kill him, but instead he had the idea of stitching him up by killing his wife, while he was asleep, as he was out of his head at the time".

"And now you think it was Sergeant Peters who did it?"

"If you are after a straight answer to that question my answer would have to be a yes, in every case Constable, but we have one serious problem on our hands regarding this case...we have to...Ugh...prove it totally, you know Constable, or we could end up with egg on our face...and you know how the powers to be feel about nailing a fellow officer...the truth becomes a probability when you look at the situation more carefully".

It was about then that a young couple entered the establishment, sending a brief gust of wind through the place as they opened the door. The young girl was complaining about the lad wanting to go to the pub and feeling threatened for being told he had a choice, *'fags or booze'*, he couldn't have both as they didn't have a lot of money, and he was demanding it was his god given right to have both, whereby she simply replied, *'if that's right then go and get a job then you lazy git'*.

Steve looked at Wendy having heard the words being said, and said to himself 'charming'.

The couple sat halfway down the cafe at a table by the wall, there was the sense that the lad wished he was somewhere else other than in this humble place. She had that smug look on her face, believing that she had got one over on him, but you sensed it was only the beginning. She took out a packet of cigarettes and offered him one; he reluctantly took one but soon lit it.

"What we need to do Constable is see if we can get a photo of Peters so we can see if he fits the person Andrew Cox met in the pub", He said as he drank the last of his coffee. "We would need to get some photos of a series of men so he didn't realise what was happening...we know he made a few mistakes regarding this case. Namely he mentions to Rose about getting a chance to go to college in

Hendon, which we know is the police college...and we know he was connected to that car that was seen several times, both outside the cinema and in the backstreet after the murder of Carol. We also know he boasted about it to Johnny King in the pub many years later...the questions at the moment are how and why he allegedly killed the girl".

"It's strange Gov how one simple act can change the course of history, for example if George hadn't borrowed his brother's car history would've been different. It is hard to come to terms with when you think of it in that light".

"I guess you're right, but again it all comes down to that little word, 'if!...If only!' if only Jack had stayed in Harlow he too would be still alive...but you are right his one little act has destroyed other people's lives. We know Alfie Green and Ian Carter are both dead, along with George Blackmore, the only one not dead is Peters".

"How come you know those two lads are dead too", she asked curiously as she ordered another coffee from the waitress, by using her fingers to gesture the request.

"Because I know they were murdered in Australia some time ago and they were with a third party, who vanished shortly after the bodies of the lads were found on the beach in a place called Townsville".

"I know Peters went abroad with some friends this year, but he didn't say where he was going; merely saying that he was off to warmer climes".

"It would appear that there is more to this Peters business than one can imagine...somehow he kills a girl in nineteen fifty eight; later he kills the wife of Cox, because the car becomes evidence that could link him to that murder. That enlightens him to the importance of that car and he realizes it could link him to the murder, because he knew he took the photo which was another one of his stupid acts in this case...at that time he was young and stupid and his own actions will lead to his own downfall".

"So what you are saying is...had he simply forgot what he did and concentrated on his job no-body else would've got hurt".

"You've got it in one", he replied as the waitress placed their two coffees on the table to the 'thank you' accompanied by a polite smile from the both of them. "The problem we have at present is proving it to be true...he thinks he has escaped the situation by killing those who were involved in the incident".

"Perhaps Gov...If Johnny King had been present at the time, maybe the girl might've still been alive today also". Wendy said calmly as she sugared her coffee.

The philosophical side of life played heavy on Steve's mind as he remembered back into his own past where that little word of 'if only' had cropped its ugly head up. He toyed with the prospect of what might've been could it have meant the future would be altered for the whole world. Her survival might've meant Sally may have married the one who calls himself the Maverick and saying to himself 'what of me in the light of this word 'if'.

If the history had not been the same, I might not have joined the police force and done something different. Who knows Peters might've been a Detective now. We just don't know. We just have to accept the inevitable in life and ponder on what might've been from time to time. The truth was; he realized he was faced with a difficult situation, one he dreaded because of the nature of the situation at hand.

"A penny for yeh thoughts Gov?" said Wendy breaking the silence that had briefly overcome them.

"Sorry I was miles away", he sighed picking up his coffee and taking a sip, "I guess this case is getting to me Constable, especially regarding this situation with Peters. The thought of arresting a fellow officer is daunting, but necessary, but it doesn't get any easier...we still need all the evidence in this case to make it stick...all I can say is, no-one could've predicted the death of George Blackmore. Even more so the fact that he had to release the truth of the past during the last moment's of his life as he did, in doing so he dug up the past and opened a can of worms...how was he to know it would spell death for the officer who had to listen to his story", he said quietly, as he removed the photo from his jacket pocket to study it yet again.

"It was a good job it wasn't Peters who went to get the message".

"That's true Constable", he said with a hint of smile.

"May I Gov?" she asked holding out her hand, hoping to see this relevant photo that has caused so much trouble. "It's hard to imagine that Carol Richards was alive and well when this photo was taken and the only thing with Peters was he was a bully at school...how ironic".

"Lets get back to the factory Constable, I'm getting concerned about the complexities of this case already", he said soulfully downing what was left of his warm coffee, before returning the photo back to his pocket for safety purposes. He knew he couldn't let Peters know about it not until he was dead sure he could get a conviction.

"You are feeling guilty about the prospect of having to arrest a colleague...especially for murder on several counts Gov", returned a concerned Wendy who had already finished her coffee.

"I guess you are right...are we ready?" he said finding his feet.

"Yes Gov!" She remarked picking up her bag she headed for the door as Steve went to the counter to pay the bill.

The usual noises and smells greeted them as they found their place in the car park of the police station in Romford, with the market in full swing full of the banter and smells which seemed never ending since time had began.

They were stopped by Reg as they entered the main reception area.

"I have a message for you Inspector", he ordered quietly.

"Ok Reg what is it?" Steve asked as he leant against the counter.

"Somebody named Frank said he wanted to talk to you and he said he'd be in the market place this afternoon, by the burger bar...he said you'd know what it was all about".

Steve just smiled at his words and nodded to let him know he knew what he meant regarding the meeting.

"I gather that's your friend who knows Sid", expressed Wendy, "would you like me to join you Gov or are you going alone?"

"I think you can join me at this point in time Constable, I gather you are keen to get to the bottom of this case", he returned as they turned around and headed for the door and a short walk to the market place. "D'ya fancy a burger now Constable?" Steve said with a laugh in his step.

The sun was hiding behind a cloud making the air feel cool; several buses were heading in both directions. A police siren echoed on the airwaves.

"I'm getting to like this Detective work, it beats hanging about in the office doing mundane jobs". She said as they walked.

"I guess you don't want to go back to that line of work then?" Steve continued to smile, tucking his hands deep into his trouser pockets to keep them warm.

The area was alive with people all milling about, some unaware of their intentions, just out to waste time looking at everything on offer. Steve tended to hate the crowds of people who seemed to get in his way. The smell of the burger bar was enticing to the nose as they headed for the smell and the thought of biting into a burger in a bun topped with a slice of cheese.

"My treat Constable", he said removing his wallet, taking out a five pound note for the purchase once they stood in a queue at the bar where Steve had stood before talking to the couple who owned it. He just gave him a smile when he noticed Steve waiting.

"What can I get you Inspector?" asked the stall holder, his wife as usual was cooking in the background.

"Two cheese burgers please mate...we were asked to meet somebody named Frank here, you wouldn't know anything about him by any chance would you Governor", Steve enquired.

"Frank you say?" he replied, pouting his lips as he took the five pound note to get him his change once he gave his wife the order.

At the same time a young man called out for a bacon roll and the owner just acknowledged the order with a fleeting smile and an explanation that it would be one pound fifty.

"All I know is that they call him the walking encyclopaedia". Steve explained.

"You amaze me Gov, you've only been here for five minutes and you already know some of the more colourful locals", commented Wendy. She stood with her back to the bar, her eyes peeled on the passing people who interested her. They seemed to look at her in a different light, now she was out of her uniform. In her clean fresh uniform she could be seen to demand respect in some quarters, while in other areas it would give her grief. The abuse was aimed directly at the uniform. In her early training days she had to put up with those hurtful chants and had to quickly learn to take them in her stride, albeit being part of her basic training. So she was now beginning to feel at ease with her new found position in life and as she had explained earlier, she was enjoying her new found status. She quickly realised that now the public didn't even give her a second glance.

"I assume you know him too", Steve uttered.

"I should do he's one of Jackson's, you know, snouts", she explained quietly as she half turned to face him. "I don't think Jackson would take it lightly if he knew you were touting one of his snouts", she explained, taking charge of her burger and proceeded to put tomato ketchup on it.

Steve took a bite of his whilst looking around him at the passing people, his eyes peeled to their faces hoping to catch a glimpse of the person named Frank.

"Inspector!" remarked the stall

holder who appeared to be able to overlook the masses in his favour, "The person you are after is sitting on the wall of the churchyard, and I just spotted him ok eh".

"Cheers mate!" Steve said between bites then headed in the general direction of the wall in question. Wendy trotted behind munching on her burger and feeling like a would be tourist, "so how long has Frank been a snout for Jackson then?"

"Years Gov", she replied.

"Right...ok...it looks like our friend is here", he said on seeing him sitting on the wall as directed. He was looking scruffy in a tatty old navy coloured track suit and toying with a bottle of cider, occasionally taking swigs from it.

"Ah, Inspector I gather you got my message then", he expressed joyfully, "your cousin told me I had to look after you on his behalf...besides there's a couple of pints in it for me if I did".

"Yes Frank, I did get the message, so what is it you wanted to tell me then?" Steve enquired as he found solace sitting on the wall beside him.

Wendy kept her distance, standing eating her burger whilst admiring a stall that had jewellery on sale. She still managed to keep a sharp eye on Steve though. She was intrigued with the thought of encountering one of Jackson's snouts like this; inside she was aware of the feelings if he ever found out.

"I managed to locate Sid for you", he explained, taking yet another swig from his bottle, then went on to add, "and I had words with him, but he said he would only talk to you if you were alone. Somewhere where no-one will know or even see him with you, because for some unknown reason he seems to fear the police. But somehow he seems to favour you over the rest and that includes Jackson...don't ask me why but he just does".

"I have my own thoughts on that theory sunshine, so don't you worry your little head about it...so the question is where and when?" Steve demanded as he took another bite of his burger and looked at Wendy with a raising of his eyebrows and a half-hearted grin.

"I gather the bird is another copper right", Frank uttered as he too watched her.

"She's with me and she's Detective Constable Fuller",

"I know, I've seen her about with her other female friends in their nice, pretty uniforms", he giggled; "You know what I mean Inspector?" he said with a little growl, then took a long swig on the bottle.

"So what about Sid, where can we meet up, it is very important"?

"He's been watching you for the last five minutes making sure you are alone, well apart from the girl that is", he said looking around himself, "He's everywhere and yet he's nowhere you could say".

"You're not making any sense, are you sure you are telling me the truth and not just pissing me off".

"Let me tell you a little bit about your friend Sid. He is Sid Atkins and during the war he was head of overseas intelligence, he went behind enemy lines to gather information about the enemy and relay his findings back to HQ. The Jerry's never knew he was there; so you see Inspector, he was so clever in his day he could be standing right beside you and you would never know it, in fact he could've eliminated you at the flick of a finger".

"So he was in the SAS", Steve snapped. "So is he here now then?" He continued looking around at the masses of people milling about in the market place.

Frank smiled at Steve's actions, at the same time he pulled back the sleeve on the left arm of his tatty track suit top to reveal a large dialled wristwatch and just simply said, "in ten minutes go into the church and sit in the end of the third row from the door, that's all I have to tell you Inspector, then it is all up to you and the lass...ok!"

"I hope you're not playing games with me Frank because...."

"Ten minutes in the church, third row", he interrupted, putting his finger to his mouth then pointing it at Steve, as he found his feet and headed off into the masses, leaving his now empty bottle on the wall. Occasionally glancing back with a cheeky little smile on his reddened face, this was due to the drink.

Chapter 34

Wendy edged slowly forward to join Steve by the wall. Both watched the cheeky departure of the wily character known as Frank, right to the time he vanished into the crowd. They were left starry eyed and amused by his cloak and dagger attitude to the situation. Steve turned slowly and stared thoughtfully at the church. The old building stood well back from the market place. Many ancient and some modern tomb stones lay in rows, their headstones facing east towards the rising of the sun.

Wendy looked curiously about her glancing at the people milling around oblivious to their problems. Suddenly she felt strange about the whole experience of working with the public in this manner. She realised that she was out of her comfort zone, because when she was wearing her regulation uniform she was looked upon as somebody in authority; where certain people were afraid of her presence; but now she looked just like everybody else going about their lives.

Steve stared at the building, remembering the past when he had to meet the Major in the church in London while living on the streets. His mind played games with him as he casually looked at his watch, with a sigh he expressed his wishes to do as he had been told and make his way into the grounds of the church yard.

Wendy exercised etiquette, by putting the wrapper of her finished burger into the same bin, along with the discarded bottle, just where Steve had placed his rubbish earlier. She was then forced to have to make a few lady like running steps to catch him up, as he was already walking the path that lead to the main entrance. He stopped briefly and half turned with a cheeky little grin as he watched her catch him up.

"This is all so strange Gov", she sighed on reaching his side, "I mean all this cloak and dagger stuff, it's unnerving to say the least", she uttered.

"Why, is it getting to you Constable?" Steve said curiously as he looked at her in a professional manner, "Just say so and you can return to the factory".

"You are joking Gov, this is what I've always dreamed of doing ever since I was a kid, but I never thought I'd get the chance though",

"Are we fit then?"

"Yes!" She replied as they headed for the rendezvous with the character known as Sid, totally unaware of who or what he looked like and assuming he would be inside.

A young couple were standing to one side of the main entrance talking about wanting to get married in the church sometime in the future.

"Are you married Constable?" Steve quizzed as they neared the entrance.

"Not yet Gov, we hope to get wed in a couple of year's time when we've saved the money for a deposit on a house", she said joyfully.

The creaking of the door echoed in the main area. The altar and the business end looked majestic in its glory. They soon found their seats along the third row in from the main entrance as they had been ordered. They looked around at the emptiness of the place where even a whisper could be heard echoing off the high walls. Steve sat back with his arms folded in front of him as he found the seat on the left side of that grand hall, while Wendy sat on the end of the row on the right. She leant forward placing her arms on the pews in front of her. A fragrant aroma of incense mingled in the air and played havoc with their senses.

"So Gov where is this character Sid then...isn't he supposed to be here?" she said turning her head in his direction. He simply shrugged his shoulders to indicate he didn't know.

Just then the far door opened and the priest entered the area and started to do things at the raised altar as if he was unaware of them sitting there. Steve's eyes were averted in his direction more out of curiosity than instinct, putting his finger to his mouth and going 'shush', when he sensed Wendy was about to say something. Putting the knuckle of his first finger of his left hand to his mouth he pondered on the prospect of the unknown future that awaited them.

Time was slipping by and Steve was getting impatient with the events occurring and was about to get up from his seat when a sudden feeling ran through his body.

"I thought you wanted to talk to me Mr. Policeman, or have I been misinformed by a certain little pip squeak?" The surprising voice came from the area around the altar.

Steve got to his feet and headed for the altar and the priest who still stood with his back to them. "You are the one called Sid...Sid Atkins?" he asked when he neared him.

The elderly priest stopped doing what he was doing and slowly turned to meet his adversaries that were slowly approaching him; at the same time he leant briefly against the altar rail. He stood around six feet tall and had receding silvery grey hair, with a matching moustache. His once reddened face now looked much more flesh coloured. "So Mr. Policeman what is you want to know?"

"You are the one they call Sid?" He again asked once he stood in front of him, Wendy stood at the end of the first row of pews.

"Yeah don't misuse it", he said sternly, "I asked you, what do you want with an old man like me eh".

"I understand you know everything about Romford since the war, is that right?" Steve pressed tucking his right hand into his trouser pocket.

"So what do you want to know, I assume you want to know who killed the copper eh?" he returned, walking to the first row of pews where upon he sat on the end seat allowing Steve to join him, sitting a couple of feet from him.

"I want to know if you can go back

to nineteen fifty eight, especially May of that year?" Steve asked as he leant his elbows on his knees and stared at the altar.

"May nineteen fifty eight you say, the year Brazil won the world cup, but I guess that's not the reason for this visit, is it or is it not?"

"In that month a young girl was..."

"The girl was Carol Richards", he interrupted him with a smile on his face as he clearly remembered the time very well, as if it were only yesterday, I know I read about it in the papers", he explained.

"So where were you that night Sid?" Steve asked with a sense of authority in his voice as he turned to face him.

"I didn't kill her if that is what you want to know". He replied feeling hurt by the innuendos Steve was embarking on.

"I asked you where you were. I have a good idea of who did kill her but I need to know the truth, that's all Sid, I'm not accusing you of anything".

"I was here back then and before you ask I saw everything that night. I was asleep in the yard near to the walls of the building. I loved sleeping near to this particular building as it was where I married my late wife Mary; it was the best day of my life I can tell you Mr. Policeman and nice police lady. I recognised her from a few weeks ago when a couple of old codgers wanted me to tell them about this area after the war. I told them to go to the library".

"May nineteen fifty eight Sid?" replied Steve, trying to get Sid back to his story of what happened that night long ago.

"Ah yes...umm...that terrible night when that poor lass lost her life. It was sad, I saw them drag her into the place and one of them produced a knife and they all had their wicked way with the poor girl. Afterwards the others fled leaving the last one alone with her; he was the one who held the knife to her throat".

"So why didn't you go to her rescue then?" Quizzed Wendy, who was feeling some resentment towards him and thinking of the girl and her plight at the hands of the killer.

"I had a few too many sherbets that night. At first it was a haze but I could hear the girl crying as they all did the business. One of the lads had her knickers in his hand but he tossed them to the ground and fled", he said softly.

"So Sid what happened next?"

"What happened next was an accident", he said looking straight at Steve, "The lad got up and began to back off when the girl got up too, but she was in a right state and started to scream at him.

He turned to try and get her to be quiet when she lunged at him with the intent of harming him for what he had done to her", he paused for a moment to regain his stature. "She flew at him but he still had the knife firmly in his hand and of course she lunged straight onto the knife. When she moved back in pain and crying he panicked and stabbed her again in the chest which stopped her dead in her tracks. She reeled forward and fell over the wall and died, the boy fled in a hurry but first he picked up the pair of knickers and waved them in the air as he rejoined his friends in an American style car that was parked at the rear of the church". He rose to his feet again and walked to the altar turning again to confront Steve. "That lad used to return to the scene several times usually late at night. He would stand under the street lamp and just stare at the spot where she died and he would smoke several cigarettes at the same time", he sat on the top step in front of the altar, his mind drifting back in time, then went on to add, "I see him on many occasions prancing about the place like he is god".

"Who are we talking about Sid?" Steve asked calmly as he sat on the edge of the seat.

"He's like you two, a Blue Bottle, you know a wooden top he thinks he's it".

"So why didn't you report it back

then?"

"Who would believe an old tramp like me, besides I was an alcoholic back then and I know any lawyer would have gone out of his way and destroyed my evidence as superficial due to my life style".

"Still you had a duty to the poor girl in this crime surely?" Steve said with an air of authority.

"I think I would've ended up like your colleague who was killed a while ago in the same spot as the girl and by the same person too", he returned with his head bowed low.

"Are you telling me you saw the person kill Jack Gould the Detective?" Steve eagerly enquired, his ears firmly fixed on this man.

"Your friend was walking to the spot where the girl was murdered when that officer approached him from behind. He put on a peaked cap and it was pulled down over his brow so he could not be recognised. Your friend took out a cigarette and was about to light it when that young officer asked him for a light, but he wasn't expecting what happened next. That officer then stabbed your friend in the stomach first and said out loud, 'I told you to forget about it, but you just wouldn't listen, would you', then he stabbed him a second time just as he did to the girl all them years ago", he said angrily then added, "If you must know the idiot killed the girl outside 'The Black Hat' night club a year ago because she told him to get lost and he got really pissed off by her words and injected the bitch with Heroin".

Steve rose to his feet and asked politely, "What did he do after he stabbed Jack?"

"He removed his cap and laughed out loud and returned to the market place where he headed for a car parked at the end of the market place, whereupon he simply vanished". Finding his feet he turned to face the altar breaking the moments silence after Steve had composed himself. Sid went on to add, "It would seem Mr. Policeman", He said turning half way to face Steve yet again and proclaimed, "right now you have a real problem on your hands, because of this sudden situation you're finding yourself in. You have a rogue officer in your midst and the little sod isn't going to come easy...all I can say is; watch yer back. If he can kill one copper, he can kill another just as easy and he will not give a toss when he does because he doesn't intend to get caught".

"By the way I'm D.C.I. Price and not Mr. Policeman". Steve remarked politely.

"I know who you are Steven Price,

but to me you're still a wooden top who needs to be watched over by a guardian angel you could say", he returned with slight smile and a wink directed at Wendy, who just returned the gesture, with a fleeting smile and a nod of her head to one side, amazed at his cheek.

"You're the second person to tell me that Sid so who and why?" Steve snapped.

"Don't loose yeh knickers Steve...you're ok...the family is who...and the truth is somebody out there wants you dead ok"

"So! This guardian angel do they have a name?" Steve pressed on determined to learn the truth behind these allegations. "And who wants me dead?"

"It's ghosts from your past, that's all I know right now, but your angel is determined to protect you, the least anybody knows about them the safer you are...ok". He said as he started for the far door so he could disappear as easy as he had entered.

"Is that all you are going to tell me?" Steve asked abruptly.

"If you want to contact me at any time Steve, just ask the pip squeak who calls himself Frank the tank".

"Were you really a killer in the war Sid?" asked a curious Wendy.

Stopping briefly just before the

door he turned slowly with a broad grin, then said joyfully, accompanied with yet another of his cheeky winks, "The pip squeak is and always will be a dreamer...so lets leave it there shall we, ok".

"Can we rely on you for a statement regarding this matter, just between us three of course? It's for Jack and Carol and even the girl outside the nightclub". Steve queried as he rose to his feet.

"I told you that if you need me just speak to Frank...ok", Sid said abruptly as he left the building.

"Well that was informative Constable", Steve remarked as Sid departed leaving them to leave via the main entrance.

"I guess he is right, we do have a serious problem regarding Peters Gov, what are we going to do about him?"

"Well if my theory is right there's been a miscarriage of justice in the case against Andrew Cox".

"So Gov what do you want me to do?"

"Get P.C. Mark Smith to run you to Canvey Island and get Rose to sign her statement and Constable mums the word about this case ok. If anyone asks it's a routine enquiry into an old case". He said as they left the confines of that church and headed for their place of work.

"Did you get to talk to the one you asked about Inspector?" Enquired the concerned owner of the burger bar who leant on his counter. "Can I get you two a coffee", he asked politely.

Steve declined the offer of the coffee, but expressed his thanks with a nod, then he simply replied to his question, by sticking the thumb on his left hand up to say yes he did meet the man in question.

"I will need a photo of Peters ASAP, so I can see if he was the person Andrew Cox encountered in the pub that dreadful night in his life".

"I'll get a series of photos of men to go with his photo Gov, that way he would have to be sure it was Peters despite you being sure about it subject to the information gathered".

Chapter 35

The next morning the rising of the sun beamed through his office window, casting a warm glow throughout the place. Its appearance brought a smile to Steve's face as he sat at his desk armed with a cup of coffee in one hand, acquired from the canteen and his typewriter mounted on the desk directly in front of him, waiting patiently to be used.

A ream of blank A4 paper stood to one side of the electric typewriter awaiting his full attention to type the report, regarding his recent findings; in relation to the crimes allegedly committed over the last twenty odd years by Peters. Starting with the loss of a beautiful young lady, up to the death of his friends in Australia and even his colleague Jack Gould who you would naturally assume had been friends.

Steve's mind was confused by his own thoughts as he toyed with the questions of his crossword puzzle in the newspaper. This was something he professed to be good at, especially the quick one which amused him, but his excuse was it helped him to think about his task at hand.

Having loaded the typewriter with

the relevant amount of paper to be typed on, which normally had to be in triplicate, he just sat motionless staring at the blank paper. His thoughts were 'where do we start with this whole bloody affair'. It would appear that it had to start with Jack and the interview with the dying George Blackmore, because it was his confession that had started this whole affair off, from the moment he had opened his mouth. Therefore his first words he typed at the top of the page read. <u>'The Death of Carol Richards'.</u>

Steve was now facing a daunting prospect of having to   piece together this story. One of the questions that plagued his mind, as he stared aimlessly at the key pad of his typewriter as his mind was hit with a mental block, was where and how to actually start.

His brain ticked over as he tried to decide on which direction he should concentrate first. Should it be either the Churchyard Murder, which had resulted in the untimely death of the sixteen year old, named Carol Richards in nineteen fifty eight... or should he start with the more recent case regarding the murder of his friend and old colleague Jack Gould? He was getting more and more confused as he stared at the blank paper whilst sipping his coffee.

Finding his feet he moved to the

window, opening the small top window to let some fresh air into the room. A light gust of wind wisped past his face making him close his eyes and take in a deep breath. A knock at the door diverted his concentration as he suddenly found his voice and with a little cough followed by the words, 'enter', but it had been opened moments before he finished saying the word. He was confronted by the chief in his uniform of rank that entered the room enquiring after his well being.

"Everything is under control Chief", Steve uttered as he moved around his desk to sit on the corner.

The chief on the other hand walked to the desk and glanced at the paperwork set up in the typewriter, the sight made his eyes light up when he spotted the heading. "I see you have headed your report the Churchyard Murder, Inspector, is there a reason for that, may I ask".

"Well Sir its simple...the same person killed Jack that is why". Steve said in a casual manner, leaning back he also looked at his own work, before finding his feet again to return to the window.

"The question one should be asking at this moment in time, is do you know who killed Detective Inspector Jack Gould?" The Chief remarked as he stood upright in a soldier like manner befitting his status, his hands held loosely behind him.

"I know who killed Jack Gould, Chief; therefore I know who killed the girl in nineteen fifty eight too, as I said they just happen to be the same person",

"I see Inspector, but how could you have succeeded now when we couldn't solve the crime back then, in nineteen fifty eight". The Chief pressed as he found himself coming face to face with Steve by the window.

"Yeah well at the time you didn't have the confession of George Blackmore to start with, back then chief...and I'm afraid to say it but certain things were overlooked back then. More importantly, certain people didn't come forward to give evidence because they hadn't realised the importance of what they had seen at the time...plus Chief, the killer at the time was so young he made so many stupid mistakes that it gave away his identity from day one".

"Do we have a name for this killer Inspector or are you going to keep me in the dark?" the Chief pursued relentlessly.

"Yes Chief I have a name for the killer. In fact I can tell you what happened on that bleak day back all those years ago. I can even tell you what happened when the girl was murdered and about Jack's murder too", Steve replied, with an air of authority.

You could feel the tension welling up in the eyes of the chief at the thought of solving something that had plagued his life from that one day so long ago. He had dreamed of the day he would solve that murder and at this point in time he felt it would elude him to the grave and yet Steve appeared to have solved it just like that. "So Inspector are you going to enlighten me to the truth you say you have unearthed in your line of investigation?"

"I can tell you that there were four people involved in the murder of Carol Richards; three of them are dead; I can confirm that two of them were killed in Australia; their bodies were found on a beach in a place called Townsville. Of course we know about George Blackmore over here in England, that leaves just the killer".

"Do they have names, these people?"

"Yes...they are Alfie Green, Ian Carter and of course our George Blackmore...Sir", Steve replied as he found his desk and sat back down in his chair facing that daunting task again of staring at the typewriter. He didn't relish the mountain he had to climb regarding the crimes that had been committed by the killer.

"I dread to think how you come by

these people and their part in this case...so do we have the name of the killer Inspector, or are you going to keep me in suspense regarding that", he said as he stood upright in front of him.

"When the time is right I will hand you the killer on a plate", informed Steve, who wasn't willing to reveal too much at this point in time out of fear of reprisals, but he went on to request, "I would like a photograph of every male officer in this station and other local stations...is that possible?"

"I will see what I can do, but more importantly I will look forward to that prospect Inspector", The chief remarked as he headed for the door only to be stopped briefly when Steve passed a comment.

"I can tell you one thing Chief, the killer boasted back then about going to college at Hendon".

There was a moments silence as the chief turned and stared at Steve regarding his last statement, then said, "Are you telling me the killer is a..." he paused for a moment to gather his thoughts, "Are you saying the killer is one of us, he's a fellow officer".

"I'm not saying anything other than I know he is Chief, but I need time to gather all the evidence in this case because it goes deeper than the girl in the fifties. She was the beginning of this life for the killer and he destroyed the lives of so many people who knew him".

"Are you saying this person is a serial killer...in fact what you are telling me is that we have a serial killer right now...here in our midst". The chief snapped, advancing towards the desk and placing his hands on the edge of it, then went on to add, "In that case Inspector you had better make bloody sure you know the truth and have the proof, because if not you could lose your badge if it turns out to be false, do I make myself clear about that...because if you are wrong Inspector you could destroy an innocent persons life, let alone his future, do I make myself clear?"

"I will say this Chief", Steve said then went on to inform; "had the killer let this case drop back then you could say he would have committed the perfect crime. Up until today he thinks he has outwitted the law again and again; but the act of killing Jack was his downfall and put paid to his safety once and for all. You see up to then his freedom was safe, because if Jack knew the killer after talking to George Blackmore he would've arrested him there and then, I know Jack well...I would suggest at this moment in time we keep it under our hat as we don't want to alert the killer to our findings. Besides I don't particularly want to end up like Jack...well not at this moment in time that is".

"I understand your concerns in this case, in that case Inspector I look forward to your final report and the person you declare to be the killer is behind bars. That way when the day comes for me to leave, I can retire with a clean sheet. I can tell you Inspector that case has been a thorn in my side. I always dreamed that one day I would solve it, as I said earlier...in that case I will leave you to it, although you should take heed and remember what I also said earlier Inspector", he said as he left the room and looked cagily back at Steve, then he gently closed the office door behind him. This left Steve sitting there, his hands together as if he were praying, his fingertips brushing his chin and his thoughts still milling over his opening paragraph of his report on the case.

Finally, running his hands through his hair with a long lingering sigh as at this moment in time he was feeling uneasy about the task he was facing. Feeling on edge he decided to go for a walk around the market place, where he hoped to get some inspiration over a burger or two, maybe even pay his cousin a visit and think over a pint of his best whilst propping up the bar.

As he was leaving the building via the main entrance he stopped at the counter and leant on the top and spoke to Reg who was manning the post. "Reg", Steve beckoned.

"What can I do for you Inspector?"

"Can you find anything out about the girl who was found dead a year ago in the car park of 'The Black Hat' night club"?

"You mean the suicide case, the bird that topped herself with a lethal dose of..."

"Yeah! Yeah! That's the one Reg", Steve interrupted him, then simply added a polite, "Thanks mate", as he left the building.

"I'll put it on yeh desk", Reg replied half-heartedly, at the same time Steve just raised his arm in acknowledgement to say thank you in the only way he knew how.

The Chief returned to his office with a strange sense of foreboding over the prospect of solving the thorn in his side that had haunted him for the best part of his life, but somehow he was feeling uneasy about the possibility of a fellow officer being the serial killer. All those years he had been in his presence and he hadn't realised. Somehow he knew Steve was right about the situation, it could've quite easily have been regarded as the perfect crime and he knew he had to remain elusive to his officers for the safety of Steve.

He stood staring out of the window of his office, with his hands held loosely together behind his back as he rocked gently on his heels deep in thought.

Suddenly he realised he was going to look at his own officers in a different light now. But not the young ones as they wouldn't have been around at that time; his eyes would be peeled on the older officers; of which there were around eight of them that flittered from each of the local stations; where ever they were needed at any given moment in time. He realised he could walk into the station canteen at any given time and be standing next to the killer and not even know it. He also knew he had to remain calm and collective about knowing the truth so as not to give the game away. All he could do was hope Steve could solve it soon so they could get on with the day to day running of the station.

Steve found himself sitting on a stool and propping up the bar in his cousin's pub with a face that could easily sink a ship.

"What's with the long face Steve?" enquired his cousin who pulled a pint for himself and joined him.

"It's this case I'm on John", he said rubbing the back of his neck. "It's getting to me now mate...you see I or we have a villain in the midst".

"Why don't you just say you have a bent copper instead of beating about the bush", Johnny said finding his seat on the other side of the bar. "If he is a villain then nail the bastard and don't pussy foot around...look if he were...Ugh...lets say...a no-body, you wouldn't think twice about nicking them there and then would you...now be realistic about it Steve...would you?"

"Yeh but it's different this time, what if I were wrong, I could lose my job over it".

"That's no hardship you can always come and work for me Steve", he grinned, then went on to add, "If I were you Steve I would do what's right and let the world know the truth...more so if he is a copper...what has he done that's so wrong?"

"Only murder that's all". Steve said softly so as not to be heard.

Johnny just whistled accompanied by the simple 'wow', as he sipped at his beer.

"I suppose I'd better get back to the factory and get on with it, it's not going to get done sitting in here Johnny", he sighed downing the remains of his pint in one gulp and placing the empty glass on the counter with the usual. "Catch yeh later

Johnny".

"Yeah...You bring Angie around next time, and then we'll go out for a meal".

"Will do!" Steve uttered with a thumbs up as he left the comfort of that establishment for the cool air outside as the sun had vanished for a while behind a large cloud.

Once back in his office and feeling more relaxed, which could only be put down to the pint he just had, he again found himself perched in his chair, staring at the empty page, with that heading that he knew was appropriate to this case he found himself working on. 'Well in for a penny in for a pound', he said to himself as he placed his fingers carefully onto the key pad and began to type. Starting with the death of Jack Gould, his opening words read like the start of a famous Agatha Christie novel where you would be expecting one of her famous detectives to suddenly jump out at you. Then gather the cast around him and solve the death without any fuss.

He realised for the first time that the incident of Jack was the beginning of the end of this case. His untimely death was in response to a crime twenty four years earlier. If George had died without telling Jack his story, Jack would still be alive today, instead he was dead and Steve was left to pick up the pieces of the story.

Maybe Carol was getting her justice after all these years and Steve toyed with the idea that she was now watching over his every move, desperately wanting her revenge. She would know that some of those who had hurt her were dead now, leaving the real culprit for Steve and the law to punish.

He was using reference numbers for the written statements of those he had talked to, ready to go into a file that he kept locked in his drawer.

An hour later and the door opened again and the chief entered with a large file in his hand, declaring these were the photos of every officer there and in local stations, making it eight as stated earlier. Steve took the file and proceeded to open it and remove the photos to check to see if Peters photograph was there and it was. "Will they do Inspector?"

"Perfect Chief absolutely perfect", Steve smiled as he put the file into his drawer with the written file he was typing.

"Are you going to tell me why it was so important to get these photos that you so urgently requested?"

"It's a little matter of a miscarriage of justice on the part of one of the witnesses to the murder of Carol Richards, the killer realised and set him up by killing his wife and making it look like he did it...very clever but not clever enough. You see Chief, I was asked by Special branch to look into the case of a Andrew Cox, who by the way witnessed the murder back then, Ok Chief...does that answer that question. So if this Mr. Cox identifies the killer I will be coming back here to arrest the culprit in question because I already have the evidence I need to nick him right now. This would then release an innocent man from prison...now do you understand?"

"I think so...it would appear you know more than you are letting on Inspector".

"You are not the first to have made that assumption Chief"

"In that case Inspector I want to be present when you make that arrest as you've intrigued me...I am still looking forward to your deliberation relating to this scenario, with the proof needed to convict this rogue officer of mine".

"If I am right Chief I will be making that arrest in a couple of days from now, as there's just a few loose ends to be tied up regarding this case, then I think you will be surprised. Even more so will the killer who is going to be totally blown away by it, because he thinks he's got away with it yet again, but I know differently...Chief".

Once the Chief left the office Steve picked up the phone and dialled the Home Office and asked if he could speak to Major

Thompson.

Moments later and the Major replied and Steve then asked him if he could make a visit to the prison the next day to see Andrew Cox again. He went on to say that he had some photos for him to look at and if his theory was right he would hopefully pick out the person who he alleged had killed his wife all those years previously. He advised the Major to meet him there at the prison, because if it was right then Andrew Cox was innocent of the crime and the killer was still at large. The Major agreed with a curious tone in his voice.

"Till tomorrow then Major", Steve said with a smile on his face as he replaced the receiver and set about his typewriter with venom.

Chapter 36

Time clicked by, with Steve constantly watching the ticking clock as it passed the minutes and patiently waited as it edged nearer to the twelve thirty mark. That was where he decided to take a rest, so stashing the unfinished paperwork in his drawer and placing the typewriter back into the cupboard where it belonged, he locked it all safely away because he didn't want a certain person to read it. Locking his office door behind him, he casually headed for the car park and his car, first letting Reg at the front desk know he was going to interview somebody in Southend. This was accompanied by one of his usual cheeky smiles and a quick wink giving the 'nudge, nudge wink, wink, say no more', type of look.

Reg simply replied touching his nose in response to Steve's remark, as he had come to recognise the meaning behind those sort of statements, which usually meant the person, was taking the afternoon off.

Steve opened the front door of his house to the sound of the radio coming from the kitchen, accompanied by the chatter of a couple of women who he found seated at the large dining table chatting over a mug of tea. Angie was blown away by Steve's sudden appearance at the kitchen door.

"What's all this about?" Angie curiously enquired, "Oh and by the way this is Lisa, Mark's young wife from next door, Steve".

"Yes I know Ange", Steve replied, as he entered the room and went over to the kettle to make himself a coffee, "I was bored and so I thought...let's just bugger off for the afternoon and take my lovely lady out for the rest of the day", he explained as he made his coffee.

"And pray, may I ask, where were we supposed to be going on this...boring day of yours", Angie pursued with a glint in her eyes and a smile as she sipped at her coffee.

Lisa sat with a smile on her face holding her mug in both hands, as it stood on the table. "I'd better make a move Ange, I think Steve has other ideas...am I right Steve? you forget I'm married to a policeman too" She commented, finding her feet she finished the rest of her coffee and went to the sink to place her empty mug there to be washed later.

"So Mr. Big shot where are we going then?" Angie enquired as she too headed for the sink with her mug, placing it alongside Lisa's.

"How about Canvey Island, walking along the beach with the autumn sun in our face and eating candy floss", Steve said as he leant against the base unit of the kitchen holding his fresh coffee in one hand and rubbing the back of his neck with his left hand.

"And pray tell me what has brought this on...Steve". Angie pressed.

"Boredom...yes that's it, boredom...and the wish to whisk you off for a moment's break, to recharge the old batteries you could say sweetheart...interested then?" He said lovingly as he went to her side and softly kissed her on the cheek.

"I'd better leave you love birds to your own devices", Lisa remarked jovially as she headed for the front door with the usual, "Catch yeh later Ange!" before closing the door quietly behind her.

"It's good to see you getting on with people and making friends...good friends that is babe", Steve remarked romantically, kissing her cheek a second time before heading for the sink to top up his mug with drop of cold water, to cool it down so he could down it faster and get on the way.

"Would you like me to change sir?" she jibed, as she gave a little twirl to show off her attire of an extra large, floral, knee length dress under a pink 'V' neck jumper.

"You look great as you are babe, but you should put on a warm jacket just in case...you never know these days, it might get a bit cold on the beach this time of the year".

"You worry too much Mr..." she said cockily then went on to add, "you forget sunshine...how I spent quite some time living on the streets in all weathers".

"Yeah well, you weren't pregnant then...were you?" Steve stated with a caring attitude in his voice.

Sometime later they drove into the car park on the Island, after a quiet journey listening to some music on the radio in the car, with Angie silently watching the countryside drift by. Her mind seemed to be on some far distant planet; still plagued by her future left in this mortal being she called Angie. Occasionally she would turn with a hint of a smile to stare at Steve as he headed for the Island and all its mysteries. Eventually pulling up at the rear of the car park, the hill loomed up directly in front of them; enticing them like every person who found themselves in this same situation; demanding you should run up it to the sea wall that waits to greet the would be traveller. Its very existence demands a look and Steve wasn't going to be put off by the thought of what pleasures lurked beyond.

"First one to the top gets the teas in", Steve laughed after locking the car, and he began the ascent up the hill, leaving poor Angie to struggle with the baby bump in tow.

After a few puffs and grunts she finally reached Steve who stood staring out over the wall at the sea. It was neither out nor in, just teetering on the ebb. People with their dogs were walking on the sands, one was throwing a ball for their dog to retrieve, and another was swimming in the sea.

A heavily laden freight liner ship was drifting out to sea, its engines droned out across the waves and mingled in the afternoon sun. The beach was awaiting its heavy wake that was heading slowly towards the sands ready to break on its shores.

"This feels great Steve", Angie finally remarked as she recovered her stature again and leant on the wall for a moment, "can we go down onto the beach...please...pretty please!?" she begged, pulling herself into Steve's side and suddenly finding her child like inner being as she headed for the slope that ran down beyond that wall, then again down onto the beach where she felt alive and ready to face the consequences of life.

Inside though she was also beginning to realise this could be the last time she might ever get to experience the euphoria of the smells and feelings of the sea air that brushed against her petite face in this lifetime. As the sea breeze gently kissed her cheeks, putting some colour (that was sadly lacking) back into her tired existence, she cuddled up to Steve as they walked the beach, stopping briefly to sit on the slope and listen to the waves gently lapping onto the beach.

"The sound of the sea is so

rewarding", Angie said as she pulled herself deeper into Steve's shoulder as they carefully sat on those boulders of the slope. He kissed her head and told her he loved her and she said, "I feel like I'm in a dream and I'm going to wake up and then reality will kick in".

"Hmm...I know how you feel, I wish I could whisk you off to warmer climes...who knows, if I solve this crime we might just do that eh". Steve said softly, then went on to say, "Fancy a coffee; I happen to know of a nice little cafe?"

"I gather this case is getting to you honey?" she enquired as they made their way to the cafe in question.

"Just a tad babe...you could say".

They were soon opening the door to the little cafe Steve had talked about. They found a middle-aged couple in the corner who just gave them a mere fleeting glance as they returned to their respective meals. An elderly portly chap with grey receding hair sat drinking his mug of tea. An empty plate sat on the edge of the table ready to be collected.

"What are you having tomorrow George?" asked Rose who was serving behind the counter.

"I fancy chilli beef and rice for lunch tomorrow Rose", he commented.

"Right oh George", she politely replied, "sorry about that

sweetheart...what can I get you Inspector...it's ok I recognise you from the other day, by the way your colleague was in earlier, I read the statement and before you ask, yes I did sign it".

"That's good Rose and we'll have a couple of coffees and two of your sausage sarnies please". Steve ordered with joy in his voice.

He paid for the meal and taking the coffees they found a seat in the window watching the world roll by. A couple pushing a child in a push chair were headed in the direction of the beach. An elderly man in the local council overalls was doing his job of picking up the rubbish which was strewn around the area and putting it into a small metal street cleaning cart, with several brooms and a shovel attached.

A number twenty one bus stopped at the bus stop and several people got off and headed for the beach area too, the cool breeze hadn't prevented them from still enjoying the presence of the warm autumn sun.

"You were saying about this case Steve, how it was getting to you", Angie enquired as she put a spoonful of sugar into her coffee and added the milk that was in a small sealed pot given to them by Rose, one per mug.

"Yeah it's a very tricky situation

I'm finding myself in babe", he said in a soulful mood He found himself staring at a young lad with a slot machine that he was wheeling along on a large sack barrow on the path that ran around outside of the Monaco pub. "It's looking more and more like the killer is a fellow officer which makes the finale even more tricky for me; as it will be me who will have the difficult job of nicking them and I'm not relishing that task one bit, I can tell you babe, life doesn't come anymore complicated than that".

"So this so called killer...does he have a name then?"

"Yes of course he does...that's what makes the task even harder for me to have to deal with".

"There you are sweetheart", returned a polite and friendly Rose, who put the two plates of sausage sandwiches on the table, "Have you found Carol's killer Inspector, or are you still looking?"

"Maybe but can we talk later Rose?" Steve enquired.

"Yeah Sorry...ok...I'll leave you to eat your food then".

"Thanks Rose...we'll talk in a while ok".

"So, this is what this little trip is all about?" Angie said quietly as she put tomato ketchup on the sausages. "And what's this about the killer being one of your lot", she continued to pursue in a discreet voice, which in turn caused Steve to suggest she should 'shush' for the sake of the situation he found himself in, but not condoning the possibility.

Instead he went on to say, "It just came to me as we entered this place Angie...I am aware that D.C. Fuller had come here this morning. Then I remembered there was something that I needed to clear up regarding Rose's statement", Steve tried to explain in layman terms.

Once they had finished the food and after Rose had dealt with a couple who chose to sit outside with their hot drinks because they had a large dog in tow, she approached Steve and enquired into what he wanted to know, as she found the seat next to Angie with a mug of tea in her hand.

"Ok Rose I just wanted to ask you about something you said in your statement", Steve said as he put his arms on the table encircling his coffee, then went on to say, "You said the lad who was tormenting you mentioned something about going to a college in Hendon...am I right?"

"That's right", she replied, then went on to say, "I told your young officer this morning that I remembered after you left before, the lad said '*he thought us girls liked men in uniform'* and I said, *'but you're not in a uniform are you?'*, whereby he replied, *'yeah but I will be soon'*, and your young female officer wrote it down in her note pad, but then added it to the statement as a post script and I signed it too".

"Right", Steve said curiously as he removed the old photograph from his jacket pocket and placed it on the table in front of her, for her to look at, "What can you tell me about this photo then Rose...anything?"

Picking up the photograph for a better look, her eyes told the story as she choked slightly, then said softly, "That's the car they were driving in, back then, and they are the lads...well not all of them, there's one of them missing...but that definitely is the car and they were definitely the lads...yeah I'm sure of it...how did you come by this photo Inspector?"

"From the driver of that car they happen to be George Blackmore, Ian Carter, Alfie Green and the missing lad who was taking this photo was the killer of Carol, he was the lad you mentioned in your statement Rose...and this photo was taken a few days before that awful night".

"Then you already know who the killer is, after all these years Inspector", she said with an air of joy in her voice as she handed back the photo before sitting back in the seat and picking up her mug of tea.

All Angie could do was sit there in awe of Steve's work, as she quietly drank her coffee leaning against the low wall under the window.

"Do you know what hurts me more than anything Inspector" she said with an air of sadness in her voice, then went on to say, "when I look back at those days I always thought it should've been me who copped it that night and not innocent little Carol, who had it all to live for...I know I was a bit of a wild one back then, unlike our Carol, she was a treasure...I guess their right when they say 'the good die young' and all that stuff...I can tell you now I was scared for years after what happened to Carol, because I believed it should've been me and not her. I even thought the killer might come looking for me, that's one of the real reasons I ended up coming to live on this island. When we moved here I felt free for the first time in ages and now you say you know who her killer was. Let's hope he gets what he deserves, the bastard...sorry for the French".

"It's always the innocent who get hurt in this world...it is so unfair", Commented Angie who up until then had sat silently on the edge of her seat. Now found herself reacting in favour of Rose's comments. For the first time she realised the importance of Steve's work, where he could bring some hope to those who get hurt in any crime.

"Too true sweetheart", Rose remarked in reply, then added, "when's the baby due honey?"

"January next year hopefully", she half-heartedly replied with a hint of a smile.

"Well Inspector are you going to tell me, how come you have the killer in your sights after all these years?"

"Simple! George Blackmore, who I've already said was one of those lads, told a fellow officer the story of that night on his death bed. Then your statement and additional information from other sources have also been a great help in building up the jigsaw puzzle that has been this case. I am sorry I can't tell you any more at the moment but it will all come out in the court case once it takes place which hopefully will be very soon, but we will keep you informed of the progress obviously", Steve reassured Rose.

Moments later and Steve was buying some candy floss and half a dozen freshly made hot sugared ring doughnuts from a small kiosk near to the cafe, before heading back up the hill to the beach.

....
....

The next day:-

Steve met up with the Major the next morning armed with his briefcase containing the file on this case and the photograph. Together they both headed off in the direction of the prison where they had put Andrew Cox for his own safety. He had been summoned to sit in the waiting room for the arrival of the two men, with the need to know more about that night. All being well it would also confirm his innocence to the crime he was imprisoned for all those years before, which was another twist in this tale; if true he could be freed sooner that expected.

Their footsteps echoed the corridors of the prison as they headed for the encounter with Cox which was to be held in a large open room with a wooden table and several wooden chairs dotting the space.

Their presence was barred by the many locked, iron barred doors for security, the heavy keys rattled endless in the many locks to be passed until they finally entered the room where they found Andrew sitting waiting. A couple of hefty prison guards stood close by but were ordered out by the Major who closed the door behind them.

"Right!" remarked Steve who found the chair by the table before placing his case on the table top and already beginning to open it. "As you are aware I'm D.C.I. Price and this is Major Thompson from the home office...he's the person who picked up your letter and authorised me to interview you...ok Andrew".

He just nodded with some quiet enthusiasm in his face and a pert smile, hoping the truth was close by.

"Continue Steve!" exclaimed the Major who happily found comfort sitting on the corner of the table opposite Steve, his left leg firmly on the table while his right leg supported him on the floor having placed his case on the floor unopened at that point in time.

"Ok then Andrew, I listened to your story and funny enough I believed you, even though the law didn't back then...so...I have got some photo's I would like to show you which will hopefully clear up this little mess and maybe send you home", he said as he removed the file from the case and placed it on the table in front of him. Finally he placed the now closed case on the floor beside him, "I want you to look at some photo's for me Andrew...study them very carefully and tell me what you see", he said as he handed him the picture of the car and the three lads.

Taking a cigarette from a packet that had been left on the table, Andrew took the photo in his hand and taking a lighter out of his pocket lit his cigarette at the same time as he studied the picture.

"That was the car I saw that night in Romford in nineteen fifty eight, two of the lads were the ones that came out of the alley that night. I can only guess that the third one was the driver who stayed in the car...am I right?...there is one missing and he was the one who was waving the knickers in the air and he was also the last to come out of the alley, that I do know Inspector".

"In that case Andrew would you like to look at these photos for me and tell me if one of them was the man you met in the pub the night your wife was murdered", Steve pressed pushing the stack of pictures across the table, in front of him.

The Major stood up from the table and asked if anyone wanted a drink, everybody asked for a coffee while Andrew carefully studied the photos that he laid out in front of him to look at each one individually.

Only the footsteps of the Major broke the silence of the room, clanging and shouting was heard in the distance as the day to day events of the prison unfolded around them. The Major asked a guard outside the door to get them the coffees.

Rubbing hands together under his chin Andrew's eyes were peeled to the task at hand, inside he was desperate to get it right and hoped that Steve had come good for him and his future that had seemed lost with time. A big old clock ticked away the seconds on the wall behind Steve.

"Well Andrew?" Steve asked, breaking the silence again.

"You have to remember it was some years ago Inspector but this one looks familiar to me. In fact I would go as far as to say he was the same guy who met me in the pub back then...he looked a bit more scruffier then but the facial features look the same...in fact...yes I can definitely say this was the villain who killed my wife back then...what I can't make out is how you come to have his photo in your collection when no-body could find him back then Inspector", he said as he held the photo in his hands ready to hand it back to Steve.

"So who have you chosen then?" Enquired the Major curiously, after taking the photo from him and looked at it first before handing it back to Steve. He looked at it quickly then smiled as he raised his eyes in the direction of the Major, then at Andrew with a quick nod of his head in approval of his choice, as if he knew he would choose the right photo. "It's Daniel Peters, just as I thought".

"You know him then...so why did he kill my wife?" Andrew asked soulfully as he dragged on his cigarette.

"Because you knew too much and he had to put you in a place where you wouldn't be heard or believed...but what you witnessed back then was the person who murdered a young girl in Romford on that night you saw that car", explained Steve.

"What we have to do now is get a confession out of Peters", informed the Major who returned to the table and placed both hands on its surface.

"And that's not going to be easy Major", returned Steve cautiously.

"So how did you find this out Inspector?" enquired a relieved Andrew who felt like the angels had answered his prayers?

"The lad who was driving that car died a while ago but confessed to the crime on his death bed, but back then you talking about that car made the killer realise that the car would lead the law to him. That is why he had to do what he did to you in order to save his own neck...now do you get it...I guess it's your lucky day Andrew", explained Steve.

"It hasn't sunk in yet Inspector...are you saying I can go free now and my crime can be dropped", enquired an excited Andrew who put out his cigarette in the ash tray then immediately lit another.

"Take the packet!" returned the Major who sat back on the table, as the door opened and the young guard came in carrying a tray of coffees, complete with a full sugar bowl and spoons." it has been a miscarriage of justice, but as Steve said we will have to get a confession from Peters first, then we can set the ball rolling for you to be freed. In the meantime I will see that you get preferential treatment until we can get your release forms sorted out, however it could take a couple of days to process then you will be free, ok", he then added, "just for your safety's sake we must ask you to keep quiet about this matter until everything has been sorted out. We appreciate you will want to tell everybody but it must remain quiet for the moment until the culprit has been arrested, otherwise things could go wrong ok".

Andrew just beamed a big smile and replied "I have been here so long already that a few more days won't hurt knowing that soon I will be out of here".

Steve packed the remaining photos in his case, keeping Peters' photo with the photo of the car in the file marked the Churchyard Murder, he then placed the file back in the case. "I think it's time to close this case once and for all Major", said Steve feeling relieved too.

Tossing the cigarette packet in the air and catching it in both hands Andrew made for the door and walked back to his cell with a sense of joy in his step, the two police guards this time just accompanying him along the way.

Chapter 37

Steve studied the situation carefully now he had learned the truth. In the meantime Andrew had been lead back to his cell. This left the Major and Steve to dwell over the interview alone in that disinfectant smelling room, drinking what was left of their coffees.

"So Steve I would like to know how or where you obtained this photograph?" enquired the Major who had picked up the old photo to examine it more closely.

"It was among the belongings of the late George Blackmore...by the way, his house was broken into shortly after his death", Steve said openly as he gathered the photos and file together ready to be replaced back into his case.

"I can assume then that you believe the killer was after this photograph when they broke into the house?" The Major returned, rubbing his chin with his left hand, whilst still looking at the photo in his right hand. "And pray may I ask, what brought your attention to Sergeant Peters being the killer and more to the point Inspector, at what time did you come to believe it to be him, Peters that is?" pursued a curious Major who now placed the offending photograph back onto the table. He then carefully slid it across the surface in the direction of a comfortable looking Steve, who in turn picked it up and carefully slid it back into the file marked 'The Church yard murder'. "And more to the point Inspector, how does this old murder case have any bearing on the murder of Jack Gould...if it's not too much to ask that is?"

"This whole case began with the

dying confession of George Blackmore", Steve started to explain, "the killer knowing George's plight and how he had talked to Jack..."

"The killer being Sergeant Peters that is", interrupted the Major who sat on the edge of the table as before.

"Yes you're right Major...Peters panicked and killed Jack out of fear of being charged with the murder of Carol Richards, because he knew George would've talked about that old case, but he also knew that car in that photograph would've been his downfall should we look into the case more closely...which I'm lead to believe Jack was about to do, hence the reason he had the old file in his case...Peters was aware that the car in that photo was a prototype that was given to a Kevin Blackmore...who by the way resides in Australia these days and he is George's older brother...George borrowed his brother's car to go out that night and by the way that photograph was actually taken by Peters himself, prior to the murder of Carol...the three lads in that picture are dead. Two of them were killed in Australia and of course there's our George, the third person in the photo".

"But what led you to thinking that Peters was the killer then?" enquired a curious Major, his piercing eyes staring into Steve's, expecting an unanswerable question regarding that matter.

"That was simple Major; you see when I interviewed Carol's friend Rose, who by the way lives on Canvey Island, she said that back then some lads in that car tried to chat them up outside the cinema, while they were waiting to go in. She had a go at the one who was trying to chat her up; in that confrontation the young Peters said he had won a scholarship to go to Hendon College, which of course we all know is the police academy. He then went on to say about how the girls loved a man in uniform, but she happened to mention that he wasn't in fact wearing a uniform, he carried on by saying that he would be wearing one soon...I can assume at the time he was talking about wearing a police uniform...now do you understand Major?"

The Major gave a slight grunt of amazement, then a sigh of contempt at the likelihood of the results Steve was presenting in his synopsis of this case, but then went on to remark, "I can see only one flaw in your surmise of this case and that is evidence Inspector...you alone should be aware no court in the land will convict on an assumption...you will certainly need all the evidence in the world to convict him on these charges Inspector, or it would be dismissed on a technicality".

"Yes Major", he snapped then

went on to add, "of that I am totally aware. That is why I have a witness that saw everything on both accounts, yes he even witnessed the murder of Carol Richards back in nineteen fifty eight", Steve replied as he neatly placed everything back into his brief case and sat on the edge of the table, then continued to say, "the witness also saw the same person kill Jack", he continued to explain, "and of course we have Andrew Cox who saw the aftermath of the murder back then".

"Yeah well that might be it, so his evidence would be fine but he never saw the actual murder...did he Inspector, but you are maybe right to convict Peters for being involved in the crime back then, but you haven't got a another Andrew Cox in connection to the murder of Jack now have you?" The Major explained.

"My witness saw everything as I've said".

"Yeah well you may be right...but does this so called witness have a name then?" pursued the Major curiously.

"His name happens to be Sid, Sid Atkins if you must know", replied Steve cockily.

"You are kidding me Inspector?"

"What makes you say that Major?" Steve enquired curiously, then went on to add, "do I get the impression you know of him?"

"I was led to believe he died years ago...so are you now trying to tell me he is still alive and kicking". The Major said in awe of the underlying statement made by a reassuring Steve.

"Yes he is alive and well...so you know of him then Major".

The Major walked around the room, his hand under his chin as he muttered, "Well I never....of all the people it has to be...it has to be good old Sid Atkins...well I never".

"I gather from your actions, you know him then?" Steve said repeating his enquiry.

"Of course I know of him, he is a legend from the past, he was once one of our great operatives who happened to have lost his family during the war...but he still managed to help the police, right up until about...the...ugh...mid fifties. I believe that was about the time when his mother died and left him a small fortune whereby he misused it getting drunk...the legend has it that he sold his mum's house to fuel his lifestyle and the last we heard we believed he was dead, but that was back in the sixties...but you are telling me now he is still alive and well?"

"Yeah and he saw everything that night in fifty eight and the killing of Jack as I've mentioned, that is the real irony of this case...we appear to have Peters banged to rights but we will need to get a full proof case in order to nail him and get him put away".

"This Peters has a bit of a reputation with the girls in his life", commented the Major who decided to pack up and leave the confines of that establishment, but stood in the doorway to talk to Steve who also had prepared to leave the place. "I see we have one real problem in this case Inspector and that is the weapon he used to kill them both, having read the pathology report it clearly says they were killed with the same weapon, a six inch wide blade with a hilt that left its mark on Carol's body".

"You are talking about a scout knife maybe, eh?" Steve said in passing as they left the room and headed for the exit, "so Major what are we going to do about Cox then?"

"I will get back to my office and draw up his release papers and have him put in a safe house so when you need him just call me...is that ok with you".

"Yeah sure...I'm sure Cox is going to really love that", Steve remarked jovially.

"Would you like to join me for some lunch at the club I go to Inspector?" returned the Major informally, then added, "you've done well Inspector, I knew you'd come good for me in this case", he said stopping briefly by a closed barred door awaiting its unlocking, "regarding this so called weapon, we need to nail him...I have my ways of getting it Inspector...the least you...ugh...hmm, know about it the better it would be for you and you're young lady police officer...lets just say I shall get somebody to find it for us, that's as far as I intend to go on this matter".

"Right In that case what would you like me to do in connection to Peters...should he be arrested now or later?"

Just then a burly guard joined them to open the door to let them pass. "I hope it all went well for you Sir", he enquired as he unlocked the door, the heavy bunch of keys rattled loudly as they entered the lock.

"Very well thank you", Returned Steve politely as he and the Major passed through into the next corridor, their foot steps echoing in its vastness, "so what do we do with Peters then?"

"It's not as if we can't find him when we need him" informed the Major casually, then added, "I understand he asked for a transfer to another area...I think we can honestly say we can forget about that. I could keep it on the back burner for now or bin it...I will have my secretary draft up a letter addressed to him, declaring that his request for a transfer has been noted and on record and that we will be informing him on that matter at a later date, with reference to his request".

"I want to ask you a question Major?" Steve said as they stopped at the next door to be unlocked, their guard walking in front.

"What is your question Inspector?"

"Have you instructed somebody to watch my back, you know a guardian angel or something?"

"What makes you think that?"

"Just a gut feeling...besides, others have seen it and told me so, but I couldn't see it at the time, but I don't know", he replied with a shrug of his shoulders.

"You sound paranoid Inspector".

"What happened to Steve, Major?" Steve returned quickly, his feelings despondent.

The Major sighed with a smile, then explained, "Protocol Steve, you have a rank that needs to be respected; before when I called you Steve you were a nobody; remember you sacrificed your status with me the day you jacked it all in, but I am glad you are back where you belong. I had high hopes for you before the tragedy of your late wife, so there you go Inspector...does that answer your question Inspector?...well there you go, that is your status now, so respect it with pride", he went on to explain as they continued on their way getting closer to the exit and fresh air.

This was something every prisoner longs for as they lounge about in their cells awaiting the day of their release. In the eyes of Andrew Cox, he could now lay on his bed with a different attitude towards his future.

"So Major what do I do about Peters then?"
There was a silence.
"Hmm...let me think...ah yes I know, there's a young woman gone missing. Her name is Sarah Brown and her mother is distraught, she seems to think she's been kidnapped by a gang of villains from the city. The mother lives in Hornchurch and I have been told by people she is not somebody to mess about with, if you get my drift Inspector, so tread carefully...I will forward the details when I get back to the office as I think you need to work on this case in the meantime".
"Does the mother have a name other than Mrs. Brown"? Steve enquired politely.
"Of course she does, her name is Eileen Brown, and I have heard she runs a pub in Hornchurch or somewhere around

there. I couldn't tell you at this moment in time as the paperwork are back in my office". The Major informed him.

"I guess she has to be tough if she runs a pub in that area". Steve smiled, then went on to enquire politely, "by the way, that lunch, is it still on offer...Major?"

"Be my guest", he laughed out loud and ordered Steve to get into his car.

Chapter 38

The weekend passed without any real incident; it was more a case of Steve enjoying a quiet time with Angie; sitting in the garden with some good food and a few bottles of wine, on a couple of warm autumn evenings.

The rising of a full moon shed light on a warm evening as the odd firework exploded in a cascade of flashing colours that crackled in the darkened sky. Thus letting the world know that Guy Fawke's night was arriving and prior to that the threat of Halloween too, with its usual trick or treating, mainly for the enjoyment of the children, who loved the thought of being up a bit later than usual and out in the dark.

Monday found Steve sitting quietly at his desk in the morning, when suddenly an unexpected phone call broke the silence. It was from Ian in Australia telling Steve he would be joining him in a couple of day's time as he was about to return to England with some good news on the front line. He declared it was now eight o'clock in the evening out there and he was booked onto the flight on the Wednesday, around mid-day their time and he should be with him by the Thursday afternoon.

Once he had replaced the receiver he was happy to return to the crossword in his daily newspaper, whilst enjoying his coffee with a few of his favourite custard cream biscuits. His pen neatly poised in his right hand ready to fill in the blank spaces of his puzzle, his mind dwelling on the right answer to the question one across, 'a card game' with six letters beginning and ending with the letter 'E'.

He was about write in the word 'ecarte' when the door opened and to his surprise Peters was standing in the doorway having entered the room.

"How's it going with the murder of Jack, Inspector?" he enquired having reached the desk.

Steve gently placed both hands

flat down on the surface of his desk. He had a steely glint in his eye knowing what he knew about Peters. However he had to keep his inner most feelings towards him in check, for fear of letting him know the true extent of his findings with reference to the death of Jack. Instead he strived to create a more relaxed attitude to the conversation.

"It has gone cold at the moment but I will be working on it at some point in the future, but at the moment the results are inconclusive. We know he was stabbed twice and we know he was looking into an old case from fifty eight, a case which I know you personally were involved in, namely..."

"The Church Yard murder", Interrupted Peters then added, "yes I am familiar with that case...and I can tell you now it was never solved back then...there was..."

"Yes I know, there wasn't anything to be getting on with, was there Peters. I mean, you should know that better than any of us", interrupted Steve again, leaning back in his chair and placing his hands carefully behind his neck having tossed his pen onto the open newspaper. "Maybe I should be interviewing you and maybe you can fill me in on all of your findings back then...like...ugh...you know...who you interviewed back then, in your line of investigations and what was the outcome of those investigations".

"There wasn't much to be getting on with back then, because most of it was done before I ever got involved with the case".

"I see", Steve uttered, biting his bottom lip as he desperately tried to think of a way around his approach to his line of investigation, without giving too much away at this moment in time. After a moment's silence, during which Peters had been looking curiously at the crossword puzzle Steve had been working on at the time he had entered the room. "I understand you were at the same school as Carol Richards?" He found himself asking, then went on to add, "and from what I have found out you were friends with the late George Blackmore whom you said was an idiot who made up stories about being a detective or something like that...am I right Sergeant?"

"Yeah I guess you're right, I did know George Blackmore but as for Carol I'm not so sure about...what I mean is, us lads didn't get involved with the girls back then...you know I was into studying criminal law. I have wanted to be a policeman ever since I could walk, but how did you know that about George?"

"You said it yourself in the beginning, when I first arrived here...remember and that isn't what your old teacher said when I interviewed him. He reckoned you liked the girls and was always trying your luck with them...anyway enough of your youth, back then did you manage to interview her friend Rose?"

"No. She had moved away when I arrived on the scene...apparently she married some guy and moved away from the area", Peters replied, after moving a chair to sit on instead of standing on ceremony.

"Tell me something Sergeant", Steve stated as he rose from his seat and headed for the window, turning to sit on the sill, his back against the window pane, he went on to pursue his line of conversation, "when you entered this establishment in sixty one...it was sixty one, yeah?"

"Yes!" Peters responded quickly.

"Yeah...right...ugh...I see. As I was saying, when you joined the force here when you did, why did you suddenly want to try and solve this murder case, when three years had passed and you were fresh out of college?"

"Oh... ugh yeah...right that...well you see", he stammered, scratching his head, as he was finding it difficult to come up with an answer, as Steve had caught him totally off guard, "I had read the story in the newspaper from the first time it appeared and followed it closely and I swore blind I would love to solve that crime, so you see when I arrived here and I learned the crime hadn't been solved...I was always lead to believe it was one of the young market stall holders".

"Ok Sergeant, what made you think that then eh?"

"Well they are always hanging about there looking for the talent; you know what I mean Inspector?"

"Yes I'm not that naive Sergeant, you are referring to the female of the sexes...so why did you assume the killer was a young stall holder then eh, besides she was raped several times before she lost her life. You see I did take the time out to study the Pathology report, plus I visited them to get some answers".

"So! What else did you learn then Inspector?" He asked curiously sitting on the edge of his seat clasping his hands between his knees; the thumb on his left hand nervously tapped the thumb of his right hand.

"I know she was stabbed twice, the first stab was in her stomach which didn't kill her but the second blow was the one to kill her. The first stab was done with such force it resembled somebody who, I don't know, may have possibly lunged at her attacker with such venom she fell onto the knife and her pain caused the killer to strike her the second time out of fear, so killing her instantly".

"And how have you come up with that surmise Inspector?"

"Because when she was stabbed the first time the hilt of the knife made a deep mark on the skin, whereas the second stab didn't. Therefore she had to have attacked her killer seeking some sort of recompense for the evil act they had done to her innocent body, not realising the knife was still there in the hand of the killer, the killer panicked and the rest is history". Steve replied.

"Ok...But what has this got to do with Jack's murder then eh and as to why I believed the killer was a stall holder was because most of them carry knives to open boxes or work with fruit and veg, that's why...it makes sense doesn't it?"

""I see thanks for your insight, now the situation regarding Jack that's a different story, now he was killed from the first blow, the killer stabbed him twice just to make sure he was dead".

"That doesn't answer the question as to why somebody killed him though." Peters edged curiously, his eyes piercing in the direction of Steve whom he suddenly became uneasy with.

"That's where I drew a blank Sergeant", Steve smiled half-heartedly returning to his chair, "the only conclusion

I can come up with at this moment in time, is that it must be linked to two major factors in this case and that is the Church Yard Murder and the recent death of George Blackmore...I get the feeling there is something missing in this whole charade and I just can't put my finger on it at this moment in time, I have this feeling it is staring me in the face and I can't see it".

"That was the feeling I had back then when I was working on the case. I too felt there was something missing and like you I too couldn't put my finger on it...still Inspector I'd better get on, I think I'm wanted by Jackson, something to do with the case of the Black Hat night club incident".

"In that case give, him my regards...I got a missing person to find", Steve said as he rested his elbows on his desk and gently rubbed his right hand.

"Before I go, I wanted to ask you, why didn't you chose me to help with this case as I was involved in it back in sixty one", he asked as he made for the door stopping briefly in his walk.

"Oh don't worry Sergeant, I did think about you, in fact I thought about you a lot but I heard you wanted to be relocated and I wanted a female perspective on this case, that is why I eventually chose Police Constable Fuller and she is proving invaluable to me, with this case that is".

"Ok Inspector good luck with the case, I hope you find your missing woman", Peters smiled as he closed the door behind him.

"Oh I intend too", he remarked quietly under his breath, with a sigh of relief at the thought of not letting on his conclusion to the case. Picking up his pen he again found the crossword a relief but his coffee was now cold so he decided to go to the canteen to get a refill, when the door opened and Wendy entered with two fresh coffees on a tray along with a couple of Chelsea Buns on a small plate.

"I see Peters was with you, so I paid the bakers a little visit on your behalf Inspector, I hope you didn't mind that is", she said as she placed the tray on his desk. "So what is the line of attack today Gov?" she asked as she found the warm seat Peters had been sitting on moments earlier.

"We have a little matter of a missing person to sort out Constable", Steve said informatively, as he helped himself to a bun and one of the coffees.

"Who's the missing person then Gov?" she enquired politely.

"A Sarah Brown, apparently her mother reported her missing and believes it has something to do with the gangland mobs of London and we have been asked, nicely, to look into it, Ok".

"Ok Gov, but what about the little matter of Carol Richards and of course our Jack Gould, or have we got to forget about that?" she pressed with some feelings of remorse at the thought of leaving the case when she knew they were so close to solving it.

"Only for a couple of days, that's all it is, to make Peters think he's off the hook, but of course you are aware of the truth about that situation aren't you constable?" Steve returned as he took a bite out of his bun.

"So how did your week-end go Gov?" She enquired changing the subject to a less formal chat.

"Quiet just some good food and a few bottles of plonk to while away the time...you?"

"Oh it was good...went out for a drink with the boyfriend", she said as she gently stirred her coffee, "by the way", she started then went on to add, "The Graduates were playing on Saturday evening at the football club in Rush Green and they were magic. The boyfriend loved them and wished he could play like the lead guitarist, who knows he said he wanted to learn to play the guitar some time ago but he dreams a lot, mind you it would be fantastic if he did. I always dreamt of being married to a pop star".

"I always dreamt of marrying

Hayley Mills when I saw her in 'Whistle down the wind', I went to the cinema nearly every night when that film was in the cinema...still we can only dream can't we", he returned soulfully.

"Oh by the way I forgot to mention that my brother may have located somebody who goes under the name of the Maverick, he reckons they come from Hoddesdon in Hertfordshire ", She said as she retrieved the other bun and begun to bite delicately into it.

"That is fantastic I come from that area so it's a strong possibility he might be the killer of my Sally...how soon can he get the address or should I say his ten forty or whatever it is", Steve eagerly enquired, giving the impression he knew something about the use of the new in thing that was CB's.

"Yeah, my brothers handle is 'the wireman' I go under the handle of 'ladybird' Gov", she smiled, then went on to enquire, "this missing person what are we going to do about her?"

"Well we are going to meet her mother who apparently owns a pub in Hornchurch, the trouble is we don't happen to have the name of the pub in question at this moment in time, so we will need to contact the Home Office and speak to Major Thompson and ask him to furnish us with the name of the public house the mother of Sarah owns, so we can pay her a visit to confirm that we are actually looking into her missing daughter?"

"Would you like me to phone him on your behalf Gov?" she asked politely placing her coffee on the tray.

"No! I will do it ", he ordered as he lifted the receiver and abruptly dialled the number for the Major's office, having dialled it several times before, "Ah is that you Chris...can I speak to the Major please?"

There was the usual few minutes silence as the secretary put him through to the Major's office where he was busy doing his daily paperwork.

"Yes Inspector what can I do for you?" returned the Major patiently, "you are aware I am a very busy man?"

"I know I want the name of the pub Mrs. Brown owns in Hornchurch, if it's not too much trouble?" Steve returned with the hint of a cheeky grin on his face only because he knew the Major couldn't see him.

"Speak to my secretary Inspector, she'll tell you what you want to know...oh...and Steve wipe that grin off your face, I wasn't born yesterday".

"You haven't got a camera here by any chance Major?" Steve replied with a more formal look in his eyes as he went on to add, "Ok put me back to Chris please...Major", he requested politely.

After a few minutes he replaced the receiver once the secretary told him the name of the pub was, 'The White Hart' in the high street.

"It looks like we are paying Mrs Brown a little visit this afternoon Constable, so make sure you have your trusty note book in your hand".

"I always do Gov so what's it all about, I heard you mention it was a missing girl?" enquired Wendy who was just finishing her coffee.

"We have been asked to try and find her daughter who been missing for the last couple of days".

"It sounds like she has run away from home, probably with a lover whom the mother can't get on with...you know...a big row...bust up and the rest is history so they say", returned a curious Wendy who went on to enquire, "do we have any clues as to her whereabouts?"

"Your guess is as good as mine, but I suppose we have to start with the so called boyfriend, she may have gone to his home...who knows?"

"I suppose I'd better take this little lot back to the canteen and get my coat and bag", she returned with a smile as she replaced her mug on to the tray and retrieved Steve's as he too finished what was left, in his hand he held the remnants of his bun, "I see Peters as he left the office and he seemed a bit bewildered when I saw him walking up the corridor, you didn't say anything to him did you?"

"If I did he wouldn't have been walking down the corridor, he'd be banged up...nah I'll catch up with him later, so don't get worried Constable I have the situation well and truly in hand...in fact I feel sorry for the lad...had he reported the incident back then, the least he would have got was a crime of mandatory rape and maybe he would've served, I don't know, maybe seven years if he was lucky. He could've been out in five and a half years, but no, instead he chose to ignore that aspect and used the police force to cover his crimes of murder...I am lead to believe he has upset a few of you young ladies in the past".

"That's an understatement Gov, he has upset virtually every girl in this station, including me...there was a point when I felt scared of him...you know it was as if he could've killed me because I told him I had a boyfriend. In fact my boyfriend threatened to come down here and beat the crap out of him...sorry I shouldn't have said that...I'll do my job Gov", She said as she gathered everything together on the tray and headed for the door and the canteen.

Chapter 39

Steve sat staring blankly into his newspaper, deep in thought, as he dipped yet another one of his custard creams into his coffee. His mind was busily toying with the idea of paying his cousin Johnny a visit, with the crazy notion that he might know this person Eileen Brown. In addition to the fact he might also know of her daughter Sarah, assuming Sarah was the only child.

Just then Wendy re-entered the office having returned the tray and her coffee mug back to the canteen. Her trusty bag now slung over her right shoulder and was held loosely in her right hand. Looking pleased with herself she commented on the fact that she had just seen Peters in the corridor heading for the rear door with a smug conceited look on his face.

Steve just returned with an half-hearted smile as he downed the remainder of his coffee, then he folded his newspaper and tossed it to one side of his desk, "I have decided to pay my cousin a little visit first Constable", he said calmly placing his pen into his jacket inside pocket.

"Cousin Gov?" She quizzed.

"Yes, my cousin Johnny he owns a pub nearby...so lets get cracking...shall we...if anybody asks we're going to see a man about a dog, ok eh". Steve said with one of his usual cheeky smiles accompanied with the wink and slight nod of the head in her direction, as he locked his office door, he turned briefly to whisper in Wendy's ear with a frown, saying, "and as for our little friend Peters, Constable we'll wipe that smug look off his face very soon, eh".

"This cousin of yours...Johnny you say?" Wendy questioned as they left the building.

"Yeah, what about him?" Steve

curiously enquired, with his right hand tucked into his trouser pocket, his left arm gently swinging in step with his right leg as if he were marching.

"Well Gov...What will he know about this case?" She asked as they entered the yard and headed for the market area.

A cool hazy sun shone through a mist that was beginning to settle around the area, when Steve explained that his cousin was a source of knowledge around this area. He then went on to explain that certain people frequented the pub with useful information, he was referring to the person he knew as Frank the tank. "You see Constable, sometimes one can get the sort of information one needs from those outside the present case...and in this case who knows, this Frank if he is there may know something about the case, besides...if nothing else we can have a drink...on me, that is ok".

"I'm all for that", she smiled with a light hearted step in her stride.

It wasn't long before they found themselves stepping into another world, a far cry from the hustle and bustle of the street life that endlessly moved about outside.

Steve casually scanned the bar, where several people sat busy chatting amongst themselves, heavily engrossed in their life stories along with all their problems to debate, oblivious to the intrusion of anybody entering that world.

It wasn't long before Johnny spotted them entering his establishment, with the usual banter of, "look what the cat dragged in". He was already pouring Steve a beer, placing it in front of him once they reached the bar. "And what can we get for the young lady...I gather the lady is with you Steve?" Johnny politely said.

"I'll have a Babycham please", Wendy asked, quietly feeling uneasy about this line of work but found one of the bar stools a welcome break from the norm.

"This is D.C. Fuller", Steve introduced, then went on to inform her that, "this is my cousin Johnny, Constable".

"Doesn't she have a name other than Constable?" enquired Johnny who poured her drink and placed a cherry on a thin pointed stick onto the edge of her champagne glass, declaring it was on the house, "So Steve what brings you to this neck of the woods then?" he enquired as he returned to leaning on the counter.

"Yeah the Constables name is Wendy mate...but we want to talk to Frank, is he in?" Steve asked as he took a sip of his beer.

"Yeah he's in the loo...sorry toilet,

he should be out in a mo", Johnny said as he poured himself another drink, "So what's the problemmo?"

"We want to know about an Eileen Brown who owns the White Hart pub in Hornchurch", Steve remarked casually.

"Yeah I know Eileen Brown, she sometimes rings me if she runs out of beer and needs a barrel or two...you see...in this game we all work together as a team, for example if there's things I need and can't get to the cash and carry she normally has it in stock...so why the interest in her, what has she done".

"Nothing, it's more to do with her daughter", Steve returned.

"Did I overhear you mention the name of Eileen Brown...Steve", came from a voice to his right. Turning quickly he found he had now been joined by Frank, with whom he had wanted to talk to in relation to his line of enquiry.

"Frank!" Steve said abruptly then went on to say, "just the guy I want to talk to".

"Why what have I done?" he grinned.

"Nothing...yet", Steve smiled as he placed a five pound note on the counter and told Johnny to give him his poison.

"So Steve what is it you want to know about Eileen Brown then eh...and that's a pint of my usual Johnny", he said finding one of the bar stools to sit on.

"What do you know about the daughter?" Steve pursued.

"Sarah!" He remarked pouting his lips with a curious glint in his eyes, "that is one mixed up lass...beautiful boobs to die for", he said waving his hands in front of his chest to imitate the breasts, then abruptly apologised to Wendy who just shrugged her shoulders with a hint of a grin but declaring she was used to it.

"Sarah!" Steve returned abruptly.

"You said she was mixed up", enquired Wendy curiously, holding the fluted glass in her right hand.

"She is in love with an Italian named Stefan Capello, if you're asking me he is a drug dealer, one of the big boys and Eileen doesn't like him playing around with her daughter and that is where the fireworks come into it".

"So what can you tell me about Eileen then?" Steve pressed on eager to learn everything.

"Eileen! where would you like me to begin...she has run a few pubs in and around the East End; she was a young bar maid during the war years; mingling with the spivs and she was also a bit of a wheeler dealer herself; that is how she come by the money to eventually purchase her first pub in the Mile End Road all legit that is".

"Legit!" remarked Wendy.

"Yeah legal you know...sorry sweetheart I'm a cockney yeh see" replied Frank.

"So Frank what can you tell me about this Stefan then?" Steve continued to pursue the story.

"Stefan", he returned taking a sip of his beer then went on to add, "he comes from a big family, rumours have it that they are after the pub. That's Eileen's pub I'm talking about".

"I gather Eileen isn't interested in selling it to them?" returned Steve.

"You hit the nail on the head Steve...no way will she part with the pub, especially to the likes of them, that is".

"I get it!" Steve snapped, "So they hitched Stefan up with Sarah, knowing in time, she would inherit the pub and they would have it in their hands for free, non-gratis and of course Eileen, who wasn't born yesterday, saw through their little plan. But Sarah being so young couldn't see it and turned on her mother and run away with this Stefan geezer...so the question is Frank...where would they go...where would this Stefan take Sarah?" Steve asked as he turned and leant on the counter pondering his thoughts. "Well Frank what d'ya reckon...any clues out there?" he asked turning back to look him in the face.

"I heard they caught a coach to somewhere in Cornwall...I think it was something like Camborne or Redruth something like that...I don't know, apparently this Stefan has family down there too".

"Where can we find the Capello family here then?" Steve enquired.

"They live in Valence Road in Dagenham, I'm not sure of the number, but I know it is around halfway down that road, ok Steve", he explained then went on to add, "if you must know, this Stefan as a reputation for grassing up those he hates especially if he's after their turf, he wants to rule the East End you see; just like the Krays did and I can tell you now...there are a few big time dealers who would love to meet him down some dark alley, especially when they get out of jail that is...if you get my drift, he should watch his back though, there's rumours going around that a certain drug baron is due out of the clink in a weeks time and I've heard he is after this Stefan", Frank said informally.

"Does this Stefan know about this drug baron getting out of prison soon...I mean could that be why he has vanished taking Sarah with him", Steve enquired curiously.

"Maybe, I don't now, but I can only assume, he might know and yes that could be why he's legged it, thinking they wouldn't go looking for him down there...maybe mummy and daddy insisted on it, who knows".

"And that sort of thing wouldn't go down to well in Eileen's pub and it certainly wouldn't do her any good now would it", Steve said as he downed the last dregs of his beer telling Johnny to keep the change from the five pound note, "Give Frank another beer on me Johnny", he said as the pair of them made for the door in order to leave the comfort of that place with the intention of paying Eileen Brown a visit.

"This Stefan seems a bit of a character Gov", Wendy said as they headed back to the factory and Steve's car.

"You're right, he is somebody that interests me and I'm sure he would also interest the drug squad should we catch up with him".

"That's assuming the drug baron doesn't get him before you...I would hate to be in his shoes right now", Wendy remarked.

"Then let's hope we get to him before he does and hope we can get some sense out of Eileen in the process". Steve replied with an air of urgency.

Three quarters of an hour later and they found themselves opening the door to the White Hart Pub in Hornchurch. It was an old building, built around the time of the Great War. Its reddish brown brickwork stood out with dark wooden window frames partly worn on the edges of the sills. Inside they were met with dark mauve Hessian wallpaper with diamond shaped flowers and a badge emblem in the middle of each diamond. A bar lay back and it was a typical London pub resembling his cousin's pub.

An elderly guy was wiping some of the glasses as they had just been washed; he was drying them and placing some of them onto a shelf; whilst hanging handled pint mugs on hooks under a high shelf, over the bar area. Another young lady was serving a couple of men in working clothes, before she made her way to Steve and Wendy who walked casually to the bar and the awaiting female.

"Can we talk to the governor please?" asked Steve politely.

The girl didn't answer, instead she simply pointed to a table in the far corner where an elderly woman sat reading a book and drinking a cup of tea. She was a tall slim woman, with short curly grey hair and her face was adorned with half round gold rimmed glasses. She wore a green floral patterned dress.

"Eileen Brown?" enquired Steve politely as they approached the table, pausing before entering her private domain.

She slowly averted her eyes from the page of her book and peered at them over the rim of her glasses with a cold look in her eyes, as if they had trespassed on her land, "Who are you?" she asked sternly.

Removing their badges Steve informed her that he was Detective Chief Inspector Price and went on to introduce Wendy as Detective Constable Fuller. "We are here to discuss the disappearance of your daughter Sarah".

"About bloody time", she replied angrily, placing her book down on the table opened and face down so as not to lose the page she was on, she then went on to add, and "She could be dead for all you care".

Steve grabbed the chair opposite her and Wendy dragged another from one of the other tables and sat back a bit from Steve.

"I see madam", Steve replied calmly, then went on to add, "I understand your daughter may have run off with a certain Stefan Capello, whom you dislike, am I correct?"

Her eyes stared at him curiously; his words had hit her like a bullet from the barrel of an invisible gun. "What else can you tell me Inspector, that I don't already know? By the way the answer to your question is...no, I can't stand the idiot, he's a toe rag, and I wouldn't want the likes of him taking over my pub when I'm dead and buried".

"Well I have been informed they were seen boarding a coach to Cornwall, as for their true destination your guess is as good as mine, but it is believed it could be Camborne or Redruth. I wouldn't know although I did hear that Stefan has family down there, so my guess is they have gone there", Steve replied calmly.

"I guess they got what they wanted all along", she returned soulfully as she bowed her head, and then added, "they wanted my daughter to go and live with them, so their precious little boy didn't have to travel to and fro from here. They also more or less demanded me to sell them this pub for their son's future, at the expense of my daughter...and I wasn't having it...lets hope the bastard doesn't hurt my little girl or I will not be responsible for my actions...do I make myself clear Inspector".

"Sure", he replied casually leaning back in his seat, "all I can do is notify the Home Office of these facts and they can make arrangements with the Bill down there to look out for them and inform them of your concern for their safety".

"Then I guess this interview is terminated Inspector", she said as she picked up the opened book averting her eyes in the direction of the page she had left, just adding one last statement of, "Good bye! - Inspector!"

Steve just smiled and left the pub with Wendy in tow declaring, 'what a nasty piece of work she is', and went on to comment, 'I wouldn't want her to be my mum Gov'.

"I know what you mean Constable", Steve uttered. "I feel sorry for Sarah too".

With that they headed for the office and some well earned lunch.

Chapter 40

The next day was just a bit of a quiet business of the day, mainly confronting the Major over his latest quest which was regarding the missing teenager Sarah Brown. She appeared to have run away with her boyfriend to the Cornish area, hopefully to the comfort of her boyfriend's relations home down there. Steve expressed his concerns that were mostly about the boyfriend who it seemed was keen to get rid of the existing drug barons in and around the East End of London and take over the area for himself.

Wendy on the other hand paid a visit to the school which the lads had attended in their youth, around the end of the fifties when the people were still escaping the results of the Second World War, the poor were the people trying to picking up the pieces of their meagre existence.

It was on the Thursday morning that Steve sat at his desk and was totally aware of the return of D.I. Dobson back on the scene, flying in from Australia with what he said was some good news, this was leaving Steve feeling restless. His mind was set on putting to bed the case he had been working on.

His moment of silence was broken with a knock on the door and the entrance of Reg with a brown envelope made out to

Steve, with the Home Office official stamp on it. After receiving it Steve began opening it after the usual pleasantries to Reg, who then left the office to continue his duties on the front desk.

Opening the envelope he found the warrant to search Peters home and arrange his arrest for the Murder of Jack Gould and Carol Richards in nineteen fifty eight. He gently placed it on his desk and stared at it with some feeling of desperation, a slight sweating of his palms made him rub them together using a clean handkerchief that he removed from his jacket pocket. His mind dictating his approach to the situation in hand; he had become more aware that Peters wasn't going to come lightly; believing he would put up some sort of fight; especially after the way he had dealt with Jack and others who had happened to cross his path.

Putting his hands together as if he were praying, he touched his lips with the tips of his fingers deep in thought, before he picked up the warrant and having taken the correct file from his drawer he slid it into the folder ready to be got at the right moment. Looking up at his clock that clicked over onto nine thirty there was an eerie silence only topped by the ticking of the clock which sounded endless in his ears, not even a sound came from the corridor as if the world had vanished, leaving him to live a life alone in that barren world. As the clock ticked over once again, he licked his lips and decided it was time for a coffee.

As Steve was passing the incident room, complete with the cream coloured wall that was covered in the crimes of the day, including that of the late Jack Gould. Steve noticed how it seemed to dominate centre stage of the room. It was decorated with several pictures taken at the scene of the crime and written text above it, declaring the time and the place of crime with a hint of the connection with the late George Blackmore and not much else. Entering the room Steve found himself staring at the wall and the picture of Jack slumped over the wall where he fell and blood on the ground around him.

'*Why, oh Why, oh Why?*' Steve said quietly to himself as several officers in uniforms moved about in the room, some with folders tucked under their arms. Steve smiled as he tucked his hand in his trouser pocket and departed from the room and headed for the canteen, where he met up with Wendy who was sitting by the window staring out into the world whilst biting into a piece of toast.

Steve stood, eyes peeled, studying the food that was on offer and dwelling on what to have for his breakfast. He was thinking that he needed a hearty meal inside him, to be able to face the events that were unfolding around him. He knew he was unable to change it, despite his dream that something might happen and everything would change for the better, but he knew that was impossible now.

Turning briefly he was surprised to find he was being greeted by D.I. Jackson who quietly said 'Hi Inspector', over his left shoulder, then went on to enquire how things were working out with the case he was working on, as he was aware Steve was working on the murder of Jack Gould.

Steve simply smiled and asked if he and Peters could join him in interview room four in an hour's time.

Jackson looked at him curiously but agreed to do so despite a heavy work load, "I do have some duties Inspector... you know I am working on this case of The Black Hat, we have a bit of an incident there with the owners of the club unwilling to come forward to be interviewed".

"So what has happened there on the scene?" Steve asked as he took a plate of cheese sandwiches from one of the shelves that he then placed on his tray and edged forward to get his drink.

"A stash of heroin was found in the office" returned Jackson who helped himself to a tuna sandwich and a ring doughnut.

"I see", returned Steve curiously then went on to ask, "Who found this so called stash of heroin then, eh?"

"Sergeant Peters did...why do you ask?" Jackson enquired, stopping to hear what Steve was getting at.

"As I said Inspector...meet me along with Peters in interview room four in a hours time and all will be revealed...but I shouldn't let Peters know what's up...preferably not at this moment in time...keep him guessing, ok Inspector", then he went on to add, "mums the word where Peters is concerned".

"How are you getting on with your side kick Wendy?" Jackson enquired wishing to change the subject to a less formal talk.

"She's good, I trust her whole heartedly", Steve remarked calmly as he handed over a couple of pound for his meal and coffee and waited for his change before heading for Wendy, "remember Inspector, one hour, interview room four, both Peters and your good self...I think you'll be somewhat surprised by this whole charade surrounding the murder of good old Jack Gould".

"In that case I look forward to your deliberation then", returned a somewhat curious Jackson who went to join a couple of uniformed officers, occasionally looking back at Steve.

Steve eventually joined Wendy at the table by the window.

"What's on yeh mind Constable?" Steve enquired as he sat down opposite her, making her turn her head quickly with a hint of a smile, "you seemed miles away".

"Just thinking Gov that's all" she uttered.

"It wouldn't have anything to do with our friend Peters by any chance?" Steve said softly, leaning on the table as he prepared to eat his cheese sandwiches.

"It has crossed my mind Gov", she replied leaning back in her seat, "What is the plan for today then?"

"I have a warrant to have his home searched for the weapon. I want you to take a couple of uniform boys and search the property for the weapon", he explained then went on to add, "it is a scout knife, usually with a brass handle and a slight hilt, you know a bit where the handle meets the blade, it is usually six inches long, curved to a point ok, eh, go in about an hours time, I'll have our friend tied up in interview room four ok, got it".

"Yes Gov interview room four...I gather you want me to bring you the weapon in that room, should we find it that is, but what if we don't find it there Gov what then eh?"

"Don't put bridges there when it isn't necessary, besides we'll cross that bridge when it arrives Constable", returned Steve who set about his meal with some sense of ease about his quest, then added briefly "You'll find the warrant in the file on my desk", he said as he handed her the keys to the office telling her to return them to him once she had the paperwork required to carry out her duties.

Wendy drank her coffee and occasionally looked at Jackson who sat with his back to them, heavy in some idle conversation with a couple of uniform boys, who seemed to chuckle at times, it seemed evident he was either telling jokes or simply taking the Mickey out of somebody.

Wendy said with a whisper so as not to be over heard, that she would have to get a locksmith to gain entry into the home of Peters. Steve agreed with her, telling her to do so. Finishing her break she did as she had been told and headed off to do her job, the office keys firmly gripped in her hand, wiping her mouth with a tissue that she finally discarded in a bin by the door.

Jackson looked back cagily over his shoulder at Steve with an element of curiosity in his eyes, toying with some crazy idea about the forthcoming event awaiting him in room four. He had been ordered to attend despite his wish to continue with his own duties, but on the other hand he was equally curious about Steve's intentions regarding the murder of Jack. However he was left wondering what did it have to do with him and Peters. Suddenly he was beginning to feel like a criminal, like a sacrificial lamb to the slaughter, despite the fact that he knew he was innocent of anything to do with Jack's murder, but it didn't stop him thinking the worst.

Wendy returned briefly to hand back the keys to his office then said she was off as requested and explained that she had retrieved two uniformed officers to escort her to the home of Peters. Steve simply nodded and gave her a half gestured smile as he took the keys from her to continue drinking his coffee.

Steve took his time finishing his breakfast, as if he had all the time in the world to do his duty, which added to the tension in Jackson's busy mind. He even took his time returning the used dishes back to the counter, glancing over at Jackson with the whisper of a smile as he headed for the incident room. Once in the incident room, he stared yet again at the board, especially the photo of Jack. Turning quickly he was ready to talk to a couple of officers who were seated at their relevant desks, writing up their reports for the morning. Steve approached them and gave them their orders to stand outside that room and not allow anyone out at all other than himself, when he gave them the go ahead, so they just simply replied 'ok' in unison, with some sense of curiosity, finding his request totally out of their normal line of duties, but agreeable to them, as it took them away from the usual duty of patrolling the local streets.

He finally returned to his office to retrieve the necessary paperwork in this case, including the photographs obtained in the course of his investigation.

He noticed that Peters and Jackson were heading for the interview room that had been requested, so Steve returned to the incident room to advise the two officers to stand outside interview room four within a quarter of a hours time. They simply shrugged their shoulders and agreed, one of them politely asked if he wanted them to knock and enter to let him know they were in place.

Steve smiled and agreed to their request, before heading off in the direction of the requested room still optimistic about his approach to this delicate situation he found himself in. He was aware that if it was a person from the streets it would've been alright, it would have been something he could do in his sleep, but when it is one of your colleagues it becomes too personal and painful.

With the files tucked under his arm he cagily approached the interview room where he had noticed the two men enter and who were now waiting patiently for the arrival of Steve. Jackson sat on one of the chairs and placed his hands on the old oak wooden table that had graffiti carved into it by previous criminals, who had also happened to find themselves in that room being interrogated by the likes of the two men now in there. Peters paced the floor, one hand tucked into his trouser pocket.

"What's going on Inspector?" Enquired Peters curiously.

"Your guess is as good as mine...so sit down, it's probably nothing", Jackson replied softly.

"Has he said anything to you about this little meeting?" enquired a concerned Peters who went on to add, "besides I thought we were supposed to be interviewing the manager of the Black Hat night club for god sake, or have you forgotten that...Inspector?"

"No Sergeant, I haven't forgotten that, so lets just hope this little intrusion is short lived so we can get on with our duties".

It wasn't long before Steve entered the room and finding Peters pacing the floor he immediately ordered him to take a seat, pointing to the one next to Jackson who sat with pouted lips and a curious look in his eyes, eager to hear what Steve was after.

Peters on the other hand slouched in the seat with his legs apart, arms folded tightly across his chest with an anxious look on his face, as he stared at Steve who took little notice of his glare.

"So Inspector, what's with this cloak and dagger stuff...meet me in the interview room in an hour, a bit school boyish to say the least", remarked Jackson.

"That is as it may be Inspector", returned Steve, who placed the file on the table after pulling up another chair on the opposite side of the two puzzled looking men. "I knew you'd be curious as to why I ordered you both in here today".

"We did wonder Inspector", returned an inquisitive Jackson.

There was a moment's silence as Steve composed himself ready for the journey into the unknown, he knew it was now or never and he had no choice in the matter, he just had to get on with it regardless of the consequences, as he briefly looked at Peters.

"Well Inspector!" Pushed an eager Jackson.

"Before I came here I was on holiday in Weymouth in my family caravan, enjoying a well earned rest from my duties, when I heard about the murder of Jack Gould. By the way I knew him some six years, hence I was shocked to hear of his death as I am aware that everybody was shocked to hear it too", Steve opened his interrogation unknown to them, then went on to add, "I was approached by Special branch with reference to his murder, but I told them to let the local plod sort it out as I wasn't all that interested in getting involved with this case".

"Are you saying you want us two to take this case off your hands so you can return to your caravan in Dorset?" returned a wide eyed Jackson.

Peters stared up at the ceiling with an air of boredom about his face.

"As I was saying Inspector", he returned gently leaning on the table his hands resting on the file.

Just then there was the signalled knock on the door which was opened by the uniformed officer who apologised for his intrusion and closed the door quietly behind him so as not to make his presence felt.

"You were saying Inspector?" Jackson pressed on eagerly.

"Yeah. Yeah. Yeah Inspector just get on with it, we have work to do", answered Peters angrily.

"Yes Sergeant!" Steve said with

his head bowed down, looking at the file in front of him and feeling despondent at the prospect ahead, "Right!" he said after a moments silence, "as I was saying before we were distracted...I didn't want this case, but then something happened to change all that.

You see a young man was banged up for life several years ago for murdering his wife, by injecting her in the neck with a lethal dose of heroin".

"Andrew Cox", said Peters in the background.

"Yes Sergeant...Andrew Cox, but...don't tell me you read it in the newspapers back then, what was it...ten years ago, something like that eh".

"Yeah well...it's what coppers do init".

"Right Sergeant", returned Steve, "so why don't you fill us in on the case then as you read the story in the papers".

Jackson turned briefly to look at his side kick sitting arrogantly and wondering where this conversation was heading.

"The guy was high on heroin and when he got home and found his wife sitting watching the television, he went mad and injected her in the neck with a lethal dose of the stuff and as she wasn't an addict it killed her outright and that is why he is serving life, ok".

"Right, do you want to fill us in on the story that Andrew was saying in his defence, Sergeant...or would you like me to tell it as it were", Steve pressed on.

Peters didn't answer, instead he gestured with his hand, to tell Steve to get on with it, complete with that bored look on his face and nearly breaking into a yawn.

"Ok! Apparently he said he met somebody in a local pub and he told this guy a story from the past; this guy said he was far from home and needed a bed for the night. Andrew out of his head on booze offered to let him stay at his address. The man agreed and said that he would head for home in the morning, which Andrew alleged he did. However when he got up in the morning he found his wife Janet dead in the lounge with a needle protruding from her neck, the stranger wasn't to be found".

"So what as this got to do with Jack's murder then eh?" Enquired a curious looking Jackson.

"Oh! It's got everything to do with Jack's murder inspector", returned Steve confidently.

"It was Lucy!" remarked Peters sharply.

"What!" snapped Steve.

"Yeah Sergeant what are you talking about?" enquired Jackson, even more curious about his friend.

"His wife's name was Lucy, not

Janet, Inspector", returned Peters confidently moving forward slightly on his chair, but soon returned to his slouched position shrugging his shoulders and raising his eyes conceitedly in the process.

"That's right Sergeant it was Lucy, you were right. I dare say you are going to tell me you read it in the newspapers back then", Steve replied quietly then went on to add, "but that wasn't the reason for this chat...no...it all stems from the story Andrew talked about that really interested me...that's the same story he told this person in the pub all those years ago and that is why I am here today...now...and here in this room at this moment in time".

"What's this... Jackanory?" snapped Peters with the slight hint of a grin, then added sarcastically, "are we all sitting comfortable then".

Steve smirked, his eyes lifted briefly to look at the actions of a fool then went on to say, "right are we sitting comfortable, there you go Sergeant just for you, ok", he said as he moved to the folder before him.

"The story goes back to fifty eight, that's May of nineteen fifty eight where Lucy...as you so pointed out Sergeant and Andrew were courting and enjoying a night out, this ended with them snogging in a back seat of a car parked in a street right here in Romford. When between kisses he spotted a car that took his fancy, it wasn't just any old car, he said it was like an American car, but in fact I can tell you, it was a Vauxhall Cresta to be more precise, one of only six made at the time...he went on to tell me about two young men running to the car laughing their heads off. A third person suddenly arrived at the car waving a pair of ladies knickers in the air, they all got into the car and it drove off, he said he didn't realise the driver was sitting in the car at the time, but only noticed him when it sped off".

Peters eyes looked cagily at Steve's deliberation of the story, suddenly he wasn't feeling right about the position he was finding himself in as he toyed with ideas of escape.

"So Inspector who or what are we referring too?" Enquired Jackson.

"Lets go back to the beginning shall we?" Steve said as he began to open the file before him. Removing the photograph of the car and the three lads, which he placed on top of the file face down.

"How do you know the make of the car Inspector?" enquired Jackson.

"Yeah come on tell us Inspector, you are driving me mad with anticipation?" pushed Peters, eager to be getting on with his duties away from this line of conversation.

"It was simple Inspector, you see that car was a prototype with only six in the country. When I checked with the DVLA in Swansea they were able to tell me that the only one given as a gift in this area was to a Kevin Blackmore and yes he is the older brother of George Blackmore who we know died a while ago. It was he who requested the aid of a detective just before his death, and the detective who responded to the plea just happened to be Jack. But of course he is dead also, so you would assume that's the end of the story".

"So...what are you saying?" pursued Jackson.

"What Andrew Cox saw was the killers linked to the death of a young attractive girl named Carol Richards in nineteen fifty eight". Steve expressed carefully.

"Are you trying to tell us the same person killed Jack?" enquired Jackson, who then went on to add, "don't look at me Inspector, it wasn't me".

Peters remained silent looking everywhere other than at Steve.

"No...the three lads in question were in fact, Alfie Green, Ian Carter, and of course George Blackmore, he was the driver of the car, George that is".

"I get the impression you know more than you are letting on Inspector", pursued Jackson eager to learn the truth.

"Maybe you are right Inspector", returned Steve, repeating it but quieter as he turned over the photograph to the amazement of Peters who quickly averted his eyes in the direction of that photo.

"The person who took this photograph is our killer Inspector...this photograph was taken by the killer about a week before the murder of Carol Richards and what started out to be a great day out turned into a nightmare for everybody concerned. A nightmare that would haunt them for the rest of their lives, with only death to release them from that one day in their life when a cruel twist of fate caught up with them". Steve said as he looked at the photo before giving it to Jackson to study.

"What you are saying Inspector", started Jackson curiously as she studied the photograph then added, "it's when the killer heard the story being told by Andrew Cox he realised his secret would be revealed if it got out, so somehow he had to set the poor sod up. So he killed his wife and departed to let Andrew take the can for his action, after all who would believe a known killer".

"I can tell you that the killer believes he is the only one left to spill the beans as they say", returned Steve sitting back in his chair feeling in control of the fate of the killer, but then went on to add, "but he is wrong, there is another, in fact there are several people he overlooked. He believes his story died with George but he is wrong, you see Inspector George had already told his story to his wife who also happens to be named Lucy. It was her who convinced him to tell the police the truth before he died. The trouble is it spelt death for who ever went to that bedside, in other words Jackson it could've quite easily have been you and you would've ended up like Jack. Now as I was saying, in this photograph the killer didn't realise that there was one other person there at the time, but hidden because he was otherwise detained with the girlfriend of George and that was a Johnny King".

"So who is the killer then?" enquired Jackson.

"The killer got George to borrow his big brother's car and go bird hunting. Looking for girls to impress with the wheels, so what started out to be a bit of fun turned into a nightmare because the killer sought revenge when he got turned down by a certain young lady who he tried to impress with his mouth, but she was wise to him".

"I get the impression you know who the killer is", Jackson said as he replaced the photograph back in front of Steve.

Steve let out a sigh as he removed

the warrant, "Sergeant Peters I'm arresting you for the murders of Carol Richards, Jack Gould and Lucy Cox and both Ian Carter and his friend Alfie Green in Australia, anything you say will be taken down and used in evidence in a court of law".

"You are joking Inspector", laughed Peters, then went on to add, "this is fairy tales, you have no proof I had anything to do with this crime...sure it was me who took this bloody photograph but it doesn't prove I killed anybody, let alone this Carol bird or Jack",

"That is why, for several years, you were seen to be putting flowers where she died, including a little teddy bear. You were also seen killing both persons by somebody who was close by at the time, they saw everything, even to the extent that the girl lunged at you for what you had done to her, accidentally falling onto the knife...you panicked and stabbed her again, before running off with her knickers in your hand and making your friends believe she was ok. Then there's our friend Mr. Cox, he picked out your mug shot as the person he met in the pub. I took the liberty of checking back then and you had just did a drugs bust, where heroin was found, so instead of handing it all in, you took some of it to set up Andrew. It is also strange that shortly after the incident with

Andrew you caused Kevin to write off that car in the photograph, thinking if it were destroyed nobody would know what happened back then. That is why after the death of George you broke into his home hoping to find this very photograph, but George had boxed clever and gave his stuff to his son to use at a later date should he need to".

"You're mad Inspector...mad as a hatter...in fact you are right out of a comic book...you can't prove a thing, I'm innocent and I'm getting out of here now", he said angrily as he found his feet and made for the door only to be met by the two uniformed officers outside the door.

"Take him away Constables and put him in a cell, he is under arrest for murder", Steve instructed but then added, "You see Peters it really was the car that was your downfall, had you not got your friend to borrow that particular car this would never have happened. Carol would be happily married and with children and of course Jack would still be alive and who knows where I would have been today...take him away".

Jackson was left in a state of awe at the events that had just evolved in his presence, then finally finding his voice he muttered "Now I can see why you are a Detective Chief Inspector and I shall now go and look more closely at the cases he has worked on with me. I guess I was here to learn about him but maybe also to protect you as he has killed so easily in the past. Thanks for letting me be in on the arrest."

Steve just responded with a final "Just check out what happened about the young girl killed outside the Black Hat last year as I understand Peters was involved in the case", he smiled grimly as he placed the photo back into the file with one final glance at it.

Chapter 41

You could cut the atmosphere in the office with a knife, after the bomb shell that Steve had unleashed. When the news of the sudden arrest of a fellow officer, especially for murder, let alone for the crime of murder of a fellow officer. It was hard for them to get their heads around the fact that Peters could even continue to work with them and yet was also part of the team to find the killer back in sixty one.

There was an eerie feel about the whole place now, with gaunt looking faces walking around like zombies, still finding it difficult to come to terms with Steve's findings. It was not just regarding the murder of Jack Gould but also the murder of Carol Richards, some twenty odd years previously. What was making it hard for them was the thought that for many years they had been working with a serial killer. It was particularly hardest for the female officers on the beat, who he had tried to befriend over the years, leaving them with the thought that they could've quite easily have become another one of his victims.

The highlight of the day was when Ian arrived at the office with his big surprise because he had brought back with him Kevin Blackmore, who when he met Peters, caused a commotion in the corridors of the station. As both of them came face to face, with Kevin finally declaring that he had tried to get his brother George to grass him up. However he had been told they wouldn't out of fear of reprisals by Peters, he had used his powers as a police officer to threaten them, claiming he could get any one of them banged up for the crime.

Bowed heads would rise when Steve walked about that place, although there was a sense of relief in some of their eyes.

Steve was summoned to the chief's office once he learned of the arrest of Peters, for the murder of Jack Gould and the murder of Carol Richards, as he had been the officer who worked on that case all those years previously.

"So Steve what's this business with Peters then, eh?" enquired a curious Chief, who sat with his pen poised in his hand ready to sign some documents.

"He murdered Jack out of fear of being captured for the murder of Carol Richards...you know the Church Yard Murder", Steve replied calmly and confidently.

"Yes! Yes! I am fully aware of the case in question, but how did you work it out Inspector when there was nothing to link him to that incident back then, eh?"

"The idiot made several mistakes when he was young...for example he boasted to Carol Richards' friend Rose that he was going to become a police officer", he explained as he edged towards the window, then went on to add, "now, had he interviewed her back then, she would've most definitely recognised him. He wanted revenge on her for rejecting him outside the cinema that night in May of fifty eight, because it was Rose he wanted to hurt not Carol, you see", he said as he sat on the window ledge, with his back against the window, then went on to explain more deeply. "Then there was this car, which was a prototype, only one of them in that area was given as a gift to George Blackmore's brother Kevin, who by the way has just come over from Australia and straight away he has ID'd Peters. So you see Chief, it was Rose and a Vauxhall Cresta, that was the killers real nightmare. Had you been aware of those facts back then he could've been banged up back then, but he thought his identity would be hidden behind his badge and for twenty four years it was. Until the death of George Blackmore that is, it was something he wasn't in control of...I hate to think what could've happened if it had been Peters who went to his bedside instead of Jack".

"The thought doesn't bear thinking about Inspector", returned the chief, feeling both elated and yet sad at the same time now, with the prospect of having the killer of Carol Richards in custody in his station, "I guess Peters isn't too happy about the situation...I gather you had D.I. Jackson as your witness Inspector...very wise of you. I must say...I mean, it could've got rather nasty had you been alone with him", he explained as he swivelled around in his chair, his left hand clenched in a fist as it rested on his green baize blotting paper.

"By the way, I had a warrant for his arrest via the Home Office Chief", he said casually then added, "so I arranged for Detective Constable Fuller to take some of the uniform boys to Peters' home and search it for the weapon, as both were murdered with the same weapon...I'm awaiting her return now, hopefully with the final piece of jigsaw needed to nail him for a long, long time, Chief".

The telephone rang on the Chief's

desk, interrupting their conversation. With a sigh of relief Steve found his feet thinking this was he cue to escape and was ready to leave the Chief to answer his phone call, when he was stopped by the door. Raising his eyes to the ceiling he turned to face the Chief, who was holding the receiver in his direction, declaring it was for him. To Steve's surprise it turned out to be the Home Office to let Steve know the Major was calling in on him, with reference to the arrest of Peters. They also informed him that the Major had Andrew Cox with him, hopefully he too would identify him as the guy he had met in the pub, regardless of the fact that he had already ID'd him from the pile of photographs presented to him whilst in prison.

Steve just expressed his utmost feelings of gratitude for the information that was being relayed to him over the phone. There was that feeling of, 'Oh my god what have I done', welling around in his mind as he replaced the receiver back where it belonged. At the same time the Chief expressed his feelings, by stating simply that he wished he had had an officer of his calibre back in the old days.

"My granddad taught me well then Chief", returned Steve.

"Your Grandfather...he wouldn't have been Detective Superintendent Derek

Price by any chance?" enquired the Chief.

"Yes! Why do you ask?" Steve returned with a sense of curiosity in his voice.

A siren echoed the room from an ambulance as it sped past outside.

"I should've guessed by the name", returned the Chief calmly, once the room became silent again, then went on to explain, "It was your grandfather who taught me after the war".

"It's a small world Chief", Steve uttered as he explained that he should go and see what's happening and to prepare for the arrival of the Major.

The Chief exercised his rights by declaring he too would like to meet the Major and be in on any actions relating to the case in question. Steve happily agreed to his request with a smile as he headed for the door and hopefully no further interruptions.

....
......

Wendy made his day when she returned with the weapon ready and bagged as evidence but that wasn't all she happened upon. Having removed the drawers of his bedside cabinet they had found to their surprise, folded up in an old white supermarket bag, the pink knickers of Carols, complete with blood stains. She also claimed that they found pictures of girls on his bedroom wall, even the picture of the girl who was killed in the car park of the Black Hat the year previously. She explained openly that they were now looking into those girls in the pictures, just in case they were reported either missing or dead.

....
......

It turned out to be quite an eventful few days after the arrest of Peters, especially when the Major turned up with Andrew Cox in tow. Andrew desperately wanted to meet the man he had met all those years previously in the pub, who had then set him up for the murder of his late wife Lucy.

What was more alarming for Steve was when the Major introduced him not as Andrew Cox but as Sammy Smith, the brother of Charlie Smith with whom the Major was aware that Steve was familiar with, Sammy's girl friend was Lucy Cox.

The Major explained that the Home Office had been inundated with letters and petitions' claiming Sammy was innocent. The family had begged him to get Steve to solve the case and that is what Steve had done and proved them right, regaining the respect of the legal system.

....
....

The climax of this story came a week later, when Steve was sitting at his desk as usual first thing in the morning, ready to do the crossword, but for the moment he was reading a story in his newspaper. However he was interrupted by a smiling Wendy who entered the room with some news regarding the person who called himself the Maverick, she was eager to spill the beans claiming that she had heard from Hertford nick and that they now had the Maverick in custody and they were requesting urgently for him to get over there and sort it out.

Steve's eyes lit up at mention of that name. The Maverick echoed around in his head as he tossed the paper across his desk to deal with later. Donning his jacket hastily he left the room and headed for his car, Wendy followed, eagerly smiling as she tried to run to keep up with him. He still managed to wait for her as he opened his driver's door and watched her hurry to his side.

"There's no need to run Constable", commented Steve who stood with his door open then went on to explain, "I was going to wait for you anyway, as I am aware of your concern in this matter and I know if it goes well we can thank your brother for his work in nabbing the Maverick".

It took him about forty five minutes to get to Hertford in a hurry. Parking up in the large car park at the front of the modern glass fronted building, which looked like a giant office block and didn't resemble a police station, it was only the blue lamp that gave it away, by the glass panelled double front doors, Steve hurriedly passed through into the lobby where they were met by a young woman who seemed irate and yelling that she wanted her son back.

"Give me back my son you bastards, he's only eleven for gods sake", she shouted.

A female uniformed P.C. was trying to comfort her, trying to tell her it was alright and that nothing was going to happen to her son and it was probably all a big mistake on their part. But the woman wasn't having it; she was determined to see her son.

"It's all go here Gov", uttered Wendy who felt sorry for the woman.

"You're telling me", Returned Steve who approached the desk and explained to the officer in charge, who Wendy and he were, there was an element of sniggers from the officer as he pointed to the door close by and said he was wanted on the second floor, room seventeen.

"Something doesn't seem right", remarked Steve softly to himself, having noticed that officers who passed him, tended to pass him by and look back at them with cheeky little smiles on their faces, as if they knew something that Steve didn't, as they headed for room seventeen on the second floor.

At the end of the long corridor he noticed a small group of uniformed officers busy talking amongst themselves that was until they suddenly noticed Steve arriving with Wendy at his side. It was as if they knew this was the person wanting to question the one who called himself 'The Maverick', they whispered to each other and chuckled, as if it were some sort of a game they were playing and Steve was the key player.

"Ok where is this Maverick guy then eh?" Steve asked politely.

They didn't answer, instead a female officer who had her back to them, turned slowly, averting her attention from the group using her thumb to point to the opened door of room seventeen, as told to them by the reception.

"Thanks", was all he mustered in response as he entered the room only to find a further two female officers sitting on the table blocking the view of the Maverick. With a grin on their faces they moved promptly, allowing Steve to see the rabbit, as the saying goes. His eyes opened wide, when he found himself being approached by a young eleven year old boy with fair hair. He was dressed in jeans and a white T-shirt under a grey V' necked jumper, waving a deck of cards sprayed out in both hands and asking Steve to pick a card.

"What the hell is going on here and where is the Maverick?" Steve snapped.

"This is the one who calls himself the Maverick", commented one of the female officers who had been keeping him company while they waited for Steve to arrive.

"Pick a card!" replied the lad politely.

"What! Eh! Hang on", Steve uttered in a softer tone, "am I right in thinking that the woman in the reception is this lad's mother and that's why she is angry".

They just nodded with a smile.

"So lad what is your real name, other than The Maverick?" Steve asked crouching down to be at his level.

"Nathan Sir...Nathan Clark and I'm eleven and I do magic tricks for my friends, that's what I want to do when I grow up". The lad explained.

"In that case Nathan I think you should come with me and put your mother out of her misery before she does something stupid", Steve said as he stood up and taking the lads hand he escorted him back to his irate mother, who was overjoyed to get him back in one piece and Steve explaining it was all a big mix-up and that it wouldn't happen again. Steve just wished the lad every success in the future with his act. "

"I want to be like Paul Daniels Sir", he uttered in reply as his mother took his hand and hurried out of that place.

It was then that Steve decided to go and pay his respects to his late wife as it had been some time since his last visit. It didn't take him long to reach the grave yard and purchasing a bunch of flowers from the stall outside the cemetery he made his way to the grave, where to his surprise he found Jenny putting some fresh flowers on the grave too. Jenny was Sally's little sister, but now a grown up, attractive young lady, unlike the last time Steve had seen her. This had been at the funeral, six years previously, when she had been only fourteen. Now she was a tall twenty year old, with long flowing blonde hair, just like Sally's had been. In fact, in Steve's eyes, she was turning into Sally with her looks and attitude, declaring that when she was young she use to fantasize about walking arm in arm with him.

"In other words you had a crush on me back then eh?" returned a curious Steve who was now crouched down, placing his flowers in the urn where Jenny had placed hers, filling it out more.

"You could say that Steve", she coyly uttered.

"What about now then Jenny?" Steve enquired casually.

"I was only a kid then Steve, I have my work these days that keeps me busy", she returned as she walked the short distance to the tap and the watering can that she half filled.

"So what keeps you busy then eh...yer boyfriend?" Steve asked as he took the watering can from her and gently tipped it into the urn, he then went on to add, "I thought you were going into the army?"

"I did join the army...I'm out on leave, so I thought I'd pay my respects to my big sister, ok", she smiled as she towered over him, resting her hand on the top of the grave stone with a picture of Sally embedded into its marble surface.

Steve kissed his fingertips and gently touched her photograph. "I live in Romford these days with my girlfriend", he said calmly has he found his feet again. He kissed her on the forehead and said he had to go, as he was working on a case and he had to get back to Romford.

"It is good to see you again Steve, and to know you are doing alright for yourself...we did worry about you when you lost, you know who".

Steve just smiled and blew her a kiss and said "maybe we could meet up some day for a chat over a coffee".

"I'll hold you to that Steve", she replied but then under her breath she said, 'one day sweetheart...one day'.

Wendy sat quietly reading a woman's magazine she'd picked up earlier.

"Everything ok Gov?" She asked tossing the magazine back into her bag.

"Perfect! Just bloody perfect!" He said joyfully as he started the engine and headed for Romford.

....
....

That night he slouched on the settee a pint mug half full with beer sat awaiting his approval as he cuddled up with Angie, the forthcoming arrival now in full view with kicking motions a marvel in Steve's eyes as he rested his hand on the bulge.

The dimmed lights gave a mellow warmth to the room as the television was on the adverts and the national news was about to start when Steve reached out for his beer, two more unopened cans stood beside the settee ready to have their ring pulls pulled.

Steve reached out and proceeded to kiss Angie gently, when the news broke and the news reader opened with the story that the naked body of a young girl had been found dead on a beach in Cornwall. This stopped Steve in his tracks when the reporter said that the police had found her bag nearby and it was believed to be the body of a missing girl from the Essex area.

It was at that time the telephone rang out, picking up the receiver Steve realised straight away who it was and why they were ringing, saying, and "yes Major I have just seen the news".

....
....

Find Steve in the next thrilling mystery entitled...

'The Murder in the Red Jacket'

18618367R00361

Printed in Poland
by Amazon Fulfillment
Poland Sp. z o.o., Wrocław